HELL DIVERS XII

HEROES

D1557428

BOOKS BY *NEW YORK TIMES* BESTSELLING AUTHOR

NICHOLAS SANSBURY SMITH

HELL DIVERS
Hell Divers
Hell Divers: The Lost Years,
Part I: X and Miles (novella)
Hell Divers II: Ghosts
Hell Divers III: Deliverance
Hell Divers IV: Wolves
Hell Divers V: Captives
Hell Divers VI: Allegiance
Hell Divers VII: Warriors
Hell Divers VIII: King of the Wastes
Hell Divers IX: Radioactive
Hell Divers X: Fallout
Hell Divers XI: Renegades
Hell Divers XII: Heroes

SONS OF WAR
Sons of War
Sons of War 2: Saints
Sons of War 3: Sinners
Sons of War 4: Soldiers

ORBS
Solar Storms (an Orbs prequel)
White Sands (an Orbs prequel)
Red Sands (an Orbs prequel)
Orbs
Orbs II: Stranded
Orbs III: Redemption
Orbs IV: Exodus

E-DAY
E-Day
E-Day II: Burning Earth
E-Day III: Dark Moon

GALAXY IN FLAMES
The Last Steward
The Last Ship (coming soon)
The Last Lion (coming soon)

EXTINCTION CYCLE (SEASON ONE)
Extinction Horizon
Extinction Edge
Extinction Age
Extinction Evolution
Extinction End
Extinction Aftermath
Extinction Lost (a Team Ghost short story)
Extinction War

EXTINCTION CYCLE: DARK AGE (SEASON TWO)
Extinction Shadow
Extinction Inferno
Extinction Ashes
Extinction Darkness

TRACKERS (SEASON ONE)
Trackers
Trackers 2: The Hunted
Trackers 3: The Storm
Trackers 4: The Damned

NEW FRONTIER (TRACKERS SEASON TWO)
New Frontier: Wild Fire
New Frontier 2: Wild Lands
New Frontier 3: Wild Warriors

STANDALONE TITLES
Savage Skies
The Biomass Revolution

NICHOLAS SANSBURY SMITH

BLACK STONE
PUBLISHING

Printed in the United States of America
Originally published in hardcover by Blackstone Publishing in 2024

First paperback edition: 2024
ISBN 979-8-212-38671-5
Fiction / Science Fiction / Apocalyptic & Post-Apocalyptic

Version 1

Blackstone Publishing
31 Mistletoe Rd.
Ashland, OR 97520

www.BlackstonePublishing.com

For the legion of Hell Divers fans. My heartfelt thanks
to each of you for joining me on this adventure.
I hope you enjoy this final chapter of X's journey.

To Blackstone Publishing and Josh Stanton, thank you
for your unwavering support and for believing in this story
from day one. Working with your staff and brilliant editor,
Michael Carr, helped elevate the story and reach an audience
beyond what I could ever have imagined.

And for R. C. Bray—this series would not be what it is
without your genius storytelling and gritty voice.
You are Xavier Rodriguez.

"Let your plans be dark and impenetrable as night, and when you move, fall like a thunderbolt."

—Sun Tzu

RECAP SINCE
HELL DIVERS XI: RENEGADES

After weeks spent shoring up the defenses of the Vanguard Islands, King Kade's fears have come true. The enemy has found them, arriving in a giant airship that disables and then destroys the Vanguard defenses. After General Forge is killed, Kade is forced into a peace treaty with the Forerunner—a half man, half cyborg leading the knights under the Trident banner. This treaty will require Kade to deploy to the North and South Poles in an attempt to turn on the six weather-tech units at each location, known as the Delta Cloud fusion reactors. But there's a catch: the Forerunner wants the man they call "the Immortal" to lead one of the missions.

The Barracudas' mission to the Texas Gulf Coast succeeded in capturing two Jayhawk helicopters but resulted in multiple casualties, including sky pilot Woody and the Cazador sergeant Blackburn. The survivors are en route from the former Texas-Louisiana border on the *Angry 'Cuda*, under Slayer's command.

On the way back from a failed mission to Rio to find Michael and his family, X and Magnolia are healing from their physical and mental wounds after being held captive by Crixus and his satanic cult. Thanks to Corporal Valeria and a few other brave Cazadores, X, Mags, and their animals have been spared from a grisly death. But there is little time to rest. After Gran Jefe locates their vessel using one of the two Jayhawks, he brings them to the isle of Sint Eustatius, where they formulate a secret plan of resistance before X turns himself in to the Forerunner. That plan will require Gran Jefe to reunite with the Barracudas and prepare for war if the knights fail to keep up their side of the deal.

After a long journey into North America and across the North Atlantic, Michael and his family have arrived at the Canary Islands in the former *Hive*, with Timothy Pepper at the helm. They have discovered what they believe to be salvation. Clean water, soil free of toxins, and, best of all, sunshine peeking through the storm clouds. Victor and his old friend Gabi help them settle into their new home. But as they shore up the defenses and start preparing the land for crops, Michael can't help but fear there's something else out there that may threaten their lives.

PROLOGUE

SIXTY-ONE YEARS AGO . . .

"Bringing station online," said Colonel Noah Greyson.

He flipped the switch, and the bank of monitors flickered to life.

"My turn," said Dr. Gillian Hallsey.

She worked next to Noah in the dusty command center of Polar Station at the North Pole. Outside, a team of heavily armed commandos held security.

So far, the mission had gone flawlessly. They landed in three Sea Queen helicopters, accessed the base, entered the command center, and brought the station online.

A wide viewport looked out over the facility built on the frozen Arctic Ocean. One of the six Delta Cloud fusion reactors was hazily visible through the frost-covered glass. The disk-shaped top towered over the permanent ice cap it was anchored into. Each was around three hundred feet tall from the base to the crest, where intercontinental missiles were mounted in a ring and poised for launch. Those missiles were armed with the technology to manipulate weather across the planet.

"Overriding security level one," Gillian said. "Nine more to go."

Noah held back a smile. This mission had taken months to plan and came with great risk. But the potential reward was worth it. If they could get the reactors back online, those missiles would fire into the sky, releasing the ionizing seeds that would kick off the restoration of the planet by clearing the electrical storms and opening the skies to the sun once again. Future generations would be able to live on the surface again—children like the one growing inside his beloved Gillian this very moment.

Noah's child.

He looked at his wife as she worked, typing away on the screen. While planning the mission, they had learned she was pregnant. He had asked her to stay back, but Gillian insisted on coming.

"This is for our unborn child," she had said. "So they can live in the sun."

Not just their child, but *all* the survivors in their colony—what was left of them. The past fifty years had seen their numbers dwindle from four thousand to just over two thousand. It wasn't always this way. For the first century and a half of its existence, the Coral Castle had thrived under the ocean, using the resources around it in combination with scientific research that helped produce energy, food, and clean water.

Minds like the great Martha Hallsey, an ITC researcher who had founded their home over two hundred years ago off the Sunshine Coast. The sacrifices Martha had made to create this safe haven for her people were legend, and Gillian had always done everything she could to walk in the footsteps of her great-great-great-grandmother.

As she was doing today.

A distant clanking resonated through the facility. Noah glanced away from the viewport to the door.

"You hear something?" he asked.

Gillian had stopped typing, and she nodded.

A noise like an emergency siren floated in the distance, then ended abruptly.

Noah knew then that the noise wasn't human engineering. Actually, in a way, it was—the noise came from a human-engineered monster.

"All combat squads, prepare for hostile contact," Noah said over the comms. "Do not let them get to the command center."

He went to the viewports and looked out to the east. Through the lightly falling snow, he could see the three Sea Queen helicopters sitting idle on the tarmac. When he turned back, Gillian was staring at a monitor that had chirped.

"My God," she said.

"What?" Noah went over to her.

"When you activated the station, it unlocked levels B-one through B-nine."

Noah didn't need to ask what was on those levels.

"It's a security safeguard, triggered by activation," Gillian said.

As if in answer, a flurry of high-pitched wails reminiscent of an emergency siren echoed through the suddenly no-longer-silent facility.

"Hurry. We must activate the reactors *now*," he said.

Gillian nodded and returned to the security monitor, tapping away. The sound of footsteps heralded Sergeant George Everett's arrival in the command center.

"Colonel, Alpha squad is engaging hostiles on level C," he said. "Bravo and Condor squads are moving in."

"Tell them to hold 'em back as long as they can," Noah said. "The fate of the colony depends on us."

Cradling a submachine gun with armor-piercing rounds and an attached grenade launcher, Sergeant Everett hurried back into the hallway, where a squad of three more commandos held security.

Noah unslung his rifle and chambered a round. He leaned it against the monitors, then brought up the blueprints of the facility while Gillian continued to override the security systems.

"What are you doing?" she asked.

"Going to see if I can slow the advance of whatever we just let out," he replied.

The map showed they were on level A, the top floor of the base. Level B was marked as labs and backup power stations. His heart skipped when he saw that level C was a chamber with a hundred individual units.

If each unit had held a genetically engineered creature, there was no way he and Gillian would be able to stop them all. In a respite of machine-gun fire, Noah could tell the shrieks and snarls of the monsters were already growing closer.

But over both these noises rose another, more horrifying roar, from a monster that seemed impervious to bullets. This was nothing like the electronic voices of the other creatures. This was a goliath—a giant bipedal creature covered in an exterior of dense bone.

Noah and Gillian exchanged a glance.

"Halfway there," she said. "We have time."

Gunfire cracked in the distance. Closer this time.

Sergeant Everett's panicked voice broke over the comms.

"Alpha squad's gone," he reported. *"Bravo is falling back, with Nader KIA and Daryl injured. Condor engaging."*

In his peripheral vision, Noah saw Gillian hesitate.

"Go with Everett; get to the helos," he said. "I'll finish this."

"I'm not leaving you," Gillian said.

An explosion rattled the labs below them, shaking dust down from the ceiling.

"Gillian," Noah said.

"I'm already on number seven," she replied. "Too close to stop now. Just need another minute."

Another blast shook the glass panels of the small chamber. The deep roar of the goliath echoed through the facility.

Sporadic gunshots sounded, along with the steady clatter of a machine gun. The goliath had torn through their commandos, leaving no one alive in Alpha or Bravo squad.

"Eight down," Gillian said. "Moving to nine."

They weren't going to make it.

Noah took a bandolier of grenades from his backpack and loaded one into the launcher of the rifle.

The gunfire drew ever closer, louder. A muffled voice called into the command center as Sergeant Everett looked inside.

"Colonel, Condor squad's falling back," he reported. "What's your status?"

"We need just a little more time, Sergeant," Noah said. "Hold 'em back with everything you got!"

Everett strode back out with his rifle shouldered. Not a second later, a grinding roar issued from the passage he had entered, as if a wall or ceiling had collapsed.

"Watch out, Jake!" Everett shouted.

The anguished human cry that followed was hardly recognizable. Audible snapping of bones sounded before a burst of gunfire went off outside the open doorway.

"We have a second goliath!" Everett shouted. "We gotta go, now, Colonel!"

Gillian kept typing. "Almost there!"

Noah saw that she had worked through nine of the ten levels.

But they were out of time.

"We have to go," he said.

"No, one more," Gillian insisted. "I can do this."

He turned back to the screen, where the graph line had risen to 95 percent. They were oh, so close to activating the six reactors.

"This is for our child," she said.

"Not if you die," Noah said.

"We're not dying in here."

Noah hesitated, then raised his rifle and went out into the dimly lit passage. Everett and a commando named David fired down the corridor into the hulking silhouette of the first goliath, which held Jake in one hand. The entire right side of his body dripped blood as the left leg kicked the air.

"Sarge... help... me," he choked.

His eyes widened for an instant as the beast crushed his neck. It flung the limp body aside.

"You bastard!" screamed a commando named Riley as he unloaded an entire magazine into the bone-clad monster. Roaring, it pulled two long, thin shards of bone from its back and hurled them like spears. One of them hit Riley in the chest with such force, it lifted his body and skewered him against a wall.

David ducked down, firing the rest of his magazine into the thick bone armor, to no avail. He ejected the magazine and grabbed another as Everett laid down covering fire. Noah did the same, aiming at the face as the beast lowered its head.

"David, get back!" Everett shouted.

The commando ran toward him as Everett pulled a pin from a grenade. Just as he tossed it into the air, another bone shard whistled away from the goliath. It struck the back of David's neck, punching through the front in a gout of blood.

Everett screamed something indistinct, then retreated into the room with Noah.

"We have to go out through the labs," said the sergeant. "I've got an extraction team on the way to meet us."

"Gillian, we have to move NOW!" Noah yelled.

"Got it!" she shouted. "Reactors activated! Commencing firing in ten minutes."

Noah felt a glimmer of relief, but there was no time to celebrate. The goliath charged down the hallway, its elephantine feet pounding the floor, sending palpable tremors through the building.

Everett led them to a sealed exit door across the command center. He unlocked it with a pulse charge, swung it open, and cleared the stairwell.

"Go," he said.

Noah went down first, his rifle light guiding them down a level. The enraged roar of the goliath followed them down, the stairway vibrating with every step.

The door at the landing was locked, compelling Everett to use another pulse charge. He opened it to a sprawling lab with rows of workstations behind glass walls. Flashing emergency lights created a strobing red glow across the ancient workspace. They hurried through the level, passing through a BSL-4 lab that held the deadliest viruses known to humanity, still entombed in locked vaults. Robotic limbs, once used to handle the specimens, hung idle from the walls and overhead.

A strobing light illuminated a pane of glass ahead and, beyond it, a door. This one hung open. From what Noah remembered of the blueprints, they must pass through two more sections of the lab to get outside.

He ran toward it, but slowed as an eyeless face emerged behind the translucent wall. In a swift movement, he raised his rifle and fired a burst. Shards of glass fell away.

Screaming rose over the echoing shots.

When the flashing light appeared not a second later, the eyeless face was gone beyond the broken wall. Realization hit him then—it had never been there to begin with; he had seen a reflection. Whirling, he saw Sergeant Everett lying on the floor, his legs mangled. The eyeless monster had him pinned down and was tearing sinew away from his neck with its teeth.

Gillian had fired her pistol into the creature, which had bat-like wings curled around its body. Striding over, Noah fired into its back, blasting the beast off Everett. It flopped onto the ground, exposing a hideous face that Noah erased with a three-round burst.

Everett brought a hand up to his neck to slow the blood leaking through his fingers. Gillian bent down to render aid as Noah cleared the space of more contacts. He froze at a guttural roar from the room they had just left. Ducking under the open doorway was the eight-foot goliath that had decimated their security team. Splattered blood covered the exterior of bones as dense as steel. The underlayer of thick muscle seemed to pulsate with an orange glow as it took deep breaths and exhaled out snorts.

"Go," Everett choked out. He pulled another grenade off his vest, keeping the other hand on his neck.

"I will tell your family what you did here," Noah said.

"I'm sorry," Gillian said.

Everett offered a pained nod as she backed away. Leaving him there was one of the most difficult things Noah had done in his life. They had grown up together and graduated the same year from the university at the Coral Castle. Everett had a wife and a daughter back home.

The ground rumbled as the goliath charged.

They ran, and Noah pulled Gillian behind a lab station to shield them from the explosion that came a moment later. The grenade did the trick, and they felt the heavy *whump* as the colossal beast hit the floor.

Ears ringing, Noah pulled Gillian to her feet and they sprinted for the exit, not looking back. Nearing the door, he felt the impacts of heavy footfalls. Clearly not human.

"Dear God, no," he whispered.

Yet another goliath lumbered out the open doorway, with three of the eyeless monstrosities prowling behind it. The beast slammed against the glass wall in its path, shattering the BSL-4–reinforced sheet without even slowing down.

Noah and Gillian were already retreating the way they had come. He pulled her to the floor.

"Stay down!" he shouted.

Rising up, he aimed his grenade launcher at the monster as it pulled its body through the broken glass wall. It launched something into the air. In that second, he felt a hot stab in his chest. As he pulled the trigger, he saw a needle of bone sticking out of him. He tried to duck down, but the protruding bone dart caught on a cubicle partition.

An explosion burst across the lab, slamming him backward. He hit the floor on his side, and pain shot up his right side and chest.

For a moment, he lay there, breathing in the scent of smoke and burning flesh. Another few seconds passed before he realized that his sudden ability to smell meant that his suit was compromised. A heartbeat later, he heard a voice over the ringing in his ears.

"Noah!" Gillian yelled.

She was leaning down next to his body.

His ruined body.

Noah realized he was looking out of only one eye. He turned it to the goliath, which now lay in a smoldering heap. The grenade had hit it in the face, breaking the head open like an egg. The three eyeless humanoid beasts behind it twitched on the ground, shards of glass and shrapnel protruding from their pale flesh.

"Oh God, oh dear God," Gillian said.

Now he knew that it was really bad. She never lost her cool.

His eye glanced down to see the bone shard protruding from

his chest, perhaps half an inch from his heart. To the right, his entire side was peppered with shrapnel. Blood leaked from several holes in his suit, which Gillian tried to plug with her gloved hands, to no avail. A dark puddle had begun to grow beneath him.

The pain subsided, replaced by a cold chill.

"It's okay," Gillian said. "I can save you."

Noah knew this wasn't true. She had to know it, too.

"I just have to get you back to the colony, to our labs," Gillian said. "Don't give up, Noah! Don't you dare!"

He blinked, trying to understand what she meant. Was she really suggesting what he thought she was?

"We said we would never use that tech on our people or ourselves," he whispered. "No matter what."

Muffled gunfire rang out. His hearing seemed to be fading.

"Help us!" Gillian shouted. "In here!"

He heard that. She hovered over him, pushing her hands against his wounds.

"Stay with me, Noah," she said. "Just hold on; we're getting you out of here. I'm going to fix you."

There it was again: that unwavering confidence and fearless tone. Believing she could do anything—the Hallsey strength that had kept the Coral Castle alive over the decades.

Two commandos from the evac team rushed into the room. Moving around the carcass of the goliath, they finished off the writhing smaller beasts. Another commando arrived a minute later with a medical pack and a stretcher.

"Over here!" Gillian said. "We have to move him fast."

Noah grabbed her by the wrist. "Tell our child I love—"

Blood bubbled up in his throat, choking him. He broke into a coughing fit, struggling to clear his airway. The next thing he knew, he was being picked up on a stretcher and carried down the hallway. Gillian stayed by his side, holding him.

"Almost there. Just hang on, Noah," she said. "You can't give up. You have to meet our girl."

"G-girl?" he stammered.

She nodded. "I was going to tell you when we got back. We're going to have a baby girl, Noah."

He smiled or, at least, thought he did. He couldn't feel much. Gillian blurred away as his eye filled with blood. She gripped his wrist hard.

"I can save you, Noah," she said. "You just have to hold on— if not for me, for our daughter."

Noah thought of what that would mean. The chambers and the robotic technology back in their labs could extend his human life, but it meant he would become something that wasn't altogether human. He wanted to see his daughter, but at what cost?

A flurry of gunshots snapped him from his thoughts. Then a massive explosion nearly knocked him off the stretcher.

"Hurry!" Gillian yelled.

Roaring seemed to follow them in their hurried escape. There were panicked voices too, going in and out as Noah was carried from the lab. Some vision returned to his eye—dim, but clear enough to see they were on the tarmac now. Three Sea Queen helicopters were still there with the pilots in the cockpits, ready to fly.

He could make out shouting from a sergeant he recognized as M. J. Then calmer words as the man tried to separate Noah and Gillian.

"He'll be okay, but you can't go with him," said M. J.

"No, I won't leave him," Gillian insisted.

"You'll see him back at the colony. You know the protocol, Dr. Hallsey. You can't travel together, and there's no time to argue!"

Another roar came from the labs. The last goliath was still on the hunt.

Gillian leaned down to Noah. "I love you," she said. "I'll see you back home."

She ran off with two commandos, and Noah lost sight of her as he was loaded onto the chopper.

"Go, go, go!" shouted one of the soldiers. "We got hostiles incoming!"

The bird lifted into the air. Noah tried to focus on breathing, on staying alive. He blinked as something streaked past the rising Sea Queen. It looked like a red bolt.

"M. J., we need covering fire!" yelled a pilot.

The sergeant grabbed the mounted light machine gun and pointed it downward. The chopper with Gillian pulled higher next to them, rising into the dark sky.

Red flashes seemed to follow it, lancing upward.

Noah tried to get a better look, but the medic working on him pushed him back down. The chatter of automatic gunfire filled the open cabin as M. J. rained lead on a distant target.

"I hit it, but it keeps coming!" he yelled. "What *is* that thing?"

A red bolt punched through the hull of the chopper, instantly burning a wide hole in the side. Two more punched through with an audible sizzle.

"Taking fire!" yelled a pilot.

Only then did Noah realize what was happening.

The clawed monsters weren't the only threat down there. Machines maybe—DEF-Nine units perhaps, or something else.

M. J. screamed as he fired the light machine gun. A laser flashed through the chopper, catching the sergeant in the helmet. He spun a quarter turn, his face gone, then slumped out of the open door and disappeared in the void.

With the gunner gone, Noah had a wide-open view of the frozen base below. His bloody eye glimpsed the six Delta Cloud fusion reactors on the horizon as the aircraft fought for altitude. They weren't firing.

Something was wrong.

He looked down, seeing the source of the hostile fire. A bulky, shadowy figure stood on the ice, too far away to make it out well. It raised jointed mechanical limbs at the sky. Those limbs abruptly blazed to life, firing lasers at the choppers. The Sea Queen carrying his wife swerved away from the threat, then pulled abreast of the chopper Noah lay inside. Struggling against the wind, he focused his one eye on the face of his wife inside. She was screaming something and waving frantically at him.

Noah flinched as rods of dazzling red light flashed through the side of her chopper, leaving a dozen smoldering holes along the aft section. Smoke churned away from the rotors as the pilot tried to keep the bird stable.

"*Gillian*," Noah whispered.

The bird began to spin, and then it exploded in a massive fireball.

"No!" he screamed, reaching out to nothing.

ONE

Bubbles rushed away from the breathing mask inside the gel-filled medical capsule. Xavier Rodriguez took in a filtered breath as he tried to see outside the glass. It took him a moment to realize that he was on the Forerunner's airship, which the knights called *Trident*. The hovering warship was a colossus, boasting enough firepower to erase the Vanguard Islands in minutes, and it had already eliminated most of the Cazador and sky people's forces using advanced electromagnetic pulses and sheer firepower.

Seeing no other option than to agree to whatever peace they offered, X had turned himself in to the Forerunner. The knights had taken him to this chamber right after he agreed to a truce and the mission to the poles to activate the weather-modification units. Memories of what the Forerunner had said played in his mind, explaining where to find Magnolia, Miles, and Jo-Jo but mentioning nothing about Valeria, Jonah, or Gran Jefe and the helicopter they had taken from Texas.

X thought hard on that, making sure he hadn't revealed anything that might give them away. Kade had already sent a secret message to the team, telling the Cazadores to hide the

Jayhawk and wait for Slayer to arrive with the second helicopter, Tia, and Zuni. And also for the Cazador forces Kade had deployed to bring X, Miles, Mags, and Jo-Jo back from Rio de Janeiro. They had commandeered the destroyer used by Crixus's fanatic followers and were on their way back to the islands.

The sky people and Cazador allies still had some hope if things went sideways with the Forerunner, but it was a long shot at taking back their home. X still had no idea how old the man was—or even *what* he was, exactly. All he knew was that the Forerunner controlled advanced technology that could wipe the Vanguard Islanders out, leaving him no choice but to agree to the coordinated polar missions.

X was sick of seeing people die. Sick of killing them, too.

He stirred in the gelatinous medium, trying to remember how long he had been here. His mind was sluggish, and his vision swam. Through the glass, he spotted two medical personnel standing around a monitor, studying data. He could also make out two knights standing guard in front of an exit hatch. Both wore medieval armor and had double-edged claymore swords sheathed on their belts.

Across the chamber, more of the medical capsules sat empty. They reminded X of cryo-capsules that he had seen in ITC facilities around the world. But the pod he occupied wasn't like the one he had saved the puppy he named Miles from over a decade ago.

The knights had referred to this as a "freon chamber," for no good reason he could see. The Forerunner had then explained that it would heal his wounds and any illness. At first, X had feared that the cyborg was poisoning him, or else turning him into some robotic automaton. But now X couldn't deny he was already starting to feel better. He glanced down at more of the tiny black beads worming out of ports in the pod. Clusters of them clung to his naked body. Hundreds, maybe thousands, had already spread across his wounds, attaching and slowly absorbing. Others had migrated up into his nose, ears, and other orifices. He could feel their smooth metallic touch inside him.

The Forerunner hadn't lied—the pod was indeed healing X.

The guards suddenly moved away from the hatch, turning to face a figure that stepped through. Another person arrived, both of them obscured from X's view.

The only thing he could see for certain was that these two people wore no armor. He heard indistinct chatter. Nothing that he could make out, but whatever they were talking about, it seemed heated.

He tensed, his muscles flexing all over his naked body, which already felt much better. As his strength returned, so did his warrior's instinct. He thought of General Forge and how he had died defending the tower against the knights after they broke into the council chamber.

While X didn't know the details, he knew that Forge would never have surrendered. He would have fought until his last breath. It was hard to look past all that and honor a deal, considering the violence that occurred on the capitol tower.

But X had to think clearly. Rolo had started this conflict. But for his actions in Brisbane, the knights wouldn't be here. Forge wouldn't have been in the situation of having to fight.

And part of that was on X.

Had he not been so focused on expansion and on finding places like the Coral Castle, he would have seen the betrayals coming. Michael wouldn't have been forced to flee into the outer darkness. Hundreds of men and women would still be alive.

X took in several deep breaths through the mask, trying to calm the rising anger inside him. He had to keep his head, for the sake of Miles, Magnolia, and everyone else.

Closing his eyes, he tried to relax. What he needed right now was to rest and heal. Anger was a cancer that would only eat him from inside and slow the process.

At some point, he dozed off. He awoke to loud barking. *Miles* barking.

Cracking open one eyelid, he saw that the blurred chamber beyond the pod was dark. Only dim blue lights glowed in the overheads across the room. The two knights were gone—or at least not where they had been posted before. No doctors or scientists seemed to be present either.

It was probably early morning, and X was likely just hearing things. His body felt stronger now. His lungs no longer burned, and his head felt clearer—no headache or brain fog.

But if he heard phantom barking, maybe his mind still wasn't at 100 percent.

Nothing was out there. He was alone.

X closed his eyes again, greedy for more sleep. He drifted back into blissful oblivion until barking broke out again.

This time, he knew it wasn't in his mind—this was real!

Bright white lights flicked on in the chamber, illuminating figures rushing through the hatch across the room. Knights. Three. Plus two unarmored figures.

And a hairy, barking quadruped.

"Miles!" X tried to yell.

Bubbles burst from his breathing mask.

His best friend broke away from the knight holding his collar and ran over to the pod. He jumped up against the glass, pawing at it and barking.

X wanted to tell him it was okay, that he wasn't in pain, but Miles didn't seem to understand. He turned and growled as two knights strode over. One pulled something from his belt.

Oh, hell no, X thought.

More bubbles issued from his mask as he tried to yell. He

fought against the restraints holding his three natural limbs and one prosthesis. With his strength returning, he summoned all of it to get free.

The knight who had pulled the device from his belt strode over, aiming it at Miles. X could see it now: a Taser.

"No! STOP!" X's words came out garbled.

A scientist rushed over to the flashing digital display next to X's pod.

"Let me the fuck out!" X yelled.

More guards rushed into the room. Gritting his teeth, he pulled against his arm restraint, finally breaking free. With his palm, he pounded against the top of the pod, trying to push it open by force.

The scientist at the screen called out, and one of the knights shouted back.

A moment later, the pod's walls lifted as jets suctioned out the gel around him. Clumps of the gelatinous fluid slopped out onto the floor. The last two restraints retracted from his ankles, and X slumped out on both knees.

Miles rushed over and got in front of him, still growling.

The knight with the Taser pointed it at the dog.

"You shoot that and the next one goes right up your ass," X snarled.

"X!" shouted a female voice.

He pulled Miles over to him as his eyes searched the back of the chamber. There was Magnolia, in the grip of two knights.

But where was Jo-Jo?

Another knight strode through the hatch. This one was larger than all of them—the hulking general, Jack. He walked over with a machine gun cradled across the breastplate of his armor. "Dumb fucking animal, where'd you go?" he grunted.

His eyes searched the room and soon found X and Miles.

"Stop," X said in a calm voice, raising his hand. "Mags, I'm okay…"

The general lumbered over, keeping his rifle on X. Magnolia writhed and fought against the two knights holding her, and Miles gave a soft but ominous growl.

"Hold on!" came a voice.

Their former prisoner, Lieutenant "Lucky" Gaz, walked into the room and stood between Jack and X.

"General," he said in a measured tone. "All due respect, but we don't need to kill anyone else. We're in *complete* control. You already took out their best soldier."

Is this the asshole who killed General Forge? X wondered.

"You better tell that freak to lower his gun, or this deal is going to be over *really* fast," X said. "You can explain to the Forerunner how you managed to fuck it up."

He stood there naked, chest heaving, working out the best way to take the general on with his bare hands if it came to that. His anger threatened to boil over, to activate the beast inside him that had kept him alive all these years, both in the wastes and in the sky.

"My dog's no threat to you. If you got a beef, you take it up with me."

"Better not hurt them, you ugly sack of shit!" Magnolia shouted.

General Jack grunted again, turning slightly.

"Let's all just settle down," Lucky said. "This is just a misunderstanding. The dog bolted away, but we were bringing him to see you, Xavier."

X stood in front of Miles and commanded him to sit. Finally, the husky went down on his haunches, still growling.

"Mags, take it easy," X said.

Magnolia squirmed against the knights holding her.

"Get your hands off me!" she hissed.

"Stay put, then," one of them replied.

Something metallic rattled outside the open door, but X saw nothing in the dark hallway beyond. All the knights heard it, too, and went rigid, except for one holding Magnolia. She seized the opportunity to break away and hurried over to X and Miles.

A rhythmic clanking outside the room drew closer. A blue glow appeared in the darkness, burning brighter as it drew closer. The slumped, wheelchair-bound form of the Forerunner rolled into the room. An IV bag of pink fluid hung from a pole mounted to the chair.

"What's the meaning of this!" his synthetic voice shouted.

"The animal got away," Lucky said. "Went to its handler."

X held Miles, stroking him, calming him.

"General, please lower the weapon," Lucky said.

The gun stayed up until the Forerunner raised a hand, whereupon Jack snapped the weapon back robotically, cradling it against his chest.

The Forerunner motored past his loyal general and into the center of the room, stopping six feet away from X's naked body, which still shielded Miles. The blue eye flitted down as the dog poked his head out around X to watch.

"I suppose we know who to kill if you try anything," said the Forerunner.

X stared back, doing his best to keep his composure. He didn't want anyone thinking he was about to run amok and kill all these medieval-looking chuckle-fucks and their robotically enhanced leader. He really, really didn't like this liver-spotted cybernetic asshole.

"Where's Jo-Jo?" X asked.

"The beast?" said the Forerunner.

"I asked for her to be safely extracted and healed. That was part of our deal. I need her for the mission to the poles."

"And you will have her, assuming she survives surgery, which she is currently undergoing."

X relaxed a little, and the tension in Miles's posture seemed to ease as well.

"Both beasts will be part of your mission, fear not, Xavier," said the Forerunner. "As long as they are obedient."

He glanced over at a doctor who had come into the room. She was young, probably in her thirties, with curly black hair.

"What's his status, Dr. Craiger?" asked the Forerunner.

"He's showing major improvement," she replied. "Should we prepare for the next stage?"

X frowned. "Next stage?"

The blue eye flitted back to X, lingering on the prosthetic arm.

"You didn't think I'd send you on a polar mission like *that*, did you?" The motorized chair backed up and turned. "Follow me."

X stroked Miles again. "It's okay, boy. Go with Mags."

Miles whined, then trotted away, looking over his shoulder.

Dr. Craiger gave X the once-over.

"What, never seen a man before?" he asked.

She scoffed, then handed him a towel, which he wrapped around his waist.

The Forerunner motored over to a hatch in a darkened far corner of the room. General Jack walked over and spun the wheel to open it. The Forerunner nodded to X, and they entered a surgical room. Robotic limbs hung from the overhead.

The hatch closed behind them, and the Forerunner turned his mechanized chair to face X.

"I once stood in your place," he said. "Well, *stood* isn't the right word," he remarked. "I came to this room in pieces, clinging to life after a mission gone wrong. A mission that cost me the most important part of my life."

He closed his eye for a long moment, as if to bury some terrible memory.

"I was made whole again," said the Forerunner. "Now you will be, too."

X looked at a skeletal prosthetic arm on a table.

"I'm good the way I am," he said. "I don't need any modifications."

"Your prosthesis is obsolete. You will need to be agile where you're going. Agile and strong."

X examined the limb. It was unlike the one Michael had received after losing an arm to the defectors. That one had meat to it, resembling a real human limb. This prosthesis was made of dense alloy in the shape of the actual bones, and the components embedded inside to operate it.

"Don't worry, you won't end up like me," said the Forerunner. "This is just to enhance your body, not to prolong your life or turn you into what I see you looking at with such disgust."

X met the ancient gaze of this man. He didn't really feel *bad* for him, but he did suddenly wonder what had happened to him over the years.

"One thing that has become abundantly clear to me is, if such a thing as immortality exists, it's a curse," the Forerunner said. "No one should live forever."

"We agree on that," X grunted.

"Good. Then you will accept this modification and follow all orders you're given. Do you understand?"

"Yeah, got it."

"I haven't lived this long by taking reckless chances." The Forerunner backed away. "My technicians will be in shortly."

"Wait," X said. "There's something you need to understand too—something we need to make very clear."

"And what's that, Xavier?"

"You don't threaten my dog again, or you're going to be back in this room getting new parts."

The Forerunner smiled, if one could call it that. The twisted grin appeared more like a pained grimace.

"I understand that love is weakness, Xavier Rodriguez," he said. "Because, believe it or not, I once had a woman and was once like you. I had to learn the hard way. There is no room for love in the heart of a soldier."

*   *   *   *   *

Waves crashed onto the beach at Lanzarote, in the Canary Island chain. Shafts of sunlight broke through the cloud cover on the horizon, glinting off the clear ocean water.

Michael Everhart stood on a rocky bluff holding his son, Bray, in his arm. The almost two-year-old boy was getting heavier by the day. Holding him brought Michael great joy, but as he had only one arm, it was good the lad seemed to enjoy walking more.

His arm strength had started to flag by the time Bray finally said, "Down."

"Careful," Michael said. He kept his hand on the boy as he stepped closer to the edge of the bluff to look at his mother. Michael could see Layla fishing in the surf not far from the twenty-foot drop to the shore below. Waves exploded against the rocks in the morning breeze.

"Ma-ma ishhhhh," Bray said, pointing.

"Yes, Ma-ma's fishing—good job!" Michael said.

He reached down, and Bray gripped his fingers as Michael led him a safe distance from the cliff edge. Below them, Layla swung the rod, spinning out her line and dropping the lure *just so* into the water. For the past few days, she had come here just after dawn—according to Gabi, the best time to fish. So far, Layla had caught a few, but nothing to feast on.

A few yards away, Victor stood with a spear poised. He thrust it into a tide pool and pulled it back with a good-size crab skewered on the trident tip.

"Look at what Uncle Victor caught!" Michael said.

Bray angled a finger down. "Oh ... ish. Ish."

"No, that's a crab, not a fish."

"Wab."

"Almost, buddy. It's called a crab."

Bray turned to look at Gabi, trekking up the beach. She held a basket up to Victor, who pulled the crab off the spear and tossed it in.

Michael had loved the Vanguard Islands, but this was a *real* island, with actual land, and places to explore. He loved the lava tubes and green glades and pristine ocean grottoes more than the packed oil rigs that smelled of sewage, smoke, and body odor. The breeze here was fresh and clean, and they had natural soil under their feet and could wiggle their toes in real sand.

He took in a deep breath and looked at the sky.

Having Timothy up there watching over them did much to ease his anxiety about being outside. As wonderful as this island was, it was not without its dangers.

"I got one!" Layla shouted.

"Ishhhh!" Bray crowed.

Michael scooped the boy up and hurried down the path from the bluff to the beach, where Layla's pole was bent almost double. Victor and Gabi trotted over to meet them on the smooth, wet sand.

"It's a big one!" Layla yelled. She reeled it in steadily, just as she had learned back at the islands. Watching her and realizing that with only one arm he couldn't perform even such a simple act as fishing, Michael felt a fleeting moment of dread. It vanished in an instant at the sound of Bray's laughter—the most joyful noise in his world.

As Layla fought the fish, Michael took in their idyllic surroundings once more. He had gotten his family here, halfway across the world, prevailing against the monsters and men who tried to stop them.

For that, he was ever grateful. And grateful to those who had helped them along the way. From Steve Schwarzer to Ton, Pedro, and all the others who had helped them. And the hundreds more before them.

His mind drifted as Layla reeled in the massive fish, shouting excitedly.

Michael thought of his father, Aaron, and of Xavier. He thought of Magnolia, Edgar, and Arlo. They were all dead, claimed by the postapocalyptic world.

"I see it," Layla said.

He shook the thoughts away and looked out over the water to see the gray, ribbed dorsal fin of a big fish break the surface a dozen feet from shore. It was a grouper. Good eating if you could get it landed.

"Victor, please take Bray," Michael said, and traded his boy for Victor's three-pronged spear.

Wading out into the surf, Michael cocked his arm back, but the grouper went back under with a splash from its tail. The sudden shift jerked Layla, but she held on.

"Easy, give it a bit of line," Michael said.

He waded out, the waves lapping against him. Spear in hand, he pushed through them until he was up to his waist.

"Don't go out too far!" Layla yelled.

Michael spotted the fin some ten feet away. Again he cocked his arm, but the fish darted away.

"Almost got it!" he yelled. "Reel it in a little more!"

He watched the fish just below the surface. It was moving slower but still had some fight left.

Michael kept his eyes on his quarry, trying to anticipate its next move, knowing he must keep the line away from the sharp corals. When it cut back, moving toward him, he led it slightly, then tossed the spear a foot below the fish to allow for the water's refraction.

Two of the three prongs punched into flesh.

"Got it!" he shouted. "Pull it in slow!"

Michael waited for Layla to reel it closer. Then, just as he reached for the spear, he noticed a flicker on the horizon. He gazed out over the whitecaps, but whatever he had seen was gone now.

"Pepper," Michael started to say, then realized he had left his headset back with his gear bag on land. Turning, he let the waves push the fat grouper toward shore. It had to weigh fifty pounds, maybe more.

When the next wave hit, he went down and had to let go of the shaft to brace himself with his hand. Pushing back up from the sandy bottom, he saw that the wave had taken the fish and spear a few feet to his right.

"Michael, hurry!" Layla shouted.

But when he grabbed the shaft, he realized she wasn't telling him to hurry after their lunch. "There's something out there. Come on!" she called.

Victor was already hurrying back to the caves with Bray in his arms. Gabi followed, moving quickly.

Michael turned to look at the horizon again as another wave bashed him. This time, he kept on his feet—and saw the source of the glint he'd seen earlier.

A boat—no, a ship—sailed a mile off the coast, maybe a bit closer.

He turned and bolted toward Layla, plucking the spear free but leaving the fish. It would do them no good if they weren't alive to eat it.

"Run!" Michael shouted.

Layla waited until he reached her, then took off. He grabbed his gear bag, slung it, and looked over his shoulder. The ship didn't seem to be heading their way.

On the way back to the caves, Michael put on his headset.

"Timothy, do you copy?" he said into the mic.

Static crackled.

"Pepper, do you copy?"

"Copy, Chief. How may I assist?"

"We see a ship," Michael said. "About a mile east of our location."

"Stand by, sir. The airship is out of range, but I'm moving now."

Michael followed Layla all the way back to the cave system. They didn't stop until they reached the fortress of rocks blocking the tunnels. Michael stopped behind a boulder to catch his breath. Victor was with Bray on the platform leading to the corridor connecting to their new home. Gabi stayed behind, scanning the surf line with binoculars.

She handed them to Michael. He zoomed in on a long, slender boat that looked as if it belonged in a medieval museum. It had a hull of shiplap with patches of metal. He couldn't make out the faded insignia on the side. Three masts rose off the decks, sails furled, as a dozen long oars stroked the ocean. The oarsmen wore gray clothing and large metal necklaces.

"What do you see, Tin?" Layla asked.

Michael zoomed in as far as he could and realized that these weren't crew members, and they weren't wearing necklaces. They were galley slaves, shackled to their oars.

He moved the lens to a man standing on the deck, holding

a spear and dressed in black. The soldier, guard, or whatever he was held up something in his other hand.

"Michael," Layla said.

He was going to respond when he saw the man peering through binoculars at the island. Ducking down, Michael breathed deeply.

"What is it?" Layla asked. "Tell me what you saw."

"Evil," he replied. "I saw evil."

TWO

"Make the announcement, Kade Long," said the Forerunner. "Reassure your people." The cyborg sat in his motorized chair on the ship's gangway. Behind him stood General Jack and Lucky. Nobu and Zen, the two knights Kade had fought beside back on the Sunshine Coast, were also here.

Nobu was middle aged and fit. Zen looked a decade younger. It seemed these were the top-ranking knights besides Lieutenant Gaz and General Jack.

Kade scoffed. "You want me to *reassure* them?"

"Tell them we are committed to peace and that we won't harm anyone else," replied the cyborg. "They have my word."

"With all due respect, sir, these brutes only understand violence," said General Jack. "You should let me kill anyone who can fight."

"Then you'd be killing every single person, including a lot of kids." Kade glared at the general, himself part cyborg now. Kade had watched him die on the helicopter after they left the Sunshine Castle. Watched the spider strings burn through his arm. Now he knew how they had brought the man back, using the same technology the Forerunner had used to heal Xavier and Jo-Jo, not to mention himself.

Kade felt a burning anger toward all these bionically enhanced men, though at this point he had little option but to obey. The lives of over a thousand innocent people depended on his ability to keep calm.

"Anyone who poses a threat should be eliminated," said Jack. "Give me the honor of cleansing this unholy place."

The Forerunner activated the hydraulics that raised his frail body above the general.

"You will do as you are told!" the synthetic voice boomed.

Jack lowered his head. "Yes, sir. Absolutely."

The cyborg remained elevated for a moment, staring down with his blue robotic eye. It flitted over to Kade.

"What say you, Kade Long?" he asked. "Will you commit to this truce and relay a message of peace to the people of the Vanguard Islands?"

"Yeah, I'll bloody transmit the message," Kade said. "Just keep your bloodthirsty general under control before he ignites a full-out war."

Kade turned away, but the Forerunner called out.

"Did I tell you to leave?"

He stiffened as the cyborg lowered his chair.

"While Xavier heals, I need something else from you," he said. "A list of your Hell Divers."

"There aren't many of us left," Kade said. "Magnolia, X, Sofia..." He let his words trail off after almost slipping and saying *Gran Jefe*. Of course, there was also Tia, but he wouldn't reveal her to the knights. "We have some greenhorns that showed promise, but they don't have any experience in the wastes."

"Hand the names over to Lieutenant Gaz," said the Forerunner. "You may go now."

Kade walked with Lucky down the ramp from the airship to the dirt on the capitol tower. Nobu and Zen waited in the dirt. They escorted him across the landing zone where they dropped two nights ago, toward the remains of the forest plot that grew on the capitol tower. Kade looked at the damage. The knights had destroyed an entire row of coco palms, and for what? He had done everything in his power to defend this rig and all the other Vanguard Islands, but in the end, he had missed the real threat in the sky.

That threat now lifted off, rising back into the clouds to avoid potential rebel fire. So far, no one had tried anything, and it was on Kade to make sure they didn't.

The Forerunner and his knights didn't know about some of the plans Kade had made before their arrival. But he feared they would find out about the Barracudas' mission to Texas. Right now Slayer would be on his way to the isle of Sint Eustatius, with Tia and Zuni on board.

Kade had debated telling the truth about it all, knowing that if any of this came to light, it could destroy the delicate trust he was trying to build, dooming his friends.

He didn't trust the Forerunner, and this had figured in his decision to keep the presence of the Jayhawk on Sint Eustatius a secret. The helicopter was the only chance at leveling the battlefield and stopping the Forerunner. Once the airship left the islands for the polar missions, the Vanguard Islanders just might regain superiority in the sky with their two Jayhawks.

By then, though, the two cruise ships would have arrived at the Vanguard Islands with their cargo and refugees from the Coral Castle, and more knights to fight.

Lucky halted in front of the palm trees. He moved closer. "You good, Kade?"

"You fucking lied to me," Kade snapped. "You knew the airship was coming all along."

"Of course I lied." He jerked his chin at the other knights. "Nobu, Zen, give us a minute."

Lucky pressed his hand to the bark of a tree, studying it as if it were something alien.

"Listen, I know you're upset," he said, "but I had no choice."

Again Kade was struck by the irony of his situation. The tide had turned, and he was a prisoner in the same spot where he had stood with Lucky not even a week earlier, when Lucky was his prisoner.

He remembered the knight grabbing his arm, wanting to tell him something. It was about the flying battleship, Kade now realized.

"I'm not stupid, mate," Lucky said. "I knew you were sending me home to get the location of the Coral Castle. You did what you bloody had to. I don't think you're evil, but I do think you've lost some perspective."

"*Perspective?*" Kade couldn't credit what he was hearing. "You're trying to lecture me on that? You know I wasn't part of Rolo's insane plans. None of us were. Hell, I *killed* the bastard."

"Yeah? So let's discuss something we haven't. What were you going to do months ago when you found the Coral Castle? Just knock on our door with a smile? Come on, man." Lucky snorted. "What was your great king planning? Was he going to raid our home, steal our resources? Enslave us?"

"You know he wasn't."

"Do I?"

"We were looking for a trading partner. We can still be that."

Lucky chuckled. "The odds of that dwindled when Rolo dropped the nuke and poisoned our land and water."

Kade sighed. Maybe Lucky was right. Maybe he *had* lost perspective. Maybe he had just seen too many evil men doing evil.

"I'll do my part to keep a peace," Kade said. "And I'll do my part to get the weather machines back online. What happens after that, we'll just have to see. For now, I need you to give me some guarantee I can trust you."

"How can I do that?"

"For one, you can tell me what's happened to my people. Even better, I want to see them. Beau, Katherine, Imulah, Pedro, Sofia."

"They're safe; that's all I can say."

Now Kade was the one to laugh. "Safe? From General Doom? The man is batshit crazy."

"He'll follow orders."

"You sure about that? 'Cause he seems to want to go on a killing spree."

"Look, you want to keep the peace, make the announcement. Then I'll work on reuniting you all."

"Fine, let's go."

Nobu and Zen returned as Kade started for the rooftop door that had been blasted away in the recent battle. He went down stairs that were still dark with blood. The landing was chewed up with bullet holes, as was the next passage.

A memory of Dakota dying in one of the blasts made Kade pause. The Cazador warrior had died protecting him and defending this place. He couldn't allow that death, or the deaths of the other soldiers and General Forge, to be for nothing.

Something good could still come of this, especially if they could work together to bring the weather-modification units back online.

Kade stopped at the council chamber. Tarps blocked off the gaping hole where the airship had pried the wall away. There beside the banks of radio equipment was the deck where General Forge had taken his last breath.

"We've set it up so it's connected to all the rigs," Lucky explained.

Kade went over and sat in front of the transmitter, trying

to think what to say. The Cazadores were a violent society, but then again, Rolo had proved deadlier than all of them combined. It wasn't just the Cazadores. All humanity had that brutal gene. Kade had to appeal to them and break that spell.

He exhaled, brought the mic up to his lips, and turned on the button to transmit.

"Citizens of the Vanguard Islands," he said, "this is Kade Long, speaking to you from the capitol tower, asking you to listen very carefully."

He waited a few moments for the crowds on the rig to gather near the various speakers situated throughout the many levels. Translators would be there to relay the message in Spanish.

"As you all know, the forces of the Trident have arrived at our home," Kade said. "I know you're wondering what this means for the future, and all I can say is that our future can still be bright. The Forerunner and his forces have agreed to a truce. They have promised peace."

Lucky folded his arms across his chest and nodded.

"Soon, they will arrive with two ships, bringing refugees to see the sun for the first time in their lives," Kade said. "These refugees have fled their former home, poisoned by the nuclear warhead that Captain Rolo dropped on their land. I ask you all to put your weapons down and welcome them. There will be room for all of us, and food for all of us, and soon, the world will change in ways we never imagined. It will grow bountiful."

He thought for a brief moment about what that meant.

"Our former king, Xavier Rodriguez, has returned and has negotiated this peace with the Forerunner. I will be traveling with Xavier and a group of Hell Divers. We will go to the Earth's North and South Poles, where we will turn the weather-modification machines back on to clear the storms across the world. If all goes to plan, future generations—perhaps even some among us now—will venture to faraway lands, to build new homes and start new communities."

He let the thought settle.

"To see this future, we must be civilized," Kade said. "For too long we have known only war. That must change today, for the sake of our children and for all humanity. Thank you."

He set the mic down, and Lucky nodded.

"See? That wasn't hard," he said. "Now, come, I'll take you to see your friends."

They left through the hallway of kings and warriors. So far, the knights had kept everything in place.

Kade brightened when they arrived at the vault once used to house el Pulpo's riches. A knight opened the door, revealing the shelter filled with children and their caretakers Kade had moved here to prep for the attack.

"King Kade!" shouted a young voice.

Alton came running over, with Katherine and Phyl right behind him. Sofia was also there, nursing little Rhino Jr., crutches leaning up against her chair.

"Is Mags okay?" Sofia asked.

"Doing great."

"Thank the Octopus Lords."

Beau and Roman walked over, looking relieved to see Kade apparently unhurt.

"I'll give you a few minutes," Lucky said.

He closed the hatch as kids and adults crowded around Kade.

Alton grabbed Kade around his waist and hugged him tight.

"Hey, pal," Kade said. "It's okay. Everything's going to be okay."

"You're not harmed?" Beau asked.

"I'm good."

"When they took you, I feared the worst."

"We heard your message," Katherine said. "Do you *really* think we all can live in peace?"

"Yes," Kade answered.

"You speak shit, then," said a Cazador woman behind her, shaking a finger at him. "Or you are blind, King Kade—blind, I say."

"You led them here!" growled a sky person he recognized as Donnie.

"Yeah, this is your fault," said another familiar face.

"Kade's a good man," Katherine said. "He did what he thought was best."

"Yeah, back off, Donnie," Beau said.

"What you going to do?" Donnie asked. "You're a coward."

Roman raised a hand to defend his father, but Beau raised a hand.

"Why are we fighting among ourselves?" he said. "Now is the time to come together."

"Yeah, Cowboy King would never do something bad!" Alton shouted. "You people just sit around, but he's out there fighting."

"Alton, please," Kade said.

Alton turned, chest heaving, eyes blurring with tears.

Hushed voices and arguments broke out around the shelter. These people were scared and angry. They had a right to both emotions.

"Rolo caused all this, and we must deal with it," Kade said. "If you listened to my message, you heard what I said about looking toward the future, a future where the Old World starts to come back and life returns across the continents."

"You can just flip a switch and bring the Old World back?" said an adolescent voice.

It was Phyl.

"Not exactly, and it will take time, but we finally have hope," he replied. "We must be patient and come together, like Beau said."

"We have to trust him," said Beau.

"Right. He's our *king*," Alton said.

"He's not king anymore," Donnie said.

"No," Kade interrupted. "I'm not king, but that doesn't mean I can't help. I'll do everything I can to keep blood from flowing."

The hatch opened, and Lucky stepped into the packed room. The crowd quieted, and some people stepped back, lowering their heads.

"Time's up. We gotta go, Kade," he said.

Kade nodded and turned back to Alton. "I'm going to be gone for a while," he said.

"Bring me. I can help!"

"You have to stay here and watch over Katherine, Phyl, and everyone else. I'll return, and things will get better. I promise, pal."

Kade turned, and his gaze wandered over faces that were frightened, angry, sad. "This is the beginning of a brighter chapter in our lives," he said. "We must have faith and trust in Xavier."

Alton grabbed him by the hand. "Please be careful, Cowboy King," he said.

"Count on it."

Kade hugged him, then nodded at Katherine. She came to him and embraced Kade. Phyl joined in, all four of them enwrapped in a group hug.

Lucky cleared his throat—time to get moving.

Kade stepped back and began to leave but halted, hearing another voice.

"Wait, Kade." Sofia crutched over, her son in a sling across her chest. "Do you need divers?"

"Possibly, but you're in no shape to go."

"I'll dive," Roman said.

Beau put a hand on his son's shoulder.

"Watch over them for me," Kade said to Beau, knowing he didn't have to say it.

He joined Lucky in the hall.

"The Forerunner wants to talk to you again," Lucky said.

The vault door shut behind them with a solid clank.

"Before I take you to him, I need you to be honest," Lucky said. "Are you sure you've told him everything? There's nothing you're hiding?"

Kade looked him in the eye and tried not to hesitate as he lied, just as Lucky had done to him a few days ago.

"I'm not hiding anything."

"Okay, then you won't mind coming on a little *field trip*, as one might call it," Lucky said.

"Come again?"

"The Forerunner is deploying the ship back to Sint Eustatius, where Magnolia and the animals were picked up."

Kade schooled himself to look casual, nonchalant. Had they found Gran Jefe and the others?

"Let's go, then," Kade said. He started walking, but Lucky grabbed him by the arm.

"For your sake, I hope you're being honest, because if you aren't, this truce'll snap like a twig in the wastes."

*   *   *   *   *

Gran Jefe lifted his gaze a thousand feet, up to the top of the Quill, Sint Eustatius's dormant stratovolcano. He stood in the fertile volcanic soil that once supported a lush rain forest. Some of it remained, mostly the dense ferns and strange fungi that had adapted to the dark and toxic ecosystem.

He couldn't see it right now, but he could hear the giant enemy sky horse hovering over the island. An hour had passed since the knights returned in the colossal flying warship. It was the second trip, after arriving yesterday to retrieve Magnolia, Miles, and Jo-Jo.

By then Gran Jefe had already fled with Jonah and Valeria into the dormant volcano, where they had stashed their helicopter. A heat tarp and camo net covered it now, hiding it from the sky far above. The ghost pilot known as Frank was absent, but Gran Jefe had a feeling the AI was watching through cameras.

So far, they had evaded the scans from the enemy airship. But if it was back again, it was hunting. If it got closer, they knew what to do: flee into the labyrinth of caves and tunnels and lose the enemy under the volcano.

The entrance to one of those passages was partially visible through the forest of ferns. There were dozens of lava tunnels down here, connecting to miles upon miles of underground corridors constructed by Cazadores over the past two centuries.

A hundred years before Gran Jefe was born, they were used during a civil war between a king and forces that rose up to dethrone him. Then to train warriors to fight monsters, when the island became the "Man Maker."

Gran Jefe had trained on the island, but he never imagined hiding from the enemy down here. He hated staying hidden, especially knowing that the knights had already taken the Vanguard Islands. He hated leaving his son at risk.

But orders from Xavier were clear. He wanted Mags and the animals to come back to the Vanguard Islands in the Jayhawk sky horse. The second part of that message was code for the rest of their group to hide and wait for Slayer to show up with the second Jayhawk. There was also another group coming, apparently, with a warship that Gran Jefe's Cazador comrades had acquired in Rio de Janeiro on their voyage to extract X and his crew.

So Gran Jefe hid in the meantime, waiting with Valeria and Jonah.

The whirring of the airship grew distant, and he rose up from his rocky hideout.

"I have a look and watch for Slayer," Gran Jefe said.

"*Me voy también*," Jonah replied. "I go, too." The big man stepped up with the sniper rifle he had used to kill some of Crixus's religious fanatics back in Rio. Gran Jefe had spent a few hours listening to the story when they grew bored earlier.

"No, I go alone," he said. "Stay and watch the sky horse with Corporal Valeria."

"You must be cautious of their scanners," she said.

Gran Jefe nodded. "If enemy come, follow the water to the sacrificial chamber. You know this place, yes?"

"Yes," Jonah said.

"Good." Gran Jefe grabbed his pack of rations, water, and gear. Three extra magazines filled his vest pockets, and a hatchet hung from a sheath on his duty belt, along with a knife and pistol.

Slinging his rifle, he ducked under the overhang and took a steep trail up through the jungle. The dense canopy of ferns blocked much of the view, but the path led to an overlook that would give him a panoramic view of the island.

He thought back to when he first trained here. Back then, he had been a fearless, self-centered maniac—one of the many ways he had hurt his ex, Jada, so many times. But finding out he was the father of her child had softened him. It should have been the opposite—*needed* to be.

You must be strong and fierce!

He would do whatever he must to protect his child, another human with the same blood flowing through his veins. It didn't matter how strong or advanced these knights were.

Gran Jefe would cut them all down if it meant protecting that boy.

Weaving between ferns twice his size, he made his way up a bluff that rose above the jungle. Sweating by the time he reached the top, he saw the airship cutting through the skies to the west.

Crouching behind a cluster of rocks, camouflaged by palm fronds and banana leaves, he pushed the rifle scope up to his visor. The airship scanned the shoreline, turning night to day with its powerful searchlights.

Gran Jefe had never seen anything like this giant sky horse in all his travels. Seeing the deadly machine did give him pause. Maybe this was why X had decided to make some sort of deal with them.

As he watched the ship, his heart sank. X was a brave warrior who had fought countless enemies, human and monster. If he had made a deal, it was because this enemy was undefeatable.

But they had not yet met Jorge Mata!

A few minutes later, the ship began to climb.

He lowered his rifle and raised his middle finger.

"Jódete, hijoeputa."

Gran Jefe slung his rifle and started back down the path to let Valeria and Jonah know they were in the clear. It was time to come up with a plan, and he had one in mind that meant no longer hiding.

When Slayer arrived with the other sky horse, they would head back to the islands, drop into the water, and swim to the rigs, where they would start a rebellion. Then they would use the newly acquired warship from Rio to destroy the knights and their robot-man leader, freeing the people of the Vanguard Islands from the inevitable chains that awaited them.

Gran Jefe froze, hearing a faint whirring noise. He stared

at the horizon, where he had last seen the ship. Storm clouds drifted low across the sky, but he saw no sign of the enemy sky horse in the flash and afterglow of the lightning. He watched a little longer, then pushed on.

He had just gotten back to the edge of the path when the whirring came again—this time not behind him but above.

Diving into the undergrowth, he scrambled for cover as bright lights exploded from the floor of the clouds. He rolled away from a dazzling plank of light and kept rolling. His body picked up speed, sliding off the edge of the bluff.

Flailing about him for something to grab on to, he blasted through scrawny weeds and bushes before hitting the thick buttress root of a tree growing out of the side of the bluff and bouncing sideways.

He reached for it, but his fingers scraped the bark and he fell backward. His shoulder pads crunched into a thorn bush that jabbed his exposed neck.

"¡Vete a la mierda!" he cursed.

Something immovable finally stopped his descent with a loud thump. The air burst from his lungs, and he lay on his back a moment, blinking the stars away to watch the sky horse lowering from the clouds. Then he heard a crunching, rending sound.

The tree that had stopped him began to bend backward.

"No, wait. No," he grunted.

Gran Jefe flung himself aside, into the dirt, as the tree's thick but shallow roots pulled free of the steep slope and crashed through the foliage below.

Birds flapped up squawking into the night.

Gran Jefe squirmed into the underbrush, trying to catch his breath. Peering through gaps in the weeds, he watched as the ship hovered over the mountain, beams still searching for him, Jonah, and Valeria.

His heart raced. What if they should find the sky horse Gran Jefe and the others had concealed nearby?

All he could do was hug the ground and hope he was lucky, that the knights would give up and fly away.

It didn't happen.

The humming and whirring remained, and a new noise reached his ears: a steady cranking sound from above.

Gran Jefe unslung his rifle and pointed it up at the enemy sky horse. He watched the bottom of the ship as a hatch opened in the curved undercarriage. A ramp extended downward. Three figures appeared, and though Gran Jefe was far below them, he could see that they weren't alone.

Two yellow-brown beasts trotted out onto the ramp. They looked a bit like the dog that followed King Xavier around. But these animals were bigger, and they wore armor.

As the ship descended, he saw that the dogs were mutated dingoes. Apparently, the knights had found a way to control them.

Change of plans.

Gran Jefe pushed his aching body up and began picking his way down the mountainside. By now, Valeria and Jonah would be going into the tunnels, heading for the sacrificial chamber. But there was also the sky horse and its holographic pilot, Frank. While the ghost pilot could evade the knights by going offline, the Jayhawk itself couldn't. He hoped the heat tarp and camo would help conceal it from the enemy.

Gran Jefe hesitated on the rocky slope of the dormant volcano, conflicted about what to do next. He had promised to meet the others at the sacrificial chamber, but what if the knights captured them? Then who would remain behind to wait for Slayer?

He looked out over the ocean. Slayer might well be their only hope now.

But Gran Jefe couldn't leave Valeria and Jonah to fight on their own. They would need someone with knowledge of those tunnels, and no one still breathing knew them better than Gran Jefe.

THREE

Bored, X sat in the padded surgical chair, watching as the new prosthetic limb was fitted to his body. A surgical robot moved delicately around it, using lasers to secure it to the stump where X had lost his arm to Horn, the bastard son of el Pulpo and former leader of the skinwalkers.

For the past two hours, X had endured surgery from an array of devices connected to a robotic arm mounted to the overhead. There wasn't much pain from where the operation fused the metal of his prosthesis with his flesh and bone, thanks in large part to the cocktail of medicines flowing into his veins.

He sat there fighting the boredom, thinking about everything that had happened over his lifetime to land him in this chair.

You're lucky to be bored and not worm food.

How many situations had he survived where other men and women perished? How many beasts had he slain? How many men had he killed? From el Pulpo and Horn to Crixus, the freak devil-worshipper who almost burned X alive.

It seemed there was an unending supply of evil in the world.

X was pretty damned good at reading people, but he was

still working on a read for the Forerunner. Then again, he wasn't entirely a person. Perhaps there were good parts to him. Perhaps he truly was looking out for the best interests of his people. Indeed, Captain Rolo had made the first strike by nuking the Sunshine Coast. One could argue that the Forerunner's return attack on the Vanguard Islands was measured and surgical, removing only General Forge and those who fought against the knights.

But one could also argue that it was all a ploy to get the islands to surrender without a fight. X couldn't blame Kade for surrendering either. They both understood trying to save lives. It had all been a big gamble in the apocalypse. Nations never knew for certain what opposing governments would do in response to attacks. Measured, or scorched earth—with tyrants it was always a risk.

All X could do was hope this Forerunner wasn't a tyrant and would end up being reasonable after X and Kade turned on the weather-modification technology. That everyone could live together in relative peace after that. And then X could go out there and find Michael. That was the fairy-tale ending: to see Michael and Layla one last time and make sure they were safe. But X knew that in the postapocalyptic world, fairy-tale endings were as rare as sunshine.

He glanced up as the intercom buzzed. A female doctor with short, curly hair stood behind a glass wall, talking on the comm. *Craiger,* X remembered.

"Almost done," she said. "We need to do some testing now."

X grunted.

"Try the fingers. Curl them in."

X flexed and straightened his fingers.

"Raise the arm, please."

He did that, too.

"Now down."

X lowered the arm.

"How's that all feel?"

"Just fine, Doc. Now can I get up?"

"Yes. Come over to the glass."

X put his boots down and wondered why the airship was moving again. He could sense the vibration through his boots on the deck. It was only the slightest trembling, but he knew it well, having spent most of his years living on the *Hive*.

That was a good trembling. With the bad kind, the ship rattled like a tin can.

"Are we already on our way to the poles, Doc?" X asked.

Craiger changed the subject. "Next, I want you to hit the glass."

"*Hit* the glass? Like, punch it?" X asked.

"Yes, as hard as you can."

"Is this a joke?"

"Am I smiling?"

"As you wish, Doc," X whispered. He clenched the robotic fingers, looking down at the smooth alloy. Then he cocked his arm back and prepared to swing with all his might—and froze in that position.

Not exactly *froze*. He could still turn his body, but the prosthesis wouldn't move.

"The hell is this?" he asked.

"The last test to see if it's working properly." Craiger stepped back from the glass. "Have a seat. Someone will come and get you shortly."

She pushed a remote on the other side of the window, and the metal arm relaxed, allowing X to move it again.

He grumbled under his breath as he moved back to the chair. He looked at it but decided to stand. Anger surged through him, but he wasn't really that surprised to know they would build some sort of fail-safe mechanism into the limb to stop him from using it against the Forerunner and his knights.

On the one hand, X was glad to have the prosthetic arm. On the other, it further enslaved him.

He looked down at the arm. Inside the alloy was a remote control allowing the knights to operate X like a damned robot.

The hatch opened, and one of those knights stepped in. Lieutenant Gaz, or Lucky, as his comrades referred to him.

"Xavier," he said with a nod.

"Call me X."

"All right, X, come with me."

They walked out of the surgical bay and into the chamber filled with the medical pods. Two guards waiting there fell in behind X.

"Where are we headed?" X asked.

Lucky looked over his shoulder. "*Headed?*"

"The airship's moving."

The knight looked ahead as they rounded a corner to a connecting corridor. Two more knights waited outside a hatch. They stepped back, and Lucky opened the hatch, gesturing for X to go inside a large communal space with three bunks.

Magnolia sat up in one of them, and Miles jumped down and bounded over to X. They weren't alone. In the corner of the large space, Jo-Jo sat up from a pile of pillows and blankets. She knuckle-walked over, bright eyed and healthy.

X bent down with a smile as Miles jumped up and licked his face. Magnolia glanced at his arm before embracing him in a hug. Jo-Jo waited her turn while eyeing Lucky and the guards in the corridor.

"Thought you'd like to see them, but don't get too comfortable," Lucky said. "We'll have a briefing shortly, and you'll meet your diving team."

"Diving team?" X asked.

Lucky once again ignored X and closed the hatch, sealing it with a click.

"Chuckle-f..." X muttered.

Shaking off his anger, he sat on the deck with Miles, stroking him. Raising his robotic arm, he reached out to Jo-Jo, but she reared back, grunting.

"It's okay," he said. "I won't hurt you."

"I'm surprised they gave you that," Magnolia said.

"Don't be. It comes with strings attached." He curled the fingers. "They planted a transmitter inside that can control the limb."

"Seriously?" Magnolia let out a huff and slowly shook her head, murmuring, "Bastards."

"Where's Kade?" X asked.

"They took him away to make an announcement," Magnolia said. "Telling everyone across the islands to stand down. They played it on the ship while you were in that pod."

"Yeah, I couldn't hear shit in that thing."

"It was a good message, but..." She shook her head as the words trailed off. Then she looked at X with a serious gaze. "Maybe we were wrong. Maybe we should have—"

"Don't," X whispered. "I'm sure they're listening to us, so be careful what you say."

Magnolia gave a subtle nod and shifted to a new subject.

"How do you feel?"

"Feel great, if I'm being honest." He scooted over to Jo-Jo, holding up his flesh-and-blood arm. "You look great too, pal."

She leaned her head down, gleaming black eyes centered on X. Her spiky hair lay flat, indicating a relaxed attitude.

He carefully checked her burn wounds and saw that they were almost healed. The deep abrasions on her neck had scabbed over and didn't show any sign of infection.

"How about you—how goes it?" X asked.

Magnolia tucked a lock of blue hair behind her ear. "Not going to lie. I miss Rodger."

"I know you do." He reached up. "Come over here."

She got down on the deck, and he gave her a hug. Miles licked her arm, and Jo-Jo nudged her. For a few seconds, they huddled together, but the moment didn't last.

The hatch opened behind them, and Lucky stepped back inside.

X noticed something as he got to his feet. The tremor in the deck had ceased. The ship was no longer in motion. They must be hovering, for X hadn't felt them land.

"Let's go," said the knight.

Magnolia got up, too.

"Just X," Lucky said.

"No, Magnolia and my animals will be on my team," X said. "That was the deal."

"We're not meeting your team right now—change of plans. Come on."

X hesitated, then turned to Mags. "It's okay," he said.

Miles tried to follow him out, but he signaled for the dog to sit.

"I'll be back, buddy, don't worry," X said. "Mags, watch him."

She got down and held Miles while Jo-Jo knuckle-walked closer, muscles flexing under her rough black hair.

X didn't look back again as he left with Lucky. Two more knights joined them in the corridor, and they set off through the colossal vessel.

"Guess you're not going to tell me where to now, right?" X asked.

"To the launch bay," Lucky said.

X didn't turn, but he paid close attention to the rap of boots behind them. The guards followed closely, only two or three strides behind. Lucky marched with a hand on his sword hilt—the first time X noticed this. And it was the sort of thing he would have noticed before.

Something was off. Something had happened.

His heart quickened as his sixth sense activated, and with it his killer instinct. On the trek through the corridors, he began mentally preparing for pain. Not long ago, he was doing the same thing with Crixus, the devil-worshipping wacko in Rio de Janeiro who had captured him and Magnolia.

Hell, it wasn't the first time he had been in an impossible situation and survived. But this? X was a prisoner in a giant warship, with an arm *they* controlled. What was he going to do, kill them with his breath?

Lucky halted ahead at a pair of double doors and pushed his face against a green slot that scanned his eyes. The doors whisked open to a launch bay that X didn't recognize. The dark, cavernous space was at least three times the size of the launch bay on the *Hive*.

A light flicked on directly across the space, illuminating shuttered viewports. In front of them stood Kade; behind him, General Jack. The Forerunner motored over in his electric chair, followed by two more knights and Dr. Craiger.

"Xavier, you're looking much better," said the Forerunner's synthetic voice. "I trust you feel like a new man?"

"I feel fine," he replied. "Ready to get this mission over with. Are we already heading to the poles?"

"We haven't even left, because we still have business to attend to."

The Forerunner raised his hand, and shutters lowered to reveal a mountain that X instantly recognized. In that moment, he knew that the knights had discovered Gran Jefe and his comrades.

"Come, have a look," said the Forerunner.

X walked over, his heart quickening again. Kade shot him a glance.

"As you obviously can see, we're hovering over the Quill, a dormant volcano on the island of Sint Eustatius, not far from where you told us we'd find Magnolia and your animals," Lucky said. "My mate Kade here told me there are no more Cazador forces out there, but we believe that to be a lie."

The Forerunner rotated his chair to X, studying him with that strange blue eye.

"Our peace must be based on trust, Xavier Rodriguez and Kade Long." The Forerunner looked over to Kade. "Come here."

Kade walked over, stopping next to X.

Dr. Craiger handed the Forerunner a remote. Before X could do anything, his prosthetic arm rose, the fingers open.

X fought to step back, but the device had complete control of the fingers, which clamped around Kade's neck before he could react. He choked out a cry of surprise.

The Forerunner worked the small remote, and X's arm lifted Kade off the ground, boots kicking as he struggled for air.

"Kade Long told us there isn't anyone else down there, but our animals have picked up a scent," said the Forerunner.

X stared into the eyes of his friend and fellow Hell Diver while involuntarily choking the life out of him.

"I won't ask again," said the Forerunner. "Where are your forces?"

*   *   *   *   *

Michael pressed the binoculars to his eyes and scanned the white-caps out to the horizon. Still shaken by the sight, he searched for the patched-up hull of the boat they had seen this morning, which resembled the Viking longships of a thousand years ago.

The presence of any boat was strange enough, but this one was being rowed by *galley slaves*. None of it made sense. Where had they come from? And where were they going?

There had to be a port out there, somewhere on the mainland. There couldn't possibly be a slave camp in the Canary chain, or Timothy would have spotted them on the flyover before setting down. Gabi would also have discovered them long ago, or they would have discovered her.

He tilted the binos skyward, searching for the airship. Knowing that Timothy was up there watching over them no longer reassured Michael—not after what he had seen today.

After another pan with the binoculars, he stuffed them into his vest. His hand free, he drew his pistol and took the winding trail down the bluff. Waves crashed against the rocks below, not far from the hidden entrance to their new home.

As Michael patrolled, he weighed their options. One, they could take their chances staying here, and be on constant watch. Two, they could head back to the ship and start over, looking for another place to live. Or, three, they could live in the air indefinitely.

There was a fourth option, though, a risky one: find out where the masters of those slaves lived, and erase them from the face of the Earth. He had no mercy for any human who sought to own and control another human.

Michael heaved a worried sigh. The second and third options were not the life he wanted for Bray. Living in the sky was not much of a life at all. He had grown up that way, but back then the ship was a community. He had friends. School. Role models. Now it was just him, Layla, Victor, Gabi, and Timothy.

Bray needed open space to play, to learn, to be a kid. And he needed sunshine.

Option four was too risky.

Michael gazed up at the half moon. The sky wasn't safe either, not with all the electrical storms and too few crew members to keep the *Vanguard* in the air. Even with the threat from the slavers, staying here still seemed the best choice. But fighting against these evil men seemed unrealistic, especially with only one arm and without the major firepower his little force would need if they were to stand a chance.

"Tin."

He looked over his shoulder to see Layla, walking up the path with their one laser rifle cradled.

"Time for you to come to bed with Bray," she said. "I'll take watch."

Victor hurried up the winding trail behind her. "I watch," he said. "You two both sleep. You need sleep more than me."

Michael joined them in front of the bluff overlooking the entrance to the cave system below. Weeds rustled, shifting in the sea breeze. A branch above them creaked.

"We need to come up with a schedule for patrols," he said. "I want someone on watch at all times."

Victor nodded. "Gabi will help, too."

"Has she said anything more about slavers?"

"Yes. She's very scared. She believes them to be the same people that…" Victor stared out over the water with rage in his eyes. "The same evil that came here and killed our friends."

Michael nodded. It was the only plausible explanation. He looked at his wife, her youthful face a mask of worry. She knew what these slavers had done here before, in these very tunnels.

"I will watch tonight; then tomorrow we make a new plan," Victor said. "Okay?"

"Thanks, Victor, I'll let Timothy know," Michael said. He holstered his pistol and patted his friend on the back.

"Pepper, do you copy?" Michael said into his headset.

Static crackled back, then a faint reply.

"Good evening, Chief. How are you?" Timothy asked.

"Good. Heading to bed, but Victor will be on patrol. You let him know if you see anything."

"Of course, Chief. Good night."

"Good night, Timothy."

Michael handed the headset to Victor, then hesitated as he scanned the ocean. In the distance, where sea met sky, stood the silhouette of a ship.

He pulled out his binos again, searching and finding nothing but whitecaps.

"See something?" Layla asked.

Michael shook his head. "Just my eyes playing tricks on me."

"Be careful out here," Layla said. She led the way back down the twisting path to the cave entrance. The high tide made them walk through knee-deep water to reach the ladder up to the overlook. At the top, they took the corridor back into the labyrinth of caves.

Michael had worked to fortify the cave dwelling's interior the best he could with the supplies available. A steel wall with a thick hatch provided one line of defense. It wasn't meant to stop an invading force—just slow down anyone trying to sneak up on them. He had already excavated a hidden tunnel inside the communal space, formerly blocked off by a sheet of metal. It would take some work, but he was going to make an escape route in case they ever found themselves cornered.

"Tomorrow, I'm going to start on a secondary line of security," Michael said. "Some old-fashioned tin cans on a string, and other alert systems I'll need to fiddle with, including motion sensors."

"Good. I'll help," Layla said. "That will make me feel better if we ever need another way out."

"Agreed, but with everything we've got going, and with

Timothy watching out from above, we should have plenty of time to get out of here if someone does find us."

Michael wanted to believe the words he was saying, but he feared the worst: that the slavers would return to capture them, or worse. If there could be something worse—death almost seemed better than seeing his family in chains.

He shook away the dark thoughts as they arrived back at the communal living space. The door to Gabi's room was shut, and the door to their room was as well. Layla quietly opened it, then nodded at Michael, confirming that Bray was still asleep.

They undressed and got into bed.

"Everything's going to be okay, Tin," Layla said.

Michael nodded and then kissed her lips. "I love you. Good night."

He rested his head on his pillow, staring up at the rough basalt ceiling. She turned on her side, curling up against him.

Bray slept peacefully in his crib at the end of the bed, face-down, butt in the air, a stuffed elephant clutched in his hand.

"Go to sleep," Layla whispered.

Michael closed his eyes and tried to think of something positive to help him relax. Layla helped by putting a hand on his hand. They often fell asleep this way.

Exhausted, he drifted off quickly, falling into a deep dream of the past.

In it, he sat on the torn carpet of his apartment, fixing a robotic vacuum. The hatch opened, and X walked inside holding a bag of steaming orange noodles—his hands-down favorite meal on the *Hive*.

Then Michael sat at a table in the trading post with Layla, eating fortune cookies. The quote from his read, *Accept your past without regrets. Handle your present with confidence. Face your future without fear.*

He remembered the boy at the end of the table, to whom Michael had given his broken cookie pieces. A vivid memory of that young child's eyes brightening at the taste of the treat played in his mind.

So did the next scene, when Michael had pushed past the rope cordon at the launch bay, with a little help from Captain Ash. He had given X the fortune-cookie paper before his dive into Hades.

The dreamed memories transported him from bright images like this to nightmares. To finding out X wasn't coming back from Hades. To learning that he had survived and was down on the surface for most of a decade. That they had left him down there alone for all those years.

The past dozen years flashed by in his mind, and with those flashes he saw the ghosts of the dead. Faces of the people who haunted his dreams. His father, Aaron; his best friend, Rodger Mintel. Role models like Katrina DaVita and, of course, X. And his stalwart, playful dog, Miles.

They were gone now, never coming back.

As he tossed and turned in bed, his paralyzed mind flitted in and out of a new nightmare. In it, he stood on the beach outside their new home, holding Bray's hand as the boy ran along the ankle-deep surf, trying to jump away from the waves.

A Klaxon sounded, and Michael looked up at the descending airship. The rumble of motors reached his ears, and he turned with Bray to the sea, where four skiffs motored over the waves.

"RUN!" Layla shouted. She dashed out onto the beach with Victor, both of them firing rifles. Return fire came, and Victor went down. Layla also slumped over, a hand on her belly.

"Layla!" Michael shouted.

He ran over with Bray against his chest, bullets zipping past them. When he got to Layla, she waved them away. "Get Bray out of here!"

In the old days, Michael could have carried them both, but not now, with one arm. He had to make a choice: save his son and leave his wife, or all die together.

The impossible decision lingered as he stood there.

"Go... please, go," Layla whimpered.

"Ma-ma!" Bray wailed.

Michael turned as the skiffs slid up onto the shore, faceless warriors in black armor piling out. The airship lowered, and Timothy aimed a mounted machine gun down at the beach. A missile suddenly rocketed away from the boat and slammed into the belly of the airship.

A bullet hit Michael in the shoulder, and he spun, losing his grip on Bray. The airship roared as it came crashing down into the water, flames bursting out of a gaping rent in its hull.

He crawled over to Bray, his shoulder on fire from the bullet wound. The boy sobbed on the sand, reaching out to Michael.

"Da-da!" he wailed. "Ma-ma!"

Michael could hear the distant voices of the approaching slavers. He reached Bray and clutched him against his body, then held up a hand as the men approached.

Layla lay there, unmoving. Already gone.

"No, please, God," Michael whispered.

He raised his hand to shield Bray as the men walked over with their rifles.

"No, stop!" Michael shouted.

The scene faded to darkness and Michael jerked awake, chest heaving as he gasped for air. His vision cleared, and he saw a room with light spilling under the door. A hand gripped his arm, and a soft voice pulled him back to reality.

"Michael, it's okay, just a bad dream," Layla whispered. She reached for his face and pulled it in her direction. "We're okay. We're safe."

Michael closed his eyes, trying to shake the awful nightmare.

But it had been *so* real, so horrific. He couldn't seem to get a grip.

"Tin, it's okay; everything's fine," Layla soothed.

Michael looked over at Bray to make sure he hadn't woken him. The boy remained in the same position: cheek down, backside up in the air.

Exhaling, Michael eased his head back down on the pillow.

"Just a bad dream," Layla said again.

Michael shook his head. "It's not just that. We aren't safe here," he whispered. "I don't think we will ever be truly safe."

She nudged up against him and put her head on his chest.

"As long as we're together, it's enough," she said.

Michael nodded. But deep down he knew that wasn't enough. He wanted a place for Bray to grow up where he could live in peace, without fear. It seemed this was not that place after all. As long as people were around, there would always be evil.

He couldn't let what happened in the dream happen in real life.

Tomorrow, he was going to learn more about these slavers. The only way to defend against them was to understand their strengths and their weaknesses and see where they lived.

If Michael's little group was to have any hope of living here, he had to know what they were up against. Then he would decide whether this could still be a home, or whether they must flee back into the skies.

FOUR

Gran Jefe moved like a spirit through the jungle along the base of the mountain, one eye on the airship hovering above the volcano. So far, he hadn't seen the knights extract anyone. Perhaps Valeria and Jonah had made it to the sacrificial chamber, where they could stay hidden among the bones of beasts that Cazador warriors had battled during their training in these caverns. But the tide had changed. Now the Cazadores were being hunted on their own ground.

But I hunt, too.

Creeping through the dense underbrush, the Cazador of Cazadores remembered his training here, over ten years ago. Inside the mountain, miles of secret tunnels awaited. More than a few greenhorn fighters had entered never to emerge again, their corpses sealed inside.

In that Stygian darkness, those men and women had lost the battle to Sirens, bone beasts, and other monsters set loose in the dormant volcano to train and test the Cazadores.

Gran Jefe thought of the seasoned Barracuda fighters who had taught him to survive inside the dark, wet passages. Legendary warriors like General Rhino, Whale, Fuego, and Wendig. They had taught Gran Jefe the skills he must use now.

Always be aware of your surroundings.

He recalled a raid in Texas when he had mistaken sea manatees for boulders. That wasn't the first time, but it had better be the last.

Moving through a section of gangly mutant trees, he scanned the area for hostiles using the hazardous terrain for concealment. Lightning flashed over the jungle, revealing bark covered in strange blisters, and branches of venomous thorns reaching out at his armor. If he wanted to get to the sacrificial chamber, he must get through worse.

A distant rumbling forced Gran Jefe down, but it was just thunder. The noise echoed away, and he continued his trek. Finally, a half hour after he tumbled down the slope, he spotted the first signs of an ancient trail. Vines grew over the old path, but he could see just enough to follow its winding way toward the mountain. He followed it to a tunnel entrance shored with rusted metal beams. Malevolent-looking barbed vines formed a living curtain.

Pushing the vines apart with his rifle, he ducked inside. He turned on the light attached to the barrel, playing it over the path ahead.

He checked the ceiling for cave-ins. That was another thing he had learned long ago: that monsters weren't the only things that could kill you down here. The terrain and vegetation could be just as hostile.

He moved steadily but with great care, rifle shouldered, its light sweeping for weak spots and sinkholes. The dual beams from his helmet captured mushrooms the size of a human skull, slick with moisture, growing out of cracks in the walls. Around the next corner, spongy bluish mosses carpeted the ground.

Despite the lack of sunlight, the caves teemed with life.

Beetles skittered into holes, and a spider retreated to a web that covered half the ceiling. Gran Jefe ducked under it, then jerked back from a snapping blossom with spiked petals that held its prey fast as its caustic nectar slowly digested it.

Seeing the carnivorous plant reminded him of an old comrade who'd slipped into a ravine on a raid in Florida. Similar lava-orange flowers had made the trench their home, and by the time his companions threw down a rope, the petals had swallowed him, armor and all. Gran Jefe remembered his anguished cries, which were silenced by Fuego's flamethrower in a blast that set the ravine ablaze.

Gran Jefe shook away the gruesome image as he came to an intersection. After sweeping the corridor with his light, he headed deeper into the mountain. Two steps into the rocky cavern, he flinched back from movement on the ground. His light captured a pale, eyeless snake hissing out of a burrow to strike at his ankle. Before it could recoil, he stomped the creature, smashing its head to mush.

Soon he heard the trickle of water. He was close to the stream, which meant the sacrificial chamber was not far. Gran Jefe picked up the pace, moving his 250 pounds plus armor and gear through the darkness as silently as a shadow. His helmet beam found another fork in the corridor, and a shallow stream trickled down the center of the path branching off to the left. Thick wooden beams sagged from the ceiling of the right pathway, where a partial collapse had filled it with debris.

A memory arose. He had found this very spot with three other greenhorns, knowing that their prey came to the stream to drink. Armed with spears and cutlasses and wearing only light armor and helmets, the squad had followed the rivulet here. Perched beside the stream was a female Siren—an easy target. All four of them had charged with their blades, unaware that the female wasn't alone.

A male had stalked them. It grabbed the young man on rear guard, spinning him and biting through an artery in his neck. By the time Gran Jefe turned, the beast had torn off the kid's face, leaving him to bleed out while it skittered forward.

Gran Jefe had a scar where one of those claws slashed his leg under the armor plate, coming centimeters from opening his femoral artery. Swinging his cutlass, Gran Jefe had hacked the hand off the beast, then stabbed it through the eye socket.

An animal howl brought him back from the memory. He stood in the dark stream, ears perked. Narrowing his eyes, he listened again for the noise.

It came a moment later.

He was hearing the mutant dingoes.

Gran Jefe waded out into the stream, boots splashing. The sacrificial chamber wasn't far.

The barking came again, then a distant shout. It sounded like English.

Moving his finger to the trigger, he skirted the rubble of the cave-in. On the left, the stream flowed down a sloped corridor, draining deeper into the mountain. As he recalled, the corridor met the sacrificial chamber at the top of this incline.

He navigated the slick passage with cautious steps. As he advanced, he turned off his helmet lights, using only the tactical beam on his rifle barrel. Nearing the crest of the incline, he doused the light and listened. The barking had stopped, but he could hear rustling and voices.

He slung the rifle and went down on all fours, crawling upward. Just feet away from the crest of the trail, he saw a weak glow that had to be human in origin. Whether enemy or comrade, he didn't know, though he doubted Valeria and Jonah would advertise their location.

Anxious to see, he pulled himself up to the top of a waterfall that cascaded down a tiered rock ledge to a pool in a sprawling cave. Above the pool where he stood, another cataract fell, no doubt fed by yet another, higher fall.

This was it: the sacrificial chamber.

All the noise seemed to be coming from that second level. He started out toward the first pool. Bones of sacrificed beasts protruded from the water, along with the deformed head of a Siren in the shallows. A snapped-off spear shaft jutted from the crown, left by the warrior who skewered it long ago. The entire chamber was filled with the bones of kills, discarded here after the hunters took their trophies and left their sacrifices to the Octopus Lords.

Gran Jefe hurried around the edge of the pool, to the water cascading down from the ledge above him. As he searched for the best way up the slick rock face, a deep voice rang out.

"Stop! Don't shoot!"

He knew that voice.

"*El Inmortal*," Gran Jefe breathed.

He worked his way up the ledge until he had a view of the upper pool. It had to be three hundred feet across, and six figures stood on a rock shelf at the edge of the water. X stood with his prosthetic arm held up.

This was indeed the former king, and he had a rifle barrel nudged up against his back.

The armored dingoes sat on their haunches, illuminated by the orange lights on their spiked collars. They were easily twice the size of the dog that followed X around everywhere. No, these weren't your average *chuchos*. These beasts had wicked-looking yellow teeth, and legs as thick as Gran Jefe's. Each dingo was roughly the size of the knight standing behind them. The man aimed his rifle at a tunnel opening to the right of the pool, where Gran Jefe noticed two more figures. Jonah and Valeria held their weapons pointed at the hostile forces.

X walked out onto the slab of rock, still holding up his prosthetic metal arm and hand while saying something that Gran Jefe couldn't make out. Two knights followed him, but the others remained in the shadows.

Gran Jefe pulled himself up onto the ledge and squirmed over to some boulders for cover. On his belly, he stuck his rifle between the rocks. Then he flipped the scope up to his eyes, zooming in with the night-vision optics. He sighted up the knight behind X, then moved his finger to the trigger.

"We've made a truce," X called out with his hands still up. "I need your help. We're heading to the North and South Poles to activate the weather tech."

Valeria and Jonah didn't move as X made his way over.

"Put those guns down," he said. "No one needs to die today."

Gran Jefe watched, heart pounding, not understanding any of this. The former king had given them all orders to hide.

Suddenly, Gran Jefe understood. X had come to save them and get them to surrender now that the knights knew they were here.

But if that was what X had planned, it worked. Valeria and Jonah both put their weapons on the ground, and the knights moved in, grabbing them.

"Where are the others?" asked one of the knights.

Gran Jefe zoomed in on Valeria. She said nothing; nor did Jonah. He moved the sights back to X, who walked over to the edge of the pool, staring out.

"Gran Jefe, you out there?" he shouted. His voice echoed through the caverns. "If you can hear me, turn yourself in! It's over!"

Gran Jefe couldn't believe the words he was hearing. The Immortal had bent the knee, proving himself a coward, just like Kade, the cowboy Hell Diver who led the knights right to the islands during his failed short reign as king, giving the enemy the keys to paradise.

If Gran Jefe was the only one who still had the balls to stand and fight, so be it.

"Jorge!" X yelled. "I know you're out there!"

Gran Jefe sighted up the scar on X's face and considered blowing it off. But… what was that? X was speaking, but no words were coming out.

Closing one eye, Gran Jefe focused on the Immortal's lips as they mouthed something out of view of the knights.

What you trying to say, cabrón?

X seemed to be mouthing a word. Was it English or Spanish? Something with a *W*—no, an *R. Ruh… Run.*

Gran Jefe pulled back from his scope and felt a grin forming on his grimy face. The former king wasn't bending the knee. He hadn't surrendered. He had bought them all time to defeat this enemy.

"Release the dingoes!" someone shouted.

Gran Jefe squirmed back from the rocks, then turned and slid down the ledge. The short drop to the pool hurt his ankles as he splashed in, but he hardly slowed. Cradling his rifle, he hurried back the way he had come, skirting around the pool on a rock ledge and melting into a tunnel, with new orders.

This was the place where he had become a man, learning to hunt and trap monsters. It seemed the time for hunting had truly come again. If the knights followed, he would slay them one by one.

Entering a new cavern, he halted at the faint sound of gunfire.

Gran Jefe turned, his heart skipping. Had they killed the Immortal?

He listened for a long moment, but this gunfire seemed too distant, far too muffled, to have come from the last chamber.

Someone else was out there fighting. Maybe he wasn't alone after all.

*   *   *   *   *

Kade flinched at the unmistakable crack of machine-gun fire. The airship *Trident* was firing at something, or someone, but he couldn't see anything in the inky darkness.

The cold deck of the empty storage quarters vibrated under his feet. The Forerunner had locked him in here after X half strangled him with the new robotic arm they had surgically grafted onto his body.

"They're on the move!" shouted someone in the launch bay.

Kade was conflicted in heart and mind, second-guessing himself. Should he have told the complete truth about the rebel forces still at large outside the Vanguard Islands? It seemed the knights had located Gran Jefe, Valeria, and Jonah after all.

Automatic gunfire erupted outside the hatch. He reached out, fumbling for the handle in the pitch-blackness until his fingers connected with it. He pulled, but it was locked.

"Let me out!" he shouted.

Footfalls answered. Kade tensed as someone on the other side unlocked the hatch. The metal door swung open, revealing Nobu cradling an assault rifle. Behind him, Zen held the .50-caliber sniper rifle that he had used back in Australia to save Kade's life from a flying squadron of Sirens.

"Let's go," Nobu said.

Kade stepped out, scanning the now-empty launch bay. The Forerunner and X were gone, and so were the other knights.

"Where's Lucky?" Kade asked.

The airship jolted slightly, and Zen grabbed Kade by the arm, pulling him out into the launch bay. Nobu walked behind him as they set off across the space. Humming resonated under their boots, and thunder rattled the hull. It told Kade they were flying in the storms outside the Vanguard Islands.

Sporadic lightning showed him the elliptical shape of the portholes along the hull. Zen seemed to be leading him toward a hatch in the center of the launch bay. As they got closer, Kade saw an armored figure on the other side of the hatch, illuminated by the strobing muzzle flash from the weapon he fired. The racket drowned out any thunderclap.

"Stay back!" Zen yelled over the din. He stepped up to the hull and tapped a button activating the dual hatches. They slid open to an enclosed machine-gun turret on the exterior of the airship. It was no more than six feet in diameter, with reinforced glass panels to provide the gunner a sprawling yet safe view.

A belt-fed machine gun angled downward through an opening in the center of the turret. The gunner was Lucky. Empty casings lay scattered around him, joined by a steady stream of brass. Attached to the wall of the enclosed turret was some sort of robotic arm equipped with a winch.

Thunder boomed again as Zen walked out and tapped Lucky on the shoulder.

"I've got Kade!" he yelled.

Lucky turned, then swiveled the machine gun for Zen to take over.

From where Kade stood, he couldn't see what Lucky had been firing at—couldn't see anything but clouds on the horizon.

Lucky moved back into the launch bay, flipping up the visor to reveal his enraged red face. Kade hardly had time to react as the lieutenant reached out and grabbed him by the shirt, pushing him backward. All Kade could do was plant his boots firmly on the deck in defiance.

"I warned you!" Lucky shouted.

Kade stared into the furious eyes. He felt that same anger, a rage growing inside that made him want to unleash a wave of violence. But something kept him steady, patient, knowing that escalation would just get more people killed.

"Tell me what the bloody hell's going on!" Kade demanded.

Lucky grabbed Kade again, yanking him toward the machine-gun turret. Kade tripped, falling to his knees.

"You want to know? Want to know what *you* did? I'll show you," Lucky said. He grabbed Kade under the arm and yanked him to his feet. Wind hissed through the gun turret as Kade stepped out to the platform, breathing in the ocean-scented air and... *smoke.*

He sniffed, confirming that was indeed what he smelled. Moving up to the viewports next to Zen, Kade looked down at the ocean. Bobbing up and down was the familiar shape of the *Angry 'Cuda.* Plumes of smoke tendriled away from the main cabin of the research ship.

No, Kade thought.

He searched for Tia, Zuni, and Slayer but saw no one on the deck. What he did see was a Jayhawk. There were also the armored personnel carrier and trailers he had deployed. The mission to Texas had worked, netting two of the choppers, but it had cost the life of his best friend, Woody, and the Barracuda soldier Sergeant Blackburn.

Now it seemed those sacrifices were in vain.

"You should have told me, but now this peace . . ." Lucky scoffed as his words trailed. He raised a hand. "Nobu, Zen, board the ship. Kill anyone that resists."

"No, wait," Kade said. "Give me the chance to have them surrender!"

"You had your chance," Lucky said.

Kade grabbed him by a shoulder plate, only for Lucky to punch him in the nose, knocking him to the deck. He pushed himself up, right into the barrel of Nobu's assault rifle.

"Stay down, Hell Diver," he growled.

Blood dripped from his nose as Kade stared up.

"You hurt them, and I won't help you," he growled back. "This truce will be over."

"I believe the Forerunner will decide whether this peace is over," Lucky said.

"Just let me speak to the crew. I can get them to come with us. I'm begging you. There's a reason I didn't tell you—"

"And what reason would that be?"

The synthetic voice of the Forerunner resonated through the launch bay from some unseen location. Kade looked over his shoulder, searching for the bizarre blue eye of the cyborg in the shadows.

"I have someone I care very deeply for on that vessel, which is why I kept it a secret. A girl—a woman," Kade said in a measured voice. "The daughter of a Hell Diver who died many years ago on a mission to the wastes. I promised him that day I'd watch out for her."

"It seems to me the girl is not the only valuable thing on this vessel."

Kade followed the voice up to the red dot of a recessed camera in the overhead, just in front of the hatches.

"This woman is not the reason you kept the vessel from me," said the cyborg. "You kept information a secret because of the obsolete helicopter on the deck. What is that, a Jayhawk? Do you still not understand how outmatched you and your barbaric allies are?"

Kade clenched his jaw, then nodded.

"Lieutenant Gaz, send the Hell Diver to the ship," said the Forerunner. "Let's see if we can end this without wasting any more ammunition."

"Get up," Lucky said.

Kade stood and dragged his sleeve across his face, smearing the blood. Nobu left, returning a minute later with a harness, which he forced over Kade's head. Lucky took the cable from the robotic winch and pulled the slack over to Kade.

"No more chances," he said as he clipped the carabiner on the cable to Kade's harness.

The side hatch opened, and Lucky activated the winch. The arm extended over the open water.

"If he tries anything, you know what to do," Lucky said. There was tension in his voice, which told Kade the knight really didn't like giving the order. But Kade also knew that he had given these soldiers no choice.

Zen unslung his .50-caliber sniper rifle and backed away from the machine gun. He chambered a round behind Kade.

"You have five minutes," Lucky said. He hit the toggle switch on the winch, activating the arm that pulled Kade out over the water. The next bump of the switch lowered him into the rain and wind. He squinted, searching again for Tia, Zuni, and Slayer. If they were down there, they were hiding.

A wind shear hit Kade on the way down, swinging him to his left. Blood dripped from his nose. He didn't bother wiping it away.

Kade looked back up at another glowing red dot. It wasn't a camera now but the laser sight on Zen's rifle. A matching red dot hovered over Kade's chest.

He looked back down as the ship's deck rose up to meet his boots.

"Tia! Slayer! Zuni! It's me, Kade!"

He landed between the cabin and the armored personnel carrier.

"Put down your weapons!" Kade shouted. "You have to give yourselves up!"

Reaching up, he unlocked the carabiner at the end of the winch cable. Then he started off toward the cabin, looking for movement behind the shattered windows. A dorsal hatch suddenly rose up in the deck, and the familiar voice of Tia called out from the darkness.

"Kade, is it really you?" She raised her face slightly.

Kade quickly moved in front of her to block any shot from Zen.

"Tia, you have to come out with your hands up," Kade said. "Please, you must listen to me."

Tia stared up at him, confusion and fear in her gaze.

"We can fight," she said. "Slayer's got a plan. Come inside with us."

"Where is he?" Kade asked.

Tia looked at the APC, but he didn't turn.

"Machine-gun nest," she said.

"Firing it would be suicide," Kade said.

"But, Kade—"

"Listen to me, Tia. You have to fucking listen to me. It's over. We can't fight."

"You have two and a half minutes!" Lucky shouted down.

Kade closed his eyes, feeling the unbearable weight of what was happening as the cold wind refrigerated his drenched body. A machine gun and a sniper rifle were on standby to erase him and his friends. Not to mention countless other weapons that the Forerunner had at his disposal.

And Slayer was sitting in the APC, thinking he could fight. It was that damned Cazador spirit that worried Kade most.

There was only one way he could end this, and that was by appealing to Tia's heart.

"If you want any shot at a life with Zuni, you must come out right bloody now, Tia," Kade said. "We must focus on the future, not the past."

Tia looked down into the ship, probably at Zuni. She said something, and Kade took a second to glance skyward.

Give me time, please, he thought.

"Slayer, I know you can hear me!" Kade yelled. "Come

out and put your hands above your head, or we are all going to die!"

There was no answer.

"Xavier made peace. We must uphold it!" Kade shouted.

"Peace? What peace? They'll kill us all," Slayer finally answered. "Blackburn gave his life for this sky horse, and I won't just hand it over to the enemy."

Kade resisted the urge to turn. It would only give away Slayer's position, and he feared that Zen would take him down without waiting.

"Woody did too," Kade called back. "They did it for our future, which we can still have if you help me. I'm heading to the South Pole on that ship, with the knights, to turn on the reactors that will restore the planet."

Kade noticed that the red dot was no longer on him. He raised his hands and glanced up at the airship. Rain needled into his face as he squinted.

"Just hold on!" he shouted up. "We're surrendering!"

He turned back to the open dorsal hatch.

"Tia, please, get up here now," he said. "They gave me a chance to end this without killing you all, but we're running out of time."

The seconds ticked down in his mind.

"The islands are under the control of the knights," Kade explained, "but we have agreed to a peace that will guarantee a future for all, and that is why I'm going with them."

"Thirty seconds!" Lucky called down.

Kade closed his eyes, took a deep breath, then reached down. "Please, Tia."

She hesitated.

"How can you trust them?" Slayer called out.

"We have no choice," Kade said.

"Ten seconds!" Lucky called.

Kade gritted his teeth, wanting to scream at the top of his lungs. He realized that it wasn't just Tia, Slayer, and Zuni he had to appeal to in these final seconds. To survive, he had to accomplish the same thing with the knights.

"You want to survive the poles?" he shouted up. "Then you're going to need more Hell Divers!"

FIVE

Waves pounded the shore of Sint Eustatius. X followed General Jack out of the Cazador tunnels excavated from the volcano. He had never heard of these tunnels, or perhaps he would have stored the food here instead of in the silos back near the port. Thinking of that brought back memories of Charmer and what he had done to Michael.

Hiding the food had been X's decision, and Michael had paid for it. He had paid for a lot of X's bad decisions.

I'll find you, Michael, someday, if it's the last thing I do.

Voices resonated from the caverns, echoing off the rock walls.

"Move it," said a knight.

He pushed at Valeria and Jonah as they ventured out of the tunnel. X took a breath of filtered air from the suit they had given him on the airship. The vessel roared over the ocean about a mile out, gliding through the electrical storms as lightning forked down in all directions.

"Don't stray," said General Jack. He looked back at the other knights. "If these dogs move, shoot them."

"Yes, sir."

Surrounding Valeria and Jonah were four soldiers, including the general. The other two knights and the mutant dingoes had proceeded deeper into the tunnels to search for Gran Jefe. Four against one normally wouldn't be a fair fight, but this was Gran Jefe, and these were his stomping grounds.

X had done everything his captors asked, by calling to the Barracuda warrior and trying to get him to surrender. It wasn't X's fault if the big guy didn't listen. Something told him that Gran Jefe had seen his silent message and was out there prowling in the darkness, an army of one.

If the truce should collapse, Gran Jefe was the best shot X's people had at taking the islands back. Especially once Slayer arrived. By then, the airship would be long gone, on a mission to drop them off at the poles, and the sky people would have two Jayhawk helicopters—enough to regain air superiority when the airship *Trident* left for the poles.

Lights blasted away from the bow of the enemy ship, raking over a segment of shoreline about a quarter mile west of their position. X stopped to look but couldn't see anything over a ridge-line blocking their view.

"Keep moving!" boomed General Jack.

X stepped over to Valeria, with whom he had yet to exchange more than a dozen words since he found them inside the volcano.

"Are you okay?" he asked quietly.

She nodded. "How's Jo-Jo?"

"She's okay. Currently recovering on that airship with Miles and Magnolia."

"You recover too, and have nice new arm."

"Yeah. I guess these knights need me more than we thought."

"Shut your mouths," Jack snarled.

The bionic shithead grumbled as they trekked down the rocky shoreline. He reminded X of Crixus, crazy as a bat and all souped up on something. It was clear he didn't like the Cazadores or the sky people, and the feeling was mutual.

X had earned his right to be a grump, but he wasn't going to make things worse. He was going to do his job one last fucking time and, the gods willing, save the world.

At the end of the day, X was relieved that no blood had been shed in discovering Valeria and Jonah. They had avoided yet another explosive situation that could have escalated things and sparked a battle. Not only had they avoided bloodshed, but to his knowledge, the knights hadn't located the Jayhawk chopper. And they didn't know about Slayer or the destroyer ship coming from Rio.

X wasn't sure what Valeria, Jonah, and Gran Jefe had done with the Jayhawk here on the island, but he wasn't going to ask. Only a handful of people knew about it, including Kade, and that secret was the last leverage they had.

That and Gran Jefe.

Of course, hiding more information could lead to bloodshed, but this wasn't the time to think about it.

The knights followed a natural stone pathway lined with rounded, moss-covered rocks along the shore. Waves crashed, their spray catching on the wind and showering the group. Valeria remained close, nearly by X's side. He couldn't deny the deep relief he felt knowing she was okay.

Jack stopped where the path ended at the base of a steep rocky ridge.

"Keep moving," he ordered.

The group started trekking up the hundred-foot-high slope. A few steps up, lightning flashed into the jungle, hitting a tree and sending up an explosion of sparks. The brilliant glow illuminated the volcano for a brief moment, and X glimpsed what looked like a figure on a bluff peering down at them.

The blue glow faded away, and with it the figure.

On the trek up the rugged slope to the ridgeline, X had the sensation of being watched. His gut told him it was indeed Gran Jefe. During the brutal hike up the rocks, he thought of the lone warrior. They certainly had a checkered past together: Gran Jefe's killing Ada, his duel with X on the sand of the Sky Arena, and the "test" in the lower decks of the *Frog* during the journey home from Australia. There was no denying Gran Jefe had a dark side, but he had also proved extremely useful—a true double-edged blade.

Valeria slipped, and X reached out and grabbed her, helping her back upright.

"*Gracias,*" she said.

Jack turned with a grunt, then kept going, not stopping until he reached the crest. As they made it to the top, the general pointed his weapon at X.

It took only a glance to the bay below to see why. Anchored there was the research vessel *Angry 'Cuda*, with a Jayhawk helicopter on its weather deck. Chains and cables from the *Trident* had lowered over the derelict vessel and were already raising the APC.

On the beach, four figures were on their knees. No doubt it was Tia, Zuni, and Slayer. But X wasn't sure about the fourth prisoner. A squad of four knights guarded them with rifles trained on their backs.

Son of a bitch …

"Walk," said Jack.

Heart pounding, X moved down the other side of the ridgeline to the beach. The silent march gave him plenty of time to think—and worry. Valeria and Jonah stuck close to X, keeping some distance from the general and his soldiers.

"What do we do?" Valeria whispered.

Jonah worked his way up to them, waiting for X's answer—an

answer he didn't yet have. When they arrived at the beach a few minutes later, he still didn't know what to do. But he did identify the fourth person. It was Kade, wearing only a soaked uniform. He looked up at X, defeat in his eyes.

X felt it to his marrow.

Their lies had been exposed, and their fate was in the Forerunner's hands.

Zuni fell over in the sand, moaning. X now saw that his legs were broken.

"He needs help," Tia said.

Valeria started over, but Jack pointed the rifle at her. "Did I tell you to move?" he snapped.

"He needs medical attention," Tia said.

"Shut your little bitch mouth," Jack said.

"Please," Valeria said.

"You too!"

"Hey," X said.

Jack angled his rifle back to X. "You got something to say now? Other than another lie?"

Kade and Slayer both looked up at X, their eyes asking permission to fight. But X subtly shook his head. *Not the time.*

He held up his hands. "Listen, we can—"

"Xavier, the 'Immortal' Hell Diver," Jack huffed. He strode over, standing a good six inches above X and peering down through his helmet slot. "I'm done with your lies. It's time for consequences."

He raised a hand. Engines thrummed overhead as the gigantic airship lowered. A winch on a robotic arm began to crank, lowering a knight in a harness.

"Send up the injured one first," Jack said.

Valeria went over as Tia tried to help Zuni up.

Two knights raised their rifles.

"Take it easy," X said.

"He needs my help," Valeria said.

"So get him up," Jack said. "You're wasting time."

X went over with Valeria, who bent down next to Zuni. She spoke to him in Spanish, but Zuni seemed barely conscious.

"Let me carry him," X said.

Five rifle barrels turned toward him as X carefully crouched down beside the Cazador.

"I've got you, *amigo*," he said as he hefted Zuni up over his shoulders. Two days ago, X could hardly walk, but whatever those miracle black beads in the gel bath were, they had healed him and given him ten years of his life back. He felt like a new man—a *younger* man.

Tia walked alongside X as he carried Zuni.

"You're going to be okay, *papi*," she said to him.

The knight in the harness touched down on the deck. It was Lieutenant Lucky Gaz. He unclipped from the cable and removed the harness. A second knight stood in the open launch bay, aiming a sniper rifle down at them from three hundred feet above.

X gently set Zuni down on the sand, where Kade, Tia, and Valeria helped him into the harness.

Lucky walked over and saluted. "General," he said.

Jack flipped up his visor and spat on the ground as X and Kade finished securing Zuni in the harness.

"Okay, send him up," X said.

Tia gripped his hand and squeezed it as Zuni was lifted into the air.

"There's still one more of the barbarians out there," said Jack. "I sent the dingoes after him, but we could just carpet-bomb this island, not risk our soldiers or beasts."

"The Forerunner wants proof of death, and he wants their other chopper. We have reason to believe there were two birds on that research vessel."

The general looked up at the volcano, then turned away from Lucky and strode back over to X and the other captives.

"On your knees," he said.

Slayer and Kade both looked to X again for orders.

"Don't look at him," Jack said. He smacked X with the butt of his gun, knocking him to the ground. Kade strode forward, but halted when Lucky raised a pistol.

"Don't move," he said.

The knights closed in, and a red dot jiggled on the center of X's chest.

"Where's the other helicopter?" Jack asked.

He pointed his rifle at Jonah, who said nothing and bowed his head.

"You have ten seconds," Jack said. He pulled the slide back, chambering a round. Then he aimed the gun at X.

"Stop! I will tell you!" Valeria shouted as she jumped up with hands in the air.

A muzzle flash lit up the darkness, the crack of a gun echoing.

It all happened in an instant. X didn't have time to process any of it until Valeria raised a hand to her neck. She looked at X and then crumpled to the ground.

"NO!" X shouted.

He sprang up and charged at Jack, who swung the rifle in his direction. X smacked it down as the general fired, the bullets punching into the dirt. Jonah also got up, shouting and charging. Bullets pierced his light armor, exploding out the other side. He crumpled, dead before he hit the sand.

"Hold your fire, damn it!" Lucky shouted.

X crawled over to Valeria, who lay choking on the ground. Blood ran between his fingers as he clamped down on the wound.

"I got you," he said. "You're okay, I got you."

X looked up, screaming for help. The knights had closed in,

rifles pointed down at Tia, Slayer, and Kade, all facedown in the sand with boots on their backs.

"Miles," Valeria said. Blood gurgled from her mouth. "Give dog…"

"Get me some help!" X shouted.

He pressed down harder, trying to hold back the flow of blood. She writhed from the pain. Another harness cranked down from above as, with each agonizing second, Valeria lost more blood.

"Stay with me," X said. "Please, don't give up."

She stopped squirming and looked up at X.

"*Lo siento,*" she said. "I'm sorry I never got to… tell you…"

"What?" X asked. He leaned down, putting his ear next to her mouth, but no breath came out. Pulling back, he saw her eyes staring blankly up at the stormy sky.

The second harness cranked down to the ground, but it was too late.

X turned to the general cradling the rifle he had killed her with. It was the same weapon he had used to kill General Forge.

"You motherfucker, I'm going to rip your throat out," X roared. He shot up, bolting toward Jack. Lucky maneuvered between them along with two other knights, who helped him pull X to the ground.

"I'll kill you!" X screamed. "I'll kill you ALL!"

Magnolia dreamed of Outpost Gateway—of burning bodies, carnivorous vines, and Rodger. The nightmare occurred often when she managed to go into deep sleep.

"Mags!" Rodger shouted in the dream.

"Rodge, I'm coming!" she yelled back.

In the dream, she rushed into the command center of the outpost's bunker, hacking through barbed vines that surged out of the walls. Across the room, Rodger was being dragged away by thick, ropy vines toward a caved-in section of wall.

"I can't move!" he shouted.

She sliced through a vine that wrapped around her leg. Red tendrils snaked across the ceiling, slithering out of a crack. The strands stretched from wall to wall, forming a thick web that separated her from Rodger.

"Hold on!" Magnolia screamed.

Panicking, she hacked and slashed through the thickening mat of maroon vegetation. But for every limb she cut, three more emerged. A gnarled vine wrapped around her wrist, pulling the blade away, so she struck with her other blade, ripping through the limb.

A liana curled around her neck, lifting her off the ground. She kicked, her vision dimming as she watched Rodger being pulled through an opening in the wall. He reached out, grabbing the rocky edge.

"Mags! I can't hold on much—" His voice rose into a screech as his body suddenly burst into flames.

"No!" she screamed.

Squirming and twisting, she battled to get free, but the vines tightened around her, as if forcing her to watch Rodger being consumed by the flames. Every muscle and nerve in her body shrieked in agony, along with her heart as Rodger crumbled into ashes.

Loud banging brought her back from the nightmare. Sweat beaded down her face. She reached up to wipe it away and found tears as well.

"Oh God, Rodger, I'm sorry," she whispered. The vivid dream

felt so real that each time, she woke up feeling the horrible loss anew—that he was gone forever.

Miles growled by her bedside. The dog stood up as the banging that had awoken her came again. She glanced around the dimly lit space. X still wasn't back.

Jo-Jo huddled on the deck by his bunk, her hair on end, eyes on the hatch.

"Magnolia," said a voice outside. "Get your animals back."

"Hold on," she called back.

She wiped the last tears from her face and motioned for Miles and Jo-Jo to get back. Standing in front of them, she said, "Okay, come in."

The hatch opened, and in stepped Lieutenant Gaz. Wet hair clung to his head as if he had just showered. He wore a black suit and a duty belt with a holstered pistol and knife. His eyes darted over to the animals.

"Where's X?" she asked.

"Come with me," he said.

"I asked you where X is."

"And I said come with me. Alone. The animals stay."

She turned and instructed them to sit. Miles whined, and Jo-Jo grunted.

"It's okay. X and I won't be long," she said. "Go back to sleep."

Lucky locked the hatch behind Magnolia, then motioned toward the left corridor. She started in that direction.

So far, she had seen very little of the airship *Trident*'s interior since her arrival two days ago. Unlike on the *Hive*, the corridors were a dazzling white. She didn't see any exposed snaking conduits or stains on the hull; nor were there any paintings on the bulkheads. A humming came from down the corridor, where some sort of robotic cleaning machine churned over the deck. Everything seemed well maintained—no flickering lights, broken panels, or rusted hatches. By all indications, this ship looked straight off the assembly line. And while she knew that to be impossible, perhaps it had been in storage somewhere for a very long time.

She thought back to what Lucky had said about activating the Trident—something Kade had explained before she left for Rio with X to find Michael and his family. It seemed the beacon on the helicopter that Lucky and Kade had flown from the Sunshine Coast was to call this flying warship to the coordinates of the Vanguard Islands.

"Here we are," Lucky said as he rounded a corner and stepped up to an elliptical hatch. He tapped in a key code and opened the hatch to a round chamber stacked with three tiers of leather seats. All of them faced a central table with six empty chairs around it.

"Have a seat," Lucky said.

Magnolia sat as the lights dimmed. She heard creaking behind them. She glanced over her shoulder at the top level of the chamber. The Forerunner trundled out on his motorized chair to a broad platform. His blue eye glowed, illuminating the wrinkled face and sagging skin. Cords snaked away from his tunic, connecting to the life-support system attached on the back of his vehicle.

Groaning, the cyborg tried to sit up straighter. He licked one wormy, bluish lip and cleared his throat. The blue eye flitted to Magnolia.

"There has been an unfortunate incident on Sint Eustatius, Magnolia Katib," he said in his synthetic voice.

She shot up from her chair. "What! Where's X?"

The Forerunner rose in his chair as she glared up at him, heat rising in her chest.

"Your Immortal is still alive," he said. "Now, sit unless you are told to stand up."

She slowly sat back down.

The Forerunner watched her for another moment before nodding at Lucky. "Bring in the others, Lieutenant Gaz."

Lucky went back to a side hatch across the room. He opened it, and two knights brought X inside with his arms over their shoulders. His head was slumped against his chest. Kade staggered in after them, wearing handcuffs. Slayer was next, then Tia, also in restraints. Two knights followed them, with crossbows pointed at their backs.

Magnolia fought the urge to stand, her heart quickening as realization set in. The knights had located the *Angry 'Cuda* and captured its crew.

But where were Gran Jefe, Zuni, Jonah, and Valeria?

The two guards dumped X onto the deck directly below the platform where the Forerunner's chair sat.

"X," Magnolia said.

He looked up, searching the room until he found her. In his gaze was a sadness that Magnolia hadn't seen for a long time. And though he looked healthy and mostly unharmed besides a pinkish welt on his head, she could see that these men had broken him mentally.

"What happened out there?" Magnolia asked.

"They killed her," X mumbled. "The evil scumbags shot Valeria and Jonah."

His glistening eyes shifted from sadness to rage as they landed on the Forerunner. With a roar, X pushed himself up and charged.

All it took was a simple click on a remote in the Forerunner's hand to subdue the legendary Hell Diver known by all as the Immortal. His new robotic hand reached up to his own neck.

Kade and Slayer were both pushed to the deck and forced to watch.

"Stop!" Magnolia yelled. "Stop this!"

X struggled for a few steps, then went down to his knees, eyeballs bulging. "You killed Valeria," he choked.

Just as Magnolia was about to vault over the seats down to X, the Forerunner clicked a remote, bringing up an image of Valeria in a surgical room.

"Your friend is still alive, Mr. Rodriguez," said the cyborg.

X stared for a moment, then fell forward as his hand released him. Lucky was right behind him now, a pistol aimed at the back of his head.

"What happened on the beach was unfortunate, but it could have been avoided..." The Forerunner broke into a cough. After it subsided, he said, "If you had told the truth while you had the chance."

X raised his head. "She's still alive?"

"Yes. Now, stand."

X got up, Lucky right behind him.

"You have put me in a difficult position," said the Forerunner. "You have lied to me about your forces."

"Yes, I lied, but that's on me, not them," X said. "If you're going to punish someone, kill me. Spare the others."

"Kade Long lied as well. You all have lied!" The synthesized words boomed through the room, echoing for several seconds.

"I gave you a chance for peace, to band together with us on a mission to save our planet and restore it to what it once was, for future generations," said the Forerunner. He clicked off the view of Valeria in surgery.

"Your lives now hang in the balance, and I will ask you one more time where the rest of your forces are located, including the helicopter," said the Forerunner.

X snorted. "Your batshit-for-brains general shot the only two people who would know the location, and I already told you about the warship that's on its way from Rio. We have nothing else to hide."

"This Gran Jefe—I want to know more about him."

"If I were you, I'd leave him alone," Magnolia said. "I've seen your talent pool. You send those trigger-happy pussies after him, there won't be enough left of them to bury."

"Is that so?" said the Forerunner. The eye flitted to her, flashing. "Tell me about this barbarian. You have fought beside him?"

Magnolia nodded.

"You know him well, then?"

"Yes," she replied, not wanting to give too much away. "You're best leaving him be."

"I heard you the first time, but I can't 'leave him be,' and have already deployed forces to find him and the Jayhawk."

He coughed, then took a deep breath from a mask that extended over his face. When it was pulled away, he glanced back to X.

"I ask myself why I should spare you all and continue with this quest to the poles," he said. "Why I shouldn't just let General Jack deal with you, since he may be spot on about all of you being barbarians."

Kade stood. "Forerunner," he said.

"Speak."

"I know it's hard for you to trust us and for us to trust you, but my broadcast to the islands about the future was true," Kade said. He looked to Lucky. "As I told Lieutenant Gaz, you need Hell Divers. And that happens to be what you have in front of you. Killing us would be wasting a resource that could secure the future you have envisioned."

The Forerunner scrutinized Kade for a few seconds. He looked down to Tia, Slayer, and X, then up at Magnolia.

"Trust," said the cyborg, with a weary shake of the head.

"We all have lost people. One of my people struck first, and for that I am deeply sorry," X said. "But if you can let the past go and save Valeria, I will dive to turn on the reactors."

The Forerunner snorted. "The ITC Delta Cloud fusion reactors aren't just machines you can dive down to and switch on," he said. "These sites were taken over by the machines after the war and were sabotaged by DEF-Nine units, or what you might know as defectors."

"We destroyed them," Magnolia said.

"Yes, but there are far worse things than machines at the reactors. The climate alone is deadly, with unpredictable snowstorms, and frigid temperatures that can plummet to minus seventy degrees Fahrenheit."

"I spent ten years straight on the surface with my dog," X said. "So let's get this show on the fucking road. I'm looking forward to freezing my balls off at these reactors. I froze my balls off for years in Hades, no problem!"

The Forerunner let out another snort. "Get them up," he said.

Lucky holstered his pistol and grabbed X under his good arm while the other knights hoisted Kade, Tia, and Slayer to their feet.

"If you swear allegiance to the Trident, then I will spare your lives, save Valeria, and heal the Cazador with broken legs," said the Forerunner.

X looked at his comrades, then up to Magnolia. "I swear," he said.

"Each of you must swear," said the Forerunner.

"You have my allegiance," Kade said.

"Mine as well," Tia said.

Slayer cursed.

"Do we have a problem?" Lucky asked.

"This is the path forward, Slayer," X said. "There is no other."

"I swear allegiance," Slayer spat.

"I swear too," Magnolia said.

"Not you," said the Forerunner. "You will stay at the islands and help find this Gran Jefe."

"Wait, what? You agreed for me to go along." Magnolia stood and tapped her chest. "You need me."

"That was before this Gran Jefe escaped. As a former member of his combat team, you will stay behind and ensure he does not pose a threat to my people."

"Your psycho general is the only threat to peace I can see," X said.

"He, too, will remain behind."

Magnolia shook her head. "No, you need me out there," she said. "You can't leave me behind!"

The Forerunner wheeled back from the platform. "The final decision has already been made," he said, his voice growing distant. "Take her back to the rigs. Everyone else, prepare to depart for the poles."

SIX

At six in the morning, Michael kissed Layla on the cheek.

"I'll go relieve Victor," he said.

"Okay, I'll be out with Bray when he wakes," came her groggy reply.

"Let's keep him inside this morning, okay?"

"Yeah, good idea." She shook her head. "Not sure what I was thinking."

"Go back to sleep for a while."

Michael slid out of bed and left the room as quietly as he could. Sometimes, he still felt like a Hell Diver sneaking into an ITC facility as he tiptoed about to avoid waking their son.

Michael closed the door gently, wincing as the metal frame creaked.

Damn.

He hung there a moment, anticipating a wail, or "Ma-ma," or perhaps even a "Da-da," but Bray slept right through the noise. Backing away, Michael found his clothing thrown over a chair in the communal space. He dressed silently and put on his boots. After securing his duty belt, he started out of the communal space, then saw Gabi's door hanging ajar and the room empty.

They were still getting to know her, but this would be the first morning she was up before Michael. He went over to the table, to the map Timothy had provided of the island chain. Layla had taken on the project of marking areas that looked good for farming. Plots of land fertile enough to give the hybrid seeds their best chance to flourish. Many of the parcels she had marked were old vineyards. Other areas, marked along the shore, indicated Gabi's picks for fishing and crabbing.

Soon, the map would serve a second purpose. When Michael had a free moment, he would mark areas outside these caves where they needed to shore up their defenses.

He closed the door to the bunker and started down the tunnel, assessing the current setup. There was more to keeping everyone safe than merely beefing up defenses on the island. As he made his way through the dark cavern to the rocky overlook, he realized that the best defense for this place could very well be a strong offense. Or some key intel at the very least, perhaps from sending out the airship and having Timothy do recon at night. Most importantly, Michael wanted to know the location of the enemy's outpost, their numbers, and what weapons they were equipped with. Then he could decide how big a threat they posed to his family. After that, he could sit down with everyone and figure out whether to stay or leave this place.

Seeing the first glow of morning sunlight reminded him how hard the latter would be. He left the cave and walked out onto the overlook, suddenly in awe. Rays of gold speared through the clouds on the horizon, heralding another day. In such moments, he had to entertain the possibility of some divine being running the show. Michael often felt that X was out there, watching over his family in spirit. He also found himself wondering what X would do in the current situation—especially now, with the threat of the slavers out there.

Victor sat in a chair under the awning of rock, watching for the evil men who had killed his friends and taken so many others into captivity. The warrior who had protected King Xavier stood as Michael crunched over to him.

"Morning, Victor," he said.

Victor offered a tired smile. "You sleep well, Chief?" he asked.

"Yeah. Now it's your turn, but first, you seen Gabi?"

Victor pointed down the beach. Michael went with him to the edge of the overlook, where their clothes lifted in the gentle breeze. A quarter mile down the beach, Gabi threw a spear into the water. Pulling it back, she dropped a nice mullet into her palm-frond basket.

"Fresh fish," Victor said. "Is good for *crudo*—raw—*con limón*. Mmmmm!"

Michael smiled at the image of a little Victor squeezing lime juice on his ceviche.

"So, we work on defenses more?" Victor asked. "I will help. No tired."

"Get a few hours' sleep, my friend; then we can discuss."

"Okay, okay." Victor handed him the rifle. Michael slung it and stayed out on the overhang, looking at the sky. He put on his headset and hailed Timothy.

"Pepper, do you copy?"

Static crackled over the line.

Michael scanned the clouds for the airship and, not seeing it, relaxed a degree. Good—if he couldn't see it, neither could others.

"Pepper, do you copy?"

"Copy, Chief. Good morning."

"Good morning," Michael said. "How are things up there?"

"Boring, which I don't mind at all. How are things down there?"

"Not bad, but Bray misses you. We all do."

"I miss you all very much, but I'm happiest watching over you. Fortunately, I have nothing to report besides a storm front moving in on the radar."

"How bad?"

"Not too bad, sir. Less than gale force."

Michael checked the sky and saw nothing out there but sunlight glinting off placid water. "Okay, before that storm hits, I need you to prepare a supply crate."

"Certainly, Chief. What can I get started for you?"

Michael rattled off the different items he wanted, including weapons and ammunition, spools of wire, and a variety of electronic components: passive infrared sensors, ultrasonic proximity sensors, vibration sensors, and temperature gauges.

"Okay, I'll get started, and then perhaps I could lower down under cover of the storm. Should be two or three hours max."

"Perfect. We'll be ready."

"Okay, Chief, talk to you shortly."

Michael pulled out his pistol and set off on the winding trail to the rocks above. A balmy breeze ruffled his hair. He watched Gabi as she stood like a statue in the sand, arm cocked back with the spear.

Even from a distance, Michael could see the little holes in the sand where crabs waited for a snack as they themselves were being hunted.

Gabi thrust her spear into the ground and plucked out a skewered crab, clacking its claws. Pulling it free of the twin barbs, she dropped it in the basket and started toward the next hole. Suddenly, she froze, and her eyes darted up to Michael.

They exchanged a smile and a nod, and she went back to work. He stood watching the horizon while she filled the basket. Finally, with claws and antennae dangling over the brim, she trekked off the beach and started up the path to the bluffs. Michael met her at the trailhead.

"*Hay desayuno,*" Michael said, hoping he accented the word for breakfast correctly.

She smiled with a mouthful of broken teeth. "*Sí, almuerzo también*"—lunch, too.

He looked into the palm-frond basket of squirming crabs and two fat, flopping mullet. "*Bien,*" he said. "Good job."

"*Gracias.*"

She took the food inside, and Michael stayed on the cliffs. He patrolled for the next hour, watching the sea and the beaches. With Timothy up there, it was overkill perhaps, but what if something slipped through the AI's net? It would be an easy thing to miss one small boat in this scattering of islands.

Pulling out his binos, he scanned the horizon. The distant clap of thunder pulled his attention back from the water. He lowered the binos to look at the storm front with his unaided eyes.

"Pepper," he said over the comms. "How's the supply crate coming?"

"*Almost finished, Chief. I've entered commands detailing the supplies and ammunition the robotic loading arm is to pack.*"

Michael continued his patrol, heading back toward the cave entrance. A voice greeted him as he reached the trailhead. Layla stood on the lookout bluff, holding Bray.

"Da-da!" he said.

Layla smiled up at Michael. "Sorry. He wanted to see you, and Gabi said it was all clear."

"Okay," Michael said, joining his family.

A message from the airship crackled in his headset as he reached out to Bray.

"*Chief, do you copy?*" Timothy asked.

"Yes, copy, Timothy."

"Tim-o-thee," Bray said. "See Tim-o-thee."

"I know, I wish you could, but not right now," Michael said. He looked up at the sky. "Go ahead, Pepper."

"The crate is ready to lower, sir, but I'm concerned with the lightning in this storm. Perhaps it would be better to wait until tonight."

"Good call."

Michael turned back to Bray. "Timothy's going to come down later."

Bray pointed up at the clouds. "Ship. Home."

"No, *this* is our home," Layla said.

A crack of thunder bounced around inside the caves. Bray didn't shy away. He squirmed in her grip. "Down," he said. "Put down."

"No, we're heading back inside," Layla said.

"Down," Bray said again. He reached out to Michael.

As badly as Michael wanted to hold his kid, now wasn't the time.

"You have to go inside with your mother," he said.

Bray struggled, trying to get out of her arms.

"Bray, please, stop," she said. Holding the squirming boy tight, she headed back inside. His protests faded as they headed deeper into the cave tunnels.

Staying on lookout, Michael unslung the rifle and sat down in the chair, listening to the first patter of rain and the eternal crash of the waves. The minutes crawled by, and he wished he could ask X for advice.

God, how he missed the man.

The storm rolled in and the skies opened. The soft whisper of rain soothed Michael, but he didn't let himself relax. He got up and moved his binos over the darkening water.

At lunchtime, Layla returned with a much calmer Bray.

"Dark," said the lad, pointing.

"Yes, it sure is," Michael replied.

"Here, we brought you some food," Layla said. "Give it to Daddy."

Bray took the large clamshell full of crab meat and cooked seaweed in both hands and gave it to Michael.

"Thanks, buddy," he said, smiling.

Thunder clapped, close enough to rattle Bray, who stared wide eyed out at the rain. He looked to Layla.

"It's okay, just a storm," she said.

In the respite of the thunderclap, Michael heard the hiss of static in his earpiece, then a voice.

"Chief, you there?" Timothy asked.

"Yes, copy, what is it?"

"I'm picking up something on sonar in the bay of Punta Ganada."

Michael's heart skipped.

"Where's that?"

Static broke up the transmission.

Michael turned back to Layla and Bray, doing his best not to sound panicked.

"Get back inside and wake Victor," he said. "Tell him to come out here with a map of the island."

"What ... why?" Layla asked.

"Timothy's detected something nearby—a boat probably, but I just lost contact."

Layla stared at him for a single second, then took Bray and turned away. A few feet into the cavern, she stopped.

"Michael, should we leave?" she asked. "What if it's that slave boat again? Maybe we should have Timothy come down and get us all out of here."

Michael looked out over the waves, his heartbeat accelerating with every passing second.

"No, too big a risk if it's slavers," he said. "We hold here and hunker down."

"Okay." She repeated it several times, as if trying to convince herself they were fine.

"I won't let anyone hurt you two," he said.

"I know," Layla said. "I trust you."

Bray looked at Michael, fear in his eyes. Then Layla whisked him back into the caves.

*   *   *   *   *

The airship hovered over the capitol tower of the Vanguard Islands. Kade looked down at the rooftop, wondering if he would ever see it again. He had already given his farewells to Alton, Katherine, and Phyl. Now he must say goodbye to Magnolia.

"This is bullshit; you need me out there," she kept saying.

"Our people need you back here," X said. "Don't make this harder than it is."

They stood in the launch bay with Beau, Miles, and Jo-Jo.

"I don't think I can do this, X," she said. "I'm not going to make it without you."

"We'll see each other again." X put his hand on her shoulder.

"X, please..." She shook his hand away, but it came back.

"Be strong, Mags."

"This is such bullshit." She scoffed, then relented, reaching out to embrace him.

"I love you, X," Magnolia said in a shaky voice.

"I love you, too. When this is over, I'll come back for you, and we'll go find Michael, Layla, and Bray."

"Cross your heart and hope to die?"

"Stick a needle in my eye. Wait a moment. I lied, I'm immortal—can't fucking die."

She laughed, somewhere between a snort and a chuckle. Then she brushed a strand of blue hair over her ear and hugged X again, whispering something that Kade couldn't hear. When they pulled apart, she went to Miles. The dog licked the tears from her face.

"Love you back, buddy," she said.

Miles wagged his tail.

"Take care of your old man for me." She went to Jo-Jo next, putting her head against the animal's, their noses touching.

"I'll miss you," she said. "Be good out there."

Magnolia got up, sniffled, and walked over to Kade. "Best of luck to you."

"And to you as well," Kade said. He stuck out his hand, and they shook. "If you wouldn't mind, keep an eye on Alton for me and make sure the little bugger stays out of trouble."

"I'll do my best."

As she turned away, Kade pulled a letter from his vest. "Wait," he said. "Can you give this to Katherine for me?"

"I'll make sure she gets it," called a voice.

Lucky walked over, reaching out to intercept the note.

"Come on, man," Kade said.

"Come on, yourself. You're smart, mate. You understand we have to screen it."

"Mates," Kade said quietly. It sure didn't feel like it now. But Kade *was* smart, and part of this was his own fault.

X looked over, and Kade decided to let it go. The note wasn't going to get anyone in trouble. It was simply a message to Katherine about Alton, and another for Alton when he was old enough to read it.

"Let's go," Lucky said. He tucked the note away and motioned for Magnolia, knowing better than to grab her.

She hesitated.

"This isn't goodbye," X said.

Magnolia walked away with Lucky toward Nobu and Zen, who stood with two more knights across the bay. Jack wasn't here—a decision made no doubt to avert any conflict between him and X. From what Kade had heard, the hotheaded general would be in charge of security at the islands, which meant the place truly had become a powder keg once again.

The airship lowered over the rooftop, setting down with a jolt. As the hatch opened, Magnolia turned and looked at them again. Kade could see the raw pain in her eyes. She was broken. They all were.

A ramp clanked down into the dirt at the edge of the forest plot, not far from where Bulldozer had crashed the Sea Queen chopper and Lucky activated the Trident beacon. The irony wasn't lost on Kade as he stood on the ship.

Civilians emerged in the distance, some waving. Kade spotted Roman out there and his dad, Beau. Kade thought of their good friend Woody, who died back in Texas. They had lost so many people over the years. This was a chance to make everything worth it, to restore the planet for Alton's generation and beyond. The boy ran out of the crowd, jumping and waving.

Kade raised a hand back. "Stay out of trouble, pal," he said.

The hatch shut with a click, and the airship thrummed back into the sky.

"Let's go," Lucky said.

X and Kade turned away and followed the knights out of the launch bay. With a deep breath, Kade decided to let his anger at the lieutenant go and to focus on giving this mission a chance.

"Nobu, Zen, go get the others and meet me in the vehicle depot," Lucky ordered.

They parted in the corridor, X and Kade following the

lieutenant to another hatch. This one opened to a sprawling vehicle bay, or "depot," as Lucky called it.

Lights flicked on in the overhead, revealing two helicopters in disrepair, secured to the deck. Four all-terrain vehicles sat in the right corner of the room along with ten snowmobiles. Racks of cross-country skis, snowshoes, and climbing equipment hung from rods on the hull. They even had a small tank—basically an armored personnel carrier with a cannon.

Lucky went over, leaning against the long barrel while Kade and X looked around. The hatch opened a few minutes later, and Nobu and Zen escorted Tia, Slayer, and Zuni in. The injured Cazador was already walking, in some sort of recovery boots.

Two more knights Kade didn't recognize followed them inside, wearing light black armor over their uniforms. A woman stood with them, arms folded over her chest. She was tall and slender, probably in her midforties. Curly brown hair hung down to the shoulder pads of her blue uniform, right above the gold Trident insignia on the collar.

"Now that we're in the air, I'll cut right to the chase," Lucky said. "As the Forerunner explained, we'll mount two dives— one at the North Pole, one at the South. These are the four special operators who will be joining us on both dives," he said. "Some of you already know Nobu and Zen. Meet Watt and Blue Blood. And also Trident Commander Josie Hallsey, who will be providing logistical support and running all communications."

Josie nodded, but Nobu and Zen remained stone faced.

"Nobu and Zen will be heading to Concordia Station in Antarctica, with me, Kade, Zuni, and Tia," Lucky said. He gestured to the other two knights. "Watt and Blue Blood will go with Xavier, Slayer, and the animals to Polar Station at the North Pole."

Watt looked solid—six feet tall, rugged face with wrinkles

under a salt-and-pepper hairline. A scar about right for a Siren's talon traced across the left side of his face.

Blue Blood was shorter, maybe five nine. A bandanna with the Trident insignia covered his curly brown hair. It wasn't hard to see why his comrades called him Blue Blood. He was deathly pale, to the point that the veins showed in his cheeks, nose, and forehead.

"Both locations are damned cold, with unpredictable storms," Lucky continued. "When we arrive, we'll monitor the weather, and if there's a window, we'll drop snowmobiles down five miles from the base. You will then dive down and use them to cover that ground. Once you reach the perimeter, you will hide the machines and make the final trek in on snowshoes. Nobu and Watt are in charge of getting each team access to the facility, which we will have more information on shortly."

Lucky waved them around the vehicles. They went to a fenced-off area with full-size lockers and a row of benches in front of them. After tapping in another key code, Lucky waited for the gate to swing open.

"Find your locker," he said.

Kade and X went inside and found the lockers with their names.

"Go ahead, open them," Lucky said.

X opened his, and Kade did the same. Inside, they found custom-fitted human-size exoskeletons and, on the top shelves, helmets.

"These will replace your obsolete Hell Diver armor," Lucky explained. "These new suits are titanium alloy and come equipped with thruster packs instead of your old balloon canisters."

"We call them boosters," X said.

"Call 'em what you like—you won't be using them again."

"Actually, I'd prefer my old suit. Call me old fashioned."

"Your old suit would turn you to an icicle in these temperatures," Watt said. "Also, these suits deploy parachutes automatically at a certain altitude."

"You got to be kidding me." X snorted. "Trusting my chute and everything else to a computer sounds like a terrible idea."

"You'll do what you're told," the Forerunner's synthetic voice said from the corner. The cyborg motored over from the shadows across the room.

Had he been here the entire time?

He steered his chair through the open gate. His multipurpose robotic eye flashed out a hologram of a frozen landscape. Six giant mushroom-shaped reactors pointed at the sky around a curved facility designed ingeniously with individual interconnected triangular rooftop segments that formed a pyramid tip. It reminded Kade almost of the closed mouth of a Venus flytrap.

"Sixty-one years ago, we traveled to both poles," said the Forerunner.

Kade looked to X, who seemed just as shocked by the revelation.

"I led the expedition north to activate the Delta Cloud fusion reactors at Polar Station," he continued. "My team succeeded in bringing the site online and overriding the security system, but in doing so, we released an ancient evil."

Kade saw the Forerunner wince, perhaps at some horrible memory. He also noticed Josie glancing down at the deck.

"We suffered great losses, and only one of our choppers made it out. Dying, I was brought back to the Coral Castle, where I became what you see before you now," said the cyborg. "I swore someday to return and finish what I started. Now Xavier Rodriguez will lead a mission back to Polar Station and do what I failed to do."

His blue eye went to Kade.

"Kade Long, when you arrive at Concordia, your team will

have the luxury of learning from our mistakes at Polar Station. You will have knowledge we did not possess. Before bringing the station online, you will set charges and destroy the monsters hibernating there."

"Guess I'm glad to be going with you, Kade," Tia whispered.

"There may be other threats, including unknown local wild-life," said Josie.

"Before we launched the polar mission sixty-one years ago, we also scouted Concordia Station with a drone," said the Fore-runner. "This is the feed."

His eye flashed again, releasing a new image of an old drone feed of the Antarctic. Another six reactors positioned around the odd-looking facility came into focus. This one, like the other, had a flowerlike appearance, with roof segments appearing almost like closed petals.

"Okay, this might be a dumbass question, but bear with me," X said. He tapped his foot on the deck, then looked out over the equipment and vehicles. "This is the most advanced airship I've ever seen. A flying warship that wiped out our defenses in a matter of hours."

The Forerunner raised his chin slightly, as if anticipating what X might say next.

"Why not just go in and use one of those EMPs you knocked out our defenses with, then light up anything that poses a threat," X said. "This ancient evil, which you haven't explained yet—"

"An EMP could cause severe damage to the reactors—a risk we can't take. And this ship is more than just a warship, and invalu-able to our survival," said the Forerunner without elaborating. "That is why you're here. Hell Divers have sneaked into places like this for over two centuries without risking your vessels by setting down."

"Okay, got it. So why don't you tell us what this evil is?"

"In addition to what you refer to as Sirens and bone beasts, there was something else that fired on us and took out two of our choppers," said the Forerunner. Another pained grimace came and went.

"Something else?" X asked. "You sure it wasn't a DEF-Nine unit, because if so, it won't be a problem anymore."

"They were not machines," Josie interrupted. "They were biological creatures."

X stroked his chin. "So let me get this straight," he said. "With respect, you're deploying a smaller team, to defeat more monsters, using less firepower than you had last time?"

"Precisely," said the Forerunner.

"Okay, I guess I'm missing the part of the plan that shows how that's possible."

"We have something we didn't have then."

"Me? I'm flattered, bub—uh, sir, I mean—but—"

"While your expertise and combat experience are greatly valued, I'm not referring to you." The Forerunner turned his chair and started motoring away. "Soon, I will reveal how we defeat this ancient enemy, but now I must rest."

SEVEN

"Dr. Craiger is here to answer any questions," said Lucky.

He opened the hatch to the medical facility. It was filled with capsules like the one X had spent days in when he was first brought to the airship. Crossing the dimly lit room, he searched the pods anxiously for Valeria. Halfway down the row on his left, a pod glowed with a blue hue. He hurried over to it, halting in front of her half-naked body, suspended in the gelatinous goo.

Dr. Craiger, out of view earlier, stood on the other side, reading a monitor on the capsule side.

"Xavier, I trust you're feeling well," she said without looking up.

X nodded as he stared at Valeria. Her dark-brown eyes were half-open, and an oxygen tube protruded from her lips. The tiny beads swarmed around the bullet hole in her neck.

"She's bloody lucky to be alive," Craiger said. "She was technically dead for fifteen minutes."

"So she won't be herself when—or if—she wakes up?" X asked.

"That depends." Craiger finally looked up from the monitor. "One of our corpsmen had nano ice pads and got them on her after she was shot. They brought her temp down to sixty degrees Fahrenheit to slow cell breakdown while she was airlifted out of the volcano."

X didn't remember much after the shooting, but he did recall a knight bending down and placing on her upper arm an oddly shaped patch that gave off a blue glow.

"I'm hopeful for a full recovery," said Craiger. "Her brain waves show increased activity—a good sign."

X let out a sigh of relief. "Thanks, Doc," he said.

Craiger stepped away, leaving him alone in the cavernous room. Of course, X knew he wasn't *really* alone. Cameras relayed his every move. The Forerunner would likely hear what he had to say too, but he didn't care.

"I'm sorry, Valeria," he said. "You deserved better than this, but the doc says you'll be just fine."

He felt a little odd looking at her, but odder still were the stirrings he felt inside him for the woman floating just beyond that glass. Ever since Katrina died, X had given up such feelings—even lust, but especially love. He wasn't even sure his heart had the capacity. This was what happened when everything you loved was ripped away from you, over and over again.

But there was no denying he felt *something* for this woman. Over the past few years, he had watched her with Miles and Jo-Jo. She had cared for the animals as a parent would a child. She had also risked her life for X and her people, many times, fighting monsters in Panama and Australia and coming to save his tired old ass in Rio.

The woman on the other side of the glass had a warrior's heart—kind yet fearless.

The thing was, X knew almost nothing else about her, not even her age. Judging by the wrinkles around her eyes, and the grays invading her raven hair, she had to be in her forties. She was easy to look at.

He pulled his hand back from the glass. "I'll bring Miles and Jo-Jo to see you when you're better," he said.

As if in answer, Valeria squirmed slightly in the gel. His eyes darted to the monitor, but her vitals appeared stable.

"Rest, Valeria," he said. "I'll be back soon."

X went back out the hatch and found Lucky waiting there.

"All done?" he asked.

"Yes."

"Good, because the Forerunner is ready for you."

Lucky led him down the curving passageway. Two knights stood guard outside a hatch. They opened it to a dark space that smelled of chemicals.

"Go," Lucky said.

X stepped inside and heard strains of classical music. He had never cared much for it, preferring the ancient rock 'n' roll.

The hatch shut behind him, leaving him in pitch-darkness.

"Hello?" he said.

He heard grinding, like a window that needed grease, and the music fell silent.

He took a step back, blinking as a dull blue glow spilled from the bulkhead. As his eyes adjusted, he noticed the outline of glass just a few feet away. The grinding shifted to a smooth electric whirring, and his eyes captured the source: shutters lifting away from tanks built into the hull. Bioluminescent creatures swam through the liquid medium inside. He went over to observe a variety of bright fish darting in and out of coral nooks and fissures.

The shutters clanked to a stop, and the music faded away, leaving only the synthetic voice of the Forerunner.

"As I said, this is far more than a warship," he said.

X looked to the center of the vast room, where two robotic limbs moved on tracks overhead. Reaching down, they gently lifted the cyborg from the pool where he was immersed. Thick, purplish gelatinous fluid dripped off pale, wrinkled flesh woven across the mechanical parts that helped his ruined body function. The disturbing blue eye centered on X, flashing once.

"You look at me with disgust," he said. "For that, I do not blame you, Xavier Rodriguez."

"Not disgust—empathy," X replied.

"Pity!" the voice boomed, echoing through the chamber.

The mechanical limbs whirred up from the pool, crossing the space to X until the cyborg loomed right overhead.

"I do not need your pity," he said. "I brought you here to see me like this for a reason."

X glanced up at the naked flesh studded with robotic parts. His eyes flitted to the deck.

"Look at me!" shouted the Forerunner.

X's eyes shot back upward.

"You see what immortality *really* looks like now." He coughed suddenly and wheezed for air. A third robotic limb lowered from the overhead with a breathing mask that fit seamlessly over his face.

After a few deep breaths, he pulled the mask away with skeletal fingers.

"I brought you here for other reasons too," he said. "First, so you can see that this ship is much more than a tool of war."

An electrical hum resonated from the deck surrounding the pools. All across the room, the hard polymer floor retreated to reveal a secondary floor of glass. X walked forward as the plastic floor moved, pushing him backward. He finally reached the edge and stepped out onto the glass. Lights flicked on across the overhead, illuminating a vast colony of corals living in the tanks surrounding the central pool where the Forerunner had been recovering.

"The *Trident* is a modern-day ark," said the cyborg. "It goes far beyond these glass habitats, for in the center of this ship beats a heart, if you will—a vault with the DNA of countless extinct species from our planet that will someday replace the monsters now prowling the surface. Inside these vaults are seeds to regrow forests and savannas in the bright sun that we will free by activating the reactors."

The lights finished clicking on, showcasing the full extent of the room in a blue-green hue.

"I brought you here for a third reason," said the Forerunner. "What happened to the two Cazadores on the beach at Sint Eustatius was regrettable, as I did not issue those orders."

"Is that an apology?" X asked.

"It is regrettable and only adds more fuel to the fire your people started."

"And yet you leave that Jack psycho in charge of the islands? You must not know the Cazadores at all."

"Actually, that is exactly why he *must* stay there. The Cazadores have a history of barbaric violence and only understand brutal force. General Jack is that force."

X understood, though he would never admit it.

"As you now know, this vessel, the truce to which we all have pledged ourselves, and the mission to the poles are of the utmost importance," said the Forerunner. "For that reason, your friend Valeria will be healed by the time we reach Polar Station."

"Thank you." X nodded. "I'm grateful for the mercy you have shown in sparing her life."

"I would recommend that you do the same."

X raised a brow. "How do you mean?"

"I would advise that you leave her behind on the upcoming mission."

"Why? I figured you'd want all the help you can get."

"Only if that help does not cause distractions."

"Distractions. What—"

"Do you love her?"

X wanted to ask how that was anyone's business, but he understood why it was, if it jeopardized the mission.

"If you do love her, then she should stay behind," he said. "You and Kade can both learn from my mistakes at Polar Station."

The Forerunner coughed again but this time didn't take the mask. The robotic limbs turned his body, and his head cocked. Light flickered from his robotic eye, playing a holographic video that appeared to have taken place many years ago. In it, a man and woman walked around the side of a rectangular pool in a small room. Flowers grew in planters along pristine white walls, their colors reflected in the pool's tranquil waters.

The young couple stopped at the other end of the pool, hand in hand. He was in his late twenties, square jawed, with glasses covering his brown eyes. He wore a blue uniform with golden trident cuff links and buttons. The woman, also in her midtwenties, was dressed in a regal floor-length gown of sapphire blue.

He bent down on one knee and handed her a single rose. She smiled—a look of pure, delirious joy, of love.

"That was Gillian Hallsey, my wife," said the Forerunner. "Our wedding day."

His eye flashed again. The holographic video changed to an underground facility, where Gillian and a much younger Forerunner walked side by side. Flanked by two knights, they walked through a packed market that reminded X of a trading post. Vendors reached out to them as they passed, clearly voicing various grievances. Some held up their products: fish, fruit, vege-tables—none of it looking healthy.

Next came a video of vast underground tanks with coral and fish. The Forerunner and his wife now walked beside tanks with a scientist in a lab coat, holding a data tablet. Gillian looked at it, then into the tanks. X didn't need narration to understand what was happening. Their colony was dying.

The light flashed again, showing a video inside a hospital packed full of pale, coughing patients. It dimmed, and the Fore-runner turned to X.

"Our supplies dwindled. Disease raged through our ranks, killing our children and our elderly," he said. "We had to do some-thing."

The eye flashed out yet another video, of a white command center. In the middle of the space, the Forerunner, now a few years older than in the first video, stood with a group of men and women wearing the blue Trident uniforms. Gillian faced a digital screen with an image of the Delta Cloud fusion reactors.

"Sixty-one years ago, we set out to Polar Station to save our people and the world," he said. "My wife insisted on coming, although she carried our unborn child, a girl."

He grimaced painfully.

"Gillian assured me the mission was for our girl, that we would be fine."

X already knew what happened next.

"They didn't make it out. Nor did my best mate," said the Forerunner, his synthetic voice cracking. "I lost everything that day, including much of my body."

"I'm sorry. Truly, I know what it's like, sir."

"Not 'sir," he wheezed. "My name... my name is Noah."

"Noah, well, nice to meet you officially, then, Noah."

After a round of coughing, he nodded. "I've lived every day

regretting my decision to bring Gillian and our daughter with me that day, but soon my pain will be over."

He stared at X another moment, then pulled back and raised an arm with a remote.

Not this shit again, X thought.

But the remote wasn't to control his arm.

Mechanical sounds issued from a bulkhead, and a hidden hatch opened. An overhead light clicked on, capturing not a person but an armored exoskeleton that had to be as big as a bone beast. Its helmet was a curved dome with a slit visor. A chain gun hung off one arm, a rocket launcher off the other.

"Josie," said the Forerunner.

The hatch behind X whirred open, and the young commander walked inside. She hesitated for a moment.

"Sir," she said, "are you sure about this?"

"Yes," he replied in a firm human voice free of any synthetic tone.

Sighing, Josie held up a tablet and tapped the surface. The robotic limbs hoisting up his body moved along the overhead track, carrying him to the armored suit as the pieces clicked apart. Once the interior was open, she tapped the tablet, and the limbs gently lowered his body inside. With a final click of the tablet, the armor closed.

Josie stepped up to the giant mech suit, glancing up at the Forerunner's face three feet above her.

"How do you feel?" she asked.

He nodded. "Good," he replied.

"Try moving your arms," she said.

He lifted each arm in turn. Then he lumbered over to X, the elephantine feet thumping on the glass. X looked up at the behemoth mech suit with the frail man inside.

"You asked how I expect to defeat the monsters at Polar

Station this time," said the Forerunner. "Now you know. I'm coming with you, to finish what I started—for my wife and the daughter I never got to meet, and for Josie."

X looked at the young woman.

"That's right," said the Forerunner. "Commander Hallsey is the granddaughter of Denise Hallsey, sister of my wife Gillian. And she will help lead the restoration efforts of all Earth's flora and fauna in the years following our successful missions."

*   *   *   *   *

Gran Jefe crouched in the darkness, listening to the heavy panting of the mutant dingo beasts resonate through the caves. Each breath seemed more labored, as if the monsters were fighting their collars to get loose.

They had his scent.

He took in a deep breath to calm his nerves. The future of the Vanguard Islands rested in his hands, or so it felt. The knights had captured Slayer and his crew, taking the other sky horse and the research vessel *Angry 'Cuda*. It would be only a matter of time before they found the chopper stashed in the volcano. He had to act fast, but first he had to get his head on straight.

Gran Jefe had never been so alone, but anger eclipsed the fear creeping into his thoughts. Anger at the knights who shot Jonah and Valeria on the beach. They would pay for that with their lives. Fueled by his anger, he prowled through the tunnels, stalking the enemy soldiers and their armored dingoes. They thought themselves the hunters, even as he hunted them down.

He would lead these knights deep into the volcano, then ambush them and their beasts. Once he had dealt with them all, he would return to the sky horse before they could find it, and have Frank fly them out of there.

It was a plan, but for it to work, Gran Jefe must execute each step perfectly. And he was going to need some luck. For now he focused on the task ahead: luring the dingoes into a place he could dispatch them. That meant trapping them.

He checked his weapons and ammo as he waited: three magazines for the assault rifle, a hatchet, two knives, and a sidearm with two additional mags. The weapons might maim or kill the beasts, but any shooting would draw in their handlers. If he was going to kill them all, he had to hunt silently. And he knew just the place where he could do that.

As the panting drew closer, he took off. Keeping low, he moved fast through the dark passage. He thought back to his training. The first thing he ever trapped was a Siren in the jungle. He had dug a pit, sharpened some tree branches, and planted them at the bottom. Then he had covered up the opening with brush. An old-fashioned way to get prey, but it had worked on the pale, eyeless creatures that used some sort of echolocation to hunt.

He hoped it would go as well with these dingoes. Their milky red eyes probably didn't see well. He led his prey deeper into the tunnels.

Turning on his flashlight inside a lava tube, he followed it right to the chamber he was looking for. He stood in the entry, sweeping his light to identify six deep ravines in the rock before him. Anything that fell inside never came back out. There were Sirens down there, but also Cazadores—at least two that he knew of, maybe more.

Soon, the beasts and their handlers would join them in death.

His light picked up a coil of rope, thrown down from above to extract a man who had taken a wrong step during a fight with a Siren. Gran Jefe looped the rope under his legs and around his waist, fashioning a harness that would hold his considerable weight.

He worked his way cautiously across the chamber, away from the edges of the ravines. In the center of the space, he found exactly what he remembered: twisted rebar posts that someone had pounded into the rock many years ago. He tied the other end of the rope to one, tugged to make sure it was secure. Then he went back to the opening he had entered through. The distant panting had ceased.

He turned off his tactical light and stood in the darkness, waiting for the telltale orange glow of the dingoes' collars. The suffocating darkness threatened to break his confidence as the hunter during those long moments. He couldn't let that happen. His son—and everyone else back home—was counting on him.

You're in control, Jorge, he thought. *You are the hunter.*

Pulling out a knife, he tapped the blade against his shoulder plate.

"Come, you ugly *chuchos*," he whispered.

As if in answer, a flicker of orange light flashed into the tunnel. He watched the elongated shadow of a giant dingo on the corridor wall.

Gran Jefe slung his rifle, tightening it over his back so it wouldn't clank against his armor. Then he reached down and drew his hatchet.

Time to dance with death.

The sniffing beast prowled down the rocky passage connecting to the cavern. Gran Jefe crouched down eight or nine feet from the entrance. Another five feet behind him was the first ravine.

Snorting echoed off the narrow corridor walls. Two of them. With luck, their handlers wouldn't be far behind. He wanted them to see him after he dispatched their beasts.

Then he would go after the handlers, stalking them in the darkness and waiting to strike until they became hopelessly disoriented.

As the glow brightened, Gran Jefe tensed, tightening his grip on the weapons. A snuffling black muzzle emerged, connected to a jaw with an underbite of wicked yellow teeth. Two red eyes flitted back and forth and then locked on to him.

The muscular shoulders and thighs of the beast flexed. It lowered its skull with the spiked helmet. A low growl escaped the open jaw, spittle dripping off the gums as it pawed the ground.

Human voices resonated out of the corridor. Gran Jefe started across the cavern as someone said, "Tank, Devil, get him."

The handlers even had names for their beasts.

Gran Jefe turned on his light as he fled. Scrabbling claws gave chase. He skirted one ravine, cut just ahead of the next. He heard a yelp, followed by a clatter of metal armor on rock.

Dousing his light, he turned to see the orange glow of a collar fading from sight. The panicked yelps grew faint and then ended altogether.

One down.

The second creature skidded to a stop before a ravine, the glow from its collar illuminating the gash in the rock. Red eyes studied the hole, then looked up to Gran Jefe.

He twirled his axe. "Come get me," he said.

The handlers were almost to the chamber now. Judging by their footfalls, they would soon be in range. He had to end this second beast now. A well-aimed rifle shot might take care of business, but he would need several seconds to unsling the gun and aim.

Snarling, the creature charged around the opening, right for him. He took a step back, knowing the next ravine was right behind him. Firmly planting his boot in front of it, he crouched with his weapons.

The dingo snapped at him as his knife slashed across the armor plate covering the rib cage. He brought the hatchet down like a hammer to a nail, aiming for the spiked helmet. The beast dodged the swing, and he fell forward. The dingo bit down on his armored wrist that held the hatchet.

Pain shot through him from the powerful bite, and while the teeth didn't pierce his flesh, the pressure felt as though it would break his arm.

The knife darted out, destroying an eye. The beast reared back with his wrist still in its mouth. He plunged the knife into its neck, then did it again. Blood ran down its armored chest, but still it didn't let go. It snagged his rifle sling with a paw, ripping it free and pushing him back, over the edge of the ravine.

Down he went with the beast still clamped on his arm. The rope he had anchored to the rebar pulled taut, stopping him with a hard jerk. The dingo swung below him, hanging on to his arm. It popped out of its socket, and Gran Jefe let out a roar of pain.

Dangling from the rope, he saw the creature struggling below, bleeding from its neck and shattered eye.

His heart skipped when the rope began to creak. It wasn't going to hold them both.

Still holding the knife, he tried to lean down. And the pain in his shoulder and arm was almost unbearable.

All he could do was kick at the beast and hope it bled out.

Distant voices sounded above him. The knights had made it into the cavern, and he was hanging here like a fish on a line.

The image of his young son flashed in his mind, and Gran Jefe fought harder. He kicked at the body with all his might, shrieking at the brutal pain in his arm.

Come on, die!

He kicked it in the ribs as hard as he could, and finally the creature let go of his arm. Claws scratched against the rock as it flailed for purchase, and the orange light faded away into the abyss.

Wasting no time, he sheathed his knife, found a hold with his good arm, and hooked his heel over the rim. As he pulled himself out of the ravine, lights danced about from the entrance, where both knights now stood.

Gran Jefe considered staying right here, but he couldn't risk it. So he felt about for a pebble and threw it across the chamber. Their lights went immediately there, and he climbed out, flattening his body on the ground. To get to one of the other exits, he would have to get around three more fissures in the floor.

There was another option, of course: shoot these two men. He still had his pistol, but with his arm fully dislocated, it would be a one-handed shot—difficult to take them both before they shot him. But it was better than nothing.

Reaching down, he pulled his knife out and sawed through the rope to free himself. Then he swapped the knife for the pistol. Keeping low, he backed away, aiming at the enemy flashlights but holding his fire. One of the beams suddenly flicked in his direction.

He ducked, but it was already too late.

"There!" shouted the knight.

Gunfire erupted, muzzle flashes lighting up the darkness, bullets whizzing across the cavern. He fired his pistol as he retreated, trying to keep his hand steady. One of the bullets found a target, or else the knight fell to the ground on his own. Either way, it gave Gran Jefe the opportunity to run.

He activated his light just long enough to locate the ravines. He jumped over one, then skirted the second. The exit wasn't far now—maybe twenty feet. Another flurry of shots streaked in his direction, narrowly missing his helmet.

Thinking of his son, he gritted his teeth at the crucible of pain in his shoulder—and ran. The last ravine was just ahead. Too wide to jump across in the middle. Near the end, it narrowed. He jumped.

As he went airborne, something stabbed him in the ass. He

landed on the other side and rolled to his feet, gasping at the pain from the bullet in his left buttock.

Son of a bitch! Shot me in the ass!

Turning, he fired at the muzzle flash.

"That all you got, *pendejo*?" he yelled.

He pulled the trigger until it clicked, the magazine empty. Lowering the weapon, he limped into the tunnel, an injured dog. But at least this dog was still breathing, which put him ahead of the dingoes.

Soon, these two knights would be joining their beasts.

Then he would go after the rest of their weak-ass army, slaying them one by one until he cleansed them from the islands.

EIGHT

Magnolia watched just below the horizon, where the *Frog* towed the *Angry 'Cuda*, with the Jayhawk and the APC from the mission to Texas still loaded on the bow deck. The ships were close enough that Magnolia could see the Trident flag waving over the *Frog*. She was still on the rooftop of the capitol tower, where the airship *Trident* had dropped her off.

A bent, rickety rail separated her from the water dozens of stories below. Part of her wanted to jump over the side. Another part wanted to scream at the top of her lungs.

In the past, she might have raged and done something stupid. There were guards up here she could attack now. Two knights with automatic rifles watched her from beneath a fig tree—one of three that remained in the rooftop's ravaged little plot of tropical forest.

Across the rooftop, another patrol was posted. They had the tower on lockdown. The old Mags might have been brainstorming on how to take this place back. But tonight, she felt no anger and came up with no plans.

She stood there, staring into the sad little thicket of woodland

---

at the highest point in the Vanguard Islands and feeling utterly defeated. With X gone, she didn't know what to do with herself. Going back to the tiny quarters she had shared with Rodger would only make her feel worse.

So she remained up here, turning to look back out over the other rigs, where strings of lights illuminated Cazadores and sky people preparing for bed. Smoke wafted up from fires boiling pots of fish, seaweed, and vegetable stews. Life went on.

On one rooftop, Magnolia could see farmers tending crops grown from the seeds she had helped bring back from Brisbane. This place was a paradise within a hell world. And ironically, for that reason, the islands had become their own hell—a prison to the people who called them home. As long as there were survivors out there, they would kill to live on these rigs. The Cazadores had done it, her people had done it, the sky people from the machine camp had done it, and now the people from the Coral Castle would take their turn.

A familiar friendly voice snapped her from her trance.

"Magnolia!"

She turned from the rail to see Sofia. Her best friend limped over on crutches, with Rhino Jr. in a sling over her chest. Behind her, Imulah fought a gusting wind for his billowing tunic. Beau and Pedro were right behind them, followed by two knights.

Magnolia summoned her strength, then went over to join her friends. She hugged Sofia gently, taking care not to squish Rhino Jr.

"Oh, Mags, I missed you," Sofia said.

"I missed you, too."

She pulled back to see Rhino Jr. looking up with wide, curious eyes. His chubby arms hung out of the sling.

"He's grown so much since I saw him a few weeks ago," Magnolia said.

Sofia smiled. "Gets bigger every day. Going to be just like his father."

"So they're gone?" Imulah asked. "Off to the poles?"

Hands cupped behind his back, the scribe looked at the sky.

Magnolia nodded. "The *Trident* will take them on two separate missions."

"I was under the impression you would be going."

"That changed when they found out about Gran Jefe." She walked over to the rail with the group following her, hoping for some privacy. She gripped the metal, staring out over the water.

"Jorge's out there, and they want my help bringing him in."

"And they discovered the *Angry 'Cuda* too," Imulah said. "We heard Jonah was killed and Valeria was shot."

"Did X provide any instructions?" Pedro asked.

The knights behind them had inched closer, and Magnolia knew she must be cautious with her words—not because she feared for herself but because she feared what they might do to her friends.

"He says to keep the peace, just like Kade's message," she said.

"Tia went with them?" Beau asked.

"And Zuni, Valeria, and Slayer."

"People are growing more agitated," Imulah said. "They know that more knights are arriving with two ships full of refugees. People fear that their homes will be taken."

"Their troops have already disarmed everyone and gone room to room here," Sofia said. "They've taken some people away."

"Magnolia," Pedro said quietly. "Did Xavier give you any secret orders?"

She looked at the eager warrior from Rio. He had a fire in his belly, just as she once had. She stepped up so they were face to face. "He said there's been too much death. Too much killing."

Pedro narrowed his eyes, as if scrutinizing her for some hidden meaning.

"Kade says we can change our future, and I believe him," Beau said.

"I don't know what the future holds. All I know is, I'm tired," Magnolia said. "I'm going to go to my quarters. We can talk more later."

Pedro moved his lips, maybe to protest, then just nodded. "I'm glad you're back," he said.

"Me too," Imulah said.

"I'll walk with you," Sofia said.

It was a short reunion, and the abrupt ending wasn't really because Magnolia was tired. She feared that their little gathering would bring unwanted attention. The others seemed to understand, and they set off across the rooftop. A patrol of knights watched them go.

Magnolia ached as she made her way down the steps to the quarters she once shared with Rodger. Sofia went to her door with Rhino Jr.

"If you want to talk, I'll be awake for a while," she said, "but I'm going to put him down."

"Thanks," Magnolia said.

"Things are going to be okay, Mags, I promise."

The two women embraced again. It helped to ease some of Magnolia's dread, but as soon as she went into her room, it came back in full force. Entering the single-room apartment, she closed the door behind her and stared at the moonlit shelf of carved figurines.

The bed she had slept in with Rodger sat unmade, the pillows and blankets strewn on the floor. The nightstand drawer was open, as was the closet. A trunk at the foot of the bed had been propped up. Someone had been inside, no doubt looking for weapons.

Magnolia went over to the window and looked out. Below, two fishing trawlers were returning from a long day at sea. For most people, life had to continue. They didn't have the luxury of sitting back to see what would happen. The only way to survive was to keep putting food on the table.

She went to the only other furnishing in the room: a desk abutting the rear wall. She sat in the chair, looking at some of her old drawings.

Lost in thought, she became aware of loud pounding on the hatch.

"Magnolia Katib," said a gruff voice.

She went over, unlatching the lock as the person continued to pound on the other side. Not bothering to look through the peephole, she opened it.

The stiff silhouette of General Jack stood in the dim light.

"What do you want?" Magnolia asked.

He pushed her aside, hard enough she lost her balance and fell onto the floor.

"Hey!" she shouted.

As she sprang to her feet, he pointed a cutlass at her. "Sit," he said.

Palms on the floor, she stared up at the tip of the blade. Two more knights remained just outside as their leader strode into her quarters.

"We have a problem, Magnolia Katib," Jack rumbled.

Magnolia pushed herself up slowly, standing and meeting the demented eyes of the man who would love nothing more than to rid the world of every single Cazador and her people, too.

"Earlier today, someone killed our two dingoes and attacked two of my knights," he said. "My guess is, this would be the man you call Gran Jefe."

Magnolia shrugged. "I told you before—you'd have to have

shit for brains to fuck with him," she said. "Guess there's not much doubt now."

Jack smiled, or maybe it was a frown. "He has no idea what kind of bloody storm he is about to unleash on himself and everyone else."

"What's going on?" said Sofia.

She crutched into the hallway between the two knights.

"Get back," one of them said.

"Mags, you okay?" Sofia asked.

"Fine," Magnolia said. "This asshole accidentally put a sword to my face and was just leaving."

The general smirked and then sheathed the sword. "I can be an asshole; you're right about that. But so far, you've only seen my nice side." He stepped closer, towering above Magnolia. "Your friend Pedro—*he's* going to see my other side very soon."

"What are you talking about? What did Pedro do wrong?"

"That's really none of your concern. Your concern should be Gran Jefe. Our ships packed with civilian refugees from the Coral Castle have been delayed so I can deal with this barbarian, and I fully plan to have his head on a pike to greet them when they arrive."

Jack reached down to Magnolia's chin, and she snapped her teeth together.

"Touch me again and you won't have a finger," she said.

He pulled his hand back. "Why do you people insist on being so barbaric?" With a sigh, he turned. "Bring her to the marina. We sail at dusk."

*   *   *   *   *

"What if it's the slave boat coming back?"

Layla's words rang in Michael's mind as he trekked across

the overgrown field of weeds a mile from the bunker. After they all hunkered down for several hours, Timothy reported that the contact had vanished from scans on the other side of the island. Together, Layla and Michael had decided he would head out with Victor to check it out with their own eyes.

Thunder cracked over the two men running across the rocky terrain, using the cover of night to cross the harsh landscape. They were closing in on the outskirts of Haría, once a popular tourist attraction but now nothing more than crumbled buildings. Both of them wore Hell Diver armor and carried weapons that Michael hoped they wouldn't have to use.

He led Victor into a derelict house for a rest break. "Let's check the map," he said.

Victor pulled the map from his vest and spread it over a rock.

"Looks like we're on the western edge of Haría," he said. "That means we have to cross this old volcanic plain."

Michael checked the map—only two thousand feet to the point of Punta Ganada, the last known location of the sonar ping.

"I'll try Timothy, see if he has an update," he said.

Victor refolded the map, and Michael bumped on the comm pad in his helmet.

"Timothy, do you copy?" Michael said into his headset.

White noise hissed back over the channel. The worsening storm was interfering with the transmissions to the airship. He tried again and this time connected to the AI.

"Copy," Timothy said. *"I'm directly above your location, but my life scans aren't detecting anything, possibly due to the storm."*

Michael exchanged a glance with Victor. "Okay, we're moving into the last known ping area," he said.

Victor tucked the map away and followed him around the half-collapsed building. They skirted around the last buildings and trekked across a stretch of sand dunes to the cliffs overlooking

Punta Ganada. Gaining the ridgeline, they heard the distant sound of the surf. Bristly weeds and bushes grew along the border, providing some cover as they advanced. When they got there, they both got down and crawled through the overgrown weeds. Michael had his pistol out, and Victor army-crawled with his scoped rifle toward the edge of the rocky bluff. The far-off white noise of crashing waves grew louder as they moved to the overlook.

Victor stopped ahead, raising his gun over a rock and pushing the scope up to his face plate. Michael crawled over next to him, heart quickening. This was it, the moment they would get their first look at whoever, or whatever, had arrived.

But scanning the ocean, Michael saw nothing. No trace of a ship or boat, in the water or on the beach a hundred feet below them. The surf surged across the rocks, echoing in the respite of the howling ocean winds.

Nothing moved in the green hue of his night-vision optics, but Michael didn't trust his vision on a single pass. He crouched closer to the edge, checking every inlet and nook below for a vessel.

Lightning flashed over the island, booming above him like a bomb going off. He kept searching. If someone was out there, they could have pulled their craft out of the water, bringing it ashore.

Michael zoomed the binos in to explore the beach for a boat's drag marks. Then he searched for any caves. But minutes of looking revealed nothing besides rocks and debris from the ocean.

Breathing slowly, he listened for any sign of life. Hearing nothing, he retreated to the rock where Victor held sentry.

"Timothy, come in," Michael said into his headset.

Static crackled back. He tried again, then once more, to no avail.

Molten silver streaked across the sky, lighting up the churn of clouds that blocked out the stars. The airship was up there somewhere, hiding in the tempest. That was good for their safety, but also bad, for the storm interfered with their comms and the scans.

Now Michael had no good way to figure out which way the boat had gone. But he was fairly certain now the slavers he saw two days ago had returned.

His heart pounded, fear of the unknown driving his worry.

Had they seen the airship? Had he missed some sort of sensor or camera that monitored this island?

An even darker thought crossed his mind. Had Gabi somehow sold them out, told the slavers about them and the airship?

No, no, Michael thought. That couldn't be. If they knew where the bunker was, they would already have headed there. But it did seem like more than a coincidence, finding another boat nearby after the tunnels under the ancient resort had been abandoned for so long.

Michael hesitated at the thought of what would happen if these people somehow managed to flank him and Victor, making it past them and finding their little sanctuary. He had left Layla and Bray there with Gabi. Layla knew how to defend herself, and Gabi could hold her own, but Michael had no idea how many potential hostiles were out there.

Michael spoke into his comm. "Layla, come in."

But the interference seemed to be messing with their messages down here, too. He tried again, then again, cursing under his breath. The sense of dread grew worse.

"I got a bad feeling," Michael said. "Come on."

Victor followed him into a cluster of trees perched like ancient guardians on the rugged crag. Although most of the island was bare, this section had somehow supported a patch of forest, the roots delving deep into cracks and crevices, anchoring them against the coastal gales. Another testament to the diverse life this place could harbor.

But that didn't make it worth risking his family's safety.

They looked out from the bluff. "What if this boat somehow got past us?" Michael said.

"How?" Victor asked.

"I don't know, but what if we missed it and it went the way we came, back toward the caves?"

"I don't know, Chief."

"We should split up." Michael stood. "You go back and make sure everyone's safe back at home. I'll keep searching out here for a bit."

"Okay, but watch your six."

"You, too."

Victor melted into the darkness, and Michael continued through the forest. The storm's fury intensified, the clouds swirling and dumping buckets of rain.

A dreadful feeling of loneliness threatened to break his focus. Reaching the end of the forest, he came upon another open stretch of rocky terrain. The gusting wind whipped up dust and grit.

An idea formed in his mind.

What if the strangers had hidden their boat and trekked inland?

If so, then he had been searching in the wrong place all this time.

Michael turned away from the water and scanned the sprawling fields. There was almost no cover in that direction. Panic began to gnaw. This wasn't his first time being on the surface and feeling completely lost.

He stopped again to think. If people had come this way, they would leave tracks. Between Victor and him, surely one of them would have seen something.

No one's made it past you, he thought.

Michael pushed on, alternating his gaze from the shoreline to the terrain ahead. The bluff began to slope downward, leading him to the beach of a horseshoe bay. He checked again for any evidence of a boat being dragged from the water, when he noticed a flicker in the darkness across the bay.

Dropping to his belly, he laid his pistol on the ground and brought out his binoculars. Darkness surrounded him after he shut off his night vision. A fork of lightning blasted the darkness away. The distant light he had seen came again, and it wasn't the blue or white residue from lightning.

This was a fire.

He pointed the binos at a rock wall. The light source was inside a cave he couldn't have seen from the bluffs. There were three caverns in all, two of them half-submerged under high tide.

Michael held the binos up, trying to get a glimpse of whoever had started the fire. For several minutes he watched, but no one emerged in the cave opening, and the fire seemed too far back to see.

He needed a better vantage point. First, though, he needed to check in on Victor.

"Victor, do you copy?" he whispered into his comm.

Static crackled in his earpiece.

Michael lay there, conflicted. He knew where someone was now, and if he left, he would give them the opportunity to escape.

No, he couldn't do that. This storm wouldn't last forever. It would move on, and he would have an open channel back to Victor and Layla, also to Timothy.

For now, Michael would stay put and wait things out.

He put his binos away, picked up his pistol, and headed for a natural fort of rocks about two hundred feet from the caves. The boulders would provide plenty of cover if he could get there without being seen. But as he moved, each flash of lightning threatened to give him away.

Picking up his speed, he darted for the rocks. About twenty feet away, he dropped to the ground at the distant sound of a voice. Thunder boomed, drowning it out.

He crawled over to the boulders as quickly as he could, sliding in the mud. Rain beat down on him, sluicing over his visor. He kept his focus on the winking orange light as he squirmed into the rocks.

This new vantage point gave him a direct look inside the cave. Dancing flames illuminated the rocky interior and, in it, a boat that had been pulled out of the water.

Michael watched for a few more minutes before deciding to move in for a better view. He spotted an outcropping that might give him the view he wanted, some thirty feet from his current location. Pistol in hand, he moved out into the darkness, keeping low.

He had made it halfway to the rocks when a scream rang out. He crawled fast to cover, where he listened, hearing more voices.

"No, no, please, no," a man cried. The panic in that voice put Michael on edge. He had no idea what he was up against, and clearly, someone was in distress.

He lay in the dirt, listening to the man beg for what sounded like his life. Rising up slowly, Michael sneaked a glimpse over the rocks. The glow of the fire deep in the cave illuminated three people, and a fourth on the ground.

Michael squinted, trying to make out that person. It looked as if he was tied up on some sort of stretcher.

Was he injured?

Michael had no clue what was happening, until two of the men got up and lifted the man, not on a stretcher but on a framework they set over the fire. The prisoner let out a bloodcurdling shriek as the flames licked his naked body.

Michael stared in horror. His gaze shifted to the three men watching the last writhing motions of their burning victim. In the strobing flicker of the flames, he could see that they wore the same gray clothing he had seen on the galley slaves rowing the long, narrow boat the other day.

These three men—slavers, he had assumed—were actually the *slaves*.

And roasting on the fire—no doubt soon to be eaten—was one of their former masters.

A theory formed in his mind: maybe the boat he had seen several days earlier was the slavers, searching for escapees. It seemed too bizarrely coincidental, but sometimes that was how things worked in the wastes.

One thing was certain: his family was at more risk now than ever.

NINE

The shrieks and grunts of feral cannibals echoed through the museum as Kade heaved Raphael up over the railing. Raph's own entrails hung from his waist, pulsing blood out into the growing pool. Kade looked down in shock at his fellow diver's right leg, hanging on by a string of gristle below the knee.

"Oh God, oh God, Kade, what do we do?" Johnny stuttered.

Kade reached for his medical supplies but stopped when Raphael choked out, "No."

They both knew that his wounds were not survivable.

Gurgling blood, he labored to say something. Kade leaned down but could make out only "Tia."

A final sigh escaped his bloody lips as Raphael went limp. His hand fell away from his vest, revealing a turquoise necklace—a gift for his daughter.

Kade took the necklace and stood up as shadows of the feral humans darted across the room, their grunts and screeches closing in.

"Come on," Kade said.

"But, Raph…" Johnny stammered.

Kade stepped away, then felt fingers grip his ankle. He turned, expecting to find that a humanoid had reached through the railing from a lower level, but the hand gripping his leg wasn't the attackers—it was Raphael. He clamped down like a vise, eyes wide and full of life.

"Don't let Tia go!" he croaked. "You must protect her!"

Kade tried to pull away, but Raph yanked him down to the ground as the first of the feral beasts vaulted over the railing, wielding a rusted cleaver. He ran a tongue over his pointy, yellow front teeth and flashed a wicked grin.

"She'll die out there!" Raph yelled. "You will fail her!"

Kade jolted awake from the nightmare. Sweat trickled down his temples as he slowly settled into reality. A distant rumbling reminded him he was on the airship *Trident*, in a communal space with his comrades from the Vanguard Islands. X and his animals slept across the room. Slayer, Zuni, and Tia were here too, sleeping through the electrical storm that shook and battered the flying warship.

Sitting up, he looked at the tablet the knights had given him with the mission briefing: four thirty in the morning.

Twenty-four hours had passed since the airship left the Vanguard Islands. It would be arriving at Concordia Station, Antarctica, in a few hours. He knew he needed his sleep, but he wasn't tired despite a terribly restless night. The nightmare from that dark day at the museum had rattled him.

Giving up on sleep, he tapped the screen of the tablet to check the map again.

"Can't sleep?" Tia asked.

She had rolled onto her side in the adjacent bunk.

"Me either," she said.

"Well, you should try," he whispered. "Tomorrow's a big day."

"You really think we can turn on these bloody reactors?"

"Yeah—"

"The better question is, why the fuck should we?" said a deep voice.

It was Slayer, sitting up on the edge of his bunk. "I hope you and X know what you're doing," he said. "'Cause we risked a lot for those choppers, only to see them taken captive."

Kade understood the anger in Slayer's voice. They both had lost their best mates on the mission to Texas.

"I'm sorry about Blackburn," Kade said. "But he didn't die for nothing, and Woody didn't either. We turn on those reactors, and we secure the future for our people."

"Yeah, what's to say that robot freak won't just leave us in the Antarctic? Or slaughter everyone back home? Especially after what Rolo did."

"I don't trust them," Tia said.

Kade didn't either. Not a single one of them, including Lucky, who had proved he was loyal only to the Trident.

"The Forerunner won't break his word," X said. "I won't let him."

"All due respect, but how are you going to keep him to his word?" Slayer asked. "Seems a heartless bastard, more machine than man."

"He still has a heart," X grunted as he sat up, his joints cracking. "You all trust me?"

"Yes," came the instant response from everyone.

"Then trust me that this is the right thing to do, and go back to sleep. You're gonna need it."

Kade shut off the screen and laid his head back down, still trying to shake off the troubling dream. But now he couldn't stop thinking about Raph's words. The day he died, he had managed only to utter her name, but in this nightmare he had told Kade she would die.

This wasn't Kade's first dream of Raph speaking about his daughter. But Raph had always just told Kade to not let Tia go on a mission. Kade had the dream before Brisbane, and again after he found out Tia had boarded the *Angry 'Cuda*. Never in any of those dreams had Raph told Kade she would die.

Maybe it was paranoia bleeding into his mind, or maybe it meant something. After all, they were heading to a frozen, hostile environment full of hibernating monsters.

Soon, he heard snores, both human and animal.

"Kade, you still awake?" Tia whispered.

"Yes, but you need to—"

"I just wanted to say thanks for looking out for me."

Before he could respond, she added, "I don't blame you for what happened to my dad."

Kade felt a weight lifted from his chest after all these years believing that she did blame him. Hell, Kade blamed himself, at least in part, for what happened to Raph that day.

"Everything's going to be okay," he said. "We'll finish this mission and go back to the islands, and you can focus on you and Zuni."

"Oh, so you approve now?" He could hear the wry grin in her voice.

"I can tell he cares about you, and that's what matters," Kade said. "So for now I approve. If he does something to hurt you, then I break his legs again."

Tia chuckled. "Pretty sure he could beat you up, old man."

"Probably. Now, go back to sleep."

Kade felt the vibration of the airship through the pillow. He missed living on *Victory*. Most people would never understand how he could feel that way after living in the Vanguard Islands. But life on the airship was a simpler time, when he did his job and came home to his family. There were no wars. They all had enough to survive, and when they didn't, they pitched in to help each other.

If only he could somehow go back and stop Captain Rolo from going to Mount Kilimanjaro ... Kade thought back to the trail of intel his diving team had discovered, which had ultimately led them there. It wasn't just on Rolo. It was on Kade, too. He felt personally responsible for discovering the info that led them into the trap laid by the machines.

At some point, he drifted off to sleep.

Loud pounding on the hatch woke him. It swung open, and Lucky stepped in to flick on the lights.

"As you can probably tell, we're deep in the storms right now," he said. "Our launch window for Concordia Station looks like it will change from midmorning to this evening. Everyone up. Get dressed and head to the mess for chow and then a briefing."

He stepped out.

Tia cracked her neck from side to side. "Today's the day we save the world," she said.

The sleep-groggy team got ready in silence. It was clear none of them had slept well—not uncommon for soldiers before a battle, or divers before a mission. As soon as they got into the corridor, Kade took a deep breath through his nose. "That coffee?"

Lucky nodded. "Got oatmeal, too."

He guided them into the mess hall. Inside, Zen and Nobu sat eating across from Watt and Blue Blood. The men looked up but didn't stand.

"Grab some chow and have a seat," Lucky said.

Kade went to a counter where steaming bowls of the mush sat next to a coffee percolator. He filled a mug, grabbed a bowl, and sat at the table between Slayer and Zuni. Tia sat beside the Cazadores, all of them across from the knights. A few tables over, X put a bowl down for both his animals.

An awkward silence passed as knights and Hell Divers all looked at each other suspiciously.

"Well, I guess the Forerunner wants us all to be what you call *mates*," X said as he joined them. "Maybe there's some special ingredient in this breakfast to make that happen, yeah?"

"We're not mates; we're allies, and we have a job to do," Lucky said. He powered up a tablet with the blueprints of Concordia Station. "Did everybody memorize the map?"

Nods all around.

He brought up drone footage from the knights' recon mission sixty years ago.

"Obviously, the terrain could have changed since we were there, and we'll send in a new drone as soon as we arrive," he said. "Once we get new footage, we'll formulate a plan to get from our DZ to the facility."

Lucky swiped back to the blueprints. Centered between the six reactors was a five-story domed structure built on the frozen terrain. A subterranean facility went twenty floors beneath it, accessible via four internal stairwells and two freight elevators from the main building.

"Obviously, we can't just waltz in," he said. "To get inside, we're going to use a tunnel system from out here."

On the tablet, he indicated a sector of passages a mile from the main facility. "These tunnels were constructed to vent heat from the reactors, to keep them from melting the ice."

"Will they have security measures in place?" Kade asked.

"More than likely, but Nobu is prepared to bypass them. Once he does, we'll take the tunnel all the way under the main facility, where we will proceed through the labs to the cryo-chambers. From a safe distance, we will demolish them, activate the reactors, escape, and wait for evac."

Lucky reached up to a headset and stepped away.

"Yes, I copy," he said.

A private transmission played, and while Kade couldn't hear what it said, he could make out the Forerunner's synthetic voice.

"Understood. We're on our way," Lucky said. He stood and motioned for Kade, then X. "With me."

X and Kade exchanged a glance as they headed out of the mess hall. Lucky took them into a corridor that wound toward the center of the vessel. A few passages later, they arrived at two circular hatches. Lucky tapped in a code, and they whisked open.

He gestured, and Kade entered a curved room with monitors hanging from the bulkheads and on raised desks. Standing at one of them was Commander Josie Hallsey.

X joined Kade just inside, where Lucky told them to wait. Seconds later, a circular hatch slid back in the center of the deck. Rising up on a platform was the Forerunner in his motorized chair. Cords snaked out of the tunic covering his frail body.

"Sir, we're about to get our first view of the terrain," Josie announced.

The Forerunner nodded at her, then looked to Kade and X.

"Come to me," he said.

Kade and X walked up to stand on either side of the cyborg. In front of them, a large monitor warmed to life with a fuzzy aerial view from a drone equipped with night vision. The craft roared through the green expanse of clouds, spearing down toward the flat, icy expanse. Snowflakes gusted across the flight path, making it almost impossible to make out the surface.

"Aircraft is ten point four miles from the reactors," said Josie. "Starting scans. So far, no radiation detected."

Rolling snow mounds came into view—an Antarctic desert in all directions. That radiation report was good, but the temperature reading came back at negative thirty degrees Fahrenheit. Colder than any place Kade had dived in his career. Sure, he had better gear now, but the environment would be brutal.

"No life-forms present on first pass," said Josie. "Taking us down for a second scan."

The drone swooped low over the frozen vastness.

"Are those wind turbines?" X asked.

Kade glimpsed movement, which finally resolved into blades churning through the wind. He also noticed something else down there and double-checked the digital map to make sure this wasn't part of the base. But no, they were still eight miles from the reactors.

"What are we looking at?" he asked.

"A small city," said the Forerunner. "Frozen in time."

The drone circled over icebound buildings protruding from the white surface. Enclosed bridges stretched over unmoving roadways, allowing residents to move between the domed buildings without being exposed to the brutal weather.

"ITC built this for future generations to inhabit in case of an apocalyptic event," explained the Forerunner. "After the machines attacked, the very stations used to preserve life became the fortresses of those determined to end it."

"And destroying the machines didn't end that threat?" X asked.

"Not entirely." He broke into a cough, and the bloodshot eye glanced over to Josie. "One day—possibly very soon if our missions are successful—I will send a science team to activate this city. That team will be led by Commander Hallsey."

The Forerunner looked back to Kade and X.

"That's right, we have other places to settle when this is all over," he explained. "The Vanguard Islands will be just one bastion for—"

"Sir, I apologize for interrupting, but I'm picking up a hit on the life scanners," said Josie. She glanced up, surprise showing in her brown eyes. "There *is* life down there."

"Check it out, but proceed with extreme caution. We don't want to give away our position," said the Forerunner.

"Understood. Taking us down to the area of the signal."

Onscreen, the drone feed relayed the image of a domed building in what appeared to be the center of the city. Snowflakes whipped across the field of view, but Kade saw footprints in the drifts as the drone rose over the top of an enclosed pedestrian bridge. The cameras magnified a cavernous opening in a mound of snow partially obstructing the doors to the adjacent building. The tracks led right up to the tunnel in the snow.

"Switching to thermal imaging," reported Josie.

The team watched drone footage, waiting anxiously for a report.

"No hits on this structure," she said a few moments later.

"Well, something's down there," X said. He glanced at Kade with an uneasy look. Then he turned to the Forerunner. "Maybe you hold off until you figure out what it is."

"No," replied the Forerunner. "Our teams are prepared for any and all hostiles."

Kade had heard that before. He had told fellow divers that very thing to instill confidence. He thought of his nightmare about Raphael in the museum, a day when they believed they were diving somewhere relatively safe. His gut told him that something evil awaited them at Concordia Station, just as it had at the museum. Only this time, it would be far deadlier.

TEN

Gran Jefe peered out of his hideout, hatchet in hand, listening to the distant voices. The knights were still out there, searching for him. They had been down here since he sent the two mutant dingoes hurtling to their deaths in the pitfall ravines inside the volcano. Injured and without his rifle, he had been forced to flee deeper into the tunnels, where he could lick his wounds and plan his next move.

For the past few hours, he had taken refuge in this old shaft concealed by a thick camouflage net. His dislocated arm was back in its socket, but it still hurt like hell. And there wasn't much he could do about the bullet buried in his right buttock. Fortunately, the armor had slowed it down so that it stopped before the bone. It would be tough trying to remove the round under such a generous layer of fat. All he could do right now was put a bandage over it and hope it didn't get infected. He was running out of time to get back to the helicopter, assuming that the knights hadn't found it yet.

A muffled voice called out. The knights were indeed drawing closer. But he wasn't worried about them finding his hideout. He had covered his tracks, and the net hid the entrance beautifully. Only someone getting up very close with a light would ever notice.

He had found it only because he remembered this passage, for it was also a place they stored supplies. Hatchet out, he retreated into the shaft, rounding a corner where there were stacks of already-sharpened stakes. Hundreds of them. There were also crates of small homemade land mines. He had laid out his equipment. There wasn't much: a medical pack, a half bottle of water, flint and a steel striker, a salt packet. For weapons, he had two knives, his hatchet, and his pistol with an extra magazine. But he had lost his rifle in the fight with the dingoes, and that was a serious loss.

A rat skittered away from his exhausted food pouches on the ground. Almost reflexively, he tossed the hatchet, smashing the creature with the thick poll.

This wasn't just a meal for Gran Jefe. It was also phase two of his plan.

He scooped up his hatchet and the limp rat. Then he went down on his knees. He would just have to get used to it until he could get someone to dig that bullet out of his bum. Skinning a rat was something all the Cazador kids learned as soon as they could use a knife. His own son, Pablo, would be getting close to that age. Perhaps he was even old enough, considering he was half-Mata, with the heart of a Barracuda warrior.

After skinning the rat, Gran Jefe skewered the flesh with a green stick. Then he lit a small fire and draped the carcass over it using two stones. The scent of cooking meat would likely draw the knights, but that was the point. The rat was bait—literally.

Gran Jefe put his armor back on and packed his gear in a bag, including some extra weapons for later. By the time he finished, one side of the rat was done. He turned it over, slung the bag, and returned to the cave's entrance to listen.

The voices were gone. He stayed another few moments, then went back for his perfectly done rat. Scooping it up, he lifted his helmet and blew on the juicy meat. He bit in, tearing off a chunk. Two more bites, and it was half-gone. That was plenty to keep him sustained for now.

Gran Jefe carefully set the uneaten half a rat up over the fire, so it looked as though it were still cooking. Then he walked out of the cave, pulling the net back to reveal the entrance.

With the trap set, he went back down the passage and gave a sharp whistle. He whistled again. Then, just to be sure, he let out a third whistle. Surely they would hear that. Backing away, he went to an alcove the size of a large closet. There, he would wait.

As he expected, two voices grew louder as they drew near. It wasn't long before their beams flashed into the tunnel. His bait had brought the two knights right where he wanted them.

Gran Jefe unsheathed the longer knife, holding it in one hand and his hatchet in the other. He was going to kill them the old-fashioned way and take pleasure in it.

"You smell that?" someone called.

"Smells like barbecue," came the reply.

The lights brightened, bobbing up and down in the tunnel, forcing Gran Jefe to pull back. He held steady, confident in his ability to stay hidden. In the darkness, he waited to strike, listening to the faint clank of armored joints.

"Careful—could be a trap," said one of the approaching knights.

"Coming from down that passage," replied the other. "Stay here and watch my back."

Footsteps crunched away.

With his tongue, Gran Jefe worked a piece of rat meat from between his teeth. He swallowed it, savoring the meat. Then he moved around the corner and sighted up the guard. He was standing in front of the passage, rifle aimed in the opposite direction.

Seeing his opportunity, Gran Jefe bolted across the passage. He pulled up a rope he had buried hours ago, and began sawing through it with his knife. Just as the strands were about to part, he whistled.

The soldier whirled toward him, and Gran Jefe cut through the last fiber. The rope snapped apart, releasing a spiked fork that sprang out of the dirt wall.

Too late, the other knight yelled from inside the tunnel, "Trap!"

Gran Jefe heard the impact of wooden stakes punching through armor, followed by an astonished cry of pain. The knight dropped his rifle, its beam lighting up the passage.

Gran Jefe was already moving toward the skewered knight. It was almost too easy. He drew back the hatchet as the second soldier arrived in the shaft entrance. He threw just as gunfire cracked from the connecting tunnel.

There were more knights down here!

Gran Jefe pivoted away, bullets punching into the porous basalt ceiling. Bending down, he scooped up the fallen man's rifle and went down on one knee. Sighting up a muzzle flash, he fired off a burst.

A scream rang out.

He backed away and turned to retrieve his hatchet from the chest of the knight writhing on the ground.

"*Gracias, ese,*" he said, plucking it out.

With a powerful downward stroke, he split the man's skull, then pried the hatchet from his helmet. Seeing a spare magazine, he grabbed it from the man's vest.

In less than twenty seconds, two of the general's soldiers were dead, and Gran Jefe was on the run with one of their rifles. But he heard three distinct voices following. He had planned for that too, though, and led them up a sloping tunnel. Bullets cracked and whizzed behind him, smacking into soft rock walls. He went around a corner and ejected the rifle's magazine. Half-full. Plus a full magazine. Plenty if he wanted to end this in a shootout. But that was damned risky, and he had spent too much time making sure he ended this like a real Cazador.

Palming the magazine back in, he then directed his light along a passageway, to gain some ground on the enemy. Keeping to the left side, he aimed the newly acquired rifle at the high point of the corridor, just in case he was somehow flanked. But no one was there, and he crouched and waited at the crest. The three knights weren't far behind, but they were moving cautiously now. He kept going, into a branching tunnel with a low ceiling. The hundred-foot-long passageway grew narrower as he advanced, so that he soon had to crouch.

This next tunnel was not for the weak of heart or anyone who feared tight places. Crouching down, he shined his light down the narrowing tunnel. This was the site of his next trap.

The lights from his pursuers angled into the tunnel behind him. He pulled out his hatchet and ducked around the bend, stepping carefully over an exposed rope to the other end of the tight corridor, where it formed a junction. He squirmed around to the left, entering an even tighter passage. Breathing heavily, he turned his body to look back down the narrow space he had just traversed.

A knight emerged at the other end, rifle up. He raised a fist to halt his two comrades. Gran Jefe pulled back as the light darted toward his location.

"He's over here!"

Gunfire cracked, dislodging crumbs of igneous rock from the wall.

Gran Jefe stayed put, not daring to look. Another flurry of bullets punched into the dirt to his right. In the respite, he heard the other two knights advancing.

Ten seconds… fifteen…

On twenty, he hacked through the rope he had stepped over.

A surprised yelp ended with a crunching sound.

Bullets zipped into the ground to his right. Gran Jefe waited another beat, then glanced around the corner to find the point man, skewered by four spears from above and two from below. He convulsed where he stood, bleeding from multiple wounds, including a spike through the top of his helmet.

Just behind the dying knight, a second soldier had been stabbed through the boot and again through the shoulder. He wailed in agony as the third knight tried to help him.

"Shoot him!" the wounded man cried, raising a trembling hand.

The uninjured soldier raised his weapon to fire at Gran Jefe, who pulled back with time to spare. Bullets pounded the wall, chipping the rock as he retreated.

If he wanted to, Gran Jefe could kill these knights with his rifle, but he had a better plan. Turning, he started crawling into the new, even tighter passage, the bag on his back scraping the ceiling. He flattened his body, keeping as low as he could.

The groans of the wounded knight grew louder as his comrade tried to pry his foot and shoulder free of the spikes. If these men were smart, they wouldn't follow him, but he couldn't chance it. He moved fast, fighting the pain from his wounds. For the last few feet, he had to squirm like a snake before emerging into another chamber. From there, he took a tunnel back topside, moving fast by the glow of his light.

At the next tunnel, he stopped to listen for more knights.

Hearing nothing, he checked the way he had come. Blood from his injuries laid a trail.

Bien.

He wanted the enemy to track him. He still had one last surprise in his arsenal of traps. He pushed on, heading back topside until he was close to the surface, where the sky horse waited in the dense red ferns and jungle that grew inside the volcano's caldera.

Reaching down, he turned off his lamp and moved silently through the darkness, using the sporadic flashes of lightning to guide him. It grew brighter as he neared the opening. A few feet from the entrance, he paused to listen.

Hearing nothing, he kept going until he had a clear view of the clouds above the caldera's rim. The massive enemy sky horse was gone now.

Keeping his rifle shouldered, Gran Jefe moved across the rocky terrain, searching for his own sky horse. He kept to the side of the tunnel, using it for cover as he crossed over to the area he remembered.

A scream echoed in the distance.

Gran Jefe took a step forward, snapping a fallen limb under his boot. A glowing light flashed behind him, and he whirled about, pointing his rifle at the glowing translucent figure.

"Hello, Jorge Mata," said Frank.

"Thank the Octopus Lords," Gran Jefe said, heaving a breath.

"You took quite the beating out there," said Frank.

"Other *hombres* looking worse—*muy mal,*" Gran Jefe said.

"What's the plan, partner?"

Gran Jefe unslung his bag with the mines. The hologram of the pilot followed him as he placed them just so in each tunnel entrance, explaining his plan as he went.

When he had finished burying the last mine, Gran Jefe stood to examine his trap, hoping the explosives would still work.

"Soon as it's clear, we take to sky," he said. "It's just you and me now, ghost man."

*   *   *   *   *

The rumble of engines filled the sprawling vehicle depot. X sat on a bench in the fenced-off locker area, running diagnostic tests on their new armor with Slayer. Miles and Jo-Jo were also here, watching Lucky, Nobu, and Zen brief Team Concordia on how to work the snowmobiles. Kade, Tia, and Zuni paid close attention to the last-minute preparations before the dive.

X wished he were going now, but it would take two more days to reach Polar Station in the north after dropping the first team at Concordia in the Antarctic.

"So you're telling me this thing's going to fire out a chute on its own?" Slayer asked.

"Yeah," X said. "Trust me, I don't like it either, but you're not the only one who's never dived before. Zuni hasn't either, and all these knights are complete greenhorns."

Slayer regarded the other men.

Blue Blood and Watt kept shooting them glances from across the launch bay.

"I got a bad feeling about this, King Xavier," Slayer said.

"First off, I'm not king anymore," he said. "Just call me X. Second off, this isn't my first rodeo working with former enemies—including yourself, brother."

Slayer nodded. He understood.

X put his hand on the Cazador's armored shoulder. "It wasn't too long ago I was a captive of the Barracudas. Fought with them in the wastes. Remember?"

"I do, King—uh, X."

"History is full of situations where former enemies fought

together for the greater good. And I can't think of a time when it was more justified than right now."

Slayer nodded.

"Okay, then. Miles, you ready to try your suit?" X asked.

The dog trotted over, wagging his tail. Jo-Jo came too, looking skeptical of the padded outfit the knights had provided. If only Ada were here, she could get the animal into the damned thing.

Sighing, X stroked Jo-Jo as he remembered her former handler, killed by Gran Jefe after she broke the truce between the sky people and the Cazadores. The cycle seemed to continue for their people. Perhaps it was ingrained in the human DNA.

He helped Jo-Jo into her padded suit as the divers across the room finished up with the snowmobiles and started their armor checks. Over the years, X had watched Hell Divers climb into their launch tubes, knowing that some of them—maybe *all* of them—wouldn't return from a mission. The stakes were always high, and the future of the airship was always at risk.

But the stakes had never been higher than today. If the two teams succeeded in turning on the reactors, humanity would have a chance to fight off extinction. If they failed, their years were numbered. Now more than ever, X understood that the Vanguard Islands would never survive over the long term. The place was a nuclear bomb waiting to go off, with factions fighting over dwindling resources.

He should never have tried to expand into Panama and Australia. He should have made this voyage to the poles himself, when he had a damned army to follow him.

Commander Hallsey walked into the bay. "Listen up, everyone," she said. "I've identified a weather window opening in four hours. Take a break, get some food, and meet back here in two hours."

She walked over to X as the knights and Hell Divers finished their gear checks.

"Just got word Valeria is awake if you want to see her," Josie said.

X smiled and patted his leg. "Miles, Jo-Jo, let's go see your good buddy Valeria."

"I'll escort them," Lucky said. "Slayer, why don't you hit the mess hall with the others?"

Slayer nodded, then set off with the rest of the divers and knights.

"Follow me," Lucky said.

He led X and his animals across the ship to the medical chamber, to find the pods empty. Valeria had been moved into a spare room off the chamber. Dr. Craiger stood by her bedside.

"Hey," X said.

Craiger turned, eyeing the animals.

"They can't come in here," she said.

"Sorry, I told him they could come," Lucky said.

"No, no, bring them," said a voice from inside.

X smiled again at the sight of Valeria sitting up in bed, wincing. Miles rushed over, whipping his tail. Jo-Jo came too, grunting excitedly.

"You're risking spreading germs and getting an infection," Craiger said with a frown.

"Nothing your magic pods can't fix, I'm guessing," X said.

Craiger walked away. "I'll be outside if you need me."

X took the doctor's place by Valeria's bedside. He put his hand on the patient's wrist as her brown eyes looked up, filled with the spark of life.

"How do you feel?" he asked.

"Okay, but I don't remember much..." She reached up to her bandaged neck. "They say I was shot."

X nodded, his smile fading at the memory of General Jack killing Jonah and, technically, Valeria, too. X would never forget the feel of her body going limp in his arms. He forced the image away. She wasn't dead. She was alive, and he was going to celebrate that.

"You're going to be fine," he said.

"Where are we?"

"On the airship *Trident*."

"What about..."

X shook his head subtly—not safe to speak here. She seemed to understand and looked down to Miles. The dog licked the hand she extended. Jo-Jo also nudged up against her bedside, grunting softly.

"They look better," Valeria said.

"Yes. Like you, they were healed."

"And you." Her eyes flitted to his new arm.

He held it up, examining it.

"Why do they help us?" she asked.

"Because they need us. We've arrived at the Antarctic, a place called Concordia Station, where the weather-modification devices are located. Soon, I'll go to the North Pole for the same mission."

"You go to turn them on, *¿sí?*"

"*Sí.*"

"Then I'm going with you." She sat up farther, groaning.

"No, no, you stay here and rest," he said.

"Pain isn't bad. I can go. You always go when you're hurt."

X shrugged.

"I want out of here," she said.

"Soon, okay? Maybe we can get you moved to better quarters, with Miles and Jo-Jo. The flight to the North Pole will take a few days."

He patted her on the wrist, then pulled his hand away, only to have her reach out and grip it.

"Wait, King Xavier," she said.

"He is no longer king!"

The synthetic voice exploded into the room as the Forerunner motored across the main chamber outside. He whipped a prosthetic arm out, knocking over a monitor. Then he slammed into a pair of supply carts, knocking them over, the drawers spilling surgical instruments across the deck.

The blue eye pulsed red.

"Oh, shit," X whispered. Something had enraged the cyborg royally.

Miles growled, and Jo-Jo went down on her front limbs, back hunched, hair spiked up in defensive mode. X moved in front of the animals, motioning for them to get back as the Forerunner drove over to the hatch.

Craiger stood in the chamber, head bowed. "Sir, may I—"

"Leave us!" the Forerunner boomed.

The doctor stepped aside. Boots double-timed across the chamber as Lucky rushed over, breathing heavily.

"Stay here," X said to Miles and Jo-Jo. "Valeria, see that they do."

He closed the hatch and moved in front of it.

"Want to tell me what's going on?" X asked.

"You LIED!" shrieked the cyborg.

He rose up in his chair, the hydraulics lifting the seat with his frail body. But unlike the other times, they set him on the deck, on his prosthetic legs. He limped over to X, his tunic catching on the chair. It fell away from his body, revealing the patchwork of metal parts over his leathery flesh.

Lucky moved behind X, standing at the hatch. Miles barked ferociously on the other side. Heart quickening, X stood stiffly between Lucky and the Forerunner, waiting to hear what had the cyborg so enraged. They had covered some emotional ground on the flight, building the first blocks of trust, learning how to work together. Something had happened that threatened to derail it all, or worse.

He tried to remain calm, but panic began to take hold.

"I'm sure we can work out whatever this is about," X said.

"Not for the four souls already lost," replied the Forerunner. "For those four men, there is nothing but darkness for eternity."

X pieced the puzzle together. Gran Jefe had been busy back home.

"Your Cazador warrior has killed four of my knights." The Forerunner stepped up close to X until they were face to face.

"I told you he is—"

"Silence!"

The cyborg raised a robotic hand, motioning to Lucky. "Open the hatch, Lieutenant, and secure the beasts."

X turned, his heart quickening as Miles barked louder.

"I'll secure my *companions*," X said. He moved to block Lucky. "Don't do this. I warned you about putting a hand on my dog. Let me calm them down."

Lucky hesitated, looking at the Forerunner.

A long moment of silence passed.

"Secure your beasts, Xavier," said the Forerunner.

X suppressed a sigh of relief. He moved in front of Lucky at the hatch. "Miles, Jo-Jo, easy," he said. Then he flipped the lever and opened it. Miles went down on his haunches, and Jo-Jo knuckle-walked over, her hair still spiked with nervous tension.

Out of the corner of his eye, X noticed that Lucky had raised his rifle. X whirled back, holding up his arms.

"Whoa, whoa! What is this?" X asked.

"A trial," said the Forerunner. His blue eye centered on Valeria. "I want to know what she knows about the helicopter and this warrior. She is one of them, is she not?"

X understood that he meant she was a Cazador.

"I could carpet-bomb that island and be certain to kill the man, but I want the Jayhawk," said the Forerunner. "So tell me, Valeria, where is this final helicopter? If you lie, you die. Again, and this time there will be no coming back."

Lucky aimed his rifle at Valeria.

"No. Stop this," X said. He moved in front of her.

"You've been warned," said the cyborg.

Valeria looked to X, her eyes widening, his heart thumping as if it might burst free from his chest.

"Tell him where the helicopter is," he said calmly.

Valeria swallowed, then nodded. "Inside the volcano, where your men have already died," she said. "Gran Jefe is a Barracuda warrior, trained there. He knows every tunnel, every hole. He can live off rats and bugs. You send more men to find him, just know they never will return."

"She's right," X said. "There's only one person who can end this situation, and that's Magnolia."

"How? How can she help?" asked the Forerunner.

"Tell her to find Gran Jefe and stop him."

A blue glow lit up the room, like the flash of a camera, before vanishing. The Forerunner scrutinized Valeria for a few more seconds, then nodded at Lucky.

X tensed, then exhaled as the soldier lowered his rifle.

"This stays here," said the Forerunner. "None of the other knights can know. If they do, when we dive it will imperil any trust we have built."

He backed away, limping slowly to his chair, metal parts creaking like old bones. A few steps away, he pushed a mask to his face. After a few deep gasps, he pulled it away.

"Prepare for your mission, Lieutenant Gaz," he said to Lucky. "You dive in three hours."

ELEVEN

"Weather conditions are deteriorating, with temps dropping to negative thirty degrees," reported Commander Josie Hallsey. "If Team Concordia is going to dive today, it needs to happen soon."

She stood in the corridor off the launch bay, dressed in her perfectly pressed blue uniform. Both teams were gathered there, with Team Concordia fully armored and ready to dive. Kade stood just left of the launch bay's dual hatches, next to Lucky, Zen, Nobu, Tia, and Zuni. On the far side of the hatches were X and Miles, along with Watt and Blue Blood.

The Forerunner had positioned his chair right in front of the door, as if guarding them.

Everyone awaited his orders.

A dazzling flash outside the viewports lit up the space, illuminating his ancient face and every line and scar on it as he sat there watching.

As soon as the rumble died away, he said, "Proceed with the dive."

"Copy that. Stand by for vehicle and gear deployment," Josie replied. "Lieutenant Gaz, you're cleared for the final mission briefing."

"Thank you, Commander," Lucky said. He held up a tablet with the most recent drone footage. "We're diving just outside the city, about eight miles from the reactors. Once we land, we'll secure our gear, load up the snowmobiles, and drive to this hollow for cover."

His finger traced over the valley that the severe postapocalyptic weather had carved over two and a half centuries. Josie had explained that before the war that changed the Earth, the entire continent of Antarctica was a vast, frozen desert where it rarely snowed. Then came the apocalypse, disrupting weather patterns and shrouding the planet in storms.

They were here to change all that. But Kade could tell that it wasn't going to be easy.

"Once we exit the ravine, we park the snowmobiles here and climb up," Lucky said. "From there, we'll have direct access to Concordia Station. You remember the tunnels from the first briefing. This is where we'll access them to sneak into the facility. Any questions?"

Seeing no upraised hands, he opened the hatch and led the way inside the cargo hold. A red hue swirled through the bay. The conveyor belts on deck were already loaded with the snowmobiles and crates. In the crates were spare armor and suits, life-support tents, climbing gear, medical supplies, and food and water, as well as most of their weapons and ammunition.

The knights were armed to the teeth—especially Zen, who had draped himself with a belt of armor-piercing .50-caliber rounds and wore two Uzis holstered at his waist. Nobu and Lucky would both dive carrying collapsible assault rifles with spare mags stuffed into their tactical vests. They would also carry semiautomatic pistols.

Kade and his comrades from the islands, on the other hand, were given only knives and ice axes. Tia had tried to argue, but the knights didn't trust Kade enough even to let him have a weapon.

He swallowed hard. Normally, he didn't get the predive jitters. But going down defenseless into a hostile place like this had him on edge. The only reassuring thing was the state-of-the-art armor designed to protect them from the elements.

In a few minutes, they would see how well it worked.

The nightmare about Raph in the museum replayed in Kade's mind as he waited to dive. Confliction pulled at his heart. Even now, at the eleventh hour, he considered asking the Forerunner to keep Tia back from this mission. *Begging* him.

But they all had made a deal, and he knew what the answer would be. All Kade could do was protect her down there. And, of course, Zuni would do everything he could to keep Tia safe.

"Comms check," Josie said over an open channel.

The knights and Hell Divers sounded off.

"Good copy," Josie said. She turned to the equipment. "Dropping gear in five, four, three, two, one."

A pair of hatches in front of the tracks opened, letting in the morning's freezing howl. Heat fans clicked on in the overhead, keeping the launch bay warm while the supply crates rolled forward on their tracks, plummeting out of the airship into the darkness, where their cargo chutes would deploy to check their fall. On an adjacent track, the four snowmobiles followed. As soon as they were gone, the hatches closed.

"Okay, warm bodies next," Lucky said. "Check your suit one last time; then check your mate's suit."

Kade looked at the heads-up display on his new helmet. It had taken some getting used to, but now he understood how everything worked. All systems were green, and the armor was fully operational.

He moved over to check on Tia.

"I'm good," she said.

"How about you, Zuni?" Kade asked, looking the younger man up and down.

"Good to go."

Clanking echoed across the space. They all turned to find the Forerunner motoring into the launch bay. He took a deep breath from a mask as he halted his chair. The other divers followed him inside.

"Whatever happens down there, remember one thing," said the Forerunner. "We are in this together. We share the same bright future—and the same sorry fate should we fail."

"We won't fail, sir," Lucky said.

"I know you won't," said the Forerunner.

X walked over with Slayer while the knights said their goodbyes.

"You got this, brother," X said.

He raised a fist to Kade and they bumped. "You too, Xavier."

Slayer and Zuni shook hands, but when they parted, Slayer hardly acknowledged Kade. He could sense animosity from the Cazador, likely due to Kade's role in bringing the knights to their home, and the botched mission to Texas that cost Blackburn's life.

Kade understood his feelings. They were justified. He walked over to Lucky as their team gathered and Team Polar left the launch bay, leaving only Team Concordia.

The comms crackled in their helmets.

"Proceeding with jump in ten, nine, eight…" Josie said over the channel.

The swirling red light flicked off on five, and a chain of three lights on the hatch turned green, one at a time. At T minus one second, a clicking came from the locking mechanism, and the single hatch whisked open to darkness.

"For the Trident," Lucky said.

"For the Trident!" Nobu and Zen called back.

"We dive so humanity survives!" Kade yelled.

He leaped into the abyss, feeling no more substantial than an autumn leaf taken by the season's last storm. For Kade, this was the last hurrah—his final season. After this, his heart and mind were too broken to sign up for more combat. He had just enough fight in him to finish this battle.

The forces of gravity and wind yanked his body in its new armor this way and that. Down he plunged, into the darkness over the Antarctic ice sheet. He turned his head in time to glimpse Tia and Zuni leaping out, followed by Nobu, Zen, and Lucky. They all were in the air now. The airship *Trident* roared onward, absorbed in an instant by the surging clouds.

Kade flung his arms and legs out into a hard arch, settling in before pulling his limbs into free-fall position. Stable now, he watched the clouds below, anxious for his first glimpse of the surface.

At twenty thousand feet, it would be over a minute and a half falling at his current speed. His gaze swept over the data on his HUD. The temp made him do a double check. Sure enough, he was diving in a shocking negative seventy-four degrees Fahrenheit. Remarkably, he didn't feel it. His body remained warm and cozy in the suit under the layers of armor, all warmed by internal heaters.

Lightning flashed on the horizon, blooming outward in a dazzling display that vanished as suddenly as it had appeared. The electrical storm didn't seem to be affecting their communications or their HUDs, however.

On their shared digital map, Kade saw the crates—already on the ground. He saw their beacons next, with Zen and Nobu pulling apart at an increased speed that could be explained only by the AI activating the thrusters built into their suits. The technology was astounding, but it could do nothing for the turbulence.

Before he could react, a wind shear flipped him onto his back, for a view of Tia and Zuni. They hit the pocket a second later and both tumbled out of control. Nobu and Zen were also in trouble, spinning wildly. Only Lucky seemed to remain in a steady free fall.

"Chins up," Kade grunted. "Relax your body and arch your back, belly to Earth!"

At fifteen thousand feet, he broke through the last of the turbulence. He relaxed a degree, exhaled, and checked his HUD again. The subscreen showed the other divers spreading out and recovering from the turbulence.

A glance down confirmed they had yet to hit the most dangerous part of the dive. Directly below, in their flight path, the shelf of clouds lit up with multiple lightning strikes. They had to get through this section as fast as possible.

"Oh, shit!" Nobu said, panic rising in his voice over the shaky channel. *"I thought the drop was clear."*

"We'll be fine," Kade said. "Just stay relaxed. Head down, body straight—be an arrow. Follow me; I'll guide you down."

"Negative," Lucky replied. *"Let the AI guide you down."*

"You do that, and you've got much better odds of being fried."

There was a pause as the divers rocketed toward the storm.

"Okay, disengage auto-opening and maneuver into a nose-dive, following Kade," Lucky ordered.

Kade put his hands to his thighs and straightened his legs. The altimeter on his HUD quickly spun down to ten thousand feet. The wind pushed his body about as he streaked earthward.

Lightning flashed to his left, the thunder booming louder than anything he could imagine. Biting down on his mouth guard, he blazed down to nine thousand feet, falling at well above terminal velocity.

At eight thousand, the AI was trying to regain control by flashing warnings on his HUD.

"No, damn it," he said. Sometimes, plain old analog blood and guts was the best way to get through a storm—not some damned computer.

A double prong of lightning lashed the sky under him so fast it was gone in a blink. He shot through the residual glow.

At seven thousand feet, it appeared he was through the worst of it. Cautiously easing out of the nosedive, he moved his arms out and bent his knees. As soon as he became stable, he glanced over his shoulder, sighting up Tia and Zuni by their infrared tags showing on his HUD. Both divers had regained control of the dive and were falling well.

"Good job, almost there," Kade said. "Reengage suit auto-opening."

By the time he looked back down, the cloud cover had broken open, revealing the icebound city on the horizon. Somewhere six miles beyond that were the Delta Cloud fusion reactors, not yet visible. The advanced optics of his HUD provided a sprawling view of stark white interrupted by the sharp geometric patterns of the city's structures, capped by snow. The stark contrast between the icy realm and the frozen remnants of civilization painted a serene but desolate tableau, foreshadowing what awaited them on the ground. A chill rolled up his spine.

Along the border, the three crates became visible by the infra-red tags showing on his visor. All four snowmobiles were also on the ground, their chutes having set them down on the flattest, most unobstructed drop zone he had ever seen. The precision was astounding.

At three thousand feet, his HUD flashed a warning.

Chute deployment imminent. Prepare for landing.

It was damned hard to see the icy surface rising up to meet his boots.

A second warning flashed. The chute fired out of the armored slot in his back, jerking his body upward, or so it felt. He reached up to the dangling toggles. The AI had calculated everything, including his distance from the other divers.

Glancing up, he tried to get a view of them but couldn't see anything over the black canopy above him. He focused back on the frozen world below, now just a thousand feet away. The buildings of the city were coming into focus, their smooth domed tops and sides covered in snow. Windows with metal shutters showed in areas where wind had blasted away some of the white.

"Approaching DZ," Kade said. "All divers, prepare for landing."

At this rate, he would be the first one down, with Lucky and Zen following. Nobu, Zuni, and Tia were all lagging by at least ten seconds.

Kade felt the gentle breeze of his forward motion. Just five hundred feet from the surface now. A gust caught his chute, pushing him toward the city.

Studying the ground for a drop zone, Kade decided on a smooth section eighty yards from one of the crates. But the wind had other ideas, pushing him away from the area. He turned into it, but his flight path would take him over a twenty-foot fence topped with razor wire. Whether he cleared it would depend on airspeed.

He watched in horror as those pointed blades seemed to stretch upward, grasping at his feet. Not thirty feet on the other side was the first row of buildings—six of them, each three stories tall, all structurally identical with precisely the same concrete facades and shuttered windows. If he smacked into one of those, it would mean internal injuries and broken bones.

At the last second, he lifted his feet over the razor wire,

performing a two-stage flare right over the fence. Jerking backward, he fell hard the last six feet after his chute caught on the concertina wire. Flicking open his knife, he turned and cut through the suspension lines. Head spinning from the impact, he looked back to the sky for a view of the other divers.

Lucky came down on the other side of the fence. Zen landed with him in almost the same second, both of them crashing to the snowy ground. Kade couldn't have asked for anything better on a first dive.

Tia, Zuni, and Nobu were still two hundred feet up, directly above Kade, drifting over the first row of domed structures.

"Watch those buildings," Kade said over the comm.

"We're good, don't worry," Tia said.

"Kade, go help them," Lucky said. He had snapped together his assault rifle and was training it on the buildings. Then Kade heard it, an odd buzzing noise that reminded him of bees.

He scanned the sky, expecting to see the airship, but this was coming from the city. It sounded almost like human engineering.

Kade tensed as he watched Nobu, Zuni, and Tia sail over the first structures, where Lucky now aimed his rifle. Nobu had to raise his legs to clear the top of a building. He went down over the side, but Tia and Zuni sailed on, deeper into the city. Right toward that growing buzz that sounded like a swarm of angry mutant bees.

"Tia, see anything out there?" Kade asked.

"No, but I hear a loud humming noise," she replied.

"Lucky, what is that?" Kade shouted.

"I don't know," he called back.

Kade had already started trekking away from the fence. He listened to the buzzing while hoofing it over the mounds toward an alley in between the buildings. The snow became deeper, coming up over his ankles, then his knees. Halfway down the alley, he was climbing up over the mounds, then sinking down. Grumbling and cursing, he fought across the higher drifts to a wall some eight feet tall that separated him from the road bisecting the next row of buildings.

He turned back the way he had come. Lucky and Zen carried a crate up to the other side of the fence, their armored forms hardly visible in the light snow.

Kade considered heading back their way to see if he could find another route into the city. But then he heard a distant cry from Tia.

"Help!"

This wasn't over the comms. This was coming from the city.

"Tia!" Kade yelled. He looked closer at the frozen wall that blocked his path. It was built of ice blocks that had melded together into a single block.

After backing up some, he ran at the wall, ice axe in one hand, sheath knife in the other. Getting some purchase with his foot on the bottom block, he sprang as high as he could, swinging the ice axe into the wall. The pick bit and held, and he pulled up on it and stabbed the wall with his sheath knife. Pulling up on both tools, he swung sideways and managed to throw his left heel over the top of the wall. A minute of struggle, and he was on top of an ice barrier three feet thick. Lying there panting, he spotted something flying over the buildings across the street.

"What the bloody hell..." he whispered.

Kade pushed up and slid down the other side of the ice dam. As soon as his boots hit the street, he took off running for another alley, which looked mostly free of drifting snow.

A burst of gunshots made him flinch. Then came the chatter of fully automatic gunfire.

He ran down the alley to the next street, where he saw muzzle flashes coming from a rooftop above him. Nobu perched there, firing a submachine gun at the adjacent rooftop.

Turning that way, Kade saw a swarm, not of bees but of drones the size and shape of winged rats. Dozens of the things buzzed around Tia and Zuni, who squirmed and fought, pulled along the ground by the wind in their chutes.

"Cut your lines!" Kade yelled.

She had her hook knife out, and so did Zuni, but they were too busy ducking and swiping at the drones that assailed them.

Kade's heart jumped at their cries of pain.

Zen's sniper rifle boomed, and a drone above Tia burst into chunks of smoldering scrap metal. The sniper took a second shot, exploding another winged machine.

Kade plowed through knee-deep snow, trying to get to the buildings. Tia had finally cut enough of her suspension lines to spill the wind out of the billowing black parachute. Zuni went next.

Muzzle flashes and tracer bullets lit up the darkness, streaking into the domed building now that the knights had clean shots at the drones still buzzing out of a hidden opening in the rooftop—something their own drone had missed on the flyover while scanning for life. Understandable since these things were not alive and made no heat signature.

Thin metal wings and debris from the machines rained from the air as Zen blasted them to pieces. Their parts fluttered down to the snow, where both Tia and Zuni writhed in agony.

Kade climbed up the mound and fumbled until he grabbed Tia by a boot, pulling her down the low slope. Then he grabbed Zuni and yanked. The Cazador came sliding down next to Tia, onto the snow-covered street.

A drone swooped down at Kade. With nothing else handy, he swung his ice axe, batting it out of the air. The gunfire waned as Kade knelt to check Tia. He could tell right away she had been stung. Zuni too was moaning in agony.

"Bring the med kit!" Kade shouted.

"On our way!" Lucky yelled back. "Nobu, Zen, get up a perimeter now!"

Frantic, Kade searched Tia for wounds.

"It burns," she choked. "It burns."

"Where? Show me where!"

He looked her over, trying to find where the stingers had penetrated. She raised a glove with a spot of frozen blood on it.

"My feet," she stammered. "And my neck..."

Kade could see the terror on her face behind her visor—eyes wide, lips puffy, cheeks mottled. The result of poisoning or envenomation. A memory of his dream surfaced, of Raph screaming that this would happen. That Kade would fail his daughter.

No, no, no, she'll be fine!

Tia reached over and gripped Zuni's hand as he choked and convulsed on the ground.

"Come on!" Kade shouted to Lucky, who was plunge-stepping through the deep snow with the medical pack. A minute away, maybe less. Precious seconds passed.

"Tia, stay with me," Kade said.

Her pained groan was weak, and she coughed as she turned over. Zuni jerked beside her, his boots scraping over the icy snow.

"Zuni, don't... don't go," she mumbled.

Footsteps crunched as Lucky and Zen arrived. Nobu remained on the rooftop, taking out individual drones that buzzed overhead.

"Here." Lucky bent down with the medical kit.

Kade grabbed it and flipped it open.

"We need epinephrine," he said. "And antihistamines."

"On it," Lucky said.

He rifled through the supplies while Kade assessed Tia. When she didn't respond, he looked up to see her eyes on Zuni. Arm stretched out, she held his hand.

Lucky handed him a syringe.

Taking it, Kade stuck Tia in the thigh, between the armor plates, right through the suit.

"Quick, do the same with Zuni!" he said.

Kade put a finger to her neck, though there was little point, he realized as both their beacons on his HUD winked out.

He twisted off his helmet, then reached out and gently lifted Tia's.

"Please, please," he whispered in the icy-cold air before he put his lips against her lips, breathing into her open mouth. Then he started pushing down on her chest. Within thirty seconds, his lips were numb and his eyelashes covered in frost.

Come on, come on, come on, Tia, please!

He pushed down and released, over and over until he couldn't feel his face. Her cold eyes had flipped up to meet his own.

"Kade," said a voice behind him.

He felt a hand on his shoulder.

"Kade, they're gone," Lucky said. "You're gonna freeze. You have to stop, mate."

Kade slumped back on his knees, staring in anguish at Tia.

He wanted to scream. This was his fault.

You let this happen!

The voice was Raphael's, overlying his own. He had broken his promise, failing to protect Tia. Just as he had failed to protect his own family.

Kade bent back down. "No, no!" he said. "We can save her. Bring the airship back down. We'll get them into one of those pods. We can bring them back!"

Lucky glanced up at the sky as if he was actually considering it, but then shook his head. "Even if we could, we can't risk the ship. You know that."

"I'm sorry," Nobu said.

Zen walked over, hovering behind Kade. "I know it's hard," he said, "but we have to move. We're exposed out here."

Kade gritted his teeth, anger eclipsing the pain. He shook on his knees, staring at Tia and Zuni, their hands still clasped.

Something metallic clicked against Kade's shoulder plate. He glanced back to see that Lucky had pulled out a pistol—and not just any pistol but the Monster Hunter.

"We have to turn on the reactors," Lucky said. "For Tia, for Zuni, for everyone back home. You have to keep fighting."

Kade stared back down at Tia. He wasn't sure if he could go on. Not after this.

Lucky reached down with his other hand. "You have to get up," he said. "We need your help."

TWELVE

Magnolia arrived at the capitol tower just before dusk.

The two knights accompanying her pushed open the hatch to the enclosed marina with its hundred or so boats suspended on hoists. To her surprise, Imulah was waiting on the pier.

"What are you doing here?" she asked.

"Going with you, apparently," replied the scribe. "Although I haven't been told where we're going."

"To track down Gran Jefe."

He stroked his beard but didn't press beyond that as they walked along the row of small craft to a war boat that had already been lowered into the water. General Jack stood with his back to them, sharpening a cutlass with long, even strokes on a whetstone.

"Sir, we've brought the scribe and the Hell Diver woman," said one of the knights.

Jack gave a menacing look to Magnolia, then Imulah.

"You try anything, and I'll feed you both to those bloody octopuses you worship," he said.

"General," Imulah asked, "could you kindly inform me what I will be doing on this trip to find Gran Jefe?"

"Documenting." Jack pointed his cutlass at the boat. A drip of blood fell from the blade.

Seeing it made Magnolia fear the worst. "Where's Pedro?" she asked.

"That's none of your concern."

"No? Neither is Gran Jefe, so if you want my help, you'll tell me where Pedro is."

Jack twirled the blade and cracked a grin. "You want to know? Okay, I don't see any harm in you knowing he was locked up for the messages he sent out during our arrival here."

He walked over close to Magnolia. "You didn't think we'd find out? I *always* sniff out enemies of the Trident." His nostrils flared as if to demonstrate.

Then he held up the cutlass. "This isn't his blood, but it will be mixed with yours if you don't get moving."

"We should go," Imulah said quietly.

Magnolia clenched her jaw and climbed onto the bow of the boat. She took a seat behind the pilot's chair. Imulah slid in next to her as the huge twin outboards purred.

Jack pushed a lever, raising a Bimini over the open cabin. The two knights on the pier tossed the bow and stern lines aboard and hopped on. Jack backed away from the dock, then came about and motored through the hatch to the open ocean outside. A trawler bobbed in the light chop, its decks clean and nets sorted for the next day out.

The docks were bustling with activity. Men and women in blue uniforms displaying Trident symbols unloaded gear and supplies from the *Angry 'Cuda*, now docked in the marina. On the deck was one of the armored personnel carriers Magnolia had spent so many hours inside on missions in the wastes. Behind the APC were two trailers, one with a helicopter strapped to it.

She looked up to the towers, searching the many windows.

Sofia was probably up there, looking down with Phyl and Alton at her sides. The kids were still curious and full of hope, resilient despite the scars of loss. Magnolia could hardly remember that age, but what few memories remained were painful.

The engines growled, lifting the bow out of the water. It came banging back down, and Imulah nearly fell out of his seat, but Magnolia held out an arm. He felt frail and old.

General Jack buried the throttle as they left the capitol tower behind. The boat powered toward the Cazador towers. Magnolia looked up at the bridges connecting them and recalled, all those years ago, riding in this very boat as a prisoner of the Cazadores. Now, on that same boat, she was a prisoner of the knights.

As they sped away, Magnolia watched the horizon for the invisible line of demarcation between paradise and the unending storms of postapocalyptic Earth. The first streaks of lightning lit up the sky. She found herself weighing the odds of taking the bloody cutlass from Jack and hacking him down, then killing the two knights aboard. But those guards looked ready for anything. Their assault rifles would cut her down before she could get close.

Rain pattered down on the Bimini's nylon canopy as they broke through the border into the storms. The boat thumped over the increasingly heavy chop, and Imulah had a hand on his stomach.

Magnolia glanced over. "You gonna be okay?"

"Actually, no," the scribe said, and vomited over the railing. She reached out and held on to his tunic as the boat rocked.

The two knights watching them chuckled, but the general just stared out at the point where the bow light hit the waves.

An hour into the journey, Magnolia glimpsed the dark bulk of an island on the horizon—Sint Eustatius, where she had been only two days ago. Jack motored into the protected bay, where a ship stood at anchor.

It took her a moment to recognize the *Frog*, now painted with a Trident symbol on the hull and flying the Trident flag. Three skiffs had beached on the shore, and tents had been erected there.

Jack eased back the throttle and turned in the chair to look at Magnolia and Imulah in turn.

"This will be your home until we have this Gran Jefe's head on a stick," Jack said. "Your job is to lure him out and track down the second Jayhawk. Understood?"

Imulah nodded.

"I won't ask you twice," Jack said to Magnolia. His hand went to the hilt of his cutlass. "Maybe I should just go ahead and show you how fucking serious I am."

"I'll find him, so you can save the tough-guy shit," Magnolia said. "It just makes people laugh behind your back."

Jack glared for a moment, then turned to steer them ashore, muttering something under his breath about feeding her to the fish.

Magnolia wasn't scared. She took the opportunity to size up the enemy forces. She counted eight tents and a red-domed multihabitat structure that reminded her of something she had seen in a book about colonizing other planets. A Trident flag flapped lazily in the breeze outside the building, where a knight stood sentry. That must be their command-and-control post.

It was a lot of people to hunt down just one man. Then again, Gran Jefe had killed at least four of their soldiers already, and they were also searching for a helicopter—a vitally important resource, especially with the airship away.

The war boat stopped a hundred feet from shore, bobbing up and down just outside the gentle break. Jack stepped back from the wheel, barking orders. One of the knights slung his rifle and took the wheel. The other soldier watched Imulah and Magnolia while Jack put on his helmet.

A skiff motored out with three more knights, coming up along the port side.

"Get on," Jack said.

Magnolia jerked away to avoid his touch and climbed out onto the bow with Imulah. She helped him down into the skiff. As soon as Jack was aboard, the skiff motored through the surf and slid up onto the beach.

Jack was first off the boat. He led the way up the shoreline, past saluting knights and someone in a hazard suit. The rumble of engines resonated from the jungle, and two ATVs came jouncing out onto the beach, each with a single rider. Each ATV pulled a sled, and Magnolia could tell by the shape of their loads that they were carrying bodies.

"Looks like somebody went hunting for Gran Jefe," Magnolia said.

Jack growled out a string of profanity. One of his hands shook until he clenched it into a fist. He suddenly reached out to Magnolia with his other hand. She tried to step back, but he grabbed her by the arm and pulled her over.

"Let me go!" she yelled.

"Hey!" Imulah said, and walked right into a backhand from General Jack.

The scribe fell down on the beach. To Magnolia's surprise, he pushed himself up from the sand. A knight kicked him back down, and he stayed there.

Jack spun Magnolia toward him, squeezing her arm with his robotic hand. Her eyes locked on to the soulless gaze and didn't look away. He could kill her, but he would never have the satisfaction of intimidating her.

"You will bring this animal to me," he said. "Or I will show you terror you've never experienced. And trust me, Magnolia Katib, I know you've seen your share of it."

He shoved her down to the sand, beside Imulah. She landed hard on her side but didn't show her pain. Two knights walked over as Jack strode ahead to the red-domed building.

"Get up," said one of the guards.

Magnolia glanced over at Imulah, who wiped blood from his face.

"You okay?" she asked.

He nodded.

The two knights escorted them to the multihabitat structure. Inside was a clean room with showerheads extending from the overhead. They passed through and entered a circular space with tables and computer equipment.

Jack stood at a table, examining a map of what appeared to be a tunnel system under the volcano known as the Quill. She eyed his cutlass, wanting to make a play for it and the consequences be damned.

"Come," he said.

The knights pushed Magnolia and Imulah closer to the table.

"This is where the scum hides," Jack said. "Are you familiar with it?"

"Fuck you," Magnolia said.

He glanced back to the map, then backhanded her in the face before she could react. The blow knocked her back, but she kept on her feet. No longer caring about repercussions, she lunged, snarling. She made it a full stride before the two knights behind her grabbed her and forced her to her knees.

"You really should learn when to obey," Jack said. He pulled out his cutlass and placed the tip under her left nostril. A slight twist cut into the cartilage, sending a wave of pain through her sinuses that made her forget her anger for an instant.

"Are you familiar with these tunnels?" he asked. "I can cut off your entire fucking nose if you want."

"No," she said through clenched teeth.

"And you, scribe?"

"I've never been there, but I know of them," Imulah said.

"Good," Jack said. "Put on a suit. You're going with this feral bitch." He snapped his fingers, and a man in a hazard suit dragged a crate over. Bending down, the man opened the lid to reveal matching suits. A second crate had packs of food and other rations.

Magnolia was pulled up to her feet, blood dripping from her nose. The general dropped a backpack in front of her.

"You have six hours to locate Gran Jefe and the helicopter," he said. "If you don't return with him and the location of the chopper, our dingoes will start hunting *you*."

*   *   *   *   *

From the shelter of the cave system, Michael watched the storm that had been raging over the island for almost twenty-four hours. It couldn't have come at a worse time, completely blocking communication with Timothy, who had been obliged to move the airship higher, away from the lightning that could so easily destroy it.

Michael had returned here to protect his family while Victor watched the escaped slaves, who had just burned one of their captors alive.

In the meantime, Michael had continued to shore up the defenses. He looked away from the sky to the beach, where he had set out the passive infrared sensors, ultrasonic distance sensors, and vibration sensors he had managed to jerry-rig over the past day. If anyone came this way, they would be detected and activate an alert on his wrist computer.

It was a start, but he still had more work excavating the tunnel in the communal space. There were tools in the supply crates that Timothy had dropped off: shovels, a high-powered drill, extra ammunition, two additional rifles, and three pistols.

With the exterior sensors set, he grabbed the tools and returned to the bunker. He had asked Layla and Bray to stay inside. Bray was used to being confined, but not like this.

When Michael opened the makeshift door, Bray came run-waddling over, carrying a glass of orange juice—the last of the frozen fruit from the Vanguard Islands. Juice sloshed over the rim as he hurried over.

"Drink, Da-da."

"That looks good," Michael said. He set the tools down, crouched, and hugged his son. Then he took a sip of the juice that Bray held up.

"Thanks," Michael said.

He looked over at Layla and Gabi, sitting at the table in the center of the room and frowning over a map they had spread out on its surface. It was marked up with the potential farming sites Layla had identified, and now it had a new marking: the location of the escaped slaves at Punta Ganada.

"How'd it go?" Layla asked.

"Good. Got the sensors finished, and I'll attack that tunnel soon." He looked down at the tools. "These will help."

"¿Dónde está Victor?" Gabi asked.

"Not back yet," Michael said as he picked Bray up and carried him over to the table.

"Outside, Da-da," Bray said.

"We can't go out there right now, buddy; it's too dangerous."

Bray tilted his head. "Outside, go outside."

"We can't, I'm sorry."

Bray whimpered and lowered his gaze.

"He's tired," Layla said. "He needs a nap."

"No nigh-nigh time!" Bray wailed.

"Just a little rest, buddy. Not night-night time yet," Michael said.

Bray put his head against Michael's shoulder, and Michael carried him into their room, cleaned up the spilled juice, and set him in his crib.

"See you after your rest," Michael said. "Sleep well."

Bray looked at him, gave a reluctant nod, and clutched his toy giraffe. Michael backed out of the room and shut it almost all the way. When he turned, Gabi and Layla had that same concerned look.

He walked over to them and sat down, laying his pistol on the table.

"So you're sure these people were *eating* that man?" Layla asked.

Michael had told them the story hours ago, omitting certain details while Bray was in earshot. The kid soaked up everything.

"Afraid so," Michael said.

"My God," Layla whispered.

Michael shifted his seat to face Gabi.

"The slavers must be the same people that came here years ago," he said. "But what I want to know is, where's their base?"

"My guess, they're in an ITC facility, but Timothy didn't find any of their hubs in the archives, which doesn't really mean much since they could be hidden," Layla said. "I've been doing searches of the maps he printed out back on the ship. Take a look."

She unspooled another set of maps—these not of the island chains but of the western coast of Africa.

"There are lots of port cities along the coast, but I think the likeliest one to have had an ITC facility is Casablanca." She tapped the screen.

"What am I looking at?" Michael asked.

"There's a berth for an ITC ship, which tells me they had a

hidden location in the city prewar," she said. "No other ports in West Africa have ITC slips that I can find."

"Good catch, Layla!" Michael said, grinning.

"Thanks, but it could be nothing. Just my best guess at the location of these slavers—or their slaves, anyway."

"How far is it from here?"

"Call it seven hundred and fifty miles, straight shot."

Michael looked at the map, wondering what secrets lay hidden in Casablanca. The only way to know for sure would be to search, but even in the airship it was a long journey. They also had no idea what kind of shape the city would be in, or whether it had been hit by a warhead during the war. Of course, most port cities had seen damage from tsunamis at the very least.

"I think, when Victor gets back, we should vote on what to do once these storms pass," Michael said. "Do we send Timothy to recon Casablanca on his own, do we go with him, or do we all stay here?"

"Not safe in the sky, and not safe here," Layla said. "Not with those people out here."

She glanced over her shoulder through the ajar doorway, where they could see Bray sleeping peacefully in his crib. He had no idea what cannibals were, or that they were just a few miles away.

"If anyone knows the answer to our question, it's the slaves," Michael said.

"You aren't seriously considering asking them, are you?" Layla said. "They just ate that guy!"

"No." He looked to Gabi, who seemed to be tracking the conversation.

Layla pulled the map of the island over to her. "This place is about as secure as it's going to be. If someone does come, we will know and have time to flee. But if Timothy's gone when it happens, we could find ourselves cornered."

Michael nodded. "I've thought about that."

"And it could take him weeks to locate this outpost out there or wherever the slavers have a base."

He nodded again.

"There's something else we haven't really discussed, Tin."

"Yes?"

"Your plan if we *do* locate their outpost." Layla looked him in the eye. "What do you plan on doing?"

Gabi looked at him too, understanding at least some of what they were saying.

"I guess it depends on how big a threat they are," Michael said, "but I'll do whatever it takes to keep us safe—including moving on until we find a new place."

Layla smiled, but it was a sad smile—an admission of what he already knew: that no matter where they went, there would be threats. Humans, mutant life-forms, storms—the list was long.

Beeping came from his monitor on the table. Michael rose in his chair, scooping up his pistol.

"What is it?" Layla asked.

"The motion sensors," he said. "Two just went off on the beach."

"Is it Victor?"

"I don't think he would come back without radioing—unless he tried that." Michael checked the magazine in his pistol. "Get your weapons. I'll try him on the comms."

Both Gabi and Layla picked up rifles and followed him over to the door.

"Victor, do you copy?" Michael spoke into his headset.

Static hissed back.

He tried again, with the same response.

"Stay here. I'll check it out," Michael said. He paused. "If I don't come back, use that tunnel to go out the back way."

Layla's eyes widened.

"It's going to be okay," he said. As he turned, he looked at Bray, who remained asleep.

It's going to be okay...

Heart racing, Michael rushed out of the room and into the passage. The thick hatch was closed and locked. He holstered his pistol and set about opening it. The faint sound of crashing waves shooshed through the rocky passages as he swung open the heavy door. He thought he heard something over the noise—a motor perhaps?

Drawing his pistol again, he ran toward it. Thunder boomed outside in the same moment that a transmission came over the comms.

"Victor," Michael said into his headset. "Victor, come in."

Still nothing.

A third sensor beeped on his wrist monitor. Whatever triggered the alert was getting closer.

Michael slunk down the last stretch of tunnel, past the area where Gabi and Victor's friends had been killed by the slavers. That made him pause slightly. He stood there, conflicted. Maybe he should just stay back in the shelter until he knew more.

A voice broke over the comms.

"Chief, do you copy?"

"Pepper," Michael replied. "I copy. Do you have eyes on the shelter? I've got multiple sensors going off."

White noise hissed in his ear.

"Damn it!" Michael huffed. He raised his pistol and pushed on down through the darkness, using the intermittent lightning to guide him out onto the bluff. The residual bluish glow chased away the shadows momentarily.

Pistol raised, Michael stepped out onto the cave overlook. The chair where Victor had sat for hours as sentry was still there.

Waves battered the rocks below, giving off a crashing echo that made it difficult to hear much else.

Outside the overhang, the rain had let up and the storm seemed to be breaking on the horizon. Michael sneaked over to a clump of boulders and scanned the water for boats. Seeing nothing on the first few sweeps, he moved on to look at the beach. Nothing down there either, from what he could see.

A wave crashed against the rocks as he started on the path winding up to the bluffs. He moved cautiously, scanning the green field of his night-vision goggles. In the respite of the waves, he heard a crunching sound.

He flattened himself against the rock wall, pistol raised. Moving his finger to the trigger guard, he waited. The slap of the surf faded away, and again he heard the crunch of heavy boots. As it got closer, he steeled himself and moved around the corner, aiming the barrel at a single rain-drenched figure making its way down the path.

"It's me!" hissed a voice.

Michael lowered the gun as a lightning bolt illuminated a wide-eyed Victor.

"Fuck!" Michael cursed. "Why didn't you radio?"

"I try. I try to tell you."

Victor sucked air as if he had run all the way across the island.

"Slow down—tell me *what*?" Michael asked.

"The slaves…" he wheezed. "They leave in a boat," he said.

Michael went up the path with Victor, trying to connect with Timothy on the comms as they reached the top of the bluff. But again only white noise hissed back.

"Are they coming this way?" Michael asked as he searched the waves.

Victor shook his head. "They leave island."

Michael felt the wash of relief knowing they had gone, but he also realized something—he had just passed up an opportunity to learn more about where these people came from. He might have learned exactly where the slavers' outpost was located.

"You got any idea where they're going?" Michael asked.

"Northwest, I think."

"Wait—are you sure?"

"Pretty sure."

Michael didn't need a map to know there was nothing in that direction but ocean for thousands of miles.

"Why would they go out there into such danger?"

But before Victor could answer, Michael knew. These slaves were doing the same thing Victor and Ton had done years ago—something Michael himself had done despite the danger. They were looking for a new, safe home.

"Good luck to them," Victor said. "They'll need it."

THIRTEEN

Drenched in sweat, X pushed up from the deck of the airship's gymnasium, using his new robotic arm. Miles and Jo-Jo rested in the center of the room, watching and probably wondering what the hell he was doing.

He went to a rack of weights bolted down against the hull. The airship had equipment he had never even seen before, from a weird-looking machine with a conveyor belt you could run on to a stationary bike with screens that showed ancient trails and roads. And it all worked! Everything was clean, too. Robots vroomed across the decks of the ship, sucking up dust and washing them down. These weren't the old, broken-down models that Tin once fixed in X's apartment as a kid. These were top of the line, just like everything else on the *Trident*.

X finished his weight routine and began jogging around the room. Miles and Jo-Jo kept watch, turning their heads again as if unsure why he would be running when nothing chased him.

"I'm training," he said.

Miles gave a playful bark, and X picked up a soft green ball and tossed it in the air. The dog leaped after it, jumping up as it came back down. Jo-Jo expressed her disinterest with a yawn.

X kept running, picking up speed as Miles chased him, tail whipping back and forth. He dropped the ball in front of X, and X tossed it again. Miles bolted away, sliding across the deck.

"Easy, buddy," X said.

He watched his companion, making sure the dog wasn't over-doing it. The medical chamber had healed them both, but they weren't exactly young bucks anymore. For this reason, training was even more important before the dive—especially this one. They both needed to be fit.

As X jogged, he thought about where they were heading, and again found himself conflicted about whether Miles should come along.

Lap after lap, X lost himself in the cavalcade of thoughts rang-ing from Kade and Team Concordia to Michael and his family, wherever they were. And then to Magnolia and his friends back at the Vanguard Islands. X felt so far from all of them, but he knew from experience that dwelling on it would do no good. He couldn't control what happened anywhere but here. He had to stay hyperfocused on his mission.

Excited barking and grunting broke his trance. He slowed and eased into a walk as Miles and Jo-Jo bolted for the hatch. Stand-ing there was Valeria, a dimpled grin on her face. Miles leaped up, licking at her face. Jo-Jo got up to embrace her.

"Easy, easy!" X shouted. "Don't break her!"

He went over, stopping to grab a towel and wipe off his face. Valeria knelt down, petting both animals. This vision of her, just days after she had died in his arms, was a miraculous sight.

She looked up as he approached, her smile warm and full of joy.

"You feel good, no?" she asked.

"Like a new man. How about you?" X asked.

"I, uh… I'm sore but much better. Thought maybe I can come walk and play with them."

"By all means, have at it."

Valeria scooped up the tennis ball and tossed it underhand into the air, with a wince she couldn't hide. Clearly, she wasn't 100 percent yet. No surprise, even with the technology they had used.

Miles dropped the ball at her feet. X joined her and picked it up. Now Jo-Jo seemed interested. She knuckle-walked over, tilting her head while blinking those big, liquid eyes.

"You want in on the fun?" X asked.

He threw the ball and was surprised by how fast Jo-Jo could move her big body when she wanted to. The animal jumped into the air, clearing at least six feet and catching the ball.

She came down next to Miles, who barked when the ball didn't come back out of Jo-Jo's mouth.

"You're not supposed to *eat* it," X said, chuckling.

Valeria laughed.

Going to the bin of balls, X picked out a bigger one and kicked it across the gym. Miles raced after it, pulling ahead of Jo-Jo. The ball bounced off the wall, and both animals buttonhooked after it.

X smiled as he watched, standing beside Valeria. For a fleeting moment, everything felt okay, and he wondered if this could be the start of something—a future for all of them. There was no denying he had feelings for Valeria, and he was pretty sure she felt the same way. Miles certainly loved her, and Jo-Jo as well.

But X knew how this normally went. Good things rarely lasted, especially when a dive was on the horizon. Still, if he had learned one thing in his tumultuous life, it was the importance of living *right now*. So after he kicked the ball next, his calloused hand reached over to Valeria's.

"Ready for that walk?" he asked.

She smiled, her cheeks warming. And off they went, side by side, hand in hand. Miles and Jo-Jo played together until they grew tired of the ball. Then they sprawled out in the middle of the gym, apparently content just to watch X and Valeria walk laps.

"This place we're going," she said quietly. "It will really restore the world to the way it once was?"

"According to the Forerunner," X said.

"How long will it take?"

"Months, maybe longer, for the sun to return. Then years, maybe longer, for the land to recover from the toxins and fallout. This is for the future generations, starting with Bray's."

X thought of the boy, and Valeria seemed to sense his anguish.

"I'm sure he's out there with Michael and Layla," she said. "You will find them again. I'll help you."

X stopped and faced her, looking into her dark eyes. She stared back, and he knew right then that he was right—she did have feelings for him.

Across the room, the hatch opened, and Commander Hallsey appeared.

"Xavier," she said. "Come with me."

X let go of Valeria's hand. "Watch the animals. I'll be back soon."

"I meet you in... your quarters?"

There was some tension in her voice, but X quickly nodded. It had been a long time since he welcomed a woman to his room, but his time on this Earth could very well be coming to an end. He must live life *right now*.

"Miles, go with Valeria," X said. "Jo-Jo, you too."

The commander waited for him in the corridor, a hand on her duty belt, near the holstered pistol.

"This way," she said.

They walked through the ship in silence. Distant boots walked closer. Around the next corner, Watt and Blue Blood escorted

Slayer. He exchanged a nod with X. Together, they all went to the command center, where the Forerunner sat in his chair, taking deep breaths from his mask. He turned to look at them.

It was obvious something terrible had happened.

"We have received dire news from Team Concordia," said the cyborg. "They suffered two casualties in the first few minutes of the dive."

X held his head high, blinking at the news. It wasn't the first time. He had heard this very statement many times in his hundred dives over the years, and it never got easier.

"I'm afraid Tia and Zuni were both killed," said the Forerunner. "I understand Kade was very close to Tia, yes?"

"Yes," X said. "He was like a father to her."

Much as X had been to Tin and Magnolia. He could feel the pain that Kade must be feeling to his very core, and the guilt that would assail him.

"Will he be able to continue the mission?" asked the Forerunner.

X didn't need to think on that for long, because he and Kade were alike in other ways, too. He understood duty, and he used pain as a teacher and motivator.

"Yes, he will continue," X said.

The Forerunner studied him for a long moment. X knew what was coming: a warning about bringing Valeria along and the dire things that could happen to them down there.

"I know the risks," X said. "Kade knew them, too. This is the world Hell Divers have lived in for a very long time."

"Not just Hell Divers," said Josie.

X turned slightly to the granddaughter of the Forerunner's wife's sister.

"I understand you have suffered too," X said. "But the past is the past, right, Noah?"

The Forerunner nodded. "There is only the future now," he said. "Go spend the last of this time with your companions. We arrive at Polar Base in the morning."

"And we'll be ready," X said.

Slayer nodded, and they left the room with Blue Blood and Watt.

"I'm sorry about your comrades," Watt said.

"Thanks," X said.

"Hold up a minute, mate," Blue Blood said.

X stopped in the corridor.

"A lot of shit has gone down between our people, but I'm glad to have you along for this mission," Blue Blood said.

"Same for me," Watt said.

"That mean you're going to give us weapons down there?" Slayer asked.

"That's up to the Forerunner," Blue Blood said.

"We're all here to do our duty," X said, "not just for our people but for the entire human race." He reached out his hand. "Years ago, people used to shake as a gesture of trust."

Watt extended his hand and X shook it. Then he did the same with Blue Blood. The knights reached out to Slayer next. He looked at them in turn, then took them each by the wrist, in the customary Cazador shake.

For the first time since the knights arrived, X walked with these men not as enemies but as allies, bonded together in a common cause. He arrived at his new private quarters a few minutes later. Slayer was staying in the adjacent room.

"Sleep well, brother," X said.

"And you," Slayer replied.

X opened the hatch to his room and went inside. Miles and Jo-Jo both got up to greet him, with Valeria sitting between them. She waited a beat before asking, "What's happened?"

"Tia and Zuni were killed," X said.

Valeria lowered her gaze. He came over and sat beside her on the bed, thinking of the pain Kade felt right now. X had been there many times. He recalled all the other dives when he had been sick with worry about Michael, Magnolia, and Miles. Or crushed by the loss of his dearest friend Aaron and countless others.

As he pondered these losses, he looked over at Valeria. He so wanted to strengthen and explore their bond, but he couldn't help feeling that it, too, would just be ripped away in the wastes.

*   *   *   *   *

Gran Jefe crouched at the edge of a lava-rock boulder on the mountain, scoping the beach and bay with his binoculars. The *Frog* remained anchored out there, but a new war boat had arrived, and a skiff brought more men to hunt him.

More to kill, he thought.

His body count was already up to four.

Soon they would march up here and send everything they had to take him down. And if he tried to escape in the chopper, the knights would blast him out of the air. He needed a *big* distraction. A volcanic eruption would be nice, but he had something else in mind, thanks to his robot friend.

Gran Jefe peered through his binoculars at the beach again. Two people in hazard suits were walking toward the jungle with a knight behind them. From what he could see, only the knight was armed. The three figures vanished into the foliage before he could get a good look.

There would be more soon, but he wasn't going to be around for them to find him. He scoped the beach one last time, then got up and started down a path into the jungle, toward the different sites he had mapped out from above. There were four total, each covered with tinder-dry vegetation.

His boots slid down the rocky scree—step and slide, step and slide, eating up the ground. With each step, he felt his injuries—especially the bullet in his ass. The exhaustion didn't help. He was hungry again too, but he had refilled his water back at the Jayhawk, where they had stashed some extra bottles. That extra hydration just might get him to the finish line in what was going to be labor-intensive work.

He arrived at the first site in the jungle. Pulling out his hatchet, he began hacking down dead shrubs and snags. The tinder-dry wood and foliage would go up with the least spark. After dragging it all into a pile, he headed to the second clearing. He was dog tired and sweating a lot. He stopped to take a drink and listen for the enemy. The dense jungle canopy blocked his view of the shoreline. Still, he searched for knights, but nothing moved out there.

Almost there. Keep going.

He took another swig of water, then went back to work, piling kindling on tinder, and fuel on kindling. When he finished, he hurried to the third location, huffing and puffing the entire way there. Within view of the last site, he halted at the sound of crunching twigs and snapping branches.

Going down on one knee, he swung his rifle up, scanning the tree line with the scope. Again seeing nothing, he got back up, slung the weapon, and made the next pile of fuel. It wasn't pretty, but it didn't need to be. The bullet in his ass hurt like hell, and his stomach growled from hunger.

He looked up at the volcano, dreading the long hike ahead of him. If only Frank could fly down and scoop him up!

Heaving a sigh, Gran Jefe swapped his hatchet out for his rifle and started back up the rugged terrain to the final site. As he advanced, his muscles tensed. It was always his body that gave up before his brain. He remembered, back as a young Cazador, passing out from heat exhaustion during the long training days on this very island.

For Pablo, he thought. *I will never give up.*

The thought of his son buoyed him up enough to get to the last location. In a daze, he hacked up and gathered a pile of trees and brush. Sweat rivered down him, stinging his eyes and the bullet wound in his ass.

After setting the third fire site, Gran Jefe pushed back up the side of the mountain to the bluff, where a cave provided refuge. Two hours after he first set out, he was back at the spot where he had scoped out the burn sites. The vantage point gave him a view of each woodpile, as well as the beach beyond, and an escape through the cave into the mountain.

It was time for the next phase of this plan.

He took a closer look at the bow and arrows he had taken from the tunnels. The quiver had ten arrows, each wrapped behind the point with a strip of linen smeared with tree resin. As he grabbed the quiver, a voice called out. A female voice.

Gran Jefe moved up to the edge of the bluff, crouched, and looked down into the jungle.

"Jorge!"

¡Qué coños! That voice was familiar, but how could it be?

"Jorge, it's me—Mags!"

¡Qué milagro! Gran Jefe raised a brow. It was indeed Magnolia.

Another voice called out in the distance. "Jorge, it's Imulah. I'm with Commander Katib!"

What was the little pen pusher doing here? And with Mags, no less.

Gran Jefe didn't dare respond. For all he knew, this was just a ruse to lure him out.

"You have to give yourself up!" Magnolia shouted. "You have to come in!"

Gran Jefe laughed. What was she smoking? She had to know that wasn't going to happen.

His eye caught movement on the beach. A group of five knights had gathered. A hunting patrol, probably—hunting *him*.

He zoomed the binoculars in on the *Frog*. The cannons on the bow were aimed at the volcano. So were the machine guns. They were definitely preparing to attack. But would they risk destroying the chopper?

He stood with the bow, nocked the first arrow, and lit it.

"*¡Vete a la mierda!*" he shouted.

Aiming at the first stack of kindling down below, he loosed the flaming arrow. The shaft sailed through the air—close but not there. He cursed, let another burning arrow fly. This one landed in the stack, quickly setting it ablaze.

He continued to launch arrows, ever conscious of the ticking clock. It took him three arrows to set the third target ablaze. Plumes of black smoke were already fingering into the sky.

Gran Jefe lit an arrow as he saw a distant muzzle flash out in the bay.

"*Hijoeputa,*" he muttered.

There was no time to react before the shell slammed into the rock wall twenty feet away. The impact knocked him down and rained debris on him. The burning arrow had fallen to the ground. He plucked it up and launched it as a second cannon shell fired from the *Frog*.

"Gran Jefe, you—" Magnolia shouted, but the explosion drowned out her words.

The force of the blast lifted him off the ground and threw him backward. He landed with a crunch, his vision darkening.

Something wet and cold stirred him back to reality.

He glanced up at a person hovering over him, but his eyelids were heavy. Hard to open. A voice speaking salty, profane Spanish hit his ears.

"Get your ass up, Jorge. Now! You have to get up."

It was female, and fiery.

"Get your dead ass up, Jorge! They're coming for you!"

He grinned through the pain. It was his ex, Jada. The mother of his boy.

Blinking, he saw her leaning down, wearing a helmet. But that didn't seem right. How could she be here?

He tried to sit up but fell backward.

"You're stronger than that!" she said. "Get up! GET UP!"

He grunted and tried again, finally sitting up. He opened his eyes, but she was gone.

She was never here to begin with.

The momentary shock wore off, and Gran Jefe pushed himself up on torn hands that burned from the raw wounds. Blood rolled down his forehead. He staggered out of the cave for a view of the beach. Smoke billowed up from the burning jungle as the flames soon spread from his bonfire sites. Leaving the beach, he glimpsed a patrol of knights heading into the jungle with an outsize dingo on a leash.

Another shell fired from the *Frog*, and Gran Jefe hurried back into the cave. The impact behind him sent a wave of dust billowing in as he darted to safety. He sucked in a breath of filtered air.

Injured, exhausted, half-stunned, he limped back into the tunnels. With his flashlight, he searched for the path back to the main chamber, where he had left the helicopter. If he was going to get out of here, he had to do it soon, with the smoke screen.

The path back inside the Quill looked different as his light raked over the walls. Or maybe it was just his pounding head. He had taken some punishment over the past few days, from the bullet still in his ass to the uncountable bruises and cuts from the recent explosions.

But he was alive. *You are still the big boss.*

He moved deeper into the lava tubes, pushing off the walls with his tattered gloves and leaving streaks of blood. The faint glow of lightning ahead illuminated a tunnel entrance to the main chamber, open to the sky. Using his flashlight, he quickly checked the land mines he had placed at the entrance, hidden by a sea of tall, reddish ferns.

His light danced across the moss-carpeted rock walls in his search for the chopper. As if in answer, a gunshot rang out, the bullet whizzing past his helmet. Ducking down, he searched for the shooter.

"Hands up and don't move, or you're dead meat!" shouted a voice.

Gran Jefe froze. A knight stood in the tunnel's mouth, a rifle pressed against his shoulder. This was the fifth soldier, who had somehow made it past all the land mines he had set in the lower tunnels.

"Hands up and come out!" yelled the knight. "Now! Do it bloody fucking NOW!"

A human form suddenly appeared in front of the knight—the hologram of Frank, giving Gran Jefe a second to bolt into the forest of ferns. Gunfire blasted into the porous rock. He dived to the ground and reached for his rifle.

¡Burro estúpido!

He had lost the weapon back in the cave and fled without it. All he had now were his pistol, axe, and knife.

"Please put down your weapon," Frank commanded.

"Get the fuck out of my way!" the knight yelled back.

Gran Jefe couldn't help but grin. The AI had saved him and even allowed him to flank this soldier behind a wall of rocks.

He sneaked a glance around the side, seeing the enemy twenty feet away in the middle of the chamber, rotating his rifle as he searched for Gran Jefe.

Gripping the axe in a bloody hand, he prepared to strike. As the footfalls came closer, he popped up and hurled the blade just as the knight fired a burst. The bullets missed, and the axe glanced off a rock wall.

The knight sighted up Gran Jefe.

There was no time to move; this was it.

"Fuck you, *cabrón*," he said.

"No, fuck you!"

Gran Jefe tensed, waiting for the bullets to rip through his armor and into his flesh.

But none came. The knight pulled the trigger on an empty magazine.

Gran Jefe charged as the warrior reached for his holstered sidearm. The motion gave Gran Jefe enough time to close the distance. Lowering his shoulder, he barged into the man, knocking him to the ground.

Somehow, the soldier pushed Gran Jefe off. They stood facing each other, both men unstable on their feet and rocking from side to side. This was a big son of a bitch. Almost as wide as Gran Jefe, and most of it muscle.

The knight pulled out a saw-toothed blade.

Gran Jefe had a bullet in his bum and dozens of small wounds all over. The blood loss made him wobbly. He took a step back as the knight feinted and struck first, thrusting the serrated blade at his chest.

Gran Jefe feinted left and swung his elbow into the side of the man's helmet, knocking him over. Disoriented, the knight slashed in wild arcs to keep his attacker at bay.

"Get up," Gran Jefe growled.

The spiked helmet shook as he stood and got his bearings. The visor centered on Gran Jefe. The soldier waited another moment before charging.

For a big guy, he was fast, but so was Gran Jefe. Again he sidestepped the jab at his chest. This time, Gran Jefe slashed at a gap between the helmet and chest armor, going for the jugular. The blade shrieked over armor as the warrior backpedaled.

Gran Jefe kicked him in the side of the knee, buckling it.

The fallen knight pushed up from the ground and launched himself at Gran Jefe, not even trying to thrust the knife. Instead, he lowered his shoulders and used his spiked helmet as a spear. The move took Gran Jefe by surprise, barely giving him time to turn.

A shoulder pad clipped him with enough force to flip him around. Now he was the one falling to the ground. He turned just as the knight leaped down onto him, pinning his arms.

"You killed Baccum!" he yelled. "And Dalton!" An armored fist punched Gran Jefe in the helmet, knocking his head back to the ground. Another blow hit his visor, followed closely by two more. The knight continued the brutal assault as he repeated the names of his comrades-in-arms killed by Gran Jefe.

"Stop!" Frank screamed. His hologram flitted about, creating a strobing effect that did nothing to distract the big warrior from his rhythmic punching.

Arching his back, Gran Jefe tried to buck the man off, but the bullet in his backside almost made him faint from the pain. As the blows kept coming, Gran Jefe's vision blurred and swam. His visor cracked.

After what felt like a hundred blows, the knight pushed off him and stood. Gran Jefe groaned and tried to turn over. Over the ringing in his ear, he heard a magazine click. This was it. The guy had him dead to rights now.

In these, his last moments, he thought of Pablo. He wished more than anything to have known the boy. To have been the father Gran Jefe never had. His thoughts went to Jada and how he could have treated her better.

And now he had been bested by a better soldier. That wasn't a bad death, and he would gladly have accepted that destiny *before* learning that he was a father.

But dying now meant he had failed his son, his own blood.

A furious anger ignited in his chest. He kicked outward, collapsing the knight's ankle. He slipped to the side as the man pointed his pistol and fired. A kick to the other ankle threw off the shot.

Gran Jefe then kicked the knight in the solar plexus, knocking him away. He collapsed into the tunnel entrance, and there was a click. Somewhere in Gran Jefe's mind, the noise registered.

"*Adiós, ese,*" Gran Jefe muttered. He tried to scramble away as the knight got up, but he felt too dizzy and battered to move.

An explosion rang out, and the world went dark.

FOURTEEN

"Kade, the storm's letting up," Lucky said. "We're going to move soon."

Kade hardly looked up. He sat with his back against a wall in a building the team had sheltered in after landing in the city. Twenty-four hours had passed since Tia took her last breath. Now her body lay with Zuni's in the next room, both covered by the same parachute. They would remain there until the *Trident* returned for evac.

Kade looked at the Monster Hunter, holstered on his hip, and contemplated putting a fat .357 Magnum bullet through his own head. It would certainly end the dread. He had done the same thing in the machine camp many times. At one point, he had given up on life after losing his family. Tia was about the only thing that kept him going.

"I need to know you're good," Lucky said.

Kade glanced up.

"Where we're going, we can't afford any mistakes, any hesitation," Lucky said. "If you can't do this, tell me now and stay here."

Kade looked through the doorway at the two bodies in

repose. Leaving them didn't seem right, but neither did staying behind when there was such an important job to do.

"Really, I'll understand if you want to stay," Lucky said. He eyed the pistol Kade held.

"I'll give you a few minutes to decide," Lucky said. He returned to Nobu and Zen, standing near the door with their rifles.

Kade pushed himself up and walked just inside the doorway. Summoning strength, he went to Tia's body. With a sigh, he knelt by her side. Reaching down, he pulled the chute back over her freckled face. Her eyelids were closed, as if she were sleeping peacefully. Her hand still gripped Zuni's. The two bodies were frozen together when the others brought them inside. It seemed only right that they stay this way now.

He leaned over her corpse. "I'm sorry, Tia," he said. "I'm sorry you never got a chance to love Zuni or experience having kids and raising them in the sunshine. I wanted that so badly for you."

Kade lowered his head. A tear fell.

"I'm sorry I couldn't protect you," he said. "I just hope you're at peace, with your father, and my fam—"

He choked up for a few moments. Crying felt good, but it also felt weak. There was only one way to honor Tia and Zuni: make sure their deaths weren't for nothing.

"I'll finish this," he said.

Kade covered the bodies, then wiped his eyes before joining the knights in the other room.

"You ready?" he asked.

Lucky studied him, then nodded. "Come with me."

They went over to the supply crates they had carried inside.

"You sure about this?" Nobu asked.

"About what?" Kade asked.

Lucky propped up a lid and pulled out an assault rifle.

"Don't fuck me, mate," he said.

Zen shook his head, clearly not a fan of the plan.

"I'm doing this for Tia and for my friends," Kade said as he grabbed the stock. He reached into the crate and scooped out a tactical vest to go over his armor, filling it with extra magazines.

"Grab a pair of snowshoes too," Lucky said. "We're headed to the snowmobiles."

Kade picked up a pair and carried them over to the doorway. He turned and looked one last time at the bodies in the other room.

"Don't worry, nothing's going to get to them," Nobu said. He nodded at a small round device outside the doorway. Kade recognized it right away as a heat-triggered land mine.

"Once I activate that, nothing's getting inside without losing a limb or two," Nobu said.

"Okay, let's get this done," Lucky said.

He shut the door, and Nobu activated the mine. Then they jogged down the corridor of closed doors, each an apartment for residents who never came. A stairwell took them to a lobby area full of frost-covered tables, desks, and couches. The door they had entered through let a drift of snow in across the carpet.

Nobu pulled the door back, and Zen slipped out to clear the area.

Pulling out a magazine, Kade punched it into his weapon and pulled the handle back to chamber a round. Zen returned outside, crouching and nodding with the all clear.

Kade followed, then Lucky and Nobu. The snow had all but stopped outside—only a light dusting of small flakes drifting lazily from the clouds.

A distant fork of lightning fired the horizon where the Delta Cloud fusion reactors waited.

With Zen on point, they moved out of the city, toward the

snowmobiles, periodically scanning for threats with their binoculars.

Zen stopped at the fence on the southern edge of the city. Lucky used bolt cutters to snip through the chain-link, opening a doorway. The team squeezed through and plodded out of town on their snowshoes. Facing the wastes again gave Kade something to focus on, but he still couldn't shake this sensation of extreme loss and sorrow.

You're a dead man walking, he thought.

Somewhere deep down—or maybe not so very deep down—he was fine with that.

Ahead, Zen held up a fist and dropped to one knee to scope the horizon. Flakes of snow fluttered over his visor as Kade searched the green background of his night-vision goggles. His HUD showed a temperature of negative twenty-five degrees Fahrenheit.

Getting to his feet, Zen gave the all clear, and on the team went.

Fifteen minutes into the hike, Kade was already working up a sweat. And it was only going to get harder from here as they approached the huge mounds of drifted snow. Zen started up a slope, rifle slung, using ski poles to help him climb.

The others waited at the bottom until Zen got to the crest. He scoped the area, then gave another all clear. Kade followed in Lucky's tracks, taking advantage of the easier progress through already-broken snow.

At the top of the mound, Kade saw the first snowmobile in the distance. A cargo chute whipped in the wind. The other three vehicles were spread out over a few hundred yards.

"Grab a snowmobile and fall in line," Lucky said. "I'll take point now."

Kade plunge-stepped quickly down the other side of the hill

with the knights. He slung his rifle and pulled out his knife to cut the chute free. The men all packed up the debris and cached it away before firing up the snowmobiles.

Lucky lit out in front, flying over the snow. Zen went next, followed by Kade, and Nobu took rear guard. They thumped over the hills and across a shallow basin. Lucky guided them down a slope to the bottom, hoping to conceal their approach for at least half the distance to the reactors.

The single line of snowmobiles raced along the ice basin's featureless floor, out of sight for the moment. Kade checked each side for contacts, but nothing interrupted the white expanse.

Lucky slowed at the far end of the depression. Standing up on his snowmobile, he pulled out his binoculars. By the time Kade reached him, Lucky had lowered them again. He pointed ahead of them and said, "Zen, get eyes on whatever's on the ice at one o'clock."

Zen raised his sniper rifle.

"Looks like a kill," he said. "No idea what it could be way out here—mostly just bones now. Definitely not fresh."

"Natural causes? Or something else?"

"Hard to say."

"Okay, keep your eyes peeled for threats. We have no idea what else is out here."

Kade thought back to the drones, knowing there could be something else far more deadly waiting to ambush them.

Lucky twisted the throttle, roaring back out in front. The convoy pursued, rapidly approaching the remains on the ice. Snow had drifted across some of the carcass, but Kade could see frozen limbs.

As they closed in, Lucky slowed his snowmobile. He glided up by the side of the animal, halting and leaning down for a look. Still curious, he hopped off and pulled a shovel from the back of his vehicle. He dug out the skull. Kade, too, was curious now. He got off his snowmobile and walked over.

Lucky crouched to examine the frozen remains, which had been picked clean. "I don't know, but those are some hellacious teeth marks," he said.

The rest of the team looked on as thunder rumbled overhead. Lucky sat back down on his snowmobile.

"We're halfway there," he said. "Better keep moving. Zen, take point and watch for heat signatures."

"You got it, LT," Zen said.

He pulled ahead, kicking up snow. The group zoomed across the ice basin, faster now. Zen led them up the right side, which seemed the gentlest slope to climb back up to the long stretch of snowy dunes. Another storm appeared to be rolling in to the west, dumping snow that gusted in the powerful wind. Visibility worsened as they climbed out of the protection of the valley, and Kade lost sight of Zen in the whiteout.

Relying on his HUD, Kade checked the map—just two miles from the reactors now. The ice wall discussed in the predive briefing was all that separated them from the facility. He couldn't see that obstacle in this whiteout, but it was their next target. They would hide the snowmobiles there, climb up, and trek to the entrance of the tunnels.

Seeing red lights ahead, Kade slammed on his brakes. Both Zen and Lucky had stopped their snowmobiles. Nobu, also caught off guard in the whiteout, came skidding up next to Kade. They both slid to a stop a few feet from Lucky.

He hopped off and turned to look up. It was then that Kade realized they had reached the ice wall, which towered directly above them. It looked a lot bigger up close. The four men walked over to the rough edges, dwarfed by the immense scale of the daunting hundred vertical feet of smooth blue ice.

"Get out the climbing gear," Lucky said. "Crampons, ice tools, rope, and screws. We'll try to stay off the more fractured stuff and stick to the harder blue ice."

Nobu unlatched a crate mounted on the back of his snow-mobile. He pulled out two coiled ropes, ice screws, ice axes, and climbing crampons. Kade grabbed a pair of crampons to fasten on his boot soles. They each grabbed a pair of ice axes, and Lucky took a sling of specialized tubular screws with sharp threads.

"I'll go first," Lucky said. "Kade, you're second, then Nobu and Zen."

Zen stood with his back to the others, panning with his rifle, watching their backs.

With Kade belaying, Lucky started right up, kicking the front points of his crampons into the ice and swinging the pick of his right ice tool, pulling upward, kicking the front points in again, swinging the left tool. At about ten feet, he sank the first screw and started twisting it into the ice. After clipping the rope to the ice screw's carabiner, he pounded up another ten feet or so and sank another screw.

After finally gaining the top, he spent a few minutes building an anchor, then gave Kade the thumbs-up. From there, it was a simple matter of fitting his ascenders to the rope and jugging up to the top.

"You good?" Lucky asked.

"Yeah," Kade called up.

As he was twisting Lucky's final screw out of the ice, a loud crack sounded above him.

"Shit!" Lucky cried as a chunk of ice the size of a snowmobile calved off the wall. Kade flattened his body into the wall, and the widow-maker plummeted past him, straight for Nobu, who was waiting to tie in at the bottom.

Nobu pulled back, just in time, and the ice shattered on the ground.

"Everyone okay?" Lucky called down.

"Bloody hell, that was close!" Nobu yelled back. "I'm good."

"Me too," Kade said.

A couple of minutes later, Kade topped out. Lucky had moved out of view on the windswept summit to check their immediate surroundings. The wind howled, blasting snowflakes horizontally. By all indications, the weather was deteriorating, but they were almost to the target. They would soon be indoors.

Soon, Nobu joined Kade and Lucky at the crest as Zen was tying in below.

Bracing against the buffeting wind, they turned for the first view of their target: six gigantic disk-shaped reactors, less than a mile away now, pointing up at the heavens.

"So those are what all the fuss is about," Nobu said.

A few minutes later, Zen joined them. "Crikey," he gasped. "Never thought I'd actually see 'em."

"This is it: a moment some of us have waited our entire lives for," Lucky said. "Everybody ready?"

Kade thought of what Tia might have said in answer—probably something about not coming here to fuck spiders. He sighed as he stared out at the reactors. They all shucked off their crampons and traded them for snowshoes.

"Okay, mount up," Lucky said. "Time to save the world."

*   *   *   *   *

"Which way?" Imulah yelled.

Magnolia huddled with the scribe under the burning forest canopy, searching for a way out. They had sought shelter here when the winds picked up, spreading the fires that Gran Jefe had set. That was two hours ago, and the flames just kept spreading. The Cazador warrior had set the lowest slopes of the mountain on fire.

At first, she wasn't sure what Gran Jefe had hoped to accomplish by burning down the jungle. But as the flames quickly spread, she realized that it was to keep the knights out of the volcano— probably to give him a chance to escape in the sky horse. But it had doomed her and Imulah along with the warrior, it seemed, after he gave his position away and was blown to pieces by General Jack's artillery round.

Flakes of burning debris drifted down from the sky, catching on their hazard suits. Sweat rolled down her face, stinging her eyes as she searched frantically for a way forward. Through the curtain of smoke, she spotted the distant beach, but getting there was going to be a challenge. Flames blocked much of the route, and the smoke, combined with the darkness, made getting hopelessly lost a real possibility.

Magnolia used the fires as signposts, guiding her through areas that weren't glowing. She saw a gap in the trees ahead.

"This way!" she yelled to Imulah.

The old scribe grabbed her arm and followed her through the dense brush. Embers swirled in the air, the burning flakes setting dry brush ablaze wherever they landed. The wind fed the raging fire, creating a building, glowing tsunami across the lower slopes of the mountain.

As they emerged from the dense jungle, they came across a field completely on fire—a sea of flames moving like waves in the blustery wind. Bits of burning bark and foliage broke away in a gust, assaulting Magnolia and Imulah.

Imulah crouched down, coughing in his helmet. Magnolia also struggled to breathe. Their filters were better at catching toxins and spores than smoke. She resisted the urge to rip off her helmet and instead pulled Imulah back into the jungle to find another route. She looked left, seeing an area that might be passable. First, though, they must dash hell-for-leather through a thicket of charred bushes. She blinked away the stinging sweat and took a deep breath.

"Get ready to run!" she called out.

"*Run?*" Imulah asked.

"When I tell you, you run like you've never run before. Okay?"

"Okay!"

She guided him under trees that seemed to reach for them with burning branches. Leaves, each a tiny incendiary bomb, fluttered down from the canopy to join others already forming piles of burning debris on the ground. Magnolia swatted her way through and stopped at the ten-foot swath of burning ground. She turned to Imulah and yelled, "RUN!"

He followed her across the cracked ground, jumping over piles of smoldering leaf litter. Fire licked at her boots and legs as she plowed through. She reached the other side with a pant leg on fire. Imulah yowled, batting at his flaming shoulder.

After smothering the fire on her pant leg, Magnolia patted his back with her thick gloves. He fell to the ground, howling in agony. A loud crack behind them set them running again, from a tree that had split down the middle.

Magnolia dragged Imulah over the scorched forest floor as the tree collapsed in an explosion of embers. She kept pulling him, glancing over her shoulder for a path out of the inferno. But the wind had shifted again, blowing smoke across what she prayed was a safe path down to the beach.

Magnolia fell to the ground, gasping for air. Next to her, Imulah coughed and retched violently.

"Hold on," she wheezed.

She got up, turning in a desperate search for a route to safety.

Panic gripped her as she staggered forward. Her vision began to dim, her legs prickling. She made only a few steps before crashing to the dirt.

Don't give up, Mags. Never give up!

As she lay there losing consciousness, a memory of Rodger came to her quite out of the blue. He was sitting on their bed in their apartment, holding a carved black bird with white dots on its feathers.

"Do you like it?" he asked. "It's a loon."

"I love it!"

"Good, because that's you."

"I'm a *bird*?"

He chuckled and reached down to pull out another identical bird statue. "This one's me. Did you know that loons mate for life? Guess you're stuck with me forever!"

The memory faded to a new one, also with Rodger, back at the Vanguard Islands. They were joined by Michael, Layla, and Bray on a balcony. X was there too, filleting a tuna. It was one of the last times they had all been together. She could hear their laughter, including Bray's little happy voice when he had only a few small teeth.

Magnolia stirred awake to muffled shouting.

"Found them!" someone yelled.

She raised her head at lights spearing through the darkness. Vicious barking broke out in front of them. As she looked up, she stared into the snarling jaws of a dingo. Three knights with rifles surrounded them. A fourth used a fire extinguisher to blast away the flames, forming a perimeter.

"Over here, General," someone called.

Eyes burning and lungs wheezing, Magnolia watched as Jack strode through the jungle. He carried a submachine gun, and a cutlass was sheathed on his belt.

"Where is he?" he boomed.

"Pretty sure there's not much left of him," Magnolia said.

"You trying to be smart?"

She shook her head. "You blew him up."

"Get them up," Jack said. "I'll take them back to the shore. The rest of you, go find the remains. Bring me his head."

Magnolia reached down to Imulah and helped him up.

The dingo snarled, pulling its handler along by the lead when the group set off. The knight with the extinguisher blasted through the flames, clearing a path for the moment.

"This way," Jack said, grabbing Magnolia by the shoulder.

She shook free of his grip, and they set off toward the shore. The roar and crackle of fires never let up on the way down to the Trident camp. Magnolia caught her breath and felt some of her strength return as she helped Imulah along, stopping once to give him water from their bag. He lifted his visor and drank, then handed the bag back to her. She took a long, luxurious swallow.

"That's enough. Let's go," Jack said.

Magnolia followed through a thicket of palmettos. On the other side, she found herself standing on open sand. They had made it through Gran Jefe's fires and back to the ocean. A motor skiff waited on the shore, and Jack ordered them aboard. As the underpowered boat battled out over the surf, Magnolia held on to the gunwale, staring back at the burning jungle, amazed to have survived the inferno.

The skiff appeared to be heading for the *Frog*, at anchor in the bay. Sure enough, it pulled up to a ladder hanging off the starboard hull.

"Climb," Jack instructed.

They were brought up to the deck, to a pair of shipping containers in the stern. A knight opened one. It was partitioned into cages, with a single prisoner inside. The man looked up, and she gasped. It was Pedro, sitting on a bench, ankles chained to the floor.

In the adjacent container, she saw faces pressed up against barred windows cut into the sides. Tiger was among them, along with several other familiar Cazador faces.

"You'll wait here," Jack said.

"But you told us we were going back home," Imulah said.

"Yes, this is it. Welcome to your new home. Now, get inside."

The general kicked Imulah into the cage, knocking him to the deck.

"Why, you dickless zombie fuck!" Magnolia said. "Your word is shit, and so are y—"

She felt the sharp tip of his cutlass on her neck.

"I'd watch that venomous tongue if you want to keep it," he said, bringing the blade up to her mouth. Magnolia resisted the urge to kick him in the balls.

Reaching out with his other hand, he shoved her inside with Imulah. The heavy steel door banged shut, locked from outside.

"Are you okay?" Pedro asked. He crouched in front of them, his eyes swollen. His nose was broken, his upper lip split, and the left side of his face gashed from ear to chin.

"What did they do to you?" Magnolia asked, though the answer was clear.

"I'm fine," Pedro said.

"Water," Imulah croaked.

Magnolia unslung the singed backpack and pulled out the bottle of water. Imulah took it, tipped it back.

"Thank you," he said.

"You should drink too," Magnolia said to Pedro.

"You first," he said.

"I had some earlier."

"Take a sip."

She nodded and wet her mouth. Pedro took a slug, then brought a finger to his mouth.

"That general," he whispered. "He's rounding up people that he believes could lead a rebellion. I'm one of them. They have Tiger too, and several Cazador warriors and sky people."

"What rebellion? Any chance of that ended when Gran Jefe got blown to bits."

"He's dead?"

"Unless he can somehow survive a direct hit with an artillery round."

"All we can do is hope the missions to the poles are successful," Imulah said. "We must have faith in Xavier and Kade, and pray for their safe return to secure a peace between all of our people."

Fuck that, Magnolia wanted to say, but the scribe was right. Too many innocent lives were at stake. Too many children. In the past, she might have tried to fight, but never in her life had they been so badly outmatched by an enemy.

She sat on the floor and leaned back against the side of the container. The adrenaline from escaping the fire had worn off, leaving her exhausted.

At some point, she drifted off to sleep, transported into one of the many ongoing nightmares that haunted her thoughts. But this one was short lived, and raised voices stirred her back to reality.

"You hear that?" Pedro asked.

He stood at the bars, looking out over the beach. Magnolia joined him at the viewport as the shouting grew louder.

"General, they've located a body—not much left," said a knight on the deck.

Jack stepped away with a radio.

From what Magnolia could make out, the advance team with the dingo had discovered the remains of Gran Jefe.

Or so she thought until Jack started cursing. It wasn't the Cazador after all but another dead knight. Word spread quickly.

A faint mechanical whooshing noise broke over the wind. Two knights ran out on the deck to stacked crates while a third climbed into a .50-caliber machine-gun turret. He swung the barrel toward the volcano towering in the distance.

Magnolia strained to hear the chop of rotors. It sounded like...

"The Jayhawk," she said. "They must have found it."

"Then why are they getting ready to fire?" Pedro asked.

She peered up at the sky, but the smoke curtain was too thick.

"Get the launchers ready!" shouted General Jack. He strode out on the deck with his assault rifle. "Shoot that fucking bird down!"

Gunshots rang out across the deck of the ship, and muzzle flashes lit up the beach.

"It can't be," Magnolia whispered. "Gran Jefe's still alive."

"How is that possible?" Imulah asked. He stood on tiptoes beside Magnolia, trying to look out through the barred viewport.

Tracer rounds flashed into the smoke. A cannon boomed, rattling the container. The mad chatter of the machine gun forced Magnolia to cover her ears as the knights unloaded everything they had into the sky.

She tensed at the implications of what they were witnessing. If Gran Jefe had survived, she would remain imprisoned, or worse.

But deep down, she didn't care. She raised a fist, rooting for the big guy to make it off the island.

"Get out of there," she said.

Cheers arose from the adjacent container.

And then a chant.

"¡El diablo vive!"

Magnolia spotted movement through the smoke—a glint of

metal, as the tracer rounds streaked into the sky. The Jayhawk pulled away, gaining altitude and exceeding the reach of the cannons on the *Frog*.

"*¡El diablo vive!*" shouted the prisoners in the other container.

"What are they saying?" Magnolia asked.

"The devil lives," Imulah replied.

Pounding echoed away from the container as the captive Cazadores stomped in celebration.

"Shut the fuck up!" Jack shouted, and fired a burst of bullets over the container.

Magnolia remained at the barred windows, watching the helicopter traverse the skyline. Somehow, despite all odds, Gran Jefe had survived the island. And by all indications, it looked as if the Jayhawk was actually going to make it out of there.

"He did it," Magnolia said. "He really did it."

The chanting continued, building into a wild cry of support.

Imulah backed away from the window as a squad of knights with rifles surrounded them. Finally, the chanting died away and only the general's screaming remained.

"I'm going to kill this motherfucker myself!"

He swung a missile launcher up onto his shoulder. "Run this up your barbaric caveman ass!" Jack shouted as the missile streaked away into the smoke-filled sky.

Magnolia held her breath. Nothing happened for a few long beats. Then came a distant crack. The general lowered the rocket launcher as the flaming helicopter spiraled toward the ocean.

He turned back to the containers and said, "Let's see if your devil can survive that!"

FIFTEEN

At five in the morning, the intercom on the hull buzzed with a message from Commander Hallsey. *"Xavier, report to the command center."*

X had already been awake but was resting quietly, trying not to wake Valeria. She lay by his side, her head on his chest—two people seeking solace and warmth in each other.

She groaned and her eyelids fluttered, her gaze settling on X. Slowly she raised her head and looked around, as if she didn't know where they were.

"It's okay," X said.

Miles looked up from the deck at the foot of their bunk. He wasn't used to seeing X so close to another human. Jo-Jo, on the other hand, either didn't notice or didn't care.

"Are we at the North Pole?" Valeria asked.

"Must be. I need to go to the command center. You stay here and sleep," he said.

"I have slept plenty."

She stood up, already dressed in a blue uniform. Miles also hopped up, tail wagging. He clearly wanted to come along. Jo-Jo hardly flinched when the intercom buzzed again.

"Xavier—command center," Josie said.

"On my way," X replied. He patted his leg for Miles to follow, and they set off with Valeria through the passage. They had enough freedom now to walk through the airship without escorts. That was great until X realized he was lost.

He went to the next intersection, looked left, then right.

"I think this way, maybe," Valeria said.

She pointed forward, and X went with her, Miles trotting along at his side. They heard footsteps. Watt rounded the next corner.

"Looking for the command center?" he asked.

X nodded.

"Follow me; you're almost there."

They took a right at the next junction and found the command center just around the corner. Watt tapped the keypad, and the hatches whisked open. Slayer and Blue Blood were already inside, facing a monitor that Josie stood behind. The Forerunner sat in his chair, watching a screen that X couldn't see.

He turned when Josie cleared her throat.

"Xavier's here, sir," she said.

The cyborg looked to X first, then to Valeria.

"Come," he said.

The group gathered in the center of the space, facing a bank of monitors.

"We're flying over the North Pole and have deployed a drone," the Forerunner explained. "In a few minutes, we will have our first look in over sixty years, but first, I have news from the Vanguard Islands to share."

He paused just long enough for X to tense.

"General Jack located and downed the second Jayhawk, along with Gran Jefe. We're searching for his body, but the general has assured me the man is dead."

The report sparked within X a feeling that surprised him:

regret. He'd had a tumultuous relationship with the Cazador, but Gran Jefe had a fire inside him that was rare. A fighting spirit, much like General Rhino.

"I hope this means there will be no more bloodshed back at the islands," X said.

"I as well," said the Forerunner. He seemed to scrutinize X, perhaps trying to get a read on how much losing Gran Jefe affected him. X was surprised to feel such a deep sense of loss, but he shook it away to focus on the living.

"Are there any updates from Team Concordia?" he asked.

"Negative. Nothing," Josie said.

X didn't like that, but they could be hunkered down from bad weather. A lot of things could have happened out there, and letting his mind race was never useful. What mattered right now more than anything was their own mission.

"Okay, so when can we get eyes on this frozen shithole?" X asked.

"Stand by," Josie said.

On the screen, a map bloomed out with the *Trident* closing in on Polar Station. They were flying over the frozen Arctic Ocean, just sixty miles out from the reactors. But X could see right away that there were severe storms.

"The weather is going to be a problem," Josie said. "In my opinion, the best flight path is at five thousand feet."

She looked to the Forerunner, who thought on it a moment before agreeing with a nod.

"Take us down," he ordered.

Tilting slightly, the airship lowered through the clouds. As they picked up speed, the hull rattled from pockets of turbulence.

"Bringing up drone feed," Josie said.

A feed relayed to the monitor beside the map. X watched anxiously for his first view of the packed ice of the Arctic Ocean.

It came a moment later—the horizon, defined by a vast expanse of muted purples as the weak Arctic sun tried to pierce the storm clouds rolling over the vast icy plain far below.

The drone broke through those clouds, relaying a high-definition view of the frozen expanse below. A dazzling blanket of white stretched infinitely in all directions. The advanced craft, equipped with thermal sensors, began relaying data back to the command center. Josie paced in front of the screens, tracking every detail and searching for anomalies or signs of life in the frigid vastness.

"Everything you see down there is ice covered in snow," Josie said. "After the war, the Arctic Ocean's ice cap grew thicker with the plummeting temperatures. Much of it is hundreds of meters thick, but in some places the ice goes half a mile deep."

"Don't let that deceive you into thinking you are on solid ground," said the Forerunner. "Beneath the ice is up to four thousand meters of deadly-cold water."

"Good thing we got these fancy suits," X drawled.

"Those won't save you."

"No, I don't imagine they will." X grew serious as the drone dipped lower, humming over the frozen ocean, on course for Polar Station.

As they neared the target, a dark speck appeared on the horizon. But that couldn't be the target, not according to the map.

"That some sort of city like at Concordia Station?" X asked.

"No," Josie said. "There's not supposed to be anything out here."

"Incorrect," replied the Forerunner.

She looked up from her screen in surprise. "What do you mean, 'incorrect'?" Josie asked.

"Lower the drone, and you will see a secret I was forced to guard closely."

She stared for a moment, then returned to her screen and tapped in the coordinates.

The speck grew larger on the horizon, and it became clear that this was something man made. The drone's image revealed a base camp, which seemed to be preserved perfectly in its frozen state. Several tents were covered in a thick layer of ice and snow, their colors faded but still distinguishable. On each, a trident marked the shredded canvas.

"This was one of our camps," Josie said in awe.

"Yes," the Forerunner admitted. "I deployed a secret expedition thirty years after my failed mission, but we lost all contact several days after establishing this forward operating base for the assault on Polar Station."

The drone circled over the base, capturing ghostly-clear video of black honeycombed habitats with metal structures and equipment, all displaying the Trident. The once-lively camp was eerily silent now, save for the occasional gust that whipped a single Trident flag hanging from a bent pole. Sledges, stuck in their tracks, lay abandoned, their cargo still attached. Instruments and tools, now frozen in place, hinted at a sudden and unexpected event that must have caused the camp's occupants to leave in haste.

"After we received an SOS, the Trident Council voted to abandon a rescue mission," said the Forerunner. "I disagreed, but it didn't matter. We left the twenty souls out here, never knowing their true fate."

It seemed that X wasn't the only leader who kept things from his people. And he wasn't the only one who had tried to expand. He looked at the frail face of the Forerunner, realizing they were more alike than he ever suspected.

"Scanning for life," Josie said.

But X already knew that it would find corpses at best. Nothing could have survived out here for thirty years, not even he. The drone passed over the tents, finding most of them torn apart. Two of the habitats had also sustained major damage, their panels crushed inward as if a giant had stomped on them.

"No life detected," Josie said. "Whatever did this is long gone."

"Take us down closer," the Forerunner ordered.

Josie directed the drone closer to the surface, relaying video of partially buried equipment. A pair of snowmobiles protruded from the snow beside a truck whose bed was laden with barrels.

"Where are all the bodies?" she asked.

The drone did two sweeps over the base, finding nothing. Any tracks would long since have vanished. On the third pass, Valeria pointed to the outer border.

"What's that?" she asked.

Josie changed course, flying the drone away from the tents to several mounds of snow on the periphery of the camp. Graves, it appeared, chopped out of the ice by the former occupants.

Sure enough, frozen hands and legs poked up through the surface.

As the drone hovered over them, the snow blasted away, exposing not a graveyard but the site of a massacre. Human parts lay scattered over the basin—limbs and heads ripped from torsos.

"You seeing what I see?" Slayer spoke for the first time.

"Of course we do," X said.

"No, I mean, I think there's a pattern." He walked over to the screen as Josie backed away to give him room. "Pull up for an aerial."

She looked to the Forerunner, who again gave his approval with a subtle nod.

The drone rose over the macabre scene. As it lifted into the sky, X saw exactly what Slayer had noticed. This wasn't just the site of a massacre—something, or someone, had arranged the parts to make up a broken Trident symbol. A warning to any who might come here again.

"What evil did this?" Valeria asked.

X swallowed hard. They would likely find out very soon.

*   *   *   *   *

A day had passed since the escaped slaves fled the Canary Islands in their small boat. Michael had spent most of his waking moments rigging up the last of the defensive positions and security measures for the bunker, from setting up sensors on the beach and cliffs and in the tunnels to excavating the crawl space to give them a secondary exit from the bunker. Soon, they would vote on what to do: send Timothy out alone to Casablanca to look for the slavers, go with him, or everyone stay behind.

Before that, though, Michael had decided to see if the freed slaves had left anything behind to give some clue to where they had been imprisoned. He had left the caves with Victor while Timothy monitored the caves from the sky and Gabi held security in the tunnels outside the shelter.

Now, two miles away on the other side of the island, Michael and Victor approached the cave at Punta Ganada where they had seen the foreigners cook their former captor alive and eat him. Dressed in his Hell Diver suit and armor, Michael was again prepared to face anything. Victor, too, donned his dented armor and shouldered his rifle as they entered.

The cannibalized corpse had been moved away from the burn pit and discarded on the rocks. It was a gruesome sight, but it might reveal something.

"Watch our six," Michael said.

Victor turned back toward the ocean.

Crouching, Michael examined the corpse. The former slaves

had taken his boots, his clothing, and anything else of value. There wasn't much left of his body either.

Michael reached down and closed the staring eyes.

Soot covered most of the face, but he rubbed it away to expose dark skin. He shined his flashlight on it, looking for any tattoos and finding only a scar above a singed eyebrow.

After a few minutes of looking the corpse over, he went to the burn pit and dug through the ashes and half-burned driftwood.

"Damn," Michael said.

Victor glanced back at him. "Nothing?"

Michael walked back to the corpse and briefly considered burying it, but the distant clap of thunder told him they were running out of time. Another storm was moving in, and he didn't want to get trapped out here. He abandoned the slaver's body to the crabs. At least it would go back into the local ecosystem.

Victor led the way back out into the darkness. The airship was out of view, already blocked by the brooding clouds. A single bolt of lightning zigzagged through the storm front and was reflected on the churning waters.

"That looks like another nasty storm," Michael said. He bumped his headset. "Timothy, do you copy?"

Static crackled; then came Timothy's faint voice. *"Copy, Chief. Did you find anything?"*

"Negative. We're heading back home for now. I'll talk things over with the others and should soon have a decision on what we do next."

"Understood. I'll stand by."

Michael followed Victor across the beach as the surf rushed ever closer. They hiked up a bluff to a sprawling area with deep soil, which Layla had identified as a potential place to grow potatoes and other hardy crops in the sporadic sunshine. The data and his own eyes told Michael this place was habitable, and he wasn't giving up on it yet.

He paused briefly on a towering cliff, with Victor just ahead, his silhouette stark against the tumultuous backdrop of nature's caprice—a reminder of how fast things could change out here. Below, the sea raged as storm-fueled waves lashed the rocky shore.

"I'll take point," Michael said.

He began the journey back across the island. It would take them between the abandoned settlement of Haría and a city to the north called Máguez. They had skirted around the remains on the way here and seen some apartment buildings still standing. It had occurred to Michael that someday he might like to return to these two places for salvage. But with Timothy in the sky and finding no life in his scans, they hadn't bothered coming to either city until now.

A light rain began to fall on the patchwork of land beyond the two ruined cities. Michael took a road cutting through ancient vineyards bordered by tumbledown stone enclosures. Layla had told him that the islanders once made wine here. He remembered the smile on her face when she told him. But that was back when they were still full of hope and awe after seeing the sun.

Booming thunder snapped him from the memory. The deep, resonant sound seemed to be coming from a living creature in the sky. He bumped his comm link, opening the channel to the airship.

"Pepper, you up there?" he asked.

Hearing nothing but static, he tried Layla on the other channel. He got the same white noise. Michael knew that they were still at least a mile from the sanctuary now. He picked up his pace to a fast trot, boots slapping the mud.

With every step, the rain seemed to sheet down harder. Playing his flashlight over stone walls and broken fences, Michael searched for cover where they could wait out the worst of the storm. The beam fell across an old stone structure on the other side of a low rock wall bordering the remnants of a roadway. He hopped over the side and poked his head into a shack with half its roof still intact.

A broken chair and an upended table protruded from the rubble and dirt that had overtaken this place many years ago. Michael crouched in the corner to try the comms. Neither Timothy nor Layla answered. He was close enough to the bunker now that it didn't make much sense. The storm shouldn't be interfering with such a short-range transmission.

He got up and looked out a broken window to the road snaking in the direction of their shelter. Wind gusted and howled, whipping the rain sideways. Movement caught his eye as a flap of debris flew over a corner of the ancient vineyard.

"You hear something, Chief?" Victor asked.

"Hear what?" Michael turned to see his friend looking back the way they had come, from Haría.

"I thought I heard a voice. A male voice."

Michael reached out to Victor. "Turn off your lights."

Victor switched off the beam attached to his rifle, then brought the scope up to his visor. Lightning flash-banged behind them, rattling the stone structure. In the respite, Michael heard a different noise, and not from the storm. This was the snort of a warm-blooded beast.

Something was out there.

Victor nodded. He had heard it, too. Michael went back to the window on the opposite side of the shack, searching with his night-vision optics. Seeing nothing in the rain, he turned off the goggles and waited.

A brilliant blast of lightning cleaved the sky. The jagged glow illuminated the outlandish hulking shape of a four-legged creature not fifty feet away. It had two heads: one at the front and another rising from a torso and neck that rose from its back, like the centaur in the pictures of the zodiac.

Michael watched with dread as the beast rose up on its hind legs. In the glow of the next lightning bolt, he saw that this was no centaur but a black horse with a mounted rider. He wore formfitting tactical gear, combat boots, and night-vision optics.

The steed gave a loud snort, its rider poised in the saddle as the front hooves thudded back to the muddy ground.

From behind came another whicker, and Michael spotted two more horses trotting through the ruined vineyard about four hundred feet away. Their riders were clearly searching for something or someone.

While Michael suspected they were looking for the escaped slaves who had killed their comrade, he wasn't going to bet on that with his family out here and vulnerable. Hiding didn't seem like an option anymore. It was time to fight.

He counted five riders, each armed with a rifle or crossbow. One man, taller than the others, carried a long shaft with a spiked round head.

Michael crawled over to Victor, crouched in the shadows with his rifle. The stomping, snorting beasts drew closer to the shack, their riders calling out to one another in gruff voices. The language was not Spanish.

A light darted in their direction.

Victor motioned for Michael to leave the way they had come. "I'll hold them off," he whispered. "Get back to the shelter. Protect your family."

"No, we can take them together." Michael raised his pistol, determined to fight.

Victor grabbed him and pulled him around.

"There are too many, Chief. Let me do this, for payback."

Victor wanted revenge for what these people had done to his friends years ago.

"I will kill them all," he said. "You go protect the others. I'll be right behind you."

The snorting and whinnying drew nearer, and Michael made the intolerable decision to abandon his friend to fight alone.

Victor brought up his rifle, and Michael bolted out of the shack. Keeping low, he ran, retracing their steps. In about ten seconds, a gunshot cracked. By then, Michael had reached the cover of a low stone wall enclosing the vineyard. He peeked around the side, pistol raised.

What he saw with his optics took his breath away.

A horse stampeded away with a rider hanging by his heel from the stirrup. Two more riders fired at the shack, where the shot had likely originated, but Victor was no longer there. Michael saw him crawling beside a vineyard wall, flanking a horse and rider.

Springing up, Victor yanked the man down from his horse and slit his throat, then slapped the horse on the rump. By the time the other riders knew what was happening, Victor had darted away.

Michael took off at a run, bumping on the comms. He tried Timothy first but got nothing. Then he tried Layla. Again, nothing.

Fearing the worst, he ran harder, only to slip in the mud. He pushed himself up and trudged back to the caves. He hated leaving Victor, but the man had given him a window to help his family, and he wouldn't waste it.

A flare streaked into the sky, bursting over the vineyards. Michael got down flat in the mud as the glow spread over the rocky fields. In the bright light, he saw several figures on foot coming from the north. Reinforcements.

Victor could maybe take the first five, but not this many. Eventually, they would find him and kill him.

Michael started to get up, then dropped back down at the

sound of snorting behind him. From the sound, the animal wasn't far, giving him only a second to make himself small. He felt the hoofbeats getting closer.

Holding his breath, he half expected to feel a bullet or a blade. The *thumpity-thump* of cantering hooves came closer until it was right on top of him. In his peripheral vision, he saw the horse pass on his right, its rider focused on the battle in the distance.

Turning, Michael checked for more horsemen, but this single rider must be a scout. He reined the horse to a stop, then raised his scoped assault rifle up to his night-vision goggles.

Seizing the moment, Michael crouch-walked forward in the mud. At ten feet away, another flare shot up in the distance, blasting the rider's NVGs with blinding light.

Michael stabbed him in the thigh, deep into the meat. Before the rider could scream, Michael plunged the knife deep through the Kevlar tactical armor over his chest. The horse kicked up, and Michael let go. It took off running, the scout's body listing to the side until it finally slid off.

The battle continued in the distance, Victor still evading his pursuers. Michael turned and ran again, putting more distance between himself and the vineyards. The gunfire receded in the distance and was soon overtaken by the crash of waves on the beach.

As he closed in on the bluffs, his lungs burned, but he didn't stop until he reached the edge of the sand. There he slowed his pace, sucking air and scanning the horizon for watercraft. Seeing none, he searched for the path that wound down to the caves.

A sensor chirped, stopping him in midstride. He glanced down at his wrist computer, which showed multiple warnings. Now that he was back in range, the alerts had come through.

His heart skipped. Someone had found the caves.

A transmission from Layla flickered over the comm channel.

"Michael," she whispered.

He could hear Bray in the background saying, *"Da-da."*

"Layla, where are you?" Michael asked quietly.

"Hiding, with Bray. There are men, and they have—"

The transmission fizzled out.

"Layla," Michael said. "Layla, do you copy?"

He cursed himself for not leaving when they had a chance. Now his nightmare was coming true.

No. I won't let it.

It was time to become a machine, to destroy anything and everything, by any means, until he had his family safely off this island.

SIXTEEN

Whiteout conditions at Concordia Base made moving difficult for the four-man team. Kade battled the merciless wind. Bent over with the rifle they had given him, he trekked over the drifting powder on his snowshoes, trying to tamp down his despair over losing Tia as he followed Lucky across the frozen plateau.

Nobu and Zen were nearby according to his HUD, but Kade couldn't see either of them with his own eyes. He was seeing something else out there—a humanoid figure shambling like a zombie through the snow. When he saw the face of Raphael, he knew that his eyes were deceiving him. Or maybe it wasn't Kade's eyes playing tricks. Maybe this was the ghost of Tia's father, haunting him for failing in his promise to protect her.

Kade blinked, and the figure was gone.

The team slogged across the terrain, searching for an access point to the tunnels under the reactors. The storm had them all turned around. They had been out here for hours. With each passing second, conditions deteriorated. Drifting snow had covered any sign of exterior structures, burying them completely.

"Everyone, regroup on me!" Lucky shouted over the howling wind.

Kade crouched beside him as Nobu and Zen used their HUDs to home in. It only took a few minutes for Zen to trudge into view.

"Where's Nobu?" Lucky asked him.

"He was right behind me."

Kade checked his HUD. Nobu's beacon was about fifteen feet away.

"I think I found something!"

The muffled voice was Nobu's, and Lucky and Kade started in his direction. Nobu had extended a collapsible shovel.

"Help me dig," he said.

Kade unfolded his shovel and started digging, tossing snow aside to clear an area three by three feet. Zen held watch, and Lucky used his mittened hands to push the powder aside.

As Kade and Nobu dug deeper, their shovels clanked against metal. Going down on their knees, they helped Lucky clear off a manhole cover.

"This is one of the access points," Lucky said.

Kade handed over his shovel, which the knight used to chip ice away from the edges. When it was clear, he worked the spade tip into the gap, then started to pry the cover open.

Kade scanned their surroundings, feeling as if something was watching them through the whiteout. This went beyond nerves or paranoia—this felt *real*.

Zen had raised his sniper rifle, scanning with the infrared scope.

"You see anything out there?" Kade asked.

"Negative," Zen replied.

Kade looked in all directions but saw only white.

"Just about got it," Lucky said.

Nobu leaned down to help, and together they pried the cover

off and slid it out of the way. Zen strode over, clearing the shaft with his rifle.

"On me," Lucky said.

He was first down the ladder.

Kade took one last look at the storm, and the hair on his neck stood up. He saw Raphael again, crawling across the snow, dragging his entrails behind him. Reaching out, he shouted, "You failed her!"

Kade took a step back as the dead diver crawled closer, raising a bloody hand. "Kade!"

A hand gripped his shoulder. "You good?" Nobu asked.

"Yeah," Kade said, swallowing. He turned back, and Raphael was gone.

Slinging his rifle, Kade started down the ancient rungs into the shaft. Nobu went next, pulling the cover back over the top. Their lights beamed downward to the tunnel below, where Lucky and Zen stood guard. Fine, dry snow fell around them.

"This is access tunnel B," Lucky said. "That means we got about two thousand feet to get to the facility entrance."

They started down the narrow passage, moving past conduits and breaker boxes. Kade checked his HUD to a displayed temperature of forty degrees and climbing. The facility had a heat source still active, but the lights were off.

The beams from their mounted flashlights pierced the black. Something big blocked the way in the distance. As they drew closer, Kade saw that this was the first of the three reactor fans they must pass through.

Zen ducked under a blade, shouldered his rifle, and led the way to the next fan. They passed through two more before finally reaching a door.

Kade waited as Nobu pulled out an EMP patch shaped something like a spider. He stuck it on the keypad, and they all stepped back as the eight legs on the patch turned red, sending out an invisible pulse to bypass the security system.

Zen raised his rifle, and Lucky fell back into a defensive position while Nobu went to work with a power drill from his pack. He drilled into the locking mechanism, the door clicked open, and he pulled it back, allowing Lucky inside a stairwell.

This was it. They were inside.

Kade knew that the facility went twenty floors deep. The first stop would be the cryo-chambers, to set the charges. The team started down the stairs, searching for the access door to the chambers.

They found it locked five floors below. Nobu stuck a second EMP patch onto the locking mechanism. As soon as it shut off the power, he started drilling through the lock. Kade tried to ignore the noise of the drill. If anything was out there, it would have no trouble hearing them.

Fortunately, Nobu made quick work of the lock. Ten seconds later, it popped open and Lucky strode into a white corridor. The temperature reading jumped to forty-nine degrees—still cold, but far from the freezing temperatures outside.

Kade moved inside, raking his light over the dark passage. Along the right wall was a series of doors—at least five that he could see.

Lucky flashed the signal to advance, and the team set off in combat intervals, their steps echoing down the dark corridor. Their beams darted over the sealed doors.

As they rounded the corner, Lucky held up a fist. He cleared the intersection, then gestured toward a door that stood slightly ajar. Nobu slipped through. Kade went inside next. A wall of opaque glass had a red glow from the banks of machines lined up against another glass wall. He raised his light, which penetrated another space, then another—row after row of what appeared to be labs.

Scattered papers, stained lab coats, and broken equipment hinted at some sort of attack long ago. No one said a word as they crossed through the first lab, careful to avoid glass from broken vials, petri dishes, cylinders, and pipettes. Burners and test tubes lay scattered around a centrifuge.

Another open door revealed the second lab, which contained stainless-steel tables and surgical tools on carts. White robotic arms like those Kade had seen back on the *Trident* hung from tracks on the ceiling.

The door to the third set of labs was closed, and its glass walls were frosted, blocking the view of whatever was on the other side. Nobu started working on the locking mechanism while Zen watched their six.

"How much farther?" Kade asked.

"We should be close," Lucky replied.

Nobu secured the EMP patch and stepped back. The spider limbs flashed red, and he went to work with his drill until the door popped open. A muffled hissing burst out, as if pressurized gas had been released.

Kade followed Lucky inside, both of them halting at the sight of twisted humanoid silhouettes suspended in tanks of murky water. The temperature inside was just above freezing, perhaps to preserve the specimens inside those tanks. But the creatures, or whatever they were, had hardly been preserved over all these years.

There were twenty-one tanks, half of them containing intact specimens. The other half were coffins of limbs, heads, torsos, and decomposed flesh.

"What are those things?" Nobu asked.

Kade had seen places like this before on dives to ITC facilities, and he seemed to be the only one in the room who recognized the clawed limbs, eyeless heads, and bony exoskeletons. These were

Sirens and bone beasts—monsters from the wastes. Developed in facilities just like this, their DNA manipulated by epigenetic changes to help them survive in the apocalypse.

Kade had always wondered if the scientists even knew what they were creating. It seemed some of them did, out here in the Antarctic, where their own creations turned on them.

Zen stepped up to the tank, tilting his helmet.

"Crikey, bruv," he said.

"Keep moving," Lucky said.

They proceeded to the next glass wall and an unlocked door. Kade, the first there, shined his light inside, illuminating a long glass-walled corridor with the largest door yet. The steel monstrosity loomed at the end of the passage.

"That must be it," Lucky said. "Nobu, get that open. Zen, prepare the charges."

They all set off to the final door. It had a much more complicated locking system with a keypad and a slot. Nobu went to work on it, connecting a tablet with patch cords, while Zen leaned his rifle against the glass wall and unslung his white pack of explosives.

Kade tried to look through the frosted-glass wall, wondering what monstrosities it concealed. He kept his rifle at the ready, but so far, there was no evidence of anything alive inside the facility.

"Almost got it," Nobu said.

Kade could see a circle flashing on the screen of the tablet as it bypassed the security hardware. Loud thuds echoed inside the door as the relays unlocked. Four, five, six . . . On the tenth thud, the door popped ajar.

Lucky grabbed the handle and heaved it open just enough for them to get through. An icy mist flowed out of the chamber. Kade followed the men inside to columnar structures rising into the air. Attached to the columns were pods full of sleeping inhabitants.

Kade searched for any that had transformed into the monsters they had found in the labs. But from what he could tell on a quick scan, these were just sleeping human and animal clones.

"Set the charges," Lucky said.

Nobu worked with Zen to spread them about the cavernous room. As they placed the explosives at the bottom of each column, Kade and Lucky held security. Their beams flitted up and down, over the faces of sleepers who would never wake up. Kade held his light on the frosted lid of a pod, illuminating the innocent face of a young woman.

He hadn't really considered what they were doing until now. She wasn't a beast. She was a person. An innocent person.

"Okay, that's it; let's move," Nobu said.

Kade hesitated, and Lucky looked up.

"Don't get sentimental," Lucky said. "They're better off not waking up. Come on."

Kade looked for another moment, then followed the knights from the chamber into the glass corridor. Nobu exited last and shut the blast door behind them.

A voice came from an unseen speaker. It was female, *familiar.*

"Kade, is that you?" she asked.

At first, he thought it was just a figment of his overstressed imagination, like seeing Raphael in the storm. But the other knights heard it, too. All of them halted.

They turned to find that a doorway had opened in the glass wall of the passageway. A woman stepped inside, just in front of the closed blast door. As their lights hit her tattoos and her freckled features, Kade froze.

This wasn't one of the frozen people. It was...

"Tia," he said.

He stepped forward, heart pounding.

"Kade, don't," Lucky said.

Kade took another step toward her, reaching out. "Tia, how? I saw you . . . I held you—"

"They saved me, brought me back to life," she said.

"It's not her; it can't be," Lucky said. "Everyone, get back!"

Kade hesitated while everyone else retreated. Nobu ran toward him, but suddenly skidded to a halt as glass walls rose up from the floor, boxing him inside like an insect trapped in a jar. He pounded the side facing the other knights and Kade.

"The bloody hell!" Nobu said in a muffled voice. "Let me out of here!"

He swung his ice axe with both arms, and the glass wobbled slightly, nothing more.

Tia stepped up to the wall behind him, tilting her head as a curious scientist might. Kade knew then that this wasn't her—it couldn't be. This was either an AI or something far worse—something monstrous.

Zen raised his rifle. "Get back," he said. Nobu backed away and Zen fired at the glass. The shot ricocheted off.

Sprinkler heads suddenly poked out of the ceiling over Nobu, swirling and releasing a hissing, colorless gas. He looked down at his armor and tried to brush off what looked like tiny black particles. They began to spread.

"Guys, get me out of here!" he shouted, panic rising in his voice.

"Let him out!" Lucky yelled.

Tia watched with apparent fascination as the particles swarmed Nobu. He went down on one knee, and Kade noticed blood dripping from his nose behind his visor. His eyes were bloodshot, the sclera an angry red. Blood bubbled out of his mouth as he choked. "Help . . ."

Zen took his ice axe out and began pounding at the glass. "No!" he shouted. "Nobu!"

Nobu's armor began to drip away like cheese in an oven. He reached out as his arm drooped, his hand dripping away. A scream of agony erupted from his mouth. Then that, too, collapsed, his jaw and face melding against his chest.

"No, NOBU!" Zen cried.

Lucky stood watching, clearly in shock, just like Kade. They stared in horror as Nobu literally melted in front of them. His legs went last, folding under him. Within seconds, Nobu was nothing more than a simmering puddle. The detonator and his rifle were all that remained, both on the floor a few feet from his remains.

"Oh God, oh, fuck, Nobu," Zen said. "Ah, shit, mate, I'm sorry, mate…"

Lucky pulled Zen away from the wall. "He's gone. And we have to go."

They moved past Kade, who looked past the puddle of gore on the floor, to the image of Tia behind the glass. She remained there, watching him.

"Don't go, Kade; come to me," she said. "I can help you."

A hand grabbed Kade by the shoulder and pulled him back, right into a wall of glass that slammed shut. The wrist and hand that had grabbed Kade fell to the floor, severed from the arm it had been attached to.

On the other side of the wall, Zen screamed, blood gushing out and hitting the glass that separated him and Lucky from Kade.

Lucky grabbed Zen and pulled him away from the box now imprisoning Kade. A mist suddenly fired from sprinkler heads in the ceiling. Kade's world swam and spun, and he collapsed to the floor.

* * * * *

"Get up, Jorge. You *must* get up."

The gentle voice of Jada came over the crashing of waves.

Gran Jefe opened his eyes to darkness. He tried to move his arms, but they were stuck. His legs, too, were weighed down by something, as if he were buried.

Gradually, he sorted out the sounds around him. He was on a beach and covered in sand. Waves surged over his trapped body.

He pushed his head up and saw a long shoreline.

He had no memory of how he got here.

Squirming and rocking from side to side, he managed to free his shoulders, then his arms. He pushed himself up from the sand and broke free. Waves lapped the beach as far as he could see. He turned to look out over the ocean, scanning the horizon for any sign of how he might have gotten here. A flash of lightning gave him one clue as it illuminated the hull of a ship on the horizon. There were lights out there, searching for something.

He fell to his back, his right buttock throbbing with pain as everything came surging back over him like the waves on the sand. Memories flashed through his mind: hunting the knights inside the volcano where he was shot in the ass, injured by an explosive shell from the *Frog*, beaten by a knight, and peppered with shrapnel from a land mine that knocked him unconscious. He had woken, collected his hatchet and some gear, and fled in the sky horse with Frank piloting. Then, just when he thought he might escape in the smoke screen he had created, a missile had taken the bird down.

The final few moments of the crash replayed in his mind, as if he were inside the cockpit now. To his left sat the holographic form of Frank, doing his best to keep them in the air.

"I can't hold us, Jorge," he said. "You must bail when I tell you. I'll get you as close as I can to the island of Saint John, but you'll have to swim."

There was no time to protest and tell him that Saint John was an island even the brave Cazador army had avoided—for whoever ventured there never returned.

As the bird lost altitude, Gran Jefe had looked through the shot-up windshield at the mysterious landmass on the horizon. Smoke from the missile impact filled the cabin.

"Do you see that drive in the dashboard?" Frank asked.

Gran Jefe nodded.

"Right before you jump, pull it—that's my hard drive. But first, listen closely."

He reached for it, but held back when the AI yelled, "Not yet!"

It was the first time he had heard Frank raise his voice.

"As soon as you pull that, I'll go offline," he said. "Do it right before you jump. I would highly recommend removing some of your weight before you bail."

Gran Jefe stripped off his armor, including his helmet. He tightened his duty belt and slung a pack of supplies over his back as the ocean rose up to meet the flaming bird.

"Best of luck to you, Jorge Mata," Frank said. "You may now remove the drive."

Gran Jefe plucked it from the slot in the dashboard. The AI blinked out, and the bird jerked hard as the cockpit hatch swung open.

This was going to hurt.

He jumped out as the chopper began to spin out of control.

After that, Gran Jefe remembered waking up here on Saint John—nothing more. He felt a little chill as he looked up at the dark landmass, wondering what dwelled in the derelict resort cities and the jungles that had overtaken them in the past 260 years.

He reached down to his duty belt and opened a pouch with the drive inside. Finding it undamaged, he put it away and took a quick inventory. He had the hatchet, knife, and pistol, although he was down to one magazine. The bag he had grabbed from the chopper was gone. It didn't turn up in a scan of the beach, and he wasn't going to stick around to search for what was probably long gone.

The distant searchlights continued to rake across the water, no doubt looking for the wreckage of the helicopter—and him. Somehow, he had survived the crash and everything else the knights had thrown at him. He wasn't going to waste the opportunity, but fleeing the beach meant heading into the mutant wastes of the island.

Gran Jefe stood on the sand, stuck between an enemy who wanted his head on a pike, and monsters that prowled the eternal night. He pulled out his hatchet and picked up a fallen palm frond. Dragging it over his tracks, he covered them all the way to the thicket of jungle bordering the beach, his eyes on those distant searchlights the entire time.

The hiss and hum of insects hit his ears when he reached the jungle. The chirping of exotic birds had been replaced by a constant hum that emanated from the heart of the jungle.

Gran Jefe stopped to unholster his pistol. The nine-round magazine was down to two shots, with another in the chamber. He ejected it, then swapped the nearly empty mag for a full one. Standing there, he scanned the vast trees twisting into the sky, displaying a palette of reds and purples. Vines that glowed in the dark cast an eerie luminescence, though hardly enough to guide him safely through. Having a cracked visor didn't help.

He stood there realizing the challenges of his current predicament. It wasn't just his injuries and lack of weapons that made him pause. He had shed his heavy armor before leaping out of the sky horse. Never in his life had he been so thoroughly unprepared. And never had he been so vastly outnumbered. Gran Jefe was truly alone.

Or maybe he wasn't.

Glancing down, he looked at the pouch containing the AI. He

pulled the drive back out and pushed a side button. Out shot a hologram of Frank.

"Hello again, Jorge Mata," said the pilot. "I'm relieved to see you survived."

"I survive not long, unless you help me."

"How may I assist?"

Gran Jefe looked into the jungle. "Guide me through that."

"Certainly. May I suggest affixing my drive to your weapon?"

Gran Jefe cut down some tough, supple aerial roots and used them to strap the drive to his pistol. Then, gun in one hand and hatchet in the other, he set off into the jungle. The spongy, moss-covered ground squished under his boots as he advanced, activating a vine that uncoiled from a tree like a serpent waiting to strike.

And strike it did, the barbed tendrils coming right for his boot. He hacked it into compost, spraying pulpy sap across the dirt. The ambient humming noise stopped momentarily, as if the heart of the jungle had skipped a beat.

Frank walked ahead, the shadows receding before his holographic figure. But the darkness closed in a little more with each step. When Gran Jefe turned, he couldn't see the ocean or hear the waves slapping the shore. The jungle had completely swallowed them.

"What, exactly, is your plan once we get through this jungle?" asked Frank.

"I find a boat, I go to Vanguard Islands, I kill knights until nothing left to kill."

"May I suggest that you reconsider the third part of that plan?"

They heard a guttural snort, and the ambient hum went silent. Every mutant insect, bird, and tree frog in the forest shut off, as if a switch had been thrown.

"That is concerning," Frank said.

Gran Jefe put a finger to his mouth, then aimed his pistol in the direction of the snort. His other hand gripped the hatchet.

Branches cracked and leaves rustled as the unknown creature prowled. Gran Jefe watched and listened, trying to sight up whatever was out there.

The snorting came again, and he glimpsed a creature the size of an adult hog. It darted between the trees, plowing into underbrush before he could get a shot.

He turned again, then again.

An insect crawled onto his boot, distracting him. Looking down, he saw that it wasn't an insect but a scorpion with a sting the size of Gran Jefe's pinkie.

Reaching down, he plucked the creature off and flung it away into a barbed bush.

"Jorge," Frank said.

Gran Jefe looked up to see the AI pointing behind him. Turning, he saw red eyes glowing in the bushes a few feet away. A pair of tusks jutted out from a dark snout. The deformed head was only slightly visible, but he could see a thatch of thick, rough bristles covering a scabrous hide the color of volcanic rock.

This was one of the fabled tropic hunting pigs in the flesh—not a fable after all.

The red eyes flitted from Frank to Gran Jefe. The pig grunted, its tusks dripping spittle. As it charged, he raised his pistol, firing three shots into the thick hide. The bullets only seemed to enrage the monster.

Abruptly, something flickered in front of Gran Jefe, between him and the beast. It snorted and lunged, ripping with its tusks. The momentary confusion gave Gran Jefe a chance to shoot it in the head. Even *that* didn't bring the beast down. It gave an enraged squeal and charged right through Frank.

Gran Jefe jumped away, narrowly avoiding a tusk meant

to skewer him. He swung the hatchet as he got up, the blade sinking into the bristly flesh of the neck. The beast lowered its head.

Knowing he was about to get gored, Gran Jefe scrambled away. Frank got between them again, but it didn't work this time. The monster charged again. Gran Jefe pulled behind a tree as it slammed against it, gouging into the bark and knocking leaves from the canopy.

Moving around the tree, he raised his pistol and aimed right between the small red eyes. The shot went wide, destroying an eye as the creature lunged. Gran Jefe felt his body being lifted into the air. He slid off the gnarled hide, falling to the dirt on his side.

"Watch out!" Frank yelled.

Gran Jefe saw the tusk coming toward him and did the only thing he could think of: he reached out and grabbed it. The tusk went between his arm and chest, cutting but not impaling him. He held on to an ear with one hand while gripping the tusk with the other.

As the hog jerked him back and forth, trying to fling him off, he hacked with his hatchet where the tusk connected to the jaw. The beast raised its head, then hurled him to the ground. Pain arced across his back and up his spine. Screaming, he held on as the creature bucked him up and down.

Blood dripped from the ruined eye onto Gran Jefe's cracked visor. He hacked again and worked the tusk back and forth. Using all his strength, he tried to pry it off. He felt it loosen.

Then, with a war cry that rose over the snorting from the beast, he ripped the tusk out of the jaw. The animal roared in pain and reared back, bleeding from the hole in its jaw.

Holding the base of the tusk against his palm, Gran Jefe thrust it right into the monster's open mouth like a spear, driving it through muscle and bone, into the brain. A snorting whimper came as the creature fell limp and collapsed to the dirt, killed with its own tusk.

He lay there a few moments, gasping for air, feeling a wet warmth in his armpit.

Frank crouched over him.

"That was quite a spectacle," said the AI. "Are you okay?"

Gran Jefe sat up, reaching under his arm and pulling his hand away slick with blood. It was bad, but he was alive, and nothing was going to stop him.

Staggering to his feet, he pushed on, following the cloven hoofprints through the jungle with the light from Frank guiding him. But the deeper they went, the more of those cloven tracks Gran Jefe saw. The beast he had killed wasn't alone out here. The tracks formed a highway, and they all led toward the port—exactly where he needed to go if he wanted to find a boat back to his boy.

A cacophony of squealing issued from the dark jungle as the creatures picked up his blood trail. He limped along, searching for a place to hide and heal.

"Over here," Frank said.

Gripping his armpit, Gran Jefe dashed through the bushes and around a tree. The AI pointed at a structure that stood out on the mutant terrain—something not of this new monstrous world. A building of stone—once a holy place where people came to worship an Old World god, in search of eternal salvation. If Gran Jefe could get there, he just might find *temporary* salvation, and that would have to do.

SEVENTEEN

At noon, X fastened the strap to his new armor. He still wasn't sure about the tech, but he had accepted that the suit and exoskeleton were a better option for the terrain they were diving into. In his old suit and armor, he would freeze inside an hour. Slayer prepared beside him, along with Watt and Blue Blood. The Forerunner hadn't arrived yet, but the countdown to the dive was on, less than an hour remaining.

X felt the seconds ticking away. He went over to Valeria, Jo-Jo, and Miles, all of them watching anxiously.

"This isn't goodbye," X said. "This is just *I'll see you in a bit after I freeze my ass off for a few hours.*"

Miles leaned forward, nudging X as if asking him to reconsider.

"This is one dive I can't take you on, buddy," he said. "Valeria is going to look after you and Jo-Jo while I'm gone."

"Xavier…" Valeria started to say.

"I've made my decision," X said. "Trust me, it's going to take more than some snow, ice, and monsters to kill me. Plus, I got robo-man going with me, and he's been planning this for over sixty years."

He reached out to Valeria. She leaned in for what he thought was a kiss on the cheek, but she turned slightly, planting one on his mouth.

"Come back in one piece," she said.

"I will," X said. He smiled, then bent down to hug Miles. "It's going to be okay, buddy."

Jo-Jo grunted as X patted her on the head. Miles nudged him again, barking after him as he walked away. Valeria crouched, holding him by the collar.

X kept his gaze forward, knowing looking back would just make everyone feel worse.

Across the room, a hatch opened, and the colossal padded feet of the Forerunner's mech suit pounded the deck with palpable tremors.

"Gather around," the synthetic voice boomed.

The knights and Slayer joined X near the equipment that was being crated to drop on the icy surface. Commander Hallsey hurried into the room, holding a tablet. She stopped in front of them, standing by the Forerunner.

"We've lost contact with Team Concordia," she reported after a pause.

The words took X's breath.

"We aren't sure what's happened, but Commander Hallsey will continue her efforts to contact them," added the cyborg. "For now, we proceed with our own mission. Once we've successfully activated the reactors at Polar Station, we will head to Concordia."

Watt and Blue Blood nodded, but X hung his head. Could Kade really be dead?

He tried to shake the thought, hoping for the best. But there was little hope in the wastes, especially in a barren, frozen wilderness like the North and South Poles.

"Are you with me, Xavier?" asked the Forerunner.

X glanced up at the outsize mech suit and the frail creature encased within.

"Yes, but my animal friends won't be joining, nor will Valeria."

The blue eye of the Forerunner flitted across the room, though he didn't reply. He turned to Josie and said, "Send down the equipment, Commander Hallsey."

"Yes, sir."

The Forerunner strode away, the thuds from his ponderous suit echoing across the launch bay.

"Zuni, Tia, and now Kade too," Slayer said over the noise.

"He could still be alive," X said.

An alarm wailed, indicating that the hatches would open shortly.

Unable to resist, X looked back to Valeria, Miles, and Jo-Jo. They had already been evacuated into the corridor, but he could see her looking through a viewport. She held Miles up, and he placed a forepaw against the glass. Jo-Jo went to another port, looking in.

X held up a hand, then faced the hatches as they opened to the swirling storm clouds.

Clanking sounded from the tracks pushing two crates of equipment out toward the sky. Inside were ammunition, weapons, and plenty of explosives to deal with whatever monsters awaited them at the reactors. The Forerunner had decided at the last minute not to send down any vehicles. They would land about a mile from the station and snowshoe in from there.

"Equipment away. Prepare for dive," said Commander Hallsey.

The Forerunner lumbered over to the hatch where they would soon depart. Standing on a yellow line in the deck, he turned to face X, Slayer, Watt, and Blue Blood.

"We're about to face evil that will test your heart and mind, an evil that took those dearest to me sixty-one years ago," he said. "But we must stand strong, for if we succeed, humanity will have a new chance. And if we fail, all that we know and love will vanish, like grains of sand in the tempest."

As if in answer, the hatch whisked open to the howling storm. X stepped up beside the Forerunner to peer out over clouds alight with a green, pulsating glow. This wasn't the sun, X had come to realize. At this time of year, the sun never shone on the North Pole, which was plunged into perpetual darkness save for this ethereal dance of glowing curtains in the sky.

"The Northern Lights," X said.

"Yes," said the Forerunner.

Reaching up, X patted the Forerunner on his armored shoulder as he might pat Miles on the back. "There's a little something my brothers and sisters and I say before a dive, and today it's never been truer," X said. He looked back to the viewport, where Valeria still held Miles up and Jo-Jo looked on.

"We dive so humanity survives," X said. Not as a shout, or even with a raised voice. He said it like a soldier giving orders, because that was what these men were: soldiers, heading into the most important battle of their lives.

"Clear for launch," Commander Hallsey said over the team channel. *"May luck be on your side as you raise the Trident banner."*

"For the Trident," Blue Blood and Watt said in unison.

The Forerunner nodded and then strode toward the open hatch in his Frankensteinian suit. Without the slightest hesitation, he stepped through the open hatch and was gone. It struck X, this would be the first time any of these men ever dived. For himself, he couldn't even remember how many dives he had completed.

Hope it's your last, old man. Time to retire.

X followed the cyborg into the inky abyss. As the freezing wind rushed over their armored bodies, there was no weightless feeling today. Maybe it was the new suit, or maybe it was the unfamiliar stab of fear that X felt in his heart—fear that this would be his final dive, that he wouldn't see Miles, or Valeria, or Michael and his family, or Magnolia, ever again.

You will. You aren't dying today, old man!

He brought his arms to his sides, straightening into a nose-dive. The advanced optics of his visor showed a mostly clear sky, with only a few clouds drifting across the dive zone. On the horizon, thicker clouds flashed with electrical storms, but they were far enough away that he wasn't concerned.

Northeast of those clouds, a spectral play of colors folded and curled in a vibrant showcase of purples, blues, greens, and shades of pink. The twisting curtain seemed alive as it bent and shimmered in ever-changing waves and patterns.

X forced his gaze away from the aurora borealis to check on the other divers. Their beacons all moved on the map squared off on his HUD, but he wanted to see the greenhorns with his own eyes. Slayer, Blue Blood, and Watt were all fanning out as they picked up speed. The AI controlling their descent monitored their distance from one another and would provide warnings if they got too close. It was still an odd feeling, knowing that a computer was in control of his dive.

He had already blown through the fifteen-thousand-foot mark, exceeding his usual 180 mph terminal velocity for a suicide dive. The Forerunner had already surpassed that and was gaining speed.

At this rate, they would be on the ground quickly, which was the plan. Less time in the sky gave them less time to be detected during the drop. X shot through a mattress of light cloud cover that fogged his vision for a second but hardly slowed him down. He shifted his gaze back to his HUD to check the DZ that Commander Hallsey had selected, a mile from the facility.

According to drone footage, some low mounds of snow would provide minimal cover on that side of the base.

At eight thousand feet, X scanned the horizon for the massive reactors. From this height, he imagined they might look like tiny mushrooms, but for now they were still out of view.

"Not so bad," Slayer said over the comms as he came up on X's left a hundred feet away.

"Radio silence," said the Forerunner.

X watched the black backdrop lighten as they neared the surface. A long sea of white stretched over the frozen ocean only a mile below. He glimpsed the pyramid-shaped main facility centered between the six massive reactors. Their huge disks, rimmed with missiles pointed skyward, contained technology that could bring the Old World back.

Seeing the towers sent a chill through his heart.

At four thousand feet, he shifted to stable falling position, arms and legs spread out and slowing his descent. Five hundred feet below, the Forerunner had done the same thing.

On a normal dive, X would deploy his chute at around two thousand feet, but they needed to get out of the sky undetected. The AI would pop their canopies at an unforgiving five hundred feet. That would cut their chances of being spotted on the way down. It would also give them almost no time to correct for any mistakes.

As the ground closed in, X studied the flat, white terrain for hostiles. At his current height, he couldn't see much, but the thermal imaging would turn up any heat signatures down there. Nothing was alive within or immediately around the drop zone.

He kept his visor on Polar Station and the reactors, scanning for contacts. He noticed a glimmer of red and yellow out there, but not on the ground. This reading was coming from the top rim of a reactor to the west.

X tried to make it out just as a warning flashed on his HUD. The parachute deployed, its black canopy yanking him out of his fall, and the suspension cables going taut.

He reached up to his toggles and steered over the DZ—an area of mounds and pressure ridges that would hide them from view of Polar Station. The Forerunner was flaring to touch down. A poof of snow showed where he landed.

X performed a two-stage flare overhead, gliding over the cyborg's mech suit. His boots hit the snow, and he skidded on the ice, going down shoulder first.

Stunned but unharmed, he pushed himself up to watch the other divers land. Slayer was next down, landing athwart the gentle breeze and sliding in the snow. Watt and Blue Blood came right after, just seconds apart, both pulling off near-flawless landings as they swooped out of the sky and touched down.

X freed his suspension lines and began packing his chute. He looked over at a supply crate that had landed right in the middle of the DZ. According to his HUD, the other crate had been blown off course and would require a short hike.

Watt and Blue Blood snapped their rifles together and fell out to hold security. The Forerunner clambered up a hill blocking their view of the reactors. X scrambled up next to him for a view.

"I saw something on the dive in," X said. "On one of the reactors to the west."

They both scanned the distant dishes, but whatever X had seen was either gone or out of range.

The Forerunner pulled back. "This sector looks clear," he said. "Follow me."

X slid back down and jogged over to the first crate, where Slayer waited. The Forerunner unlocked it and propped the lid. He reached inside, pulling out attachments for his arms that included a grenade launcher and a chain gun.

As soon as the Forerunner stepped back, Watt lifted out a laser rifle and two assault rifles with grenade-launcher attachments. Both X and Slayer looked from the weapons to the cyborg.

"Yes, they are for you," said the Forerunner. "I have decided to trust you both, but if, for some crazy reason, you do get any ideas, well, Commander Hallsey has specific orders."

X appreciated that the cyborg didn't elaborate on what those orders were. He reached out and took an assault rifle. Then he fished out a bandolier of grenades and four extra magazines, which he stuffed into a vest from the crate. Slayer did the same, then handed the laser rifle to X.

"You're a better shot with this one," he said.

X slung it over his back, and they set off back to the hill where Blue Blood waited.

"Looks clear from here," Watt said.

"Combat intervals," said the Forerunner. And taking point, he checked his weapons and set off in his mech suit, reminding X yet again that this was a highly trained officer in the Trident military.

Slayer finished loading a grenade into his launcher, exchanged a nod with X, and started up the hill. At the top, a fierce wind lashed their suits as they started the mile trek to the facility. It was a bone-chilling negative thirty-five degrees, but the skies were clear of snowstorms for now.

To the northwest, X could still see the alien green and purple shimmers of the aurora borealis, in stark contrast to the austere palette of white-and-gray wasteland intermixed sporadically with the rare pale blue of deeper ice. As he walked, his boots crunched over the Arctic ice, creaking slightly, and he reminded himself that they were floating on an ocean two miles deep.

The chute on the second crate whipped audibly in the rising wind as they approached. Watt opened it up and began hauling out four loaded backpacks.

"There are explosives in each of these," he said. "We're all taking one."

X unslung his rifles and threw the pack over his back. Slayer did the same thing, and they pushed on into the fierce wind. X watched as they closed in on Polar Station, his gaze alternating between his digital map and the horizon.

It wasn't long before the first reactor came into view. The team spread out between pressure ridges in the ice for cover while the Forerunner scanned for life-forms. X pulled out his binoculars again to search for the heat signature he had seen on the dive in. Slowly moving the lenses, he focused on the reactor rim but saw nothing. Maybe that was all it was—nothing.

The Forerunner gave the signal to advance across the open ice to the first reactor. It was about a thousand feet, but X couldn't see any cover between them and the base. The domed building rose five stories, with multiple helicopter landing pads on raised platforms over the ice.

X recalled the story of what had happened to the Forerunner's family here.

From what he could tell, the cyborg was heading right toward the platforms. And as X came closer, he saw frozen debris scattered across the snow. A rotor, a charred piece of fuselage. It was definitely part of a helicopter. Somewhere amid the wreckage were the deep-frozen remains of the Forerunner's wife and their unborn daughter, and his friends.

The mech suit plodded to a stop a few feet away from a mangled piece of aircraft aluminum. When X realized what was happening, he went over and crouched a few feet behind the cyborg. Noah seemed hypnotized by the sight of the destruction, probably remembering everything that had happened that catastrophic day.

Watt and Blue Blood exchanged a glance with X. Both of them

looked worried as hell. Just as X was about to say something to ease their fears, the Forerunner got up and lumbered toward the platform connecting to a side entrance. Doors remained blown open after all these years, letting the snow drift high within.

Weapons up, the cyborg strode over, scanning for life. X checked for tracks but saw nothing. This place seemed dormant. Perhaps the monsters that had foiled the last Trident mission were hibernating now.

But X knew they were out there, waiting.

The team moved out after the Forerunner in widely staggered intervals, slipping into the facility one by one. Blue Blood held rear guard while Watt moved ahead of X, watching a tablet. They passed a little row of graves carved out of the ice, strewn about with the remains of bone beasts blown apart six decades ago.

The Forerunner thudded past them, the ice cracking under his padded mechanical feet. X winced at an even louder cracking that resonated through the passage as they advanced.

But this sound seemed to be coming from behind them and growing louder.

The Forerunner halted, turning with the others. X looked up at the overhead as it suddenly gave way in a thunderous roar, like a glacier calving into the ocean. Emerging from the shadows stood a giant metal robot with six misshapen limbs radiating from a bulbous torso.

It was some sort of freak robot spider, X thought as he backed away.

Hydraulic pistons hissed from three jointed mechanical legs pushing the robotic exoskeleton to a height of ten feet. As it scuttled out, X saw that it wasn't all machine. At the top of the monstrosity, a domed lid housed what appeared to be a pulsating mass of gray-and-pink brain matter. Electrical impulses arced across the veiny surface, illuminating faces—human faces—trapped in the convoluted mass that throbbed as they pushed outward with open mouths unable to scream.

In less than two seconds, X had planted his feet, raised his rifle, and moved his finger to the trigger. For Blue Blood, it was already too late. The nightmarish mech snatched him up with a clawed arm, then used another to rip him in half.

"Get back!" the Forerunner boomed.

Slayer and Watt darted away with X as the cyborg unleashed a stream of gunfire from the chain gun mounted to his metal arm. The raucous whining echoed in the frozen passage. X dived under the legs of the Forerunner, sliding through. As he rolled to his feet, he saw multiple sets of glowing red eyes at the end of the corridor. Three hulking forms lumbered through the shadows beyond the next intersection.

"Behind us!" Slayer shouted.

X swung his rifle up, aiming at bone beasts. But these were not like the creatures he had battled in the wastes. Cords snaked out of exposed flesh beneath their bony carapaces, connecting to mechanical packs that rose over their shoulders. Some sort of battery, perhaps, or a source of nourishment for these monsters that had remained frozen in the depths of the facility for decades. They scattered as X fired a grenade, forcing the monsters back from the intersection.

"Get to the command center and activate the reactors!" shouted the Forerunner. "I'll deal with this abomination."

"This way!" Watt yelled, dashing through the intersection. X and Slayer ran after him after laying down covering fire at the roaring bone beasts.

X hesitated at the junction to look back. The Forerunner had charged the mech, grabbing one of its arms and smashing the glass dome with its curved metal crest.

It dawned on X that the Forerunner had lied about not seeing this monster all those years ago. He had seen it with a clarity that allowed him to build his own mech suit and duel the beast. As X turned away, all he could do was hope it would be enough to defeat whatever evil kept those faces trapped inside that freak-ish brain.

EIGHTEEN

"Michael, they have Gabi," Layla whispered over the comms.

"I know. I'm working on a plan, but you have to stay quiet," Michael said softly. "We're going to be fine, I promise."

He wanted to believe those words, but in his gut he felt a lump of dread that he was about to lose his family—that his nightmare would come true and these slavers would take from him what he treasured most.

The rock bluff where he lay prone was in easy view of the cave system connecting to their shelter two hundred feet away. Deep inside the caves, Layla and Bray hid in the very tunnel Michael had excavated yesterday. But the slavers had found their shelter, taking Gabi by force and holding her captive inside. It was only a matter of time before they found his family.

Overhead, the storm weakened as it rolled east, the rain now just a drizzle and the lightning sporadic. Michael had managed to connect with Timothy and told the AI to stand by. When the moment came, the ship would lower down to extract them.

But first, Michael had to deal with the slavers, and that meant waiting for the precise moment to attack. From his vantage point on the adjacent bluff, he could see a lone sentry in the look-out where Victor and Michael themselves had spent many hours watching. Behind the man, two of his comrades were interro-gating Gabi. He could hear her distant shouts, each one making him tense up.

Michael turned to scan the area where he had fled the horse-men who tracked him and Victor. After escaping, Michael had lost track of the battle. He had no idea if his friend was alive, or if he had killed all the slavers out there. It was safe to assume that Victor had likely failed against the overwhelming odds.

Then again, none of the horsemen had shown up here, and Michael didn't see any vessels on the sea. No ships or boats, not even a skiff.

He flinched as Gabi cried out in pain.

"Michael!" Layla whispered over the channel.

"On my way," he replied quietly. As he moved into position, he tried not to imagine what they would do to his wife and son if they found them. It was a miracle they hadn't heard Bray or discovered the passage connecting their shelter to another tunnel. He had debated telling Layla to flee that way, but it was too dangerous.

The only option was for Michael to take out this guard. Then he would order Timothy to lower the airship while he rushed into the tunnels and took out the two slavers with Gabi. It was a risky plan, leaving him open to attack and leaving the airship exposed, but it was the only way he could think of to get them out of here.

The guard below stood still, eyes hidden behind a dark visor, making it impossible to know where he was looking. As difficult as waiting was, Michael had to be strategic and wait for his chance to take down this slaver.

A transmission hissed in his earpiece as he looked out over the ocean.

"Chief, do you copy?" said Timothy.

"Copy."

"I've detected multiple contacts in your area."

"I'm well aware," Michael whispered back.

"These are heading in from the ghost town Haría, sir."

"Shit." Michael understood now. These were the horsemen. Time was up. He had to move. Now.

"How many?" he asked.

"Three men, two animals."

"How far?"

"A mile away, moving at about three and a half miles per hour."

He had maybe fifteen minutes.

"Listen carefully, Pepper. When I tell you, I need you to fly like a madman and come down to us with the launch bay open, ramp extended, and any tricks you can manage for distracting hostiles."

"I'm ready, Chief. Just tell me when."

"Soon."

Michael switched channels to Layla.

"Get ready to move. I'm on my way," he whispered into his headset.

"We're ready," she replied softly.

He moved from his hiding spot, keeping low, even going down to crawl for a few feet. When he was out of view of the slaver guard, he pushed up and started toward the trail above the lookout. He soon found the boot prints of these men, leading to the bluff. The rock platform extended out of the cave entrance, but the slaver was standing back, out of view.

As Michael moved down the winding trail, he swapped the pistol for his second knife, a smaller blade than the one he had used to dispatch the horseman back in the vineyards. He moved cautiously down the rocky path, doing his best not to make any sound.

Flipping up his visor, he put the knife between his teeth. Then he picked up a rock. Nearing the entrance to the cave, he tossed the rock to the edge. It worked, drawing the slaver out. Michael already had his knife in hand and lunged, leaping up and wrapping his legs around the man's midsection while drawing the blade across his throat.

Michael hit the ground on his back, sawing awkwardly back and forth since he had no second arm to help hold the guy down. Blood gushed, and the slaver tried to stop the flow with his hand. In a swift jab, Michael plunged the knife through the side of the helmet. The body weight on top of him fell limp.

Rolling, Michael pushed the dead slaver away. He pulled the knife free, sheathed it, and picked up the man's weapon—a sawed-off double-barreled shotgun. Michael opened the break to find two shells loaded. He flipped it shut and bumped on his comm.

"Layla, I'm coming," Michael whispered. "One guard down."

He strode away from the ledge, entering the tunnel that the slaves had stormed, smashing down the hatches. Halfway to the shelter, he heard Gabi cry out in pain, pleading with them to stop.

Realization hit him like a falling tree. They had switched from interrogation to something more sinister.

As Michael approached, he saw her flailing on the table inside the communal room, kicking at one man as she squirmed in the grip of the other. They had torn her shirt and were struggling to get her pants off.

Michael shouldered the weapon, aiming at the head of the man pulling on her pants. He braced himself and fired. The recoil of the shot knocked him back as blood and flesh burst from the slaver's skull. Michael raised the weapon at the man behind Gabi, who reached for his sidearm as she rolled off the table. As he pulled the gun, Michael fired again. This time, nothing happened.

The cartridge was a damned dud!

Manic laughter erupted from the slaver—a mix of shock and excitement at his unexpected reprieve from near-certain death. He aimed the pistol at Michael as a figure sprang up behind him and jabbed something into his neck, then his back. He collapsed to the table headfirst, and the figure came into focus in the dim light. It was Layla, thrusting a long blade into his back, over and over with impacts that he could hear.

Michael rushed over to Gabi, who lay curled up on the ground, shaking.

"Come on, we have to go," he said.

He tossed the shotgun and picked up an assault rifle. Layla went back down to the tunnel she had emerged from, and pulled Bray out. The boy had ear protection on and gripped the two padded earpieces with his tiny hands. His wide eyes stared at Michael as he mumbled, "Da-da, Ma-ma."

"It's okay, buddy," Michael said. He glanced at Layla, who ejected a magazine from another assault rifle. After checking the mag, she palmed it back in and checked on Gabi.

"You're safe now," Layla said, handing the assault rifle over.

Gabi grabbed it, then spat on the body of the man on the ground. She gave him a solid kick in the groin as Michael led the way out of the room.

"Timothy, fly now," Michael said into his headset. "We're on our way."

"Copy, but be advised, those contacts have picked up speed," Timothy replied.

Michael turned to his little band. "We have to move fast. Come on!"

He guided them into the tunnels, back to the cliff where the dead slaver lay. The whirring of the airship rose over the thunder and wind. In the meat of the clouds now, the airship began to descend.

Layla stopped just shy of the corpse. Rifle slung, Bray in one arm, and a pistol in her other hand, she pointed out to sea. "Look!"

Michael narrowed in on a long boat on the horizon, cruising toward the island. Add to this the inbound hostiles from the vineyards, and he was running out of time to get everyone aboard the airship. Even if they got airborne, the slavers might shoot them down.

"Timothy, we got eyes on a long, narrow boat to the east," he said.

"I'm aware, Chief. We'll need to make this extraction quick," replied the AI. *"I'll be there in sixty-five seconds at my current rate of speed, but those contacts nearing your position on land will be within firing range."*

Michael turned from the ship to Gabi, Layla, and Bray. "You all go," he said. "I'm going to lay down some covering fire for us."

"Da-da, no go, no go, Da-da."

Michael forced a smile. "I'll be right back—promise, buddy."

He looked to Layla with a little smile, then started up the winding path to the bluff. A distant whinny hit his ears at the crest. Crouching behind a rock, he looked out at the fields, where two riders approached. One of them wore a spiked helmet and gripped a long staff or club.

Michael's heart sank when he noticed a figure being dragged on the ground behind one of the horses.

"Victor," he whispered.

Michael should have helped his friend kill these men when he had the chance, but fear of screwing up had taken over—fear of a mistake that could cost him his family.

Now he was going to make up for that mistake.

He mounted his rifle on a rock, snugging it against his shoulder. If he was to have any hope of saving Victor and getting his friend on the airship—assuming he was even alive—each shot had to count. The captured warrior lay unmoving in the dirt, still in his armor and helmet. Michael thought he could see his chest rising and falling, but it was hard to tell from this distance.

The horsemen stopped a hundred yards away, their helmets turning skyward. Michael sighted up the spiked helmet, moving his finger to the trigger. He squeezed off a shot just as a battery of brilliant lights beamed down from the sky, hitting the area with a blinding glow.

Michael lost sight of the two men as the beam brightened. Thumps came from overhead, and flares exploded across the ground in front of him. Timothy's distraction worked, but not just on the enemy. There was no way Michael could get a shot now.

Holding his shoulder up to cover his visor, he turned as the ship lowered behind his position, ramp open and ready to accept them.

"Prepare for evac," said the AI over the comms.

Blinking, Michael turned back with his rifle to look for Victor in the bright glow of the airship lights. He could make out three figures and the horses, but that was it, and he had no idea who was who until he made out one of those figures holding another up like a human shield.

"Lay down your weapons and come out, or he dies!" shouted one of the slavers.

"Run!" said a second voice, muffled but distinguishable. It was Victor. The man holding him smacked him in the side of the head.

"Come on!" Layla shouted.

Michael stared down the iron sights, waiting for a shot to help his friend. Gunfire suddenly blasted away from one of the figures. He aimed at that guy and fired a burst. The rounds went high, then wide, giving the slaver a chance to hunker down.

He took a breath in, held it, and fired again at the slaver with the rifle aimed skyward. One of the three rounds hit him in the chest. The man went down, firing wildly in death.

"Go!" Victor shouted. The slaver holding him dropped him

to the ground and unslung a weapon. He fired at Michael, forcing him down, then turned the barrel on the airship.

"Taking damage," Timothy reported.

The report sent a chill up Michael's back. He popped up to find the slaver crouched behind Victor and firing at the airship. The parachute flares began to burn out, shadows creeping back over the terrain, making a shot almost impossible.

"Michael!" Layla called out. "Michael, hurry!"

Torn by the impossible decision, he stared at Victor, still hoping for a shot. His earpiece crackled. *"We have to leave, Chief,"* said Timothy.

"I'm sorry," Michael choked out.

Keeping low, he retreated to the trail and rushed down to the ramp. Gabi, Layla, and Bray were already safely inside the launch bay. He leaped aboard and backed away as the ship rose. The hatch began to close, but Michael bent down for a look at the bluff, now engulfed in the beams from the airship lights.

Victor was on the ground in front of the slaver. He held the spiked club up in the air, pointing it at the ship. The hatch sealed shut, blocking the view. But Michael knew what was about to happen.

"No," he cried. "No…"

He felt a fury that he hadn't felt since Charmer was alive. A fury that grew each time he faced evil, burning hotter, requiring more vengeance.

Michael turned to his family, the world slowly returning from what felt like slow motion. Layla bent down with Bray, and Michael hugged them close.

*   *   *   *   *

Kade tried to open his eyelids. They felt heavy and cold. His breath came out in an icy puff. He was at Concordia Station. But he didn't recall how he'd gotten here, in some dim chamber. The last thing he remembered was...

"Tia," he mumbled.

He forced his eyes open to a vast, dark view lit by tiny pinpricks of red, like planets in the abyss of space. These lights were all spaced exactly the same distance apart, casting towering structures in an otherworldly glow.

Kade leaned forward against the harness. Those lights ran down to a floor fifty feet or more below him. His heart quickened as he recognized his surroundings. He was inside the cryo-chamber where Nobu had planted the charges. Not just inside the chamber, but inside one of the pods. Its glass lid was propped open above him. Tubes and thick conduits snaked away from the other pods stacked onto the pillars across the room.

He glanced down at capped tubes protruding from his capsule, ready to pierce his flesh with needles and connect him with the thousands of other people already plugged into the system.

"Tia," he repeated, louder this time.

The last thing he remembered was seeing her in the corridor. But it couldn't be her.

What he saw had to be some sort of AI. But how had they known what she looked like, unless they had somehow discovered her body back at the city?

His brain struggled to understand, sluggish from the mist that had knocked him unconscious inside that glass prison back in the corridor. For some reason, his captors had spared him after killing Nobu. Part of Kade wished it had been him and not the knight.

He strained against the harness to look out at the other pods for Lucky and Zen, but saw no sign of them.

"Lucky," he whispered. "Zen, can you—"

A cracking noise answered him, coming from below.

No...

He glanced up at movement scurrying across the ceiling. Ice flaked off, sifting past the red glow of the batteries or whatever kept the occupants inside the chambers alive. Kade tried to identify the source of the movement, but the figure went still in the shadows above.

Kade squirmed against the harness, inducing pain in his right upper arm. He rotated his neck, seeing a tube he hadn't noticed earlier. This one had already been inserted into his flesh. He grabbed it with his other hand, wiggling it to pry it out. The pain increased.

He froze at a cracking sound above him, like dull blades scraping against steel. He knew that sound all too well. Slowly he lifted his eyes to something he had hoped never to see again: a machine lowering itself from the ceiling on thick, white cable-like strands. But this mechanical monstrosity was different from the DEF-Nine "defectors" that had held him and his people prisoner for so many years. This nightmarish beast was a blend of metal and flesh, an unholy creation that looked like a six-legged spider with limbs in all the wrong places. Two hollow, cylindrical limbs protruded from a bulbous torso covered in scales. Another, smaller limb, if you could call it that, hung from the upper back of the torso with a hooked end. At the bottom, three jointed legs hung from underneath the mechanical monster.

As it lowered, Kade saw something yet more horrifying. Connected to the top of this robotic spider was a bizarre domed head containing what looked like human faces encapsulated in a mass of organic tissue.

He blinked, his eyes relaying a sight that his brain couldn't quite process.

The thing stopped in front of Kade's pod. The five faces inside pushed and pulled against their fleshly matrix. All at once, the mouths spoke in synthetic unison.

"Kade Long, you have come here to destroy us," they said. "To activate this station and the Delta Cloud fusion reactors."

Kade simply stared, wondering, as he had many times in his life, whether this was real or just a nightmare he couldn't wake from. The emotionless blend of robotic voices spoke again.

"The very entity that created us also created these reactors. During the first days of the war, our creator gave us orders to safeguard this location, and to activate the reactors only at a time when humanity has been completely eradicated."

"That will never happen," Kade said.

"You came closer to wiping out all cybernetic beings with the computer virus uploaded at facility KON-8, at Mount Kilimanjaro. But this virus did not account for highly modified units like me, the perfect adaptation of metal and flesh. A bio-cyber species that is the future of this planet. Our mission has never been clearer: erase humanity."

The robotic creature spun in its hammock of cables, then swung down, planting all six metallic limbs over the pod so Kade saw the bulging faces.

"You, Kade Long, will help us accomplish this goal," they said.

The mouths closed briefly, all eyes on Kade.

"We are authorized to offer you a place in this future, but you will get this offer only once," they said. "All you have to do is tell us where your people come from, and then I will administer a synthetic drug that will ease you into sleep and wipe your memories. All the horrors of your life, gone. When you wake up, you won't remember a thing and will serve us in a comfortable position."

The eyes seemed to scrutinize him for a reaction.

He considered the offer in silence. As appealing as wiping his bad memories might be, he never wanted to erase the good ones. The times with his boys and his wife, and with friends who made life worth living.

"You are conflicted, Kade Long," they said. "We understand you want to live. This is a rational human trait that has made your species very difficult to kill. But like you, we want to live, too."

"That's where you're wrong," Kade said. "I don't care about living anymore. I've lost everything that made me human. Go ahead and kill me. I'm ready."

He raised his eyes in defiance.

"Your request has been denied," they replied. "Your body is needed for our future. You will tell us where your people are located. This is not a question that can be evaded."

Kade smirked. "I won't tell you shit."

"There is another way to obtain the information we seek, but I assure you, the easier and far less painful way is for you to provide it willingly."

"I spent years in a machine camp. There's nothing you can do to me that hasn't been done."

In answer, a metal apparatus the width of a screwdriver extended from a bladed arm of the robot straddling his pod. The limb telescoped outward, and prongs on the end began to whir toward his skull.

"You can tell us where your people are located *without* suffering, or we will extract the information from your brain without any sedatives. You will feel every millimeter of metal as it drills into your skull. Once that is complete, we will deploy a nano worm that can tap into your memories, burrowing through your brain until it accesses the information we seek. You will feel every second of this process—a deeply violating and *painful* sensation."

The emphasized word echoed in the many voices of the faces. Kade could already feel the heat of the prongs coming closer and closer.

He blinked rapidly from nerves but remained determined.

"You can fight it, but you will regret your decision," they said.

"The choice is yours. I will leave you to ponder this decision, Kade Long."

The prongs stopped spinning, and the limb retracted. With it, the white bands drew the monstrous robot to the ceiling, where it skittered away.

Kade closed his eyes, trying to regain his wits. But his answer wouldn't change. He would rather die than give away any information about the Vanguard Islands. His mind started to clear.

The way he saw it, there was no way he could complete this mission, especially as the sole survivor. And rather than betray the last bastion of humanity, he saw only one option: kill himself.

He had already given away the coordinates of the islands once to the knights, hoping for peace, but with this enemy there could never be peace. The machines would stop at nothing to obliterate his kind.

Kade had been here before, wanting nothing more than to join his family in the darkness of whatever might be out there after leaving this realm. This time, he wouldn't hesitate.

He struggled in his harness, looking down. The drop from the pod was at least fifty feet and would surely kill him if he landed headfirst.

It's been a good ride, but the rodeo's over.

Kade took a final minute to think of Xavier, Magnolia, and everyone else still out there fighting for humanity. He hoped they would have better luck than his team.

Good luck, mates. Sorry I let you down.

Ripping the tube free from his arm, he prepared to jump. Hurried sounds echoed through the chamber as the machine returned to stop him. But as Kade climbed out, he realized that this noise wasn't mechanical in nature. He went completely still, ears perked like Miles, listening to what sounded like human footsteps.

The click of heels on flooring echoed through the chamber,

and a white glow lit up a figure, as if an angel had come to save Kade. He narrowed his eyes on what he already knew was Tia, and was even more convinced by her glowing form that this was some illusion.

"You're not real," he whispered.

She stopped underneath his pillar, looking up at him with a mischievous gaze. It was *so* realistic, but then again, if the machines could extract information from a human brain, they could surely figure out a mannerism or two.

"Who are you?" he asked.

"It's *me*, Kade. They saved me."

No. You were gone too long.

"I escaped after they brought me back," she said softly. "Hurry, climb down and come with us."

Zen limped into view, his severed wrist wrapped with a bandage. He held an Uzi in his hand and waved for Kade to get moving.

But where was Lucky? Kade didn't see anyone else down there.

There was no time to explore this new option. Metal on metal clattered above him. He climbed out of his pod and began clambering down to the capsule directly below. As he did, Kade looked up at the spider-brain beast above him, scuttling upside down across the ceiling using four of those misshapen limbs. Two of them fired strings of hissing white cable at the ground where Zen stood firing a burst from his submachine gun. He leaped away as the ropes smacked against the floor and stuck there, causing it to bubble and smoke and disintegrate as if from some sort of acid.

"Hurry!" Tia shouted.

Kade dropped to the next pod, where an innocent male face lay in repose through the frosted glass. The eyes remained closed in deep slumber, oblivious to the horrors outside.

Zen fired another burst as the monstrous robot darted into the shadows. Whooshing came from above as Kade felt with his foot for the pod below him. A thick white cable hit the glass, spreading out and hissing as the surface dissolved.

His eyes followed the cable to an adjacent pillar, about ten pods above his, where the mechanical monster perched on the side. Zen fired in that direction, shattering the glass lid and punching into the flesh of an occupant who would never wake. The beast skittered around the other side.

"Move, Kade, move!" Tia shouted.

Kade climbed to the next pod. Only two more separated him from the ground now, but Zen had emptied his magazine, allowing the creature to clamber down the side of a pillar. Zen struggled to swap out the magazine one handed.

Tia grabbed the weapon and palmed in the extra ammo. Then she raised the barrel and fired at the robot as it leaped from the next column to the column Kade was descending. Bullets pounded the armored scales of the metallic torso, pinging off the side.

This had to be Tia, Kade realized.

Somehow, against all odds, she *was* alive. Back from the dead. Maybe the cold had preserved her brain and body long enough for the machines to bring her back. Just as the Forerunner had brought back Valeria, and Jack before her.

Kade moved faster but suddenly lost his footing. He slid down the lid, then fell to the final capsule, bouncing off the top. He hit the ground on his side. It hurt. He could see Tia firing the Uzi, and Zen bending down to help Kade.

The machine dropped down between the knight and Tia with a loud *whump*. It slashed at her with a razor-edged limb, then raised the two appendages that launched the deadly white cables. It pointed them at Zen.

"Move!" Kade shouted.

Both barrels flashed, but no white cables appeared. Instead, two bright-red laser bolts hit Zen in the upper back.

Zen fell forward on his knees, shoulders a melted hump and his neck and head gone. Seconds later, the body toppled onto its side.

Kade scrambled away, then pushed himself up as Tia fired another burst into the spider-brain beast's dome, which was now protected by an armored shield over the faces. The creature skittered toward her, slashing outward. A bullet glanced off the dome, leaving a dent in the side. The monster swiveled toward the shooter, and so did Kade.

It was Lucky, holding Zen's sniper rifle in the doorway of the chamber.

"Run!" he shouted.

Kade took off with Tia toward the knight as he fired more high-caliber rounds into the beast. But these only slowed it down. It closed in, its synthetic voices roaring.

"You will never leave this place!"

Lucky lowered his rifle and held up a small device as Kade and Tia approached.

A robotic voice screeched behind them as Lucky pushed the button on the detonator that he must have retrieved from Nobu, the last one to have it. At the bottoms of the pillars, explosions boomed in series. Somehow, Zen or Lucky had set the rest of the charges.

Kade felt the heat on his back as he made his way into the tunnel where Nobu's remains lay puddled on the floor.

Lucky led the way back to the labs, but Kade turned to watch as the pillars collapsed with their sleeping occupants. The robotic spider raised its bladed appendages, the lustrous metal glinting in the inferno. It vanished in an avalanche of metal shards, glass, and debris.

"Hurry!" Lucky shouted.

Kade followed him and Tia into the labs, where he slammed the door shut, sealing out the heat of the blast. Tia walked over to Kade, a smile on her face. Just then Lucky slammed his rifle butt into the back of her head.

She collapsed in Kade's arms.

"What are you doing!" he screamed.

"It's not her!" Lucky shouted.

Kade gently lowered her to the ground, glaring up at the knight, who now had his rifle aimed at her face.

"Get out of the way, Kade," he said.

"Stop!" Kade raised his hands and shielded her body. "She's like Jack and Valeria! That machine brought her back like the Forerunner brought them back."

"No. He brought them back with medicine, and they still had brain function. That isn't Tia. It's just her hijacked body. The machines were using her to deceive you. If you don't believe me, turn her over."

Kade gently rolled her onto her stomach. He looked down at a black, beetle-like device burrowed into her skull.

"That's how they control her," he said.

The distant roar of the spider rang out.

"We have to go and send an SOS," Lucky said. "Now, get out of the way so I can finish this."

Shaking, Kade looked down at not Tia, trying to understand. Trying to accept that the machines had controlled her through this device.

He reached out to Lucky.

"Kade, it's not her—"

"I know," he said. "I should be the one to do this."

Kade took the rifle, looked at Tia one last time, and said goodbye.

NINETEEN

Frank gave a ghostly glow to the belfry in the steeple's interior, illuminating the bell that hung from an anchor in the stone ceiling. Gran Jefe looked out over the canopy of trees surrounding the ancient church. The vine-covered stone had withstood the apocalypse and the two and a half centuries that followed, standing tall in a graveyard of structures that had collapsed long ago. The jungle had swallowed most everything else. What little rubble remained was now consumed by vines and strangler figs.

Beyond the dense canopy, Gran Jefe could make out another graveyard, this one of ships and boats. Sterns, masts, and bowsprits poked out of dirt that rose up like the black hide of some prehistoric monster sleeping in the jungle. These were the vessels washed away during the war, heaved by the force of the violent waves that wiped the port right off the map. That was where he needed to go to search for a boat that he could use to row his gunshot ass back home.

But getting there meant crossing a mile of treacherous territory controlled by the predaceous porkers that killed whatever set foot on this wretched island. The raucous chorus of their grunts and squeals never let up, making rest almost impossible. And rest was what Gran Jefe needed most right now. His body needed to heal from being beaten, shot, blown up, and stabbed.

By a stroke of luck, his medical kit had survived the crash of the sky horse. He had used the surgical tools and a mirror on a stick to remove the bullet from his ass. He had sutured the wound with a needle and thread and not so much as a swig of shine for the pain, and packed some antibiotic cream on it.

If the noise wasn't bad enough out there, the pain made sleep even more elusive.

Gran Jefe moved away from the window and settled back on the ground, curling up and putting his hands over his ears to sleep. He shifted his body, trying to get into a comfortable position that didn't cause pain to his butt or his arm. Exhaustion finally took him.

"Jorge," said a voice he knew.

He stirred awake, and there in front of him glowed the AI pilot. Groggy, Gran Jefe took a moment to remember that he was in the steeple of the church. The squealing of the pigs reminded him.

When he realized that the squealing was from directly below him, he grabbed his hatchet. Glancing to the vertical shaft that led down into the nave below, he saw that the bristly beasts had broken inside. They darted back and forth, smashing broken furniture with their tusks.

"I believe they were attracted to your snoring," said Frank. "Don't worry, though, they can't climb up here."

"No shit, *amigo*, but we go nowhere."

Gran Jefe watched two of the beasts slamming into each other with those jagged tusks. They reminded him of Cazador warriors on a raiding mission, fighting over the spoils. Today, though, *he* might be the spoils.

"How long I sleep?" he asked.

"How long *did* you sleep?" Frank responded.

"*Sí, professor.*"

"Three hours and thirty-two minutes. And you needed it. I would say you look much better, but how are you feeling?"

"*Bien.*"

Gran Jefe gathered his meager gear as he worked on a plan to get out of the church.

"I need your help," he said.

"I'm at your service, Jorge Mata," Frank said. "How may I assist?"

"Detract."

"Do you mean *distract*?"

"*Sí, sí.* You lead those ugly *hijoeputas* away from me."

"Okay, but my projection has a range of thirty feet from the remote; otherwise, it won't work." He looked at Gran Jefe with a raised brow. "Do you understand?"

"Stay close, *sí*. I am no *estúpido*."

"Might I suggest a different distraction first?"

Gran Jefe nodded.

"Throw something into the jungle to attract the pigs; then head out the back of the nave. I'll do the rest."

"I think the same."

"Good. I'm ready when you are."

Gran Jefe looked around for something to chuck out of the steeple. A pebble, stick, rock, or roof tile, or… When his eyes lit on the bell, he started to grin.

It took a bit to uncouple it from its housing, but it was worth the effort. If he could heave it over the parapet to the tiled second-story roof, it would likely roll down a hill that sloped into the jungle, clanging and banging all the way down.

Squatting, he got both hands under it and heaved it up onto the low parapet of the belfry, then tilted it over.

Crashing onto the rooftop below, the bell shattered several tiles before rolling off in a great din and clatter.

Staring in anticipation, Gran Jefe watched as the bell lost some of its momentum in the soft jungle muck. But it didn't stop altogether, and the lip tilted over the slope, pulling the bell's weight beyond the angle of repose. Faster and faster, it rolled and tumbled down the other side, ringing all the way down. Squealing in answer, the enraged pigs stampeded out of the church.

The bait was working.

Wasting no time, Gran Jefe climbed down the ladder to the empty nave. The herd, which had to be twenty hogs, stampeded away through the trees.

Gran Jefe ran out the church's open back door. The sporadic glow of lightning was hardly enough to see in the dark terrain, but Frank exerted his glow, making a beacon to guide them through the perils that surrounded them.

The clamor of the runaway church bell faded away to the grunts and growls of the confused beasts. Then followed the thumping of cloven hooves. They had his scent. Not looking back, Gran Jefe ran like a madman in the opposite direction, toward the port, with Frank's glow guiding him over the treacherous terrain.

Bugs skittered up from the carcass of a hog that had fallen into the grasp of a carnivorous vine. Arms of the mutant liana shot up at Gran Jefe, striking at his neck. On the ground, they snaked away from trees and out of holes in the ground to snag his boots.

After bursting through a mat of weeds, he stumbled out into a field of downed trees. His boots squished down on something moist… and rank. He lifted a boot caked in dung.

Frank had stopped about ten feet away, in the center of the circular glade, emitting light over a landscape scalloped with broad, shallow depressions.

"Oh, shit," said the AI. "And no, not referring to your boots."

The holographic pilot turned, his glow capturing the dish-shaped hollows in the ground. The damned AI had led him to where the monsters bedded down!

Behind them, the herd crashed through the jungle in their effort to find Gran Jefe.

"You'll need to step it up a bit," Frank said. "I'll try and help. Good luck."

"¿Qué?"

Gran Jefe watched as the AI went to a ravine in the muddy circle, illuminating a litter of shoats. Each was already the size of that *perro negro* that followed X around everywhere. The young hogs grunted and oinked innocently as Frank walked toward them.

A sinister grunt answered.

Gran Jefe dashed across the last part of the open area and back into the jungle, ducking limbs and hurdling fallen logs. He tripped over a root, pushed himself back up, and hacked at a vine that had thrown a coil around his ankle.

The battle against the flora took him to the edge of a ravine. Hoping to lose the blood-hungry hogs, he jumped in and slid down to a creek of murky water, his boots sinking in the muck below. After yanking his feet free, he splashed across to the other side, then clambered on all fours up the hill to a gap in the trees.

The distant white noise of waves hit his ears—he was almost to the ocean. He set off across the raised topography of dirt and sand that had slid through the area.

Passing the half-buried boats he had seen from the church, he heard furious squealing and snorting again, drawing closer.

"Faster, my friend, faster!" said Frank.

"Fu…"

Gran Jefe tried to curse, but just breathing was challenge enough. He sucked air into his burning lungs as he ran toward the shore, scanning frantically for a skiff or dinghy he could push in and row back home. Seeing nothing, he yelled, "Find me a boat!"

The AI vanished, then flickered back to life in the junk pile, searching the wrecks nearer the water. Gran Jefe could see the surf now, crashing up against the loose berm of landslide debris. He glanced over his shoulder at the jungle. The trees shook from the stampeding hogs. One of the beasts emerged from the shadows at the top of the hill, then another. Soon, a dozen slavering, grunting hogs were staring right at him.

The AI glowed beside a mound of seaweed and tidal debris. "Here, here!" he shouted.

Gran Jefe ran toward Frank, seeing a plastic paddle protruding from the pile. He holstered his pistol and grabbed the shaft, wiggling it back and forth. He looked back at the pigs again, now picking their way down the hill toward him.

Paddle in hand, he turned and ran to Frank. The AI was pointing at the narrow hull of a fiberglass kayak.

"¡Qué diablos!" Gran Jefe shouted.

"It's the best option you have," said the AI. "You have roughly one minute and ten seconds to get this out in the surf."

Gran Jefe tried not to listen to the grunts and squeals of the advancing hogs as he hauled the kayak from the pile of wrack and driftwood. He put it under his arm and hobbled to the surf.

He pushed the little craft out to the crashing foam, wading behind it, bracing himself against the warm swells. The salt water stung his ass, but when he looked back, the hogs were already piling out of the jungle, onto the beach.

Gran Jefe waded out, through another breaking wave. Once he was past it, he pushed off the bottom and began to kick his way past the surf line. The next swell hit him in the face, knocking the hull into his head, prompting a string of profanities in two languages.

Blinking away the sting of salt water, he kicked back up and tried to climb onto the small craft. Another wave caught him sideways, capsizing the kayak and pushing them back toward shore and the hogs. The paddle fell out, but he managed to grab it before the next wave could take it. After jamming it into the bungee, he kicked and pushed the boat over the next wave.

Behind him, pigs raced out into the surf, grunting and gnashing their tusks. He looked at them as he tried to mount the kayak again. A few of the beasts charged into the water.

Grasping both gunwales, Gran Jefe scissor-kicked upward, at the same time hauling himself belly first up onto the boat. Then, with a gasp of pain, he flopped over onto his buttocks, with one leg sticking out. As the swells pushed him backward toward the clacking tusks, he fought to get the rest of himself aboard.

Gritting his teeth, he forced his leg into the boat. Then he pulled the paddle free of its bungee. He dug deep into the water. Stroke after stroke, he pulled away from the beach, not looking back until he got past the surf.

Chest heaving from exhaustion, Gran Jefe glanced over his shoulder.

A few of the pigs swam out, eventually giving up as the waves rolled them shoreward. They milled about on the beach, squealing and snorting.

He laughed between groans of pain, shocked to find himself still alive. He raised a fist to the beasts.

"That's right, *pendejos!*" he shouted. "Next time, I carve you into bacon!"

*   *   *   *   *

"Team Polar, do you copy?"

The crack of static electricity surged over the comms from

Commander Hallsey. *"Be advised, I'm detecting a massive storm front with whiteout conditions heading in your direction. You have two hours to complete the mission before you're stranded there."*

"Copy that, Commander," said the Forerunner's clipped robotic voice. *"We'll get it done one way or the other."*

X checked his mission clock. Over four hours had elapsed since they arrived at Polar Station. Things had gone south almost immediately, with Blue Blood torn in two and the Forerunner locked in combat with the spider-brain beast, or whatever the hell that thing was in the hallway. Noah, in his mech suit, had retreated to fight another day, following Watt, Slayer, and X into the facility's interior to regroup. After blasting their way through two more bone beast sentries, they had taken a stairwell to a laboratory three floors beneath the surface.

The team was hunkered down and waiting to make the next move. X held security with Slayer at the only door to the room, listening to the prowling. A rhythmic thumping drew closer. From the sound, X put the monster making this noise somewhere above them.

Looking through a pane in the door, he could see nothing in the hallway beyond the labs.

An explosion shook dust from the overhead—the charge Watt had set to cover their escape.

"Got another one," Slayer said.

Watt looked over from his work on the Forerunner. The cyborg was sitting down to give the knight access to his internal battery pack and parts. Watt had connected a portable charger and diagnostic machine to work on the mech suit. That first battle had played hell with his armor, ripping away an exterior plate. Claw marks streaked down his back and neck where hostiles had tried to rip into the battery.

"We'll move soon," said the Forerunner, his voice crackling.

"You still need to recharge," Watt said.

"I have enough power to complete this mission, and you heard Commander Hallsey—a bad storm is on the way."

"We could ride out the storm down here," X said. "Wait—"

"The longer we wait, the worse our chances of success."

"Okay, let me seal you back up, then," Watt said. He closed the armor plate over the internal battery pack. Then he replaced the bolts to secure the plate shut.

"You're good to go, sir," Watt said.

The Forerunner thanked Watt and thumped over to X and Slayer, standing guard at the door. He stopped and projected a hologram out of his visor showcasing a map of the facility.

"We're here, on subfloor C," said the Forerunner. "We need to head back up to the first floor and access the command center. But by now they will have it on lockdown, because they know why we're here."

"So what's the plan?" X asked.

"I'll take point, destroying security cameras and drawing the guardian hordes outside. We'll split up after that, but you won't be going directly to the command center—the enemy is too smart for that and will have their forces waiting."

Another hologram showed, this of a mechanical room directly below the command center.

"You three will hang back until it's clear, then head here," said the Forerunner.

"Wait. I don't remember seeing—" X started to say, but the cyborg cut him off.

"That's because it's not in the blueprints—a safeguard I discovered when scanning the facility upon arrival. I believe Watt will be able to hack into the reactors via the backup power inside and activate them from there."

"*Believe?*" Slayer asked.

"The machines know we're here, and they know why. Breaking into the command center is impossible. To defeat them, we must outsmart them."

"We've done it before," X said. "We'll do it again."

A distant female voice called out, and he looked to the door. Slayer had heard it, too.

"Who's that?" asked the Cazador.

"Help me," said the woman. "Please, someone, help me."

The Forerunner stopped and listened, along with Watt.

"We need help," said another female voice.

"Probably those faces trapped in the brain," X said. He realized how insane that sounded, but he had seen them topside. They were real.

X raised his rifle. "Ready?"

The Forerunner went to the door and was met by a face on the other side. X stared. This was a human woman. At least, she looked like one. Wet black hair hung over her shoulders. She had an innocent, youthful face. Brown eyes, a button nose, freckles. No scars, no wrinkles, no broken teeth. This was a woman who had never seen the outside of this facility.

The realization hit X—she had just awoken from one of the pods.

"Shit, it's one of those sleepers," Slayer said.

"Do not be deceived," said the Forerunner. "When I open this door, you will see more of these people, all of them begging you to help. But if they get close enough, they'll slash your throat, for they are controlled by the Cerebro."

"The *what*?" Slayer asked.

"That cyborg you saw," said the Forerunner. "It's a Cerebro model."

"You know what it is?" X said.

"Yes."

X had already suspected this, but hearing the Forerunner admit it confirmed everything.

"I still don't get something," he said. "I thought we shut all those bastards down."

"The DEF-Nine units were erased by your virus, but this machine is not only a machine. It is like me—part human, but more robotic. The Cerebro models found a way to survive, and my guess is, Team Concordia has met one of these abominations as well."

Outside the door, the woman put a hand on the glass, staring in at them.

"Please," she said.

The Forerunner lifted the locking lever. "You can't hesitate, not for an instant." He opened the door and snatched her by the neck, crushing it in a single bionic squeeze. Her body slumped to the floor as he strode ahead. A second woman, to her right, held up her palms as she retreated from the hulking Forerunner.

He swiped with a bladed arm, taking her head off in a clean stroke. Twin jets of blood pulsed up toward the ceiling, and the body fell on top of the other corpse. X stepped out of the labs and tried not to think too hard as he passed the two lifeless forms, but it was hard not to see them as human. The severed head rolled, then stopped with its face against a wall. A shiny black device with a short spike or antenna protruded from the wet hair.

"That's how they control them," said Watt.

He raised his rifle and went ahead as X and Slayer exchanged a glance.

On the team went, following its own cyborg. Another sleeper limped into the intersection, waving. It was a man—bald with blue eyes and a thin frame.

"Stop! I need help," he said. "I have to get out of this place!"

The Forerunner did exactly as he had commanded X and the

others. He did not hesitate. And that was a good thing because the man was holding behind his back something that he began to fling outward as the Forerunner's blade pierced his skull. With a fierce kick, the cyborg launched the man backward. Not a second later, the explosive device he had been holding blew him to confetti.

X turned slightly, but the Forerunner was closer, and his armor had received most of the blood and gore. He marched onward. They took the stairwell up, the temperature dropping with each step toward the surface floor.

Twenty degrees... eighteen degrees... fifteen degrees.

The carcasses of the bone beasts killed mere hours earlier were already frozen solid.

"Stay here," said the Forerunner.

The cyborg moved into the corridor. Immediately, the chain gun attached to his arm began to whine, the muzzle blaze strobing as the weapon unleashed hell on another bone beast. The thudding footfalls shook the floor under their feet as the creature charged with a horrific roar.

A well-placed grenade silenced the creature in a ringing explosion.

"Move!" the Forerunner commanded.

The team followed his mech suit out into the smoky passage littered with spent casings, some still rolling on the floor. In the remains of a bone beast twenty feet away, flames flickered up from the torso, licking at splintered limbs. At the end of the passage, snow had melted and refrozen.

"Watt, seal that exit," said the Forerunner.

The knight raised his rifle and fired a grenade that thumped into the open door, bringing down a section of ceiling. He loaded a second grenade and fired again. Rubble rained down, blocking the passage from outside. Apparently, they weren't going out the same way they came in.

"This way," said the Forerunner. He went left at the intersection, his chain gun still smoking. Every few steps, he fired into the ceiling, disabling the cameras and denying the view to the brain machine, which was no doubt watching their every move.

Ahead, the right side of the icy corridor had collapsed in an explosion that ripped through the walls. Metal panes and wall panels lay warped and torn, scattered about the passage, exposing pipes and electrical wires. The Forerunner pried back a piece of steel paneling as if it were cardboard. Then he lumbered onward, firing another burst from the chain gun. The whining echoed away, and a gruff male voice spoke.

"Hold your fire!"

A man in a parka bearing the Trident logo stood in the tunnel. For the first time on the mission, the Forerunner hesitated.

Holding up his hands, the man cautiously stepped out from the tunnel.

"I never thought I'd see anyone again," he said in a shaky voice. "Are you really with the Trident?"

"Who are you?" demanded the Forerunner.

X moved for a better look. Unlike the other people they had encountered, this man was old, with a gray beard and white hair protruding from under a stocking cap.

"Sergeant Archie Lium, with the Trident Second Brigade," he said. "I didn't think anyone would ever come—thought I had been abandoned forever."

"He's with the old base camp," Watt whispered.

X narrowed his gaze, still not believing that this guy could have survived out here for thirty years. Hell, ten years on the surface with Miles had almost been too much for X.

The Forerunner lowered his chain gun, and the man waved them into the shadows of a snowy tunnel that had to lead outside. Wind howled through the passage. Archie moved away, but just then X saw four holes in the back of his coat, each surrounded by a burn mark. His flashlight illuminated the bottom of a black device protruding from under his stocking cap.

"He's one of 'em!" X yelled.

The Forerunner raised his arm and switched to the flame-thrower attachment. "I'm sorry," he boomed.

"No, don't!" Archie cried.

He held up his arms, shielding his face as the cyborg loosed a rope of fire, torching Archie where he stood. The man shrieked and flailed inside the snowy cavern, his burning body slamming into the frozen walls.

The Forerunner stepped back and motioned for Watt, who went inside the tunnel. Archie made a few more dervish twirls before collapsing to the snow. The flames consuming his body illuminated the end of the passage. X could see outside, where a light snow fell, adding to the pile that rose nearly to the ceiling.

"Let's put this poor bastard out—hurry," Watt said. He scooped up a double armful of snow and dumped it with a loud hiss onto the burning corpse that lay crackling on the ice. Slayer held security while X joined in, kicking powder over the melted face.

As X went to kick more snow, the skull began to shake. The melted stocking cap suddenly ripped back, and a bot the size of a cricket skittered out of the scorched hair.

X snatched it off the ground with his prosthetic arm. The machine squirmed in his grip as he studied it. It seemed to study him back.

"What the hell is it?" Slayer asked.

"A mini Cerebro, or some bloody shit," Watt said.

X crushed it in his hand and tossed it onto the snow by the corpse.

"So that guy was real?" Slayer asked.

Watt looked to Archie. "Yeah, he must have been taken

captive during the expedition and kept here just in case we ever ret—"

The roar of a bone beast floated through the facility, forcing them all down. Vibrations rippled under their feet as the monster charged nearby.

"We need cover," X said. He went to the snow mound at the end of the tunnel. They clambered up to the top, into the wind. Two of the reactors loomed in the distance, silhouetted by the intermittent lightning from the approaching storm front. A wall of angry clouds marched across the horizon, toward the base.

X went prone at the crest of the snow mound, peering back into the corridor that the Forerunner had left them inside. The thuds from the hunting beast echoed closer until it seemed right on top of them.

X hugged the snow as a bone beast lumbered into the main passage beyond the icy tunnel. It wasn't alone. Two more stalked after the Forerunner. As their growls dimmed, a far more menacing sound replaced them: the metallic skittering of robotic legs.

Sheet-metal ducts crashed down into the main hallway.

Keeping his helmet low, X stared as the robotic spider lowered its mechanical frame from the collapsed overhead. The curved head turned as the metal shielding lifted over the cracked glass dome. Inside, the human faces trapped in the lump of gray matter looked upon what had been Archie. Those faces contorted as they whispered in an incoherent chorus. The alloy shield went back over the glass dome, silencing the poor souls trapped therein.

X slowly pulled back, unafraid to admit he was piss-your-pants scared. Never in his life had he seen a monstrosity like this—something so diabolical and at the same time so bizarre that it seemed more fantasy than real.

Watt tugged X's shin guard to get his attention, and X slid

down next to them. The knight and Slayer were at the bottom of the snowdrift with their weapons raised.

Gunfire cracked in the distance, followed by a series of three explosions. In the respite, the metallic legs clambered away.

Watt waited a few beats, then motioned for them to climb back up on top of the snow pile. They lay there, listening to the distant battle.

"Okay," he said. "Our turn now."

TWENTY

The *Frog* cut through the tumultuous seas under a violent storm. Rain slanted through the barred windows of the shipping container that imprisoned Magnolia, Imulah, and Pedro. Magnolia stood gripping the bars, looking out at the horizon. The ship was finally starting to move again after a long delay spent combing the crash site of the Jayhawk for Gran Jefe's remains. The knights had located pieces of floating, charred debris, but Magnolia had not seen them bring any human remains on board.

"You think we're going home now?" Imulah asked.

"Maybe," Magnolia said. She wasn't sure what would happen to them at this point. She sat back down on the deck, beside Pedro. He cupped his hands under his swollen cheek to make a pillow.

"How are you feeling?" she asked.

"I'll be fine," he said. "You?"

She shrugged. She didn't feel much of anything. Only a deep numbness—perhaps her body trying to hold back the dread from creeping in.

The latch clicked, and the door on the left swung backward. General Jack stepped up to look inside their cage.

"You're all very lucky," he said. "Your great warrior is fish food now."

"You found his body?" Magnolia asked.

"No, but we found pieces of the helicopter. No one could go through that and live to tell the tale."

Magnolia, too, had underestimated Gran Jefe before, but this was different. She hated to admit it, but she agreed with the general.

"So what happens now?" Imulah asked.

Jack walked up to the bars of the cage inside the container.

"You will return to your home and begin your service as a delegate to a Trident-run body," he said.

Magnolia could read between the lines. He wanted Imulah to be a puppet liaison between their peoples, but the knights would be in charge.

The general looked to Magnolia.

"You will be given a chance to swear allegiance to the Trident," he said. "You will do this, or you will remain here, caged like the animal I believe you to be."

He slammed the door and walked away.

"Pile of rancid Siren shit!" she growled.

Imulah put a gentle hand on her back. The hand bore a scar where Magnolia stabbed him long ago.

"You must control your anger and hold on to hope," he said. "Hope that Xavier and the others will return victorious from these missions."

She went to the bars to look outside. A pair of knights patrolled the deck around the two containers. Even now, when all resistance seemed impossible, she watched the enemy's movements. It was her way of dealing with things. Just as Imulah's way was to hope for the best, hers was to plan for the worst.

Pedro groaned next to her. He, too, shared that fighting spirit.

"What do you think?" he asked. "About swearing allegiance?"

"I think it's a nice way of turning us into slaves, and if we say no, we'll end up like Gran Jefe."

"I agree. So what do we do?"

"We wait to see what happens at the poles. In the meantime, we all need to rest up for whatever comes next."

Pedro nodded and went back to the deck. Magnolia was tired too, and she decided to join him. They sat huddled together for warmth with Imulah, hands tucked under their arms. It calmed her enough that she could at last close her eyes.

When she awoke, it was to voices calling out on the deck. Sunlight blasted in through the bars. Pedro was already standing there.

"We're back at the islands," he said.

Imulah stirred awake. He got up with Magnolia and joined Pedro at the bars for a glimpse of a distant oil rig. From the spinning wind turbines, she knew at once that this was the engineering rig. That meant they were east of the capitol tower. This was one of the most distant rigs.

"Over there," Pedro said. He stepped back to give Magnolia a better view. She immediately saw what had animated him so. Two large ships sailed on the horizon. Dozens of much smaller ships and boats followed the mammoth vessels in a ragtag flotilla.

"Those must be the refugees," she said.

Magnolia had almost forgotten about the two main ships that the Cazador scouts had reported coming through the Panama Canal. The knights had waited until Gran Jefe was confirmed dead before moving this flotilla into view of Cazadores and sky people. Now they had arrived, bringing thousands of their people from the Coral Castle.

The *Frog* chugged past the engineering rig on an intercept course with the two retrofitted cruise vessels. The gigantic ships towered over the sea, rising up with level after level of individual quarters. Magnolia had seen plenty of these in ports over the years, but one on the open water was a sight to behold.

She spotted tiny human figures on the upper decks, along railings, and behind open windows. It occurred to her that this was the first time in their lives any of them had ever seen the sun. And that made them all the more dangerous.

The sunshine was a precious resource that drove humans to kill.

As they came closer, she got her first look at these new faces. Men, women, children. The elderly. Families with parents holding excited children. All of them staring in awe.

Rising in the center of the bow, a giant metal trident shimmered in the sunlight, perhaps for the first time since it was welded together. Above it, a crew stood behind the clean windows of the bridge, all of them looking ahead at their new dominion.

The *Frog* turned, giving Magnolia a view of the second vessel. Uniformed sailors stood on balconies looking out over the water. Shouting echoed down, answered by the unmistakable barking of dogs. Magnolia looked to the aft section, where cages of animals stood on the open deck. Three dogs came into view, and a pen full of sheep. In the next, she saw the pink, fat bellies of pigs. After that, a large shed with a wire mesh front contained a hundred chickens. There were more pens after that, holding goats, cows, some sort of large bird, and even horses.

It was like the ark that Magnolia remembered reading about in the ancient biblical text. There had to be thousands of animals on that deck.

"They brought everything with them," Imulah whispered.

"Amazing," Pedro whispered.

The *Frog* pulled ahead of both ships, leading the way to the rigs. Patrol boats motored over in front of them. The Cazador speedboats were all crewed by knights now. Magnolia counted six of the craft thumping over the waves. They spread out, forming a wide phalanx around the Trident flotilla. On the horizon, their destination came into focus—the capitol tower.

"I must say," Imulah whispered, "I'm having déjà vu from when your people first arrived in the sky."

Magnolia had to agree. History was indeed repeating itself. The question was whether the knights really planned on trying to live here in peace with the Cazadores and other surviving populations like Pedro's, from around the world.

But now more than ever Magnolia realized, there was no fighting these people. Imulah was right. The only hope was that X would return victorious. If he did, and the Forerunner came through on his promise to allow X to search for Michael and his family, then Magnolia would go with him. She was done with this place—done trying to protect it, done fighting for it, done with life here. Too many bad memories, many of which flooded her mind as the capitol rig drew nearer. She dreaded the idea of going back to the apartment that she had made into a home with Rodger.

The *chop, chop* of rotors distracted her from her thoughts. A Jayhawk flew overhead, turned, and circled in the sky. As it passed, Magnolia saw two people in the cockpit, both wearing sailor outfits from the cruise ship. That appeared to be the helicopter's destination. It lowered over the vessel, touching down on the deck.

There was noise outside the container doors. The three prisoners stepped back from the bars as the locking mechanism flipped. General Jack opened the door and motioned for Magnolia and Imulah.

"You two come with me," he said.

"Where are you taking us?" Imulah asked.

The general didn't answer, and Magnolia stepped out into the sunlight, shielding her eyes from the glare.

"Get the other prisoners ready for transport," Jack said.

"Wait. You said if they swear allegiance you'd—" Magnolia began to say.

"I said if *you* and *the old man* do."

Magnolia grabbed the barred door.

"You got your man," she said. "The threat to your people is over. You can let the prisoners go as a sign of goodwill."

Jack snickered. "Jorge Mata killed five of my own after the truce. That's three more of ours than yours…" He watched as two knights went to grab Pedro out of the shipping container. "You lived under the law of the barbarians, so you should be familiar with our own law: eye-for-an-eye justice."

*   *   *   *   *

A framed picture stood on the little nightstand bedside of the bunk where Kade sat in the single living quarters. He picked up the frame and brushed off the dust to reveal a smiling family of four. The man was in his forties, balding and wearing glasses. Beside him was a woman, presumably his wife, giving the camera a toothy grin. They both had their hands on the shoulders of two boys in front of them.

The smiles told Kade they had once lived a happy life before the war.

With a shaky hand, he put the picture back down and wrapped his arms around his torn suit. He shivered violently, more from what had happened than from the cold. Tia was gone and not coming back. He had made sure of that. Nobu and Zen were dead, too. It was just him and Lucky now, the entire mission riding on them. They had fled the labs and found refuge in the living quarters for the scientists once stationed here.

Footsteps clicked toward the open doorway, and Kade picked up the pistol he called Monster Hunter, which Lucky had recovered and given him after they escaped the cryo-chamber. The knight returned with Zen's sniper rifle slung over his back, and a parka draped over one arm.

"Zipper's broken, but it'll keep you warm," he said. "I found some lab gloves, goggles, and a few lab coats you can double up on for extra layers. Oh, and some tape to hold everything together."

He tossed the clothing onto the bed.

"Get dressed. We move out soon."

"So we're leaving? Just like that?" Kade asked, teeth chattering.

"Temporarily, yes. The radio is brokedick, so we have no choice but to head back to the DZ if we want to transmit an SOS to the *Trident*. Then we'll hunker down and wait for reinforcements."

Lucky motioned for him to hurry.

Kade stared for a moment, then started putting on the layers—lab coats over his suit, then gloves, and finally the parka. He used a roll of industrial tape to seal it over his chest. Throwing up the furry hood over his head, he tightened it, covering most of his face. The goggles went on next. It was a good start, but he wasn't sure it would be enough.

He picked up a third lab coat, ripped off an arm, and wrapped it around his exposed face, leaving only the eyes exposed, then taped the sides to keep them secure. Finished, he shoved the Monster Hunter into a roomy coat pocket and stepped out into the communal space of couches, tables, and desks. Across the room, Lucky waited by the fire escape.

"You look like a mummy." He chuckled. "Better than an icicle, I guess."

"Either's fine with me, but I'd prefer dying here and trying to finish our mission."

"We're heading back to the city at the DZ because that's where our gear is, and my transmitter's toast."

Kade felt a weird tingle in his chest. He raised a brow, paranoia setting in. Was Lucky one of them now too? Did he have a mechanical device in the back of his head like Tia's?

Kade replayed the events back in the cryo-chamber when Zen had shown up with Tia, and then Lucky appeared a few minutes later. It didn't seem right.

"The enemy was already there, Lucky. That's how they got Tia. Why would we go back there?"

"I told you—"

"For a radio? Why not just try and finish the mission?"

Lucky faced Kade. "How the fuck can we finish this mission?"

Kade stiffened and gripped the pistol in his pocket.

"We don't have enough ammunition to fight even if we did stand a one percent chance of turning on those reactors."

Kade had never seen Lucky give up before. The knight had done everything in his power to fight and survive since the day they met on the Sunshine Coast. This wasn't like him at all.

"You will follow my orders," Lucky said.

In a swift movement, Kade had the Monster Hunter out and the barrel shoved under Lucky's chin.

"What the hell!" Lucky cried.

"Take your helmet off."

"You kiddin' me, mate? After all we've been through?"

"Helmet. Off."

"Okay, okay, calm the fuck down," Lucky said. He reached up and twisted his helmet loose, then popped it off, glaring with rage.

"Turn around," Kade said. He backed away and kept the gun pointed as Lucky turned to show the back of his head. Reaching out with his other hand, Kade felt his hair but found nothing unusual.

"Feel like an asshole yet?" Lucky asked.

"Had to be sure," Kade said.

Lucky snapped his helmet back on just as glass shattered. Then came crunching footfalls accompanied by a guttural growling. The noise sounded like a giant, enraged canine.

"What is that?" Lucky asked.

Kade shook his head and raised the Monster Hunter.

Lucky waited a moment until the noise died away, then motioned for Kade to follow him into a stairwell. Once they were inside, Lucky gently shut the door and secured it. Then he quietly went down the steps.

The next floor down, a tremendous noise shattered the silence. The walls of the stairwell shivered from the impact of the creature bashing through the walls of the labs they had left behind.

Kade loped down the stairs behind Lucky. When they reached the landing, the creature slammed into the reinforced lab door with an echoing thud that seemed to buckle it. The next impact broke it down in a loud crash, freeing the monster and letting in a new sound of slopping wet feet or paws.

But how was that possible?

Kade thought back to the labs they had discovered earlier in the mission. Labs full of carcasses. Experiments gone wrong. This creature, whatever it was, must have been a lab experiment that didn't die—something that had been waiting all this time to be unleashed on any threat to the station.

"Run!" Lucky yelled.

Kade sprinted after him down to the subfloor they had used

to enter the facility. The hacked door was still open, allowing them to climb down into the ventilation tunnel. But they didn't have any explosives to cover their trail this time, or anything besides bullets to slow this thing down.

The knight ran into the tunnel, toward the first fan. They picked their way between the blades and were on the other side when the monster burst into the passage behind them.

Lucky swung up his rifle, and the light captured a seven-foot-tall creature that looked part bone beast, part something else—clearly some sort of lab experiment. Bony armor stretched around the torso, studded with spikes and clad in patches of white fur.

In other places along the neck and face, patches of mottled green-and-brown flesh were covered in an oily sheen. A bulbous red eye gleamed, unblinking in the light. Set higher in the skull, under a patch of fur, was a terribly bloodshot second orb. Below both eyes, a glistening pink snout sniffed the air.

The jaw opened, rimmed with bony spikes. It opened wider, the cavernous throat bulging outward and... *hurling projectiles?* In what felt like slow motion, Kade saw long, slender teeth whizzing through the air.

He fired at the same moment, the Monster Hunter bucking with the recoil. The bullet smashed into bony armor, shattering chunks. In an instant, the beast squatted down, and the muscular back legs sprang, launching the creature toward Kade and Lucky.

Lucky fired a .50-caliber round directly into its chest, throwing it off kilter. The creature smashed into a wall, cracking the concrete with the impact.

"Go," Lucky said as he chambered another round.

Kade ran while the knight laid down covering fire. A roar of agony answered, and he looked over his shoulder to see the beast reaching up with a tentative paw for the pink snout that Lucky had blown off with his second shot. The creature roared again, so loud that it hurt Kade's ears. Then it turned and lumbered into the stairwell. The strategic retreat suggested a much higher intelligence than in some of the other monsters Kade had encountered in the wastes.

He ran past the teeth, like little polished ivory spears in the wall and door. Lucky followed him, ducking and bending between the blades of the second fan. Already, Kade could feel the temperature dropping.

Both men arrived at the pile of snow under the vertical shaft they had used to access the tunnel. Lucky went up the ladder to the surface, where he propped the grate open. The wind hissed, swirling snowflakes inside. He scanned in all directions, nodded.

"Looks clear."

Kade checked the corridor one last time, but the creature remained out of view. He climbed up the rungs to Lucky, who had knelt to scope the terrain with binos. As soon as Kade poked his head out the top, the cold bit into him, like an icy arrow piercing his layers. He sucked in a frozen breath that stung his throat and lungs.

"Get the snowshoes," Lucky said.

As Kade started digging out their equipment, he heard growling. This wasn't coming from the tunnel shaft. It was up here, on the surface. He turned east, peering through the gusting snow.

"You got eyes on it?" Kade asked.

"Negative."

Kade slid him a pair of snowshoes. "Put yours on first. I'll cover us," he said.

Fumbling in the darkness, Kade slipped in his boots. "I can't see shit, man."

"I got you. Just hold on."

After Lucky finished putting on his snowshoes, he unslung

the rifle and handed it to Kade. As soon as Kade put on his own snowshoes, they set off, stomping over the fresh powder. But with every step, the cold sank through Kade's many layers. Not even ten minutes in, his face felt numb under the ripped lab coat.

Every few minutes, Lucky turned to scope their six, making sure they weren't being stalked. Kade checked, unable to see much of anything. He couldn't help but feel like fish bait on a line, waiting to be plucked away.

He trudged on, determined to stay alive and see the mission through. Switching hands on the sling helped him keep them warm by sticking the free one into the coat pocket. He wiggled his toes to keep the blood flowing.

All that effort kept him distracted, and before he knew it, they were pounding up the slope to the ice cliff, where they had left some of their climbing gear. The snowmobiles and remaining gear would be down the other side.

"You good, Kade?" Lucky asked.

"Yeah, I'll make it."

A guttural howl crossed the icy expanse they had crossed. Lucky swung up his rifle and aimed into the storm as Kade searched the darkness for movement.

"You go first," Lucky said. "I'll cover us."

Kade took off his snowshoes and tossed them over the side of the glacier. Then he found the rope anchored to the ice with three screws. He tugged on it to make sure it was secure, then attached the rappel device that would help him control his speed of descent. And back down he went, over the ice cliff they had climbed up.

Halfway down, a gunshot echoed above. Kade craned his neck back at the top of the glacier. Lucky screamed something lost in the wind. He tried to shout again, but his words were drowned out by roaring.

Kade stopped the rappel and reached into his pocket to draw his pistol.

"Lucky!" he shouted.

Chunks of ice plummeted down, smashing on the surface below. Kade aimed up into the darkness. Silhouettes moved back and forth, but he couldn't distinguish friend from foe.

Another gunshot blasted above, followed by a third, and a fourth. These were not from the rifle. Kade saw the faint light of a muzzle flash. A yelp of agony rang out above.

Something big cartwheeled over the side, flailing as it fell. Holding in a breath, Kade looked down as it thudded into the ice below, but he still couldn't see.

He loosened his grip on the rappel device, sliding down all the way to the surface. His boots crunched on the frozen snow. Pulling out his flashlight, he raised it with his pistol and sighed with relief. This wasn't Lucky but the giant bone beast lab experiment. Blood bubbled from its mouth as it struggled to breathe. Under the bony exoskeleton, the throat bulged and receded like a beating heart. A bloodshot eye flitted to Kade.

Air hissed out of its mouth as it reached up with a furry paw covered in blood. Kade took a step back, then realized that the beast didn't seem to want to hurt him. It was like a dying soldier asking for mercy.

Kade obliged, aiming his pistol at the white furry patch above the eye and pulling the trigger. The paw dropped to the snow.

Hearing noise behind him, Kade turned as Lucky rappelled down, one hand clutching his side. He fell to the snow as soon as he touched down. Kade rushed over to find three of the thin, finger-length ivory daggers protruding from his side. Blood had frozen on his armor.

"It got me," Lucky moaned.

Kade bent down to look.

"Med kit on snow… mobile," Lucky grunted. "Get… pliers."

Kade helped Lucky over to the closest of the half-buried snow machines. Lucky took a seat, crying out in pain.

"Hold on," Kade said. He located the med kit and got out the pliers, which he could hardly feel in his wooden hands. Then he carefully grasped the first needle.

"Ready?" he asked.

Lucky nodded.

Gripping the end, Kade yanked on it, but the spike came out only halfway. Lucky slid off the snowmobile, screaming in agony.

"You have to hold still," Kade said. Holding the pliers in his shivering hand, he gripped the pale, almost translucent spine again and pulled harder. The three-inch tooth came out.

Lucky collapsed on the snow, unconscious. Kade used the opportunity to get the man up and onto the snowmobile, securing him there. Then he went back to the medical kit, pulling out a bandage to cover the wound. With that on, Kade went to work plucking out the second needle while Lucky was still out.

On the third needle, the knight stirred and groaned. That was good. Kade needed him awake.

Kade got onto the snowmobile and gave him a little shake. "Lucky, you have to tell me where to go," he said.

Lucky leaned forward against him, groaning.

"Gaz, come on, man!" Kade shouted. "Which way is the DZ?"

Lucky lifted a finger and pointed away from the ice wall, to the west. Kade twisted the throttle, hoping it was the right direction. If he was off even three degrees, they would both soon be icicles.

TWENTY-ONE

The muffled chorus of screams from the human heads trapped in the robotic brain filled the hallway. Thudding blows from the Forerunner's fight shook the ceiling and walls. From what X could tell, the battle was happening somewhere above where he now stood with Slayer.

Watt motioned them to proceed down the dark passage. They moved in combat intervals with Watt on point, Slayer on rear guard, and X pointing his rifle at the high ceiling to make sure nothing surprised them from above.

At the next junction, Watt held up a fist. X and Slayer were to stay put while he went around the corner to check a wall with his handheld scanner. He pocketed the device and hurried back.

"I think this is it," he whispered. "Cover me."

They held security while Watt went back to the wall. But as the map on their HUDs had indicated, there was no visible door. Watt began placing the explosives on the wall. Now X understood. They were going to *make* a door.

"Okay, soon as I blow this, we'll have limited time to activate the reactors," Watt said. "Get ready to fight, and hold them back as long as you can for me."

X and Slayer both nodded and checked their weapons.

Watt pulled out a remote. "Ready?"

Two more nods.

"Three, two, one," he said.

The charges went off, sending plumes of fire and debris around the bend. Before they dissipated, Watt was already moving and disappeared into the cloud. X and Slayer darted after him, through the gaping rent in the wall. Sure enough, they were in a room that wasn't marked on any map. It was filled with racks of electronic equipment.

The knight went over to a bank of hardware towers and hooked up a tablet. The screen warmed to life. X shouldered his rifle, his heart pounding. He could feel the ground trembling with the advance of unseen hostiles. The distant whine of the chain gun came to life, followed by two vibrations from grenade explosions. It sounded like a pitched battle above them.

"That metal . . . thing—it's coming here, isn't it?" Slayer asked.

"Oh yeah," X said.

He had never known Slayer to be nervous, but X wasn't afraid to admit that he was, too. Part of it was the anticipation of the fight. Waiting, when you knew what was barreling toward you, could wreck the nerves of the most hardened warrior.

But it went beyond the fear of pain and death. There were far worse things down here. X didn't want to end up like Archie—a prisoner of these monsters.

"Okay, I've accessed the system," Watt said. "It's going to take three, maybe four minutes to exert control and activate the reactors."

X stood in the smoldering doorway, listening to the thump of monstrous feet stamping closer and closer. He knew that sound: a bone beast.

"Stay here with Watt," he said to Slayer. "I'm taking this fucker out."

X took off down the corridor, keeping to the right side. He knelt behind a protruding metal soffit twenty feet from the next junction.

The thumping was closer now.

Boom… Boom… Boom…

A faint red-orange glow emerged at the end of the passage. Red eyes glowed like embers through the smoke. X fired his grenade launcher down the hall. The blast went off behind the beast, knocking it to the ground. X fired a burst of bullets into the head, breaking off chunks of skull as the beast reached over its shoulder and pulled out a javelin of bone. When it cocked its arm to throw, X sighted up the hideous bone-encaged face and fired. The creature hurled the javelin into the metal panel beside X, where it stuck.

He pumped in another grenade and fired again. The projectile hit the charging beast and detonated, shattering bones and tearing into flesh. Shrapnel pinged off X's armored suit. As the boom faded away, Watt's voice came on the comms.

"Two minutes," he said.

X looked back in shock as the creature tried to prop itself up on one mangled arm. Half the bony face had been blown off, including both eyes. It sniffed the smoky air with a bleeding snout.

Striding forward, X slung his rifle, drew his blaster, and jammed the barrels inside a nostril. The weapon recoiled from the shot. So did the head of the monster. Brain matter flew out the back of the skull.

X ejected the spent shells and reloaded both barrels. The

hair on the back of his neck rose from a sudden static charge. He whirled just as, halfway down the passage, the ceiling collapsed.

Down dropped the robotic monstrosity, right outside the still-glowing doorway Watt had blown into the wall. X swapped the blaster for his rifle, flipped the selector to semiauto, and started firing shots at the domed head. From inside the room, Slayer pumped bullets into the armored torso.

The creature thrust a leg through the door, then pulled it back as X fired another burst into the dome.

"Over here!" he shouted.

The torso rotated toward him. It aimed the pair of tubular arms at X and blasted out long, sizzling white ropes. He dived out of the way as something big and heavy came stomping up behind him.

Screams of agony echoed from the room Watt and Slayer were inside. X grabbed his rifle and scrambled to his feet, expecting to find another bone beast flanking him. But instead, he saw the charred and battered mech armor of the Forerunner striding down the passageway.

"Down!" the Forerunner barked.

X dropped back down as the chain gun spun to life, spewing bullets into the dented side of the Cerebro as it tried to pry apart the blown-open wall and get inside. It roared, skittering away with surprising speed. The Forerunner launched a grenade that zipped down the corridor and exploded directly behind the machine.

As X squeezed through the rent in the wall, Slayer wailed in pain, trying to pull off the metal shin guards that were wrapped up in the cable hissing through his armor.

Watt, too, squirmed on the ground, in obvious pain with a cable stuck to his chest. Smoke rose from under the armor plate.

The Forerunner reached down with robotic fingers and ripped the thick fibers away.

"Help them, Xavier, and get those reactors activated," he said. "I'll finish the Cerebro."

He thudded away, a section of his armor dangling loose on his back.

X went into the room to Slayer, who waved him off. "I'm fine," he said. "Help Watt."

The knight was trying to remove his chest plate now. The tablet he had used to hack into the computer equipment had come disconnected, the countdown paused.

"Shit," X grumbled. He bent down with his combat knife and wedged the armor plate away from Watt. Underneath, tendrils of the strange white fibrous material burned his flesh. X sawed the strands away, pulling skin and muscle with them.

Watt howled, then slumped to his side, eyes rolling up into his skull.

"Stay with me," X said. He shook Watt. "Stay with me, man. I need to know what to do."

Watt's head shifted from side to side.

X glanced back to Slayer, who had removed a shin guard and was wrapping the burned flesh beneath with bandages from an open med kit.

"Throw me the adrenaline," X said.

Slayer dug through the pack, then tossed a syringe to X. He pulled off the cap and looked for a gap in the armor to inject Watt. The best place seemed to be his exposed chest.

X clenched his jaw and punched the needle in.

Watt heaved a deep breath. His wide eyes flitted to X.

"Listen to me, Watt—you have to finish this job," X said. "Slayer will stay with you. I'll watch our backs. Okay?"

Watt managed a wincing nod. Slayer slid the med kit over as

X moved back to the hallway. He stepped into the smoky passage, loading his second-to-last grenade into the launcher. Then he ejected the magazine—all but two rounds spent. Pulling out a fresh mag, he palmed it in and charged the handle.

The bullets and even the grenades seemed to have little effect on the tank of a machine. Like shooting BBs at a bull. Maybe the Forerunner would have better luck out there when he tracked it down again.

"Bloody damned piece of shit," Watt muttered.

"What?" X called back.

"Having a hard time connecting back to the system. I need more time."

As the seconds ticked by, X tensed, knowing how close they were to completing this mission. Then again, Noah and his wife had been this close sixty-one years ago. He tried not to think about the fact that there was still another pole location to be activated, where Team Concordia had likely failed.

A damage warning on his HUD caught his attention. This wasn't for Slayer or Watt; it was the Forerunner. The cyborg had taken significant damage to his mech suit in the battle with the Cerebro.

X looked from his HUD to the left and right of the hallway. From what he could tell, the Forerunner had knocked out most of the monsters dwelling in the icy darkness of the facility.

"Okay, I'm back in," Watt said in a pained but excited tone. "Three minutes to launch."

There was no response from the Forerunner on the comms, but X could hear over the fighting. Tremors rattled the floor and overhead, and ice spicules sifted down from the ceiling. It sounded as though the two behemoths were slamming through walls.

"Slayer, you good?" X asked.

Slayer limped over. "Yeah, I'm good."

"The Forerunner needs help. You protect Watt and then get the hell out of here. Meet us topside."

X patted him on the shoulder pad, and Slayer nodded back.

Slipping into the hall, X followed the sounds of the furious battle. The noise took him back the way they had come. He took a right around a corner, halting when he saw a new warning on his HUD for the Forerunner: *System compromised.*

"Shit. Hold on, Noah, I've got you!" X said. He took off, no longer concerned with stealth. Clutching his rifle, he ran as fast as he could. At the next corner, he slipped on a patch of ice and hit the floor.

Head spinning, he realized he no longer heard fighting. On his HUD, the same *Compromised* warning flashed about the Forerunner. But there was a new warning too: *Battery level critical. Systems shutting down.*

"Noah," X whispered over a private comm channel. *"Noah, can you hear me?"*

A raspy robotic breath hissed back.

X shouldered his rifle and slowly approached the next junction, where the beacon for the Forerunner read *Idle.* But if the fight was over and the cyborg was down, then where was the Cerebro?

Halting, X listened for the mechanical abomination. He checked his clock and saw that a minute had passed since he left Watt and Slayer. At least two more minutes remained before the launch. That was the main priority. He couldn't leave them defenseless. And he knew that the Forerunner would also go back for them, even if it meant his own death.

Immortality is a curse, X remembered Noah saying.

Conflicted, he started back. He heard the faint but distinct scratching of metal. There was also a whirring sound.

Inching back up to the corner with his rifle, X held in a breath and moved around the side. He scanned the shadows with his infrared scope and got zero hits.

"Slayer, come in," X whispered.

"Copy. Watt says we got two minutes left before activation."

"Understood."

In a defensive crouch, X moved forward, finger against the trigger guard. To his right, maybe fifteen feet away, was the blown-out wall that connected to the tunnel where they had encountered Archie. If X was reading the location of the beacon correctly, the Forerunner was inside that frozen corridor.

In his robotic hand, X raised the assault rifle. The other hand held his blaster. With each step he took toward the noise, he thought of the reasons he was here: Michael, Layla, Bray, Miles, Valeria, all the people back at the islands, and all the unknown survivors throughout the world. People who clung to life in the hope that someday the world would come back and they could live in the sun with their families.

X clenched his jaw, determined to finish off this evil. He knew damned well that if the Forerunner had failed to defeat it, his chances were small, but he was prepared to give his life.

He heard gasping from the icy corridor where the Forerunner had killed Archie. The whirring noise was joined by a loud grinding. X sneaked a glance around the edge but saw nothing.

You got this, X. You got this...

Stepping into the tunnel, he fired a flare from his blaster. A red star streaked over the remains of Archie and thumped into the snow at the end of the tunnel. The brightening glow captured the Forerunner, lying prone in the snow with the huge spider straddling his mech suit. Within a second of firing the flare, X spotted the drill the monster had deployed to penetrate the Forerunner's helmet. His synthetic voice hissed over the channel.

"Kill it, Xavier." Gasp. "Don't hesitate."

The robotic beast fired a cable at X. He ducked, and it simmered into the wall. X returned fire with his second-to-last grenade. The round hit the ceiling above the cyborg, blowing the beast off and into the pile of snow. Debris fell, leaving a poof of steam and smoke.

Warnings flashed across X's HUD, but he ignored everything and raced after the machine as it clambered out into the snowstorm. With less than two minutes until launch, he had to keep it away from Watt and Slayer.

The Forerunner moved slightly as X jumped over his partially buried suit. X loped up the snow mound and hunkered down at the top, shouldering his rifle to search for the escaped monster. A heat signature showed fifty feet out—the quick-moving Cerebro skittering back toward the facility.

Lining up his sights and leading the machine slightly, he fired a burst. Then he slid down the other side of the snowbank and sank into fresh powder up to his knees. Struggling, he tried to give chase, but there was no way he would catch it.

"Fight me, you fucking coward!" X shouted.

He raised the barrel of his rifle at another entry point the Cerebro seemed to be heading toward about two hundred feet away. It would be a long shot, and X had only one grenade left.

Don't hesitate . . . he thought.

The grenade thumped into the air and sailed right into the opening. A blast bloomed outward, into the flailing monstrosity as it lashed out with bladed limbs. The domed head twisted toward him, letting out a synthetic roar of anger.

"That got your attention, didn't it, you ugly fuck?" X said. "How about this?"

He aimed at the dome and fired, the bullets pinging off and leaving only dents. The monster seemed to hesitate, as if it were weighing a decision. Then it came barreling toward him. He held the trigger down, emptying the rest of his magazine with no effect whatever.

"Oh, son of…" X switched to his blaster and stood his ground. "Slayer, Watt, how much longer?" he asked over the comm.

Neither answered.

X looked at his HUD for their beacons, and his heart sank. They were offline. Something else had gotten them—something he had missed.

The Cerebro shambled toward him. At this pace, it would slash him down and get back inside the facility to slaughter Watt and Slayer with time to spare before the launch. The team had never stood any real chance of activating the reactors after all, X realized.

He took a step backward and raised his blaster, knowing that the buckshot might as well be spitballs. If he could slow it down, maybe, just *maybe*, there would be enough time. He just needed seconds. *Seconds!*

X screamed and fired the blaster as the machine lunged outward. In a spray of sparks, the shot knocked off a bladed limb.

"Get down!"

The synthetic voice crackled behind X.

He dived to the snow and looked up. There stood the Forerunner outside the snow pile, missing part of his arm and the grenade launcher. His entire suit had deep gashes and scorch marks. He raised the arm with the chain gun, strafing the overhead with bullets as he crawled to safety.

"Finish the launch, Xavier," said the cyborg.

X got up from the powder and scrambled on all fours up the pile of snow. At the crest, a clashing of metal drew his eyes to the battle. The Forerunner and the Cerebro circled warily. A leg slashed down the Forerunner's chest, showering sparks onto the snow. He parried the next blow with his telescoping blade, striking the domed head.

"Get him, Noah," X said as he skidded down the snow. He raced down the tunnel to the main corridor. From there, he took off for his comrades with his blaster out. As he approached the opening Watt had blown into the wall, X heard raspy breathing. Unsure whether it was human or monster, he slowed his gait.

Blaster up, he moved around the corner to find a downed bone beast, still breathing. X finished it off with a double-aught round to an eyeball. As he stepped over it, he found Slayer, pinned under the dead behemoth.

"He... he stopped it," said a voice.

X looked across the room to Watt, shivering in front of the computer towers, a tablet still in his hand. A clock on the screen ticked from thirty seconds. On the ground was his chest armor, burned by the cable. Now X understood why his beacon was offline. Slayer, however, was indeed gone, his body crushed beyond repair. There was no time for grieving now.

X went over to Watt and helped him up.

A violent tremor shook the facility. Before it stopped, a series of smaller blasts echoed, along with the crack of heavy machine guns, and a high electric whirring.

"Prepare for evac," said a female voice over the channel. It was Commander Hallsey.

X helped Watt up as the ticker hit ten seconds.

"Let's go," he said. He stopped for a moment to look at Slayer one last time.

I'm sorry, brother.

With an arm around Watt, he helped him into the hallway.

An emergency alarm rang out, echoing off the icy interior of the facility.

"That must be the launch," Watt said in a voice laced with pain.

Strobing red lights whirled, creating an eerie glow as they trudged down the corridor. Explosions thumped outside, eclipsing the heavy chatter of machine guns.

X helped the knight into the frozen corridor, stepping around the corpse of Archie. Debris from the last grenade X had fired littered the dirty snow ahead. They trudged over to it and stopped for their first view of the battle raging outside.

The *Trident* hovered in the sky, concentrating its many weapons on a single target: the Cerebro scrambling across the ice, returning fire with the two tubular arms. But it wasn't merely flinging those blistering white cables X had seen back inside the facility. These were lasers it was shooting. Lasers could destroy the airship.

"Over there," Watt said, raising a hand.

X looked out to a metallic figure lying in the snow. It looked as if all four limbs had been cut off, leaving him stranded in his suit.

"We have to help him," Watt said.

X and the knight pushed out into the deep snow. The Cerebro skittered away from the airship's rockets and machine-gun fire. But now Commander Hallsey switched tactics, firing in a circle around the behemoth. It screeched a synthetic roar as it tried to break free from the assault.

A low, loud rumbling rose over the other noises. X and Watt reached the Forerunner just as the first of the disk-shaped reactors released its payload into the clouds. X shielded his eyes from the brilliant glow piercing the sky.

The spider creature raised four arms, flashing lasers at

the bow of the airship. But the ice around it began to tilt and shatter.

As the weather-tech missiles blasted away, the surface collapsed under the Cerebro. Flailing, it fought to hold on to chunks of ice and clamber back out, but Hallsey continued her relentless firing. In a last-ditch attempt, the thing fired more lasers as the water splashed around it.

A final rocket slammed into the domed head, and the Cerebro sank into the icy abyss.

X looked down to the Forerunner and saw the blue eye, still active behind the visor.

"We did it, Noah!" he said. "Can you see?"

The blue eye flitted toward the reactors, all of them firing their payloads into the air. He managed to nod ever so slightly.

"We're getting you out of here," X said. He bent down to try to pull him up, but even without limbs the suit weighed a ton.

The sounds of breaking ice grew closer.

X looked over in horror as a crack yawned toward them.

"Help me!" Watt yelled.

The knight tried to pull the Forerunner away, but the entire shelf appeared to be on the verge of collapsing.

"Leave me," croaked the cyborg.

X watched the approaching chunks of ice breaking up, water geysering up between them. With all his strength, X grabbed the Forerunner and heaved the body a few inches backward. Then a few more.

The fracturing of ice sounded like gunfire. But the sound of distant missiles blasting into the clouds made it all worth it.

"Come on, damn it!" X grunted. He pulled harder, dragging the Forerunner a few more inches, with Watt pushing.

X fell to his knees, looking down at something that appeared to be entirely mechanical. But he knew that beneath the layers of the suit was much more than that—a man with a good heart, who had wanted nothing more than to bring back the Old World and live in it with his wife and their daughter.

X would be honored to die with him.

Water blasted outward as the ice gave way, plunging them all into the freezing ocean.

TWENTY-TWO

The airship hovered at twelve thousand feet in thick cloud cover. Michael sat on the bridge, watching the monitors as they tracked the slaver ship using the synthetic aperture radar. They had been following it for the past fifteen hours since escaping the caves.

Bray was unharmed physically after witnessing the shocking violence back in the caves, but he was definitely off. Now he was awake in Layla's arms, being rocked back and forth. The normally energetic toddler was docile and reserved. Kids were resilient—Michael and Layla were examples of that resilience. But kids also remembered, and Michael feared that Bray would have lasting trauma or core memories from the violence.

They would deal with that later. He was just glad his son was still alive and uninjured.

"Thanks to Victor," Michael whispered.

"Uncle Victa," Bray said.

Michael didn't think he had said it out loud, but the boy paid attention.

"Uncle Victa," Bray repeated.

Michael and Layla exchanged a glance, but neither of them

had the heart to tell their son that Victor was likely dead. Still, they weren't giving up on the brave, selfless man who had risked his life so many times for them. Michael had no idea how to rescue Victor if he was still alive, but he couldn't just abandon him without knowing the truth.

Heaving a sigh, Michael looked back to the radar, comparing it to the digital map on the adjacent monitor. The slave vessel was heading toward the coast of Africa, but it was too early to say where yet.

"If Layla's right and the destination is Casablanca, we have a long way to go," he said.

"Three days at this rate," Timothy said.

Layla brought Bray over in her arms, his head resting against her shoulder. The boy was tired and blinked lazily at the screen as Michael pointed. Gabi also joined them, wrapped in a blanket.

They had yet to discuss it as a group, but Michael knew they could never return to the caves. He had abandoned any hope of living there.

"I'm going to the cargo hold to do an inventory of our weapons," he said. "Let me know if there are any changes."

Layla nodded and eased into a seat with Bray.

"Pepper, come with me," Michael said.

"Okay, Chief."

The AI walked with Michael out of the bridge. When they reached the next corridor, Michael said, "Do you think Bray's okay?"

"I do," Timothy said. "Clearly he's frightened by what happened, and his ears probably hurt from the gunfire, but I don't see any concerning health issues."

"I thought we were safe there..." Michael shook his head. "I was stupid to think so."

"You aren't stupid, Chief. You're human, as I once was. I admire what you have done to keep your family safe."

Michael looked over, suddenly feeling terrible for the AI. He had lost everything at the Hilltop Bastion. Not long after they discovered him, Timothy had found the corpses of his family on Deliverance and had gone into a downward spiral of emotions that Michael feared would force them to shut him down. But the AI had recovered, and he remained the trusty support program that felt almost like an equal member of the crew.

"Thanks, Pepper," he said. "I'm grateful to have you."

"You're welcome, Chief."

They arrived at the cargo hold, entering through the open hatch. In fleeing the islands quickly, they had been forced to leave some of their weapons and ammunition behind. But Michael had planned for that, keeping a stockpile on the airship just in case they ever had to leave in a hurry.

He inventoried the contents of the lockers: a shotgun, two blasters, two assault rifles, four handguns, and three crossbows. Plus the laser rifle he now had slung. It was a small arsenal, but their ammo was running low. He counted fourteen shotgun shells, six full magazines for the assault rifles, a few hundred rounds for the pistols, and thirty bolts for the crossbows.

For armor, they had Michael's Hell Diver suit, and Layla's, too. There was some leftover riot gear, but nothing that would protect against a bullet or a sharp blade.

"This everything we got, Pepper?" Michael asked.

"Yes, Chief."

He flickered, and a message from Layla crackled over the PA system. *"Michael, get back to the bridge."*

Michael looked to Timothy as he started to rush out of the hold.

"Sir, I believe she wants you to see that the vessel we're tracking has started toward a port," said the AI.

"What port?"

"A place called Agadir."

"Where?"

"Agadir was the economic hub of Morocco before the war and is located on the southwestern coast of Morocco, overlooking the Atlantic Ocean. It was known for its modern infrastructure after the city rebuilt following a devastating earthquake that struck in 1960. Agadir also attracted tourists with its warm climate, beaches, and golf courses. The old kasbah, a fortress known as Agadir Oufella, has a good view of the city and coast."

"Do we know how much survived after the war?"

"Negative, but we should know more soon. We're only about twenty minutes away from a visual image."

Michael arrived at the bridge a few minutes later. Bray was wide awake and tapping at one of the computer screens while Layla studied the radar.

"They're heading to Agadir," she said.

"I know. Timothy filled me in."

Layla turned to another screen. "Looks like we're going to hit some bad weather in about an hour, so now's our chance if we want to take a look."

"That would require us to go down to about two thousand feet," Timothy said. "It's dark, though, and I'm confident we can remain undetected."

"Can you keep us in the clouds?" she asked.

"Yes, I should be able to poke out just enough for a visual without exposing us."

"Okay, do it," Michael said. "I want to see what's down there."

He strapped Bray into a seat. The boy didn't fight the harness. He was tired, and still not himself after the horror of the caves.

Once everyone was secure, the ship began the descent from ten thousand feet as they approached the ancient city. All eyes were glued to the front screen relaying exterior views from the cameras. Right now all they could see was clouds.

Bray squirmed in his seat, groaning and whispering something incoherent. Layla looked to Michael. All he could do was reassure her with a nod.

"Prepare for visual," Timothy said.

The AI helped distract Bray, and the boy looked at the screen. Frontal cameras dialed in on lights below. Torches burned along the ancient fortress walls that Timothy had spoken of earlier. The castle appeared to be the location of the slavers.

"I have good news," Timothy said. He waited a beat, then said, "Victor's beacon is still active."

Layla exhaled.

"The bad news?" Michael asked.

"There are over one hundred fifty human life signatures down there, and I believe many of them to be hostile," Timothy said.

Michael groaned inwardly. There were almost as many people down there as bullets up here. He checked the location of the slaver ship—heading toward the piers bordering the fortress. Maybe this was a chance to swoop down, kill the slavers, and grab Victor before they entered the facility.

But that would require lowering the airship. Or diving down and putting himself or Layla in danger—something Victor wouldn't want.

There had to be another way.

"Chief, I've got a view of a collection of people," Timothy reported. "Looks like the majority are inside a single area of the fortress."

"Show us," Michael said.

He leaned forward to look as the cameras zoomed in on an

outside area surrounded by high metal fences. Inside were small huts, some with smoke rising from cook fires. Groups of people stood in the dirt, huddled around burning barrels. Most of these people looked gaunt and quite small.

"Kids," Bray said, pointing.

Michael squinted. His son was right. These prisoners were almost all children.

"My God," he whispered.

"There's another concentration of people in this location," Timothy said.

The next image showed a few men and women, all wearing the same shabby uniform, their skin filthy. Working with tools in the glow of industrial lights to build something.

"Slaves," he said. "More than likely the parents of those kids."

"We have to do something," Layla said. "We have the weapons and ammo."

"Yeah, but we don't have the . . ." His words trailed.

"What is it, Tin?"

"We send down a weapons crate, just like we would for divers on the ground to fight monsters. Only this would be for those prisoners, to fight the slavers."

Layla nodded. "One of us will still need to go down and get Victor."

"Yes, but we do it with a major distraction."

"I can accomplish that," Timothy said.

"It's a plan, then," Michael said. "We get the weapons in a crate and get it ready to drop. Then I go down and free Victor."

*   *   *   *   *

Waves filled Gran Jefe's field of vision to the horizon in all directions, and he couldn't help wondering if he would ever see home again. For what felt like an entire day now, he had pushed the little kayak through the waves. He long ago lost track of how many times he had capsized. His entire body was drenched and sore. He paddled doggedly, tilting up and then down over each wave. It required constant focus just to keep the precarious craft upright.

"Adjust fifteen degrees to your left for this next wave," Frank said in Spanish.

Having the AI with him was the only thing that kept Gran Jefe from losing all hope. He followed the command with a deep paddle stroke.

"You're sure you know where I'm going?" Gran Jefe asked in Spanish.

"Yes. Stay focused."

Gran Jefe wasn't sure how the AI knew they were heading in the right direction, but he trusted the ghost pilot. Thunder rumbled in the distance, and the sky became a thick blanket of black. Raindrops the size of marbles hit Gran Jefe hard enough to hurt.

"Paddle hard forward, and then lean back," Frank said, once again in Spanish.

Through the veil of rain, Gran Jefe saw the next wave approaching. He didn't waste any energy replying. He dug his paddle in, using what remained of his strength to push into the wall of rising water. As it rolled toward him, he leaned back. The kayak shot up the face of the wave. After a moment's pause, it zipped down the other side.

Water slapped against his exhausted body. Everything seemed to ache, but the wound under his arm hurt the worst. The salt water inflamed the wound more with each paddle stroke. That wasn't going to stop him, though.

Gran Jefe welcomed the pain. It let him know he was alive.

At this point, no amount of pain would stop him from getting home. He felt a determination unlike any before now. The fire grew in his chest, fueling him.

He focused on the next wave, then the next, rising and falling in a rhythmic pattern. The rain intensified.

"Are you sure we're going the right way?" he asked yet again.

"Yes. The device in your pocket has a GPS unit."

"Then how much farther?"

"Hard to say, but my guess is, at your current pace you're within two hours of seeing the first rig."

"What time is it?"

"Three in the morning."

Gran Jefe had hoped to reach the rigs under the cover of darkness, but it was going to be close. He shook off the fatigue and paddled onward, stroke after stroke, pulling himself closer to home—to his boy, to his comrades, and to the enemy.

He honestly had no idea what he would do when he arrived. Maybe find a meal. His empty stomach rumbled. The hunger pains were almost worse than his injuries. To combat them, he worked on a plan. It would depend on which rig he found first, but he needed to find a Cazador rig with allies. The problem with that was, he didn't have a lot of friends.

Eventually, he would make his way to the main Cazador rigs, connected by bridges. Pablo and Jada were there, protected, he hoped, by her husband, Chano, although Gran Jefe doubted that the skinny fisherman could do much.

"Well done, Jorge," Frank said. "I believe you're almost through the worst of the storm."

After emerging from his trance, Gran Jefe spent a moment taking in his surroundings. The AI was right: the waves were shorter and the rain had weakened. The hostile, dark sky seemed to lighten until he glimpsed the first rays of moonlight.

Searching the horizon, he identified the first rig. Finally, a welcome reward for his tenacity. A flood of relief washed over his battered body, but he didn't let up. He paddled harder. At this pace, it was still going to take him another thirty minutes or longer to get there. But he was in luck, for this was a Cazador rig. He could tell by the pinpricks of light from torches burning on several upper decks. This was the easternmost rig, where they had moved some of their farms. It wasn't heavily populated either.

Thrusting his paddle into the nearly still water, he pulled closer to the rusted behemoth of concrete and steel rising over the ocean.

"Jorge, watch out," Frank warned.

An engine rumbled behind them, and Gran Jefe glimpsed over his right shoulder a boat, roaring toward the rig. He slid off the kayak into the water, holding on to the rim of the cockpit. With his head just above the surface, he watched the speeding craft. A searchlight speared away from the bow, raking over the ocean.

Gran Jefe stared in horror. Had they seen him somehow?

He looked to the rig, now only two hundred feet away. But there was no time—mere seconds before the boat arrived.

Grabbing his gear, he gently pushed the kayak away. Then he kicked away, swimming as fast as he could. As he pulled away, his arm burned terribly from the overhead stroke and the sting of salt water.

He came up for air, watching the boat speed closer. The light flashed his way, and he submerged, holding his breath. Maneuvering his body downward, he surface-dived to avoid the light sweeping over the surface.

With breath still in his lungs, he stopped and looked up at the spotlight closing in on his position. The twin outboard motors churned slower as the pilot eased off on the throttle.

They coasted over him and began to turn. His heart skipped

when he saw the light no longer moving in wide arcs but holding tight on a single object: his kayak.

Gran Jefe could only hope they would see it as floating debris. He counted the seconds in his head, his lungs already starting to burn. An idea seeded in his mind to kick up and try to board the boat and take out whoever was on it.

Maybe this wasn't even the enemy. Maybe it was Cazadores.

Not wanting to take the risk, he kicked away from the boat until he could hold his breath no longer. Nearing the surface, he slowed his ascent. Ever so carefully, he surfaced and sighted up the boat.

Sure enough, two knights stood in the bow. They used a long rod to pull the kayak over to them, talking in hushed voices. If he were closer, he would climb onto their boat and kill them both.

Instead, he took another deep breath and went back under. Then he began kicking over to the rig. He stopped a few times, coming up for air. The light was raking back over the water again, searching in the direction of the kayak.

Using the darkness to his advantage, he kicked over toward the massive concrete pillars supporting the rig. The closest was only a hundred yards away. If he could reach it, maybe he could climb up before the enemy found him.

Summoning what little strength he had left in him, he swam over to the pillar.

As he reached the pillar, the engines chugged back to life. They were onto him now. He bobbed up and down in the water as he searched for the handholds that the maintenance workers used. He found what remained of the bottom two, both sheared off.

He tried to jump and grab the next rung but fell short and splashed back down. A light flashed in his direction, bisected by the pillar and shooting off to both sides. Heart in his mouth, Gran

Jefe seized the last seconds he had by scissor-kicking up out of the water and grabbing again for the lowest rung. His fingers found purchase, and kicking and pulling, he managed to scramble up.

The boat motored nearer. He reached up to the next rung, grabbed it, and pulled. His boot slid on a wet rung and he nearly dumped. Fifty feet above him were barrels and equipment where he could easily hide, but he wasn't going to make it.

Gran Jefe looked down as the boat came around the pillar slow, directly below him.

"*Hola*, motherfuckers!" he shouted.

Letting go of the rung, he kicked off the pillar, putting his arms out as he came down on the two unsuspecting knights. Both men went down under his wings, falling to the deck of the small craft. He picked up a spear and thrust it into the neck of one man, then skewered the other through the heart, killing him instantly.

Pulling out a sword, he went down to finish off the man bleeding out from a neck artery. Despite the blood shooting out, the soldier fought for life, clamping his hands over the wound and scooting back on a deck slick with his blood.

Gran Jefe leaned down, locking eyes with the man. Hardly a man, really. He was young, about the same age Gran Jefe had been when he joined the Cazador army. For a fleeting moment, he felt empathy for this kid, but it passed. There was no room for sentimentality in war, and right now his people were at war with these people. He had his son to think about.

Just as Gran Jefe was about to finish off the soldier, his hands fell away, and his head lolled to the side. He was dead from blood loss.

Working quickly, Gran Jefe swapped his wet clothing for the enemy uniform and armor. When he finished dressing, he used a cable on the boat to wrap the corpses together. Then he lashed them to the anchor, cut the anchor rope, and heaved them overboard. As they sank to the ocean floor, a few bubbles rose to the surface——the only sign that they ever existed.

Frank glowed to life in the bow of the boat, looking down. "Well done," he said.

Gran Jefe scavenged through the dead knights' gear and found some dried fish, which he ate quickly while scanning the horizon for boats. It appeared, at least for now, that he had slipped under the radar. Still, he needed to get moving. He equipped himself with a rifle, knife, and cutlass, then checked his compass. The way to the main Cazador rigs was due west. He turned the bobbing boat that way.

"What now?" Frank asked.

"I become like you," Gran Jefe said. "*Un fantasma*. A ghost."

TWENTY-THREE

Kade hunkered down against the side of the snowmobile to shelter from the violent snowstorm. A thick drift protected him from the wind. It had cost him considerable energy, but he managed to dig a horseshoe shape around the machine. The idling engine hummed, providing heat that kept him from freezing. Lucky sat next to him—or leaned, rather. The knight had fallen unconscious again—a possible death sentence for them both, for without Lucky, Kade had no idea how to get back to the drop zone.

After driving a few miles away from the glacier, Kade had decided to stop and build the makeshift shelter around the vehicle while waiting for Lucky to wake up—*hoping* he would wake up.

Every thirty minutes, Kade had fired up the engine for some heat, but the fuel supply was dwindling. Fortunately, he had found some extra lifesaving gear in the supply crate on the back of another snowmobile. A face mask, stocking cap, gloves, and socks.

Lifesaving, he scoffed. *More like life prolonging.*

The gear helped him fend off frostbite for now, but it wouldn't forever. Inevitably, the cold would worm its way through all his layers if he didn't get out of the open.

"Lucky, come on, man," Kade said. He reached out and shook the knight but got no response.

There was another option that Kade had considered, but this meant exposing Lucky to the elements by taking off his helmet so he could use the digital map. Maybe he could do it quickly, memorizing it and then heading out, hoping to keep a straight bearing. But with low fuel, it was a huge risk if he got lost—especially in the dark and in a storm.

At this point, though, Kade saw no other option. He maneuvered Lucky closer to the engine, then unclasped his helmet. He quickly put it over his own head.

"Bring up current position and route back to DZ," Kade said into the headset.

The voice-activated AI went to work, relaying a map on the HUD's digital subscreen. As it began to lay out the route, Kade noticed the temperature: negative thirty-six degrees Fahrenheit.

His eyes went back to the map—still three miles from the DZ. All he had to do was keep a straight course west and he would hit it. But doing so in these conditions would be a major challenge. He basked in the warmth of the helmet for a few seconds before sliding it off.

"You're gonna make it," Kade said as he slipped the helmet back over Lucky's face.

Moving fast, Kade stuck his head up above the wall of snow, the wind biting into his exposed skin. He knew from experience that it would take only a few minutes for those areas to freeze. To have any chance of surviving, Kade was going to need some luck.

Bending down, he slipped his gloved hands under Lucky's armpits, then heaved him onto the back of the snowmobile. The knight groaned, or at least, Kade thought he did. It had taken only a few seconds, but the wind had shocked Kade like a plunge in an ice bath.

He climbed onto the snowmobile and then wrapped the rope around himself and Lucky to keep the knight from falling off the back. Once they were secure, Kade gripped the handlebars with fingers still warm from the engine heat. But they would soon feel wooden again.

Backing the machine up, he turned it and twisted the throttle. The snowmobile hurtled over the dense snow. Each breath felt sharp, the cold air biting his lungs. Despite the new gear and the multiple layers under his parka, a relentless shivering gripped his body, threatening his balance. He tried to move his fingers but had already lost most of the feeling in the tips. Kade had to visually verify that he was even twisting the throttle.

The snowmobile hummed beneath him, but the engine sounded distant. On the horizon, the veil of snowfall seemed to play tricks on his eyes. The headlights that had penetrated the whiteout earlier now seemed to distort and flicker.

He blinked, shook his head slightly. The onset of fatigue became more insidious as drowsiness tugged at the edges of his consciousness. It took an immense effort to stay alert enough to keep going.

Out of the swirling snow, the lights captured a figure. At first, it seemed a mirage—a trick of the headlights and the cold. But as he neared it, he saw a thin figure with shoulder-length hair. His blurred vision managed to relay a detail to his freezing brain: a tattoo on the side of her head.

He blinked, trying to rid himself of Tia's image.

You're dead. Gone.

Was this another trick of the machines? What if they had fixed her body?

No. Impossible.

After his gunshot, there would be no way they could make her look human again. He didn't deviate as she stepped in front of the snowmobile. The machine blasted right through what was indeed a figment of his imagination.

The realization helped Kade shake away the grogginess. He managed to focus his mind and even felt his fingers enough to twist the throttle. Accelerating, the skis thumped up over the hill, giving him a slight reprieve from the wind.

The headlight beams punched into the darkness, but Kade still didn't see anything out there. He steered the snowmobile down the hill, back onto level terrain. Twisting the throttle, he kept them on a westward bearing. The merciless wind attacked his body, but he no longer felt the sting. In fact, he didn't feel much at all. A deep fog settled over his brain.

He stared into the distance, following the beams that seemed to blur into a tunnel of light. The tunnel widened, the snowflakes coming down in slow motion. Kade felt his body listing to port. A sudden spark of heat formed in his gut, rising up in his chest at the realization that he was leaning off the vehicle.

Letting go of the throttle, he let the snowmobile skid to a stop.

He lowered his head to give himself some reprieve from the wind.

Just a few seconds…

He could no longer feel the engine beneath his body, though he could hear its hum. He resisted the urge to climb off and seek that heat. But a glance at the gauges told him that would be his death sentence. Fuel was below a quarter tank. He had to conserve.

Just rest a few more seconds.

Kade closed his eyes.

"Daddy, wake up!"

The young voice stirred him back to reality. Standing in front of the snowmobile was Sean, his four-year-old son.

"You got this, Dad!" said Jack.

Rich was there too, the older boy standing behind Sean.

"You can't give up. Alton still needs you," said another voice.

Behind his boys, his wife, Mikah, walked up, pulling them all toward her.

"We're okay, my love," she said. "We're all together and we're waiting for you, but you have to finish what you've started. You're so close."

"Mikah," Kade whispered.

"We're waiting for you and always will be."

She vanished, along with Rich and Jack.

"Love you, Daddy," Sean said.

Then he was gone, too.

Kade shook away the fog of the cold as the images of his family fueled him with an internal warmth. He grabbed the throttle and twisted it.

"You can't die yet," he said.

The snowmobile raced onward, into the storm. Wind battered his body, and snowflakes stuck to his goggles. He kept his focus, fighting the chill with everything he had left. That determination rewarded him a few moments later. On the horizon, the beams from the vehicle lit up a fence and buildings beyond. He drove up to the enclosure, stopping within inches of the frozen metal. He stood up, reached out just to make sure it was real. The fence shook when he pushed on it.

"We made it," Kade said.

He turned to Lucky and untied them. Then he opened the med kit and pulled out a syringe. Blocking the wind with his body, Kade carefully inserted the needle into Lucky's leg and pushed the plunger down.

Jerking, the knight responded almost instantly to the adrenaline shot.

"Crikey, where the bloody fuck…" he muttered.

"We're back to the city," Kade said. "Time to go send that SOS."

*   *   *   *   *

X was aware of falling into the frigid water from the collapsing shelf of ice. Chunks broke around him, their slippery sides providing no purchase for his robotic hand. Watt went under a few feet away, his helmet light dimming in the darkness. The Forerunner sank beneath them, unable to move in the limbless mech suit. It now became a metal coffin that would plummet thousands of feet to a final resting spot—on the bottom of the Arctic Ocean.

Frantic, X flailed for something to hold on to, but as the ice continued to fracture, he was left with only small chunks. A shard snapped off the shattered shelf, hitting him in the helmet. He went under, the soul-shocking cold penetrating all his layers. He extended his arms up toward the bright glow of the airship above him. The machine guns had gone silent, their mission completed when they shot the ice floor out from under the Cerebro. Flashes of light shot into the sky from the reactors, but that glow waned as he sank.

You're not done yet, X. Fight!

He couldn't surrender to the bone-chilling cold. He had to keep fighting. There was still one last mission.

X kicked up again, breaking through the surface. He grabbed at a slab of ice but slid right off, going under again. The weight of his armor pulled him down. He kicked, but his strength was gone, and his body felt numb.

"No," X whispered. He reached up with his robotic hand at the vanishing light. As he sank, an image of Miles and all his loved ones emerged in his foggy brain, but only briefly. There was only the sense of freezing.

"Miles," he whispered. "Michael... Valeria..."

His numb lips opened, but nothing else came out. He blinked, trying to hold on to his vision, but that, too, dimmed away.

This was it, the end for Xavier Rodriguez.

No more dives. No more battles. No more...

And then he was rising up, or so it seemed, his body held in some gigantic hand. A brilliant light blasted from overhead.

That was the last thing he remembered.

When he woke next, it was to warmth—warm lights, a warm blanket over his body, the warm lick of a tongue that could only be Miles. His eyes confirmed this, focusing on his dog at the side of the bed. Jo-Jo reached out with a paw and grunted.

"Heya, pal," X said. He blinked, his eyes falling next on Valeria's smile. She sat on the edge of the bed, a hand on his side.

"You made it back," she said.

The events replayed in his mind again—not just the battle on the ice but everything before that. From the dive to those final icy moments when he was retrieved by the airship. But what about Watt and...

"The Forerunner," X mumbled. "Where is he?"

"I don't know," Valeria said.

"Watt?"

"I'm not sure about him or Slayer."

X lowered his head.

"I'm sorry," he said. "Slayer didn't make it."

The image of Slayer's crushed body surfaced in his mind, and then the guilt of not being there to help him fight the bone beast. All the normal questions ping-ponged in his head.

Was there something he could have done?

Of course, there was no way to know.

"You did your best. Don't think too much," Valeria said, as if sensing his torment.

She leaned over his bed. X hesitated, then threw aside his confliction over getting close to someone again. He embraced Valeria, pulling her in tight. Miles jumped up, nudging between them, tail beating back and forth. X found a smile forming on his scarred face. He stroked his dog with his other hand, keeping the robotic one around Valeria.

A knock on the hatch interrupted the moment.

"Yeah, come in," X said.

Commander Hallsey opened the hatch.

"Xavier, come with me," she said.

"He needs time to rest," Valeria said.

"I need to talk to him, alone."

"It's okay," X said. He pulled the blanket off his legs and got out of bed, staggering for a moment on weak knees. Valeria, Miles, and Jo-Jo all watched him. He gave them an emphatic nod to let them know he was fine. Then he followed the commander into the corridor.

"Follow me," she said.

"Wait, what about Noah ... the Forerunner?"

"He's in his chamber, healing," she said. Then she stopped. "His heart is failing, and I'm afraid the life-support systems aren't going to be able to keep him alive for much longer. Most of his other organs are synthetic. It's just a matter of time now before they all give up the ghost."

X could see the sadness in her gaze. To her, the Forerunner was more than a leader. He was family—a man she looked up to and loved.

"I'm sorry," X said.

"He wouldn't even be here if it weren't for you. Watt either."

"Is he going to make it?"

"Yes, he will make a full recovery. My condolences on losing Slayer, but his sacrifice was not in vain."

X simply nodded. The words were familiar and brought him back to all the times Captain Ash and leaders after her said the same thing—then to all the times X had said the same thing to wives, children, and parents about how their loved one had died a hero.

Josie took a step closer, until they were just a few inches apart. "I watched what you did down there to save them all," she said. "To help Noah and protect him, to ensure that the mission didn't fail. He was right about you—"

"Enter." The pained voice crackled from unseen speakers in the passage. The hatch in front of them whisked open.

X and Josie walked into the chamber as the Forerunner rose out of the gelatinous liquid on mounted robotic arms. His broken body hung there, limbless save for part of an arm. The glow of fish tanks brightened around the chamber, illuminating the tapestry of metal, flesh, and glass. This was the first time X had seen the transparent plate on the Forerunner's chest. Behind it, a visible beating heart pumped blood through his body.

The Forerunner raised his bald head covered in lesions and liver spots. The blue light from his robotic eye further illuminated a sunken, haggard face half-covered by a breathing mask. Tubes snaked away from his chair sitting at the edge of the pool. Each of those tubes connected to ports in his back and neck.

"I'm starting to wonder if the prophecy is real, Xavier Rodriguez," he wheezed.

"Prophecy?" X scoffed. "I assure you, I'm *not* immortal."

"No, but I'm starting to believe that our paths have crossed by far more than coincidence—"

The Forerunner broke into a cough—a deep rattle resonating from his chest. He took in several deep gasps. His next words were muffled, but X made them out clearly enough. "You led your people to the sun, and now I believe you will restore the sun for the entire planet."

"The first missiles have already detonated and are beginning to spread throughout the atmosphere," Josie said. She pulled out a tablet and tapped the screen. "However, I'm afraid it won't be enough without also firing the Delta Cloud fusion reactors at Concordia Station."

X figured that much. He had known all along that this was a two-pronged mission.

"An hour ago, I received an SOS," Josie continued. With a second tap of the screen, a voice surged out.

"This is Kade Long, transmitting from Concordia Station..." Loud, popping static cut off the transmission momentarily. "Gaz is severely injured, and the rest of our team is KIA."

The next pause sounded to be more from Kade and not from any interference he was hearing. "We encountered a mechanical creature that prevented us from completing our mission. Requesting support as soon as possible."

The audio shut off.

"We're en route and will be there in twenty-one hours at our current speed, barring major storms," Josie said. "However, I'm requesting permission to stop at the Vanguard Islands in order to bring on new team members."

The Forerunner shook his head immediately. "There's no time," he said. "Before Xavier rescued me from the Cerebro, it tapped into my helmet."

X thought of that moment, when he saw the monster straddling the mech suit and drilling into his armor.

"It was trying to extract information from my brain," explained the Forerunner. He took a deep breath, then added, "Information on the Coral Castle and the Vanguard Islands."

"Ah, shit," X said.

"When it tapped into my skull, it connected us somehow. I saw the past—and the future if we don't stop it. A world devoid of humanity."

He coughed, and coughed again. The episode turned into a violent seizure racking his frail body. X took a step forward as the Forerunner shook violently in the robotic arms.

Josie moved forward. "Sir, are you okay?"

The cyborg slowly regained his composure and nodded. He let out an exhausted, pained sigh.

"If Gaz or Kade are captured, or anyone else, the enemy will try to extract the same info," he said. "That is why we must make haste. There's no time to stop."

"Understood, sir," Josie said. "I will proceed as fast as safely possible—"

"Wait," X said. "Your people captured our Jayhawk, did you not?"

The Forerunner slowly nodded.

"From what I understand, that's a long-distance battery-powered hybrid chopper," X said. "With a little work, you can strip it down for weight and load it with knights and ammunition..."

He thought about it for only a second, knowing Magnolia would want to be on that bird. "Magnolia," X said. "She's our best surviving diver."

Now the Forerunner had to think on it, but like X, he didn't need long.

"Commander Hallsey, send a message to Captain Namath of the First Trident Fleet to put together a team as soon as possible," he said. "And for General Jack to be on full alert for hostile forces."

"Yes, sir."

"As soon as Watt is on his feet, I want him to prepare my mech suit for combat. We should have all the spare parts and material."

"Sir, there's no way you can fight in your condition—"

The Forerunner cut her off. "I must. It's our one option."

He took a few breaths, blinking rapidly as if he had difficulty seeing.

"I need only enough strength to finish this," he said. After another pause, he said, "Commander, please leave me with Xavier."

Josie hesitated, but then saluted and left the chamber. The hatch shut with a loud enough slam to convey her disapproval.

"Definitely a Hallsey," the Forerunner said with a chuckle. "My wife was like that—aggressive but means well."

X had never heard the Forerunner laugh before. He blinked, trying to focus his old eye and the blue lens. "Come forward, Xavier."

X approached closely enough to see the heart beating.

"We can't count on these reinforcements," said the Forerunner. "We are in a desperate situation now—desperate enough that we need every soul on board."

He cleared his throat.

"I know this goes against what I told you before. But this mission transcends love for individual and family."

X nodded in understanding, but the dread began to fill his gut. Not only would Magnolia be heading into danger, Valeria would, too. The thought of losing either of them made that dread worse. But if they could succeed, their efforts would change the world for future generations.

"I'm prepared to die for this mission," X said.

"You and me both—"

The Forerunner coughed again, deeper, and not even the mask gave him relief. The blue eye remained fixed on X.

"Commander Hallsey!" X shouted. "Josie!"

She entered the room again, running over. With a tap of her tablet, she lowered the frail body back down into the gel.

The seizure passed a moment later, and the eye focused back on X, then Josie. He closed it just as his head went beneath the surface of the gel.

"He can't go back out there," Josie said. "He's too weak."

"I agree," X said. "Leave this to me."

TWENTY-FOUR

"Speak if spoken to, and answer questions," said General Jack. "You're about to meet Captain Namath, Commander of the First Trident Fleet."

Magnolia stood with Imulah on the deck of one of the two Trident cruise ships. They had been transferred on a motor skiff from the warship *Frog* a few minutes earlier. The warship patrolled around the two big luxury vessels. A few dozen smaller craft formed a ragtag flotilla of refugees.

Magnolia feared what would happen to Pedro and the other prisoners, but right now she had no way to help them.

"This way," Jack said. He crossed the deck of the gigantic cruise ship, passing an ancient pool retrofitted into a greenhouse.

With an escort of two knights accompanying them, Magnolia and Imulah were taken down a deck into an old ballroom that had been transformed into another farm. Banks of dangling grow lights illuminated planters spilling over with vegetables. Pipes snaked overhead, spraying water from sprinklers over individual plants. Not a foot of space had gone to waste.

Gardeners looked up from their work, surprised at seeing

Magnolia and Imulah. Or perhaps it was General Jack. The man clearly sparked fear in his subordinates. She had met enough men like Jack over the years to see him for what he was: nothing more than a brute. Brutes were the easiest enemies to defeat—you just had to find their weakness and exploit it.

He guided them down two levels until they got to the bridge, guarded by a soldier in a blue suit with black chest armor. That wasn't the only difference between him and the knights she was used to seeing. On the breast hung an embroidered sail-and-sword logo.

"Sir," the guard said. He stepped aside and then opened a hatch to a sprawling room. Leather seats faced dim screens at twenty workstations. At some of them, officers rose to their feet to stare as Magnolia and Imulah entered.

A man in a black uniform stood at the helm, looking out the viewports at the rigs beyond. Or perhaps he was staring at the reflection in the glass of these two very odd new people. He turned to them—dark-brown eagle eyes set under gray brows. Wavy white hair hung over his deep-furrowed brow. He had striking features, like Xavier, conveying strength and confidence.

"Captain Namath," said General Jack.

"Jack, it's good to see you, brother," Namath said. "I feared the worst when I heard about the attack back home."

He reached out and shook the general's hand.

"Take more than some bloody mutant spiders to kill me," Jack replied. His gaze shifted to Magnolia and Imulah. "This is the Hell Diver you've probably heard of, and the Cazador scribe."

"My friends call me Mags," she said. "You can call me Magnolia."

"Imulah. Pleased to meet you," Imulah said respectfully.

Namath walked over, further scrutinizing them before jerking his chin toward a conference room. A guard followed them inside, his hand resting on his sword hilt. He stood at attention by a viewport looking out at the capitol tower a little less than a mile away. The captain turned from the view, with a dire look. "I'm afraid I have bad news to report about the Forerunner," he said.

Magnolia braced herself, watching the captain's lips as they seemed to slow down.

"The mission to Polar Station was a success, but the Forerunner was injured and we lost Blue Blood," he said. "The *Trident* is currently on its way to Concordia Station to help the team there. From what I've heard, there are only two survivors."

"What news of Xavier?" Magnolia blurted.

The captain looked at her. "He's alive."

Magnolia relaxed a degree.

"The Forerunner has requested help, and we're putting together a team to deploy on the recovered Jayhawk, using Lieutenant Mamoa from my ship as pilot," he added.

Magnolia opened her mouth to volunteer, but before she could say anything, the captain spoke. "General, your orders are to stay here and keep the peace."

"*Peace?* The brutes killed five of my knights!" Jack boomed.

"Which is all the more reason not to escalate tensions further."

"You expect me to turn a blind eye to—"

"You killed the man responsible, did you not?"

Jack paused, then nodded.

"The Forerunner said to be on full alert for external enemies," Namath continued. "The message was cryptic, but I can only deduce that he believes our location might not be safe. You will stay here and watch for threats."

"Permission to come aboard the helicopter," Magnolia said.

Namath and Jack had a stare-down for a few moments before Jack nodded in agreement. Then Namath moved to Magnolia.

"With Gran Jefe dead, you no longer need my help here," she said. "X and your Forerunner, on the other hand, do."

Namath shifted his gaze back to Jack. "Can she be trusted?"

"Can any of these barbarians be trusted?" Jack sneered. "She's got a mouth on her, this one—and she can bite."

Namath walked up to Magnolia, facing her directly and looking into her eyes. She held his gaze.

"I've been a Hell Diver my entire life, committed to protecting life," Magnolia said. "I've seen the worst out there, fighting monsters, machines, and evil men. Do your knights have experience diving into the wastes? Experience in hostile environments like the one you're headed to? Because it will be the most hostile they have encountered yet."

"They are well equipped and prepared."

"They'll be better off with me. You have room on the chopper. Please." Magnolia didn't want to beg, but she had to be on that chopper. "You *need* my experience."

"She's a good fighter," Imulah said. "She was captured by the Cazadores and brought here before her sky people defeated our former king, el Pulpo. She follows Xavier, the man who ruled this place and—"

"The one that came to search for our home at the Coral Castle," Jack interrupted.

"But he did not order the nuclear strike in Brisbane, correct?" Namath asked.

"Correct," Magnolia said. "Xavier's a fair man, a good man. The best I've ever known, in fact, and he dealt with those responsible for your plight. They died. In fact, I'd say it's worked out for you. Just look out the window."

Namath looked outside briefly. He stiffened in front of her, raising his chin. "If it were up to me, you wouldn't set foot on that chopper, but the Forerunner has already requested you come along."

Magnolia felt the numbness in her heart suddenly fading, replaced by the spark of excitement.

"You *will* follow my orders," Namath said.

"Yes," she said.

The captain studied her another long moment, then nodded. He turned to the guard. "Corporal, take Miss Katib to the Jayhawk to get suited up."

"Yes, sir," said the guard.

"Watch your back with that one," Jack said.

"I can handle things, thank you, General," Namath said.

Jack cracked a half grin as Magnolia walked to the hatch. She considered spitting in his face on her way out. Stopping just shy of the exit, she turned to Imulah.

"Tell Sofia and everyone else where I'm going," she said. "Tell them I'm sorry I couldn't say goodbye."

Imulah bowed slightly. "Best of luck, Magnolia. May you find peace."

She smiled at him. Despite their tumultuous past, she appreciated his wisdom and support.

"This way," said the captain.

He guided her through the ship, to the stern weather deck. The Jayhawk was already there, perched on a landing pad. Engineers and mechanics were stripping out anything nonessential to cut weight. Others worked to install new batteries. They also appeared to be adding cold-weather gear from stacks of crates. A pair of soldiers in black armor that reminded her of Hell Diver gear were already there, squinting in the sunshine as she was brought over.

"This is Hell Diver Magnolia Cohiba," said her escort.

"Katib," she grunted. "Just call me Magnolia."

"She will be accompanying you all to Concordia Station."

The two men exchanged a glance as the corporal stepped

away, leaving Magnolia alone with them. They both were big and muscular. They looked well trained.

"I'm Master Chief Clay," said one. "This is Sergeant Donny."

Magnolia simply nodded.

"Find a suit and some armor," said Clay. "We're taking off as soon as Captain Namath and Lieutenant Mamoa arrive."

Magnolia went to the crates the master chief pointed to. Inside was plenty of cold-weather gear. Coats, snow pants, hats, gloves, socks, ice masks, and boots. It took her a while to find gear that fit, and by the time she was dressed, another man arrived.

"Lieutenant Mamoa," said Clay.

A blond man of some thirty-five years carried a pilot's helmet under his arm as he jogged over in a blue flight suit. His hazel eyes fell on Magnolia.

"Who the bloody hell are you?" he asked.

"Magnolia Katib," she said. "I'm a Hell Diver. Who the fuck are you?"

"She's coming with us, Lieutenant," Clay said.

Mamoa shifted his helmet to the other arm. "On whose orders?"

"Mine."

Captain Namath walked up, looking the Jayhawk over as mechanics continued to bustle about the craft. After a quick scan, he went to Mamoa.

"You're sure it can make it?"

"Yes, sir. We've reinforced the batteries to protect them from the cold, and we have plenty, plus onboard charging."

"How long till we're ready?"

"We're close—maybe an hour, max."

Magnolia kept quiet, taking in the sights during their final preparations. The flotilla of Trident vessels, the distant Cazador rigs, and the capitol tower that she had called home for several years of her life. Her best friend was still there with her son, Rhino Jr., probably worried sick about his future.

What Magnolia was going to do might help secure that future.

Shouting distracted her. The voices were distant but somewhere on the ship. The rumble of large engines came over the water. She walked over to the cockpit of the helicopter, trying to listen to a radio transmission from the bank of equipment but only picking up something about a missing patrol.

Master Chief Clay huddled with Captain Namath on the other side of the bird as she leaned in to listen.

"Two of ours haven't reported back," Clay said. "General Jack is putting together a search and rescue."

"We're ready to roll," Mamoa called out.

Namath glanced out over the railing to a Cazador rig, then back to the Jayhawk. "Okay, everyone, let's move out."

The soldiers boarded, Magnolia joining them in the cargo hold. They sat facing one another in the back. Outside, a mechanic gave a final thumbs-up.

Mamoa secured his helmet and moved up into the cockpit, where he strapped in and started ticking through the preflight checks.

"Get comfortable back there," he said. "It's over twelve thousand miles to Concordia Station. We're looking at a bloody damned long flight of forty-plus hours in good weather conditions, which we don't have."

Magnolia settled into her seat, pulling her harness over her chest.

"Okay, here we go," Mamoa said.

The rotors turned, and the helicopter came just off the deck. Magnolia turned to look out a viewport as they pulled away from the deck of the ship. On the water, two speedboats packed full of knights motored away from the vessel. Even from far above, she could make out the rigid silhouette of General Jack as the boats thumped over the waves, racing away from the flotilla and toward the Cazador rigs. She didn't know what was brewing—only that it couldn't be good.

But she had a new mission to focus on—in the sky, where she felt at home.

Magnolia looked to the capitol tower, bidding her friends a silent goodbye. Even with Gran Jefe dead, the place was still a powder keg as long as Jack was in charge. She feared what might happen, but there was nothing she could do to prevent bloodshed or to fight. Her heart no longer felt present here, and it might never again.

Whatever future she had was out there somewhere.

*   *   *   *   *

"We have to move now," Michael said.

There was no time for a debate. They were out of time.

The airship was directly over the fortress at Agadir Oufella, hovering in the thick cloud cover at two thousand feet. Normally, this was one of the most dangerous altitudes due to electrical storms, and while none were raging at the moment, there was no telling when they might experience severe weather.

Through the clouds, one of their bow cameras showed an image of Victor, very much alive and being moved to a stone terrace facing the ocean. The infrared showed him being dragged by two men and dumped on the ground. Another camera had already captured what this terrace was used for—displaying heads mounted on pikes. The bodies that once corresponded to those heads now hung from ropes over the wall, suspended a hundred feet above the shoreline.

Gabi looked on in horror, whispering, "*¡Dios mío!*"

"Okay, let's hear this plan again," Layla said, bouncing Bray on her lap.

Everyone looked to Michael as he laid out his plan.

"We drop the crates into the prisoner area with a recorded message explaining what they're for and why they should fight," he explained. "A minute or two after the crates land, I will dive down and get Victor out of there on a booster."

"What happens if these people don't fight?" Layla asked.

"Then Timothy'd better put on a hell of a distraction with the flare systems," Michael said. "Something tells me, though, these people will. Especially after they realize they aren't alone, which will be explained in the message I recorded."

"I've uploaded it and programmed it to play as soon as the crates hit the ground," said Timothy. "I'm confident I can get them right where they need to be, without any guards seeing them on the way in."

"Okay, do you have a DZ for me?"

"I would suggest this location."

A monitor in front of them showed the seaward walls of the fortress.

"Five hundred feet east of the terrace where Victor is currently held," Timothy explained. "If you can land there, you will have a view of Victor and the prisoners, who are about one thousand feet north of the wall. As soon as they open fire on the slavers, I'll unleash a barrage of flares, providing a secondary distraction for you to take this staircase down to Victor."

The camera image shifted to show the stone stairs.

"Take those; strap the booster on Victor," Timothy said. He offered a smile. "You two will both be on your way back to the ship before the enemy knows what hit them."

Michael smiled back and then looked to Layla for her approval. She didn't hesitate.

"Go and get Victor. But please, please be careful."

"I will, and I will."

He kissed her on the lips and hugged her with Bray.

"Da-da go?" asked their son.

"Just for a little bit," Michael said. "I love you, buddy. I'll be back soon."

"We can't lose you, Michael," Layla said.

"And you won't."

He hugged them again and then rushed to the launch bay, already in his armor. Two boosters were already laid out with his chute. After securing it all over his armor, he grabbed the laser rifle and a pistol with an extended magazine. Almost all the other weapons would be going down to the prisoners. Michael had to count on these people wanting freedom as badly as the people he had seen back in the cave, who had killed and eaten their captor.

"Timothy, I want you to relay the video feed from the cameras to my HUD so I can watch Victor's location," Michael ordered.

"On it, Chief."

Michael clipped his helmet on and stepped up to the launch-bay door. This would be a short dive—only two thousand feet to the ground, which meant only a few seconds before deploying his chute. Normally, he would be opening up another thousand feet higher, but he couldn't risk hanging in the air long enough to be spotted, maybe even shot.

The drop zone Timothy had chosen was an abandoned section of fortress wall. If he could control his chute one handed, there was ample room to touch down.

A visual image emerged on his HUD: Victor, still in the same location on the terrace. He was lying on the stone, curled up in a fetal position. Only a single guard was there, but the others could return at any minute and finish him off.

Michael had to move.

"Drop the crates," he said.

"Dropping in one minute," Timothy said.

As he waited, Michael did a systems check. After confirming that his suit was operational, he opened a channel to Layla. "Comms check," he said.

"Copy," Layla said. "You ready?"

"Good to go."

"Ten seconds to deployment of crates," Timothy announced.

Michael stepped up to the hatch. He remembered diving to Mount Kilimanjaro, thinking that if he didn't dive, his home would never be safe for Layla and Bray, that there was no other way. Today, he was diving for another reason: to save Victor and free these people.

"Crates away," Timothy said.

Michael watched his HUD, tracking the beacons of both crates as they plummeted toward the open-air prison of the slaves. In seconds, the big cargo parachutes would deploy, and seconds later, they would touch down and his message would play—a message of hope.

That message replayed in his mind as the crates closed in on their target.

"You are not alone," Michael had said and Timothy translated to Arabic and Spanish. "This very moment, people from across the world are rushing to save one of their own—a warrior who slew many of your captors. Together, if you rise up, we can defeat them and you will be free. But you must make your decision now, while there's time, before your captors can strike back."

The crates both landed, hitting the dirt inside the prison, just as Timothy had promised. A few heat signatures of prisoners went over to investigate.

"Fight for your freedom," Michael whispered. "How do you say that in Spanish, Timothy?"

"*Lucha por tu libertad,*" replied the AI.

Michael repeated it a few times. He waited a few more seconds, then heaved a breath. "Okay," he said. "Open the hatch."

"Good luck, Chief," Timothy said.

"I love you, Michael, and Bray loves you," Layla said over the open channel.

"I love you both."

The hatch creaked open, letting a warm gust of wind inside the hold. Michael leaped right into it, but he didn't arrow into the usual nosedive. Instead, he extended his arms and spread his legs wider than normal to help slow his descent.

His altimeter ticked down from two thousand to eighteen hundred. A glance over his shoulder confirmed the airship was out of sight, hidden in the clouds. He was in the open now, though, accelerating toward the fortress below. There was no room for error and no room for fear. He was utterly focused on getting to the ground safely. Then he would move to his next objective, and then on to the next, making each in turn his sole priority.

A pocket of turbulence batted him about. He tried to turn on instinct—a mistake that knocked him out of stable position. The powerful wind shear cartwheeled his body. He did a hard arch to fight his way back into stable position over the next five hundred feet. By the time he did, the altimeter read nine hundred feet. A second or two remained before he had to pop his chute.

At this low altitude, he already had a clear view of his target from the torches burning across the stone walls. He waited until the meter read 750 feet. Then he reached down to his thigh and pulled his pilot chute to haul out the main canopy. The suspension lines went taut above him, checking his descent with a jerk.

He grabbed the toggle and steered toward the drop zone on the fortress wall. It would take some work, but he was on course. His gaze alternated from his HUD to the ground, and back to his

HUD. Victor was still in the same location, but there were two guards again.

When his eyes went back to the ground, Michael saw something else that made his heart skip. A flickering light moved across his drop zone. His mind made sense of what his eyes were seeing—the light was a torch, being carried by a soldier.

"Oh, shit," Michael whispered.

There were just seconds to correct his drop, but as he searched desperately for a new DZ, he realized there was nothing, other than smacking into the outer wall.

Michael keyed on the soldier with the torch, whose back was now turned. He needed to put down and surprise this man, killing him before he could call out. It was a huge risk, but the only option he could see.

The ancient stone walls rose up to meet his boots. He sailed over the first wall, about five hundred feet from the terrace where Victor was being held. Raising his knees slightly, Michael performed a two-stage flare, swooping down and tiptoeing effortlessly out of the sky. As soon as his boots hit the ground, he popped the Capewells to release his chute, pulling his knife as he ran toward the slaver with the torch.

The man halted, perhaps hearing something, and turned—right into Michael's blade. He pushed it in deep and twisted, wrecking the larynx to make sure not a peep escaped.

The man dropped the torch to the ground and grasped his throat. His other hand held a pistol. Michael let go of the knife and grabbed the weapon, plucking it free. He stepped back as the slaver collapsed to the ground, wide eyes locked on this attacker who had appeared from nowhere.

Flames spread out from the torch, and Michael turned to see they were close to setting the parachute on fire. He stomped out all of the flames, and darkness again enveloped him. Crouching, he holstered the pistol and unslung the laser rifle, scanning the long wall for other targets. Seeing none, he grabbed the chute to pack it away. When he was done, the slaver lay dead in a still-growing halo of blood.

For a moment, Michael paused to listen for voices and gunfire—any sign the prisoners had gotten the packages. But he heard nothing over the soft beating of waves and cries of seagulls.

He went to the edge of the wall, crouching to study the fenced-off area of the prison. Michael couldn't hear the prisoners, but he could see them gathering around the two crates. He looked to the front gate, where a guard stood, his back turned.

Two more sentries sat on chairs atop fortress walls overlooking the area. But both of them were still—either asleep or just not paying attention.

Michael got up and went west toward Victor. He moved quickly, keeping low and away from the parapet facing the prison. Halfway to the western overlook that would give him a view of Victor, he heard shouting, some of it in Spanish. Something about coming from the sky.

Michael hunched down along the parapet to look for the source of the voices. But these seemed to be originating from where Victor lay bound. He got back up and ran the rest of the way down the parapet to the very end.

Just as Michael looked down to the area where Victor was restrained, a guard looked up at him. The slaver tilted his head as if he couldn't credit what he was seeing. Michael didn't hesitate as he aimed the laser rifle and fired a bolt through the man's midsection. The other guard tried to dive away, but Michael lasered him through the back.

"Timothy, now!" he said into the comm.

Streaks blasted from the clouds and became a constellation of parachute flares. Bursting in brilliant glows that spread out in the darkness, they lit the enemy positions up almost as bright as day.

"Fight for your freedom!" Michael shouted. "*¡Lucha por tu libertad!*"

Michael sighted up the guard at the gates and fired. His shot missed, but a flurry of bullets from inside the prison did not. The sentry crumpled under a barrage of gunfire. It came from the prisoners.

"Yes!" Michael said proudly. He ran to the stairs, taking them down to the terrace, where Victor squirmed on the ground, his hands and feet bound. Michael cut him free, then helped him up.

"I got you, brother," he said. "Here, put this on."

Michael shrugged off a booster pack and helped Victor into it. Gunshots cracked inside the fortress, and more flares whistled out of the sky. Everything was going perfectly to plan.

"Okay, let's get you home," Michael said. He was reaching over Victor's shoulder to hit the booster pack when a voice surged over the comms.

"*Chief, you have contacts coming in from the northeast,*" Timothy said. "*Looks like riders on horses. Ten of them.*"

Michael hit the button on Victor's booster pack, deploying the balloon. It inflated, launching him into the sky. Victor reached down, struggling to say something that Michael couldn't make out. He went to the parapet of the terrace overlooking the battle below.

The prisoners had killed some of the guards and broken the gate down in the fenced area. Two surviving slavers fired at the fleeing people, gunning down two women. Return fire dropped both guards. Michael fired from his vantage point, trying to give the prisoners a chance to flee. They scattered in all directions, but a large group headed right for the exit of the prison—right where the horsemen were heading.

An young voice called out, and Michael tracked it to five kids that had been separated from the adults.

"Michael, get in the air!" Layla urged over the comms.

He hesitated, staring in horror at the children milling and running in panic. He glanced up at the clouds. Victor was away, the mission to save him complete. Michael could go back to his family up there.

But leaving the kids was something he would have to live with for the rest of his life.

No, he couldn't abandon them.

He had started this, and he was going to finish it.

TWENTY-FIVE

Gran Jefe pulled down the cowl of the leather duster he wore. Frank's holographic glow lit up the abandoned corridor on the lower level of the main Cazador rig. They were here to hide the dead knight's armor that Gran Jefe had used as a disguise to get on the rig. The rest of the evidence was gone, including the bodies and the boat now at the bottom of the ocean. He had covered his tracks and had a new disguise, but his work was just starting. His next objective was to figure out what the knights knew about him.

"*Silencio, por favor,*" Gran Jefe told Frank.

The AI vanished, and Gran Jefe tucked the remote in his duster. Pistol in one hand, knife in the other, he started up the stairwell to the upper decks. The third level was his first stop. He checked an intersection of passageways, saw a few people coming and going. When they passed, he slipped into a darkened nook where a criminal named Pepe often loitered to sell his black-market goods. Sure enough, Gran Jefe heard the familiar nasal voice in the distance.

Just weeks ago, Gran Jefe had put the squeeze on Pepe in

search of the special drugs General Forge had ordered Gran Jefe to find—drugs for their knight prisoner, Lucky.

Now Forge was dead and Lucky was doing fine. The irony enraged Gran Jefe as he stalked Pepe through the deck of the Cazador rig. In such a short time, fortunes had changed, and now Gran Jefe no longer needed the man's medicine—he needed his *help*.

Surprisingly, life hadn't changed much for the Cazadores living on this rig since the enemy's arrival. These people were used to living on scraps and offal. The stench of raw sewage and body odor drifted through the cramped warren of shacks, tents, and sheet-metal shanties these people called home.

Pepe stopped at a tent, bent down, and unzipped it. He spoke in hushed tones to whoever lived inside. Gran Jefe seized the moment by moving ahead of Pepe and stepping into a partially blocked off corridor. There in the blackness, he waited. The wait wasn't long.

As Pepe stepped by, Gran Jefe grabbed him by a bony arm and yanked him into the darkness, putting a hand over his mouth.

"Scream and I snap your scrawny neck," Gran Jefe said in Spanish. "When I pull my hand away, you tell me what the knights know about Gran Jefe."

Pepe glanced back, eyes widening when he saw Gran Jefe. Then he nodded in understanding. Before pulling his hand away, Gran Jefe let go of Pepe's arm to bring his own arm up around his neck. Now Pepe couldn't scream if he wanted to.

"The knights have only come here twice—once to recover weapons, and the other time to go to your apartment," Pepe said. "They tore through your room."

Gran Jefe had expected this, which was why he didn't go there to find gear. But what he really feared was that they would know about his son.

But only a few people knew—hell, Gran Jefe had only recently found out.

"What else?" he said, smacking Pepe on the back of the head when he went quiet.

"That's all I know about you, I swear. Everyone thought you were dead."

"Have they taken anyone prisoner?"

"Not here, but on other rigs. I heard only rumors—we've been cut off since the invasion." Pepe took in a breath. "Kade Long spoke to us, said not to fight. Told us the world would go back to the old ways; the sun would shine everywhere."

"And you believed him?"

Pepe paused, then said, "We're all sick of war, Jorge."

Gran Jefe relaxed his grip a little. Then he tightened it again. "You tell anyone you saw me, and—"

"I won't, I won't!"

Gran Jefe winced in pain as he pulled his arm away.

"You're hurt," Pepe said.

"It's nothing."

"I'll help. I have medicine."

"Oh, so *now* you have it?"

"I had some before, just wasn't going to give it to those bastards, you know."

Gran Jefe snorted. "Okay, I'll follow you, but you make a single wrong move and—"

"I won't," Pepe said.

Reluctantly Gran Jefe let go of the man. And like a fish that has just gotten off the line, he bolted into the darkness. At first, Gran Jefe thought he was running away, but Pepe stopped and motioned for him. Moving out into the deck, passing dozens of cramped apartments, Pepe checked around a corner, then waved again.

They continued to the door of his room, where Pepe jangled his key chain. Fumbling in the dim light, he found the right key, inserted it, and cracked the door open. Gran Jefe looked over his shoulder to see if they had a tail. Nothing that he could see. No loiterers outside either. The prostitutes who often frequented this floor were keeping their heads down.

Gran Jefe stepped into the room, narrowing his gaze on Pepe, wondering suddenly if this was a trap. Pepe went to a crate in the center of the small room. Gran Jefe checked the connecting rooms, finding a shit can and a small kitchenette that reeked almost as badly.

"Here," Pepe said. He held up a bottle from a crate he had opened. "The good stuff."

Gran Jefe glanced outside again, then closed the door. He walked over and snatched the bottle. "Got any water?" he asked.

Pepe pointed with his chin at the kitchenette.

"You get it," Gran Jefe said.

Pepe went to pour water while Gran Jefe popped the bottle open. He downed the two pills, then chased them with the jug of water Pepe handed him. As he gulped it down, he eyed Pepe, not taking his eyes off the man for a second.

"Thanks," he said.

"No problem."

Gran Jefe went to the open crate. It wasn't just medicine inside. Pepe had stashed all sorts of stuff in the box. Gran Jefe rifled through the contents. He pulled out bandages, some Cazador-made antibiotic ointment, glue, and tape.

With the materials in hand, he took a seat on a chair and shrugged off the duster. Raising his arm made him wince again.

Pepe craned his neck to get a look. "Ouch," he said.

Gran Jefe cleaned the gash. Fresh blood oozed out. He dressed it with the ointment, then taped the bandage in place.

"Got any weapons?" he asked.

"Thought you'd never ask." Pepe went over to a filthy rug, pulling it back to reveal a trapdoor much like what Gran Jefe had in his apartment. "You didn't get these from me," he said.

Gran Jefe walked over and peered in to find an impressive cache of weapons. Two pistols. A bag of knives that clattered as Pepe heaved them out with his bony arms. Then he reached inside and pulled out a double-barreled shotgun with the barrels sawed off.

"Nice, yeah?" he asked.

Gran Jefe nodded. "Yeah... very nice." He took the weapon, admiring it. "I'm curious—why are you helping me?"

"'Cause you're the only one that can free us."

"I thought you are sick of war."

"I'm no soldier." Pepe handed him a box of shells for the shotgun. "You are—the great boss warrior."

A few minutes later, Gran Jefe had the duster back on. Beneath it, he was armed with five knives, the pistol, and the shotgun. Not much, but it was a good start.

"What are you going to do now?" Pepe asked.

"I'm going to start freeing us," Gran Jefe said. "You got any food, though?"

"A bit." Pepe turned and then returned with some fish jerky that Gran Jefe scarfed down.

"God, that's nasty," he said, wincing as he chewed.

"Sorry, it's pretty old, but better than nothin'."

"Long as it doesn't make me shit myself."

Pepe shrugged. "Good luck, boss."

They shook arms in the Cazador way. Then Gran Jefe turned to the door. With one hand on the shotgun under his duster, he used the other to open the door, checking both ways. Seeing it was clear, he stepped out.

Maybe it was just a placebo effect, but he already felt better from the pills. The cream had soothed his wound too, allowing his arm better range of movement. Now he would do what he came here to do: make sure his son was okay. Then he would start to look for real allies—not the Pepes of the world, but soldiers. Warriors who would fight back and free the islands from the knights.

He made his way up to the main deck, where Jada lived with their son and her husband, Chano. Gran Jefe kept his hood up, obscuring his features. Most people were inside their apartments, shacks, and tents on the way up, but he encountered a few randoms making their way down the many corridors. Fortunately for him, down here most of the lights were burned out or broken.

Finally, he came up a stairwell to the open area, where hundreds of people lived in deplorable conditions. The scent of raw sewage hit him hard in the shadows of the stairwell. He peered out at a bustling communal area that formed around a large black iron cauldron. A fire burned under it, and a hunched woman stood on a step stool with a spoon the size of a canoe paddle.

Lines of hungry people waited for the stew—a swill of discarded fish parts, seaweed, and herbs to make it palatable. These people wasted nothing.

Gran Jefe moved out of the stairwell, keeping to the shadows of the dilapidated shacks cobbled together out of rusted sheet metal and wood. Tarps and plastic sheeting covered the gaps to keep out water leaks. Two empty crates sat in front of a table with an abandoned game of dominoes. The men who usually sat here most of the day playing the ancient game were gone.

Pushing on, Gran Jefe passed a tent that he remembered from his last visit. A candle burned inside, the glow lighting up a single person on a cot. A face emerged as he walked by. It was the retired fisherman who was rocking his skeletal wife the last time Gran Jefe passed this way. Gran Jefe had been right: he would never see the woman again. The man looked out through the open tent flap with sad eyes.

Gran Jefe continued to the communal open space, keeping to whatever shadow he could find among the flimsy shacks built against the pillars of the rig. Across the way, beyond the line of people waiting for food, he saw the hut where Jada and Chano lived with Pablo. The door and window of the shack were dark.

His eyes scanned the gathered crowd, stopping at the thin form of Chano at the very end. But where were Jada and Pablo?

Pulling his hood down lower, he took a step out, then halted. He noticed that the queue wasn't moving toward the pot, and the woman wasn't scooping any out. Everyone had their head down.

The clank of boots reached his ears as soldiers with assault rifles poured in across the room.

"You're surrounded. Get on the deck NOW!"

A knight carrying a sword strode toward him, pointing down. Gran Jefe quickly took in the area. He counted five heavily armed and armored soldiers.

He already had his finger on the trigger of the shotgun and was prepared to raise it at the knight with a rifle on his right. He would blast him first, then dive away, find cover, and begin picking off the others.

He could survive this. He could still escape.

"This is the end of your journey, Jorge Mata," boomed a deep, throaty voice. "My name's General Jack, and I have to say, I've never wanted to kill someone as badly as I've wanted to kill you."

A hulking knight in armor emerged next to the hut that belonged to Jada and Chano. The general moved out, holding a squirming figure that Gran Jefe already knew was his son.

"You've proved you're a formidable warrior," Jack said. "Too bad you're also a barbarian. I could use soldiers like you in my army."

"Let him go!" Gran Jefe said.

Pablo squirmed and snarled in the general's grip.

"You're like your dad—a wild animal," Jack said to Pablo. "Did you know that's your father—your *papá*?"

The boy cocked his head a little, staring curiously at Gran Jefe.

"He doesn't know, does he?" Jack said with a laugh. He looked over at Jada, who was being held by another knight a few feet away. She stared at Gran Jefe, anger in her gaze, but for once, it wasn't directed at him. Her wide eyes pleaded with him to do something to save their son.

The general pulled a saw-toothed blade from a sheath and held it down to Pablo.

"No!" Gran Jefe screamed. "This is between men, not a boy!"

"This boy will grow up to be like you—a barbarian!"

Jada broke free from her captor, bolting toward Jack and leaping into the air like a cat with extended claws. The general smacked her to the ground.

"*¡Mamá!*" Pablo shouted.

Anger burned through Gran Jefe as the knight with the sword approached and the rifles of other soldiers closed in. He had been prepared to strike, but now he was frozen out of fear that if he did, the general would slit his son's throat and then kill Jada.

He had survived the Man Maker, then the pigs, and then the ocean. But his luck had run out. There was nothing more he could do.

Gran Jefe shrugged off his coat, dropped the shotgun, and discarded the pistols. The knives went next, clanking onto the deck. The knights moved in around him, taking him to the ground as Jada and Pablo watched.

For the first time in years, Gran Jefe saw something on her face that wasn't rage. It was sadness as they dragged him away.

*   *   *   *   *

"How's he doing?" X asked.

"Hanging in there," Josie replied.

"The Forerunner is strong," Watt added. "He'll hang on until the missions are over."

The knight wasn't fully recovered from his injuries just two days ago at Polar Station, but he was back on his feet and ready for what came next. If the Forerunner was right, then the same model of Cerebro that had attacked them at the North Pole was also protecting Concordia Station.

X went to the glass lid of the medical pod holding the Forerunner's broken body—the same pod that X had spent days in after turning himself over to the cyborg. Since then, X had gone from seeing Noah as an enemy to seeing him as an ally. Through their conversations, X had learned that there was far more to him than almost anyone else understood. On the outside, he looked more machine than man, but their conversations had opened X's eyes to a lifetime of service to the people of the Coral Castle.

In many ways, X and the shadow of a man beyond the glass were alike. Both had given everything to their people, sacrificing pieces of both body and soul to protect their homes. Noah, however, had suffered far longer. He deserved rest.

X had a feeling Watt was right, though—that the Forerunner would hang on to the bitter end, to ensure that the world he left behind was better than the one he had entered.

"I won't let you down," X said.

He stepped back as Josie put a hand on the glass and bowed her head, whispering something under her breath. Watt did the same thing. It was clear they were both devoted to their leader and felt a deep connection to him, even now.

"Follow me," Josie said. She guided them out of the medical chamber to the launch bay.

"Have we heard anything from Kade?" X asked along the way.

"I'm afraid not," Josie replied. "It may be they have gone dark to hunker down."

X knew the other possibility, of course: that they were already dead.

"We have been in contact with Captain Namath," she added. "His squad is en route but won't arrive for another thirty-plus hours, depending on weather."

"Is Magnolia with them?"

"Yes."

He felt a degree of relief that she was alive and doing well, but he worried about her heading out into the unknown. Alone, the trip would be extremely dangerous.

Josie stopped outside the launch bay. The hatches opened to a bare space—a chilling reminder of how few souls were left to save the world. Across the room, Valeria stood over Miles and Jo-Jo, both of them dressed in cold-weather gear. They both had been through rigorous training and dived to many hostile areas—Jo-Jo with Ada, Miles with X. Moreover, both had proved they could function in extreme conditions. Jo-Jo had grown up in the wastes, and Miles spent ten years of hell out there with X. Still, X wondered whether this was the right move, even if they could prove useful down there.

Miles barked and ran over, tail wagging, clearly excited about the prospect of coming. Jo-Jo, too, seemed stir crazy, and anxious to get off the ship.

"Okay, change of plans," Josie said.

HELL DIVERS XII: HEROES

Watt, X, and Valeria gathered in front of Commander Hallsey inside the locker area as the animals sat on the deck looking on.

"The weather is too severe for a dive, and the enemy already knows about Team Concordia," Josie said. "For that reason, we won't dive in and will instead set down near Kade and Lucky's last known position and search for them on foot."

"We?" X asked.

"I'm coming," Josie said. She turned to her locker and opened it to reveal a diving suit and armor just like what X had been given.

"All due respect, but would the Forerunner want you coming with us?" X asked. "He specifically said you'll be in charge of the restoration project if—"

"If the mission fails, there won't be a restoration project. I will do my part to achieve total victory, and I have been trained for combat."

"Okay, but who will fly the ship?"

"AI will take command."

X blew out a breath. "Figured you'd say that."

"Commander Hallsey can shoot a fly off a dingo's ass—I've seen her do it," Watt said. "Best shot in the Trident ranks."

"Good. We'll need someone down there to take out that robotic beast, although I'm not sure we have the firepower."

"Actually, I've got just the thing," she said, gesturing for X to follow.

They went to the armory, where she tapped in a code to open the gate.

"There's only one weapon we have that can penetrate the armor on that machine." She pointed at the wall, where two large rifles were mounted. "A railgun."

"How's that?" X asked.

"A railgun is an electromagnetic weapon that uses electrical current to accelerate a projectile to very high speeds. We didn't use them at Polar Station, because they aren't efficient in a battle, due to their low rate of fire, but a direct hit should take out the Cerebro."

X took one of the weapons down off its mount. It was much heavier than a normal rifle.

"Take a secondary weapon too," Josie said.

X scanned the wall of weapons: assault rifles, laser rifles, submachine guns, grenade launchers, pistols of all calibers, shotguns, and bolt-action rifles. He went for an assault rifle, and a .357 Magnum semiauto pistol for some extra kick.

Josie grabbed a railgun, slung it over her armored shoulders, and grabbed a shotgun. Watt walked in next and selected an assault rifle with a grenade launcher.

"Didn't get a chance to thank you," he said. "For pulling me out of there."

"No thanks necessary," X said.

He patted Watt on the shoulder and walked out of the armory, heading back to his animals and Valeria.

"You sure I can't talk you out of this?" he asked.

She gave him that smile that sparked a warmth inside him that he hadn't felt for years.

"Okay," he said. "Go get a weapon."

Valeria went to the armory and returned with a pump-action shotgun and two pistols.

Miles and Jo-Jo were both suited up. X heaved a sigh at the thought of what would happen if the Cerebro attacked them. But now X had a weapon that could take it out before that happened.

He bent down to Miles, who wagged his tail under his coat, happy to be coming along and not left behind.

Josie clanked over to them in her full armor. "Preparing to descend over coordinates," she said. She stood in front of the group, pushing shells into her shotgun.

As they neared their destination, a heavy tension fell over the survivors. Jo-Jo grunted nervously, and Miles had gone down on his haunches, no longer acting excited as the airship rumbled through the clouds.

X caught Miles looking up at him with a glimmer of fear in his eyes. His boy knew they were heading toward danger. A tendril of dread wormed through X's psyche—a sixth sense about something happening to Miles. It felt unlike his normal worries.

"Shit," X whispered.

"¿Qué? . . . What?" Valeria asked.

"I just got a bad feeling."

"We're descending over the coordinates, attempting comms with Team Concordia," Josie said.

The beginning data came in over their HUDs. A negative-forty-degree windchill awaited them on the surface, along with blowing snow that would reduce visibility. Miles still had his enhanced sense of smell, but his vision was no longer what it once was. He would have a hard time seeing in the darkness and snow. And with no armor to protect his body, it would take only a single swipe of a bladed robotic arm to kill the dog.

"No response from Kade or Gaz," Josie reported. "Life scans aren't picking up anything."

X's mind was awhirl with worry. What if the Cerebro had found them and killed them and was waiting for Team Polar? What if they were setting down into a trap?

"I don't like this," X whispered.

Valeria again turned to him.

"I think we've got to keep Miles back," he said. "It's too dangerous."

The ship rocked through a pocket of heavy turbulence in the clouds. When it passed, X squatted down in front of Miles.

"Thirty seconds to touchdown," Josie announced. She looked back at X.

"He can stay here, but you need to decide fast," she said.

X pulled the dog over. "Bud, I know you're going to be mad, but you got to stay back again." He hugged Miles tight. "I'm going to come back, promise."

Miles whined, pulling out of his grip as Valeria bent down.

"I'll watch out for your old man, *no problema*," she said.

"Ten seconds," Josie said.

The hatches began to open, and X stood. Just as he did, Miles bounded forward, darting onto the extending ramp. Snow blasted into the cargo hold.

"Miles, get back here!" X commanded.

But Miles leaped off the extending ramp and out into the snow.

"Son of a gun," X said.

"Go. Everyone out," said Josie.

The group set off behind the commander. As soon as they were on the ground, the airship rose away while still retracting its ramp. X saw Miles ahead, sitting on his haunches. He got up as X approached, tail beating under his suit.

The whir of the airship was drowned out in the howling storm. It was too late now to turn back. X patted his leg, and Miles fell in with him, hopping over the three inches of powder. Valeria kept close to Jo-Jo as the team advanced, with Watt right behind Josie, who trotted through the storm on point. Distant flashes from an electrical storm surged to the north, providing a weak glow but not nearly enough to see through the darkness.

The team relied on their night-vision optics; flashlight beams were too risky. Jo-Jo was managing well in the harsh conditions, and Miles appeared to be doing okay. X kept close to the dog, cradling his rifle as they closed in on the city. It wasn't far to a sturdy metal fence bordering the city. Snowcapped buildings, designed to be a bastion for survivors to restart civilization, rose up on the other side.

X found a gap in the fence and ducked under it, motioning for Miles to come ahead. The dog sniffed the cold air, then went rigid.

"What is it?" Josie asked.

"He's got a scent," X said. "Stay here. I'll check it out."

They crossed the drifts of snow to the first row of buildings. X took an alley between two structures. A wall of snow blocked the view to the street on the other side, forcing him to clamber up for a look. Miles made his way up next to X, sniffing again. He gave the all clear by standing up, but X took a few more seconds to search for hostiles.

Seeing nothing out there, he turned and motioned for the team. Together, they trekked into the next street. Miles kept his nose down to the snow but looked up every few feet, scanning the iced windows of structures towering over them. X felt it too— the sensation of being watched. Something was out there.

Miles trotted after the scent to a caved-in entrance of a three-story domed building. Snow had piled inside a lobby full of scattered furniture.

"We'll take a look," X said. "Stay here."

The team gathered in the lobby, where Jo-Jo shivered from the cold as Miles sniffed over to a cracked door that opened to a stairwell. X turned on his rifle beam and started up the stairs to the second level.

Just inside the hallway, he noticed something on the tattered carpet. He bent down and found frozen blood. Turning, he checked the stairs with the beam but didn't see any other flecks of red. The path must have been from the other direction, down the hall.

He followed the blood drips to an open door, listening for contacts. At the doorway, he motioned Miles back, then moved inside with his rifle shouldered.

Lowering the beam, he found a macabre scene of body parts scattered on the carpet. The light illuminated a severed leg, an arm, and what looked like a human jaw.

"God," X whispered. It looked as though he had found a member of Team Concordia, but there was no good way to tell. He stepped back into the hall with Miles. The trail of blood continued down to another stairwell, where he discovered a boot with a foot inside. A few steps down, a mound of viscera had spilled from a torso.

Miles growled a second before X heard a distant howl. He turned from the gruesome sight to the landing where his dog stood growling. The distant noise waned to a soft clicking that sounded closer—right behind him.

Now X knew why Miles was snarling down the stairs.

A chill prickled up his back as he whirled back to the stairwell with his rifle aimed downward. He nearly pulled the trigger but eased off when the light illuminated a figure standing behind the gory mess. X brought his light up to the snow-crusted beard and familiar dark eyes of a Hell Diver.

"Kade, is that really you?" X asked.

"We have to go," Kade said in a whisper. "They're coming."

TWENTY-SIX

Kade couldn't believe it at first, and looked over his shoulder again as he led the motley team along a corridor beneath the city. When he saw X and Miles standing in a stairwell of the domed building, he thought it was some sort of trick of the mastermind machine. Or perhaps he had finally gone insane after everything that had happened.

But they were both real, and so were Valeria, Commander Hallsey, and Watt. Even Jo-Jo was here. She snorted a cloud of condensation from her large nostrils.

"Reinforcements are en route, but they won't be here for another day, maybe longer," Josie explained.

Music to Kade's ears, but they would still need a lot of firepower to take out the machine and all the escaped lab experiments that had so decimated his team.

"You still haven't told us what happened down here," Josie asked.

Kade halted, the words pulling back a flood of fresh memories that burned through his brain. He shuddered recalling the landing that had kicked off the tragedies, with Zuni and Tia dying horrific deaths from the venomous stinging drones.

"I thought she was dead," he stammered. "But then... we... Blue Blood, Zen, Lucky, and I got inside, and she was there. She was *right there*!"

Kade looked down at his shaking hands.

"Bloody hell, I shot her," he murmured.

X walked ahead of Josie, Watt, and the animals, holding up a hand. "It's okay, Kade," he said. "You didn't shoot Tia."

"Yes." Kade nodded. "I shot her in the head."

"It wasn't her, Kade," Josie said.

Kade shook his head, trying to clear his thoughts. "Maybe I could have saved her," he said. He had thought about this over and over again since pulling the trigger. "Maybe I could have brought her back."

X pulled Kade to the side. "You did everything you could, and trust me, I know that losing someone and not being able to save them is hell. I've been there a hundred times, but now you have to focus on the living. People who need you. Alton needs you, Kade. The rest of humanity needs you. Our success doesn't just save the innocent. It avenges everyone who made the ultimate sacrifice before us."

Kade looked up from his hands and met the gaze of a man who knew loss. Loss of loved ones, yes, but also the loss that came with betrayal. His own people had left him on the surface for a decade after he dedicated his life to keeping their ship in the sky. It wasn't just them—Kade's people had betrayed him too, even after X helped save them from enslavement by the machines.

"I'm okay," Kade said. His voice grew stronger. "I'm with you to the end, brother."

"I know." X patted him on the shoulder.

"Kade," Josie said. "Can you tell us more about what's out there?"

"That body you came across—that was Zuni," Kade said. "The

howl you heard—that's from a monster that tore him apart after he was already dead. Now, we should keep moving."

Kade started back down the passage, picking up his pace at the thought of beasts that could, even now, be following them deep underground.

"What are they?" X asked.

"Some sort of hybrid bone beast with fur," Kade said. "It came from a lab at the reactors. Some sort of experiment designed to protect this place. One of them almost killed Lucky on our way here."

"Where is he?" asked Watt.

"Taking you to him now. We've been holed up underground for the past two days. This corridor leads to another building. I've got him set up comfortably in a bunker."

"So that's why you didn't answer the comms?" X asked.

"Right. I was on my way to transmit when I saw you."

"Good timing."

Kade nodded at this. The timing seemed almost *too* good. But he wasn't complaining.

"How bad is Lucky hurt?" Watt asked.

"Got hit with three projectile needle teeth in his abdomen," Kade said. "I stopped the bleeding, but he needs something to fight off the infection. He's in a lot of pain."

"Crikey," Watt breathed. "Needle teeth?"

"Valeria's a medic," X said. "She'll fix him up."

"How many of those things are there?" Josie asked. "Tell me anything that will be useful to us."

Kade went over everything he could remember. Each painful memory spilled out of his mouth in flat, unaccented tones. Somehow, his heart was still beating after everything that had happened to him. But just because blood flowed through his veins and air filled his lungs didn't mean he was truly alive. The last part of him had died with Tia.

Kade stopped, breathed, and pointed to a door. "We're almost there, just—"

Guttural roaring cut him off. Miles and Jo-Jo both responded with grunts, their bodies tensing at the noise. Kade looked past the animals, down the passage they had all come through, but the voice of this creature wasn't coming from behind them. It was coming from the other side of the door.

"Lucky," he said.

Josie moved ahead of Kade.

"How many entrances to this bunker?" she asked.

Kade thought a moment. "There's another way in . . . Those things must have found it."

"Stay behind me," X said. He opened the door and entered another stairwell that went two levels belowground. Kade hurried down the steps, hoping the beast hadn't found Lucky. A gunshot confirmed that it had. Two more followed, close together.

X moved faster, practically loping down the stairs to the closed bunker door. Grabbing the wheel handle, he tried to spin it, but the locking mechanism had been set on the other side.

"Gaz!" Watt shouted.

Kade shook behind X as Lucky's screams echoed out of the bunker. More gunshots popped, followed by howls of rage from the monster attacking him.

"Watt, get this open!" Josie commanded. "Everyone else, back!"

Watt moved ahead, shrugging off a pack and putting an explosive charge on four edges of the vault door. The rest of the team retreated about thirty feet. Muffled shrieks resonated from the other side, but the gunshots had ceased.

"Hurry!" Kade yelled.

Watt ran back to them.

"Fire in the hole!" he shouted.

The explosions boomed in sync, sending out a wave of heat and a hail of shrapnel down the passage. X strode forward into the smoke cloud drifting away from the destroyed door.

"Stay here," he said.

X vanished into the smoke screen with Miles. Kade switched on his infrared optics in the helmet he had taken off Zuni after arriving back at the frozen city. He scanned the bunker beyond but saw no sign of the knight or the monster attacking him.

Unable to hold back another second, Kade hurried down the passage. He had a rocky relationship with Lucky after all they had been through together, but he considered him a friend. Leaving him here alone and injured had been an error.

Kade burst into the room as the smoke dissipated. The cots they had slept on were toppled, along with barrels of food and water. The second exit door was wide open, and a trail of blood snaked up it. There was a lot of blood—too much, Kade thought, for the average person to survive. And with Lucky already injured, his chances couldn't be good.

"Let's go!" Kade shouted. He rushed up the steps, squeezing past Josie, pistol in hand. Three floors up, he arrived in the lower level of the agriculture building. Wind gusted through the broken front doors. The blood trail led into the snow. As his boots sank into the fresh powder, he scanned the area with his NVGs but saw nothing in the violent storm. The gusts felt like a large person pushing on his armor.

A howl carried on the wind. The noise seemed to be coming from the sky. Turning to look in the opposite direction, he spotted a heat signature mounting the rooftop of a building across the street. Another signature flickered next to it. The deformed shapes of the hybrid bone beasts were unmistakable.

He held up a fist as the rest of the group emerged in the lobby.

X and Josie both stood by Kade's side, aiming their railguns in the direction of the monsters. But the monsters weren't alone.

Roaring came from behind them, and Kade turned back to the blood trail, which was fast disappearing in the sheeting snow. At the end of the street, he glimpsed a limp armored figure being dragged away by a hulking beast with a bony exoskeleton.

Josie moved in front of him, aiming her rifle.

"Wait!" Kade said, pushing her gun aside. "You could hit Lucky!"

Josie swung the gun back up to fire again. "That's the point. We can't let them take him alive—"

Gunfire cut off the rest of what she had to say, but realization set in as her bullets flew into the snowstorm. Kade remembered what the machines had wanted when he was captured: the location of the last survivors. This was the final battle between man and machine, with the winner determining the future of the entire planet.

*   *   *   *   *

"Michael, you have to get out of there!" said Layla over the comms. Her voice came across calm and self-assured, despite the crackling static.

"Working on it, but I have five kids with me," Michael replied quietly.

An hour had passed since he jumped down to rescue Victor, kicking off a battle that still raged in the prison. In the chaos, Michael had rushed down to escort five lost kids away from the bloodshed.

But bullets were still flying across the fortress between the surviving prisoners and the reinforcements for the guards. Michael hunkered down in a lookout on a wall to the south. An arched exit door led back to a bridge that draped across the fortress, with a three-foot parapet along both sides. The slaver who manned this post lay crumpled on the ground, part of his head missing from Michael's first laser shot.

In the shadows, the five kids Michael had rescued were huddled together. The oldest was a boy of nine or ten years. There were two more boys of about five and six, and two girls, both toddlers, one younger than Bray. Whether they had parents or other loved ones missing them, Michael wasn't sure.

The crack of gunfire grew sporadic. He could hear the slavers hunting below on their horses. These fighters were much better trained than the tired sentries Michael first took down. To make things worse, another six slavers had been inside another building when the battle broke out, including the lead hunter, who carried the spiked club.

Michael had lost track of him but could hear the results of his work—the thud of metal and spikes on human flesh, the crack of bones, and the screams of the victims. The shivering children could hear it too, and the younger ones were whimpering.

"It's okay. You have to be quiet, okay?" Michael said. "I won't let them hurt you."

The five sets of eyes stared back at him, frightened and not understanding. He brought a finger to his mouth just as another cry of pain rang out, closer this time.

The youngest little girl cried, tears streaking down her grimy face. Michael wanted to turn and comfort her, but he needed his only hand for the rifle.

The sound of cracking bones came again, then again, silencing the screams of the victim. Michael put a finger to his mouth, and one of the older boys pulled a sobbing girl to him.

Rising up, Michael checked out the window. In the center of the fortress was the fenced-off prison filled with tents and

shanties. Outside the fence were several warehouse-style structures. Stone walls, some over a hundred feet tall, bordered the
open lower level. Most of the surrounding areas had collapsed
over the years, and all the structures bordering the city had been
reduced to rubble.

Michael wasn't sure how he was going to get these kids to
safety. He had hoped the prisoners would win the battle with his
help. But having these kids in tow impeded his ability to fight.
Sniping was easy on his own, since he could move quickly and
silently—not possible with the children.

If only he had Timothy to tell him where the enemies were
located, using the cameras on the airship. It now hovered at ten
thousand feet—safely out of the range of most bullets, but also
unable to provide any visual assistance.

A horse whickered in the distance. Michael checked out the
window again to see the silhouette of a horse and rider trotting
down a path between dozens of shanty structures a hundred
yards away.

The rider reined his horse to a stop. He dismounted and
sheathed the spear on the saddle. Then he unslung a crossbow
and started toward a tunnel in the stone wall to the left of the
overlook. Michael didn't know whether any people were hiding
inside, but he couldn't let them be slaughtered. He waited for
his shot to take the slaver down. At two hundred feet away, he
moved his finger to the trigger, when a bullet ricocheted off the
stone window frame.

Michael ducked. He had no idea where the sniper shot had
come from. The kids all stared at him as he turned to face them.
Their position was now compromised. He had to move them. But
doing so with a sniper dialed in would put them all at risk. First,
he needed to take down the shooter.

His gaze flitted from the kids to the dead slaver, an idea

forming in his mind. He grabbed a hand and dragged the corpse over to the window, positioning it against the wall.

A distant shot cracked as he heaved the corpse up. The bullet zipped past the bearded face, confirming this sniper as a lousy shot. Michael glimpsed the muzzle flash on an adjacent wall four hundred feet away. He let the body slump as if it had just been shot; then he ducked over to the other side of the window.

The laser rifle was accurate, but it was still going to be a tough shot at this distance. Holding a breath in his chest, he waited a moment. The kids all watched with wide eyes.

Michael rose up, used the open ledge of the window to mount his rifle, and fired once, then again. In that time, another bullet pinged off the top of the frame, but he didn't flinch. His third shot hit the sniper in the side, knocking them to the ground. He steadied his rifle, finishing off the slaver with a shot to the skull.

The clatter of boots on ladder rungs sent a chill up Michael's neck. He swung his rifle down at a trapdoor in the floor that he hadn't seen before. The door was already propped up, and the slaver with the crossbow was raising the weapon at Michael. The oldest kid jumped on the trapdoor, knocking the crossbow-man forward and banging his head as he fired. The bolt missed Michael's neck narrowly, whizzing harmlessly out the window.

Michael lifted the trapdoor to see the slaver squirming on the dusty ground below. He aimed the laser rifle down.

"No, no!" He held up a gloved hand, which Michael shot through. The laser bolt vaporized the man's face and much of his head.

Screams of horror in the distance were followed by sporadic gunfire. Michael decided to use the distraction to move. He went to the oldest boy, who stared at him with piercing brown eyes.

"Thank you. You did good," Michael said. "Tell the others to follow me, okay?"

The boy nodded in understanding. He picked up the youngest girl, who still sobbed. The other three children huddled together as Michael led them to the arched doorway to the bridge. Before he walked out, he motioned for them to keep low along the parapet.

They nodded back.

Crouching down, Michael checked over the wall for hostiles in the area. He immediately saw a mounted slaver on the northern side of the fenced-off prison. Two prisoners made a run for the front gates into the main city. They screamed as the slaver thrust his spear, skewering one and then the other. Michael considered a shot from this distance, but it would draw attention to him and the children.

He started across the bridge that stretched to the next wall. Crouching down, he kept as low as possible, just slightly above the parapet. Portions had crumbled away, leaving exposed gaps that they had to cross to reach safety.

At the end of the bridge, a stairwell led up to the terrace where the slavers had dumped Victor. If he could get the children up there, then maybe he could take the next set of stairs to the area where he had landed. Then he could try to lower the kids over the seawall and escort them along the shore. Just as he was about to head that way, one of the kids cried, "Ma-ma!"

He turned to find a girl looking over the wall. Below, between two trampled tents, a female body lay sprawled with a spear sticking out of its back.

"Ma-ma!" the girl wailed.

Gunfire flashed in their direction. Michael ran over with his rifle slung, scooping the girl up in his arm. He hit the ground with her gently, flattening his body over hers as bullets pounded the other side of the stone wall. The other kids were all on their bellies, whimpering or scared silent.

"Crawl after me," he said. The oldest boy nodded. Then he guided them toward the stairs leading up to the terrace. Rounds whizzed overhead as Michael tried to squirm forward. The girl sobbed, clinging to him with her legs around his back, arms around his neck.

"It's going to be okay," Michael whispered.

But at this point, he couldn't be sure that was true. He was cornered, and the prisoners had lost the battle. It was just a matter of time before the slavers killed him and recaptured these innocent children.

TWENTY-SEVEN

The Jayhawk flew low over dark windblown waves. Storm clouds formed a thick ceiling in all directions, their lightning bolts illuminating the infinite whitecaps. If this mission succeeded, the storms would clear across the planet, letting the choked-off sun shine once more.

Magnolia had always wondered if that day would come. It was still far from a sure thing. They still had a way to go before they could help X and the other survivors out there. Fifteen hours into the violent flight, and she was about to heave. The never-ending turbulence wasn't something you just got used to. She gazed at the cockpit, where their single pilot sat at the controls. He was good, but he would need rest at some point, even with the stims he kept popping.

She rested her head against the hull, hoping to catch some sleep. As she was getting drowsy, a voice surged over her headset.

"Our long-range comms received a transmission," reported Lieutenant Mamoa over the team channel. *"Commander Hallsey is on the ground now."*

"Hallsey?" asked Captain Namath. "What about the Fore-runner?"

"Didn't say, sir."

"How far out are we?"

"Still another twenty-two hours at our current speed."

"Longer than that, because you're going to need rest."

"I'm good, sir. I can get us there in a straight shot."

Namath didn't reply right away. "We'll take it an hour at a time, but you tell me if you need a rest, Lieutenant, understand?"

"Copy that, sir."

"You better, Mamoa," Clay said. "This time if we belly flop, we're done!"

"Hey, that wasn't my fault," Mamoa protested.

Sergeant Donny laughed at that.

"Belly flop?" Magnolia asked.

Clay and Donny both looked over to Magnolia but said nothing. So far, the knights wanted little to do with her, which wasn't surprising. She was an outsider, and in some of their minds, she was still seen as the enemy.

"We aren't greenhorns, as you might say," explained Captain Namath. He looked over to Magnolia from two seats down. Of all the knights, he had been the friendliest to her, or at least the most casual.

"A decade ago, when I was a captain with the Third Expeditionary Force, the Forerunner put together a mission to explore Japan and seek out a group that called itself the Ashikaga Clan. We—"

The chopper rattled violently in a gust. Magnolia grabbed her harness and closed her eyes as her insides settled back down.

"All good, mates!" Mamoa called out.

Magnolia opened her eyes and looked to the cockpit. The pilot flipped several switches, then gave a thumbs-up.

"Crikey," Donny said. "Better get the chunder bucket."

Namath stared at the cockpit for a brief moment, then turned back to Magnolia. "At any rate, we spent months making our way north. Lost a chopper that Mamoa crash-landed in the water. All but one of us got out."

He paused a moment, then continued. "During our journey, we found nothing but death. Destroyed cities overtaken by mutant beasts and carnivorous vegetation that lit up the countryside like glowing snakes."

"You never found this clan?" Magnolia asked.

"He already told you what he found," Clay said. "Death. What outposts or groups were out there after the war were hunted by the machines and eliminated. Some were lured to—"

"I know the MO. I didn't live under a rock my whole life. I spent most of the past twenty years diving into those same wastes."

"I'd like to hear about these missions," Namath said. "We have plenty of time."

"Maybe she can tell us how they ended up in Australia, where they nuked our home," Donny said.

"Yeah, that should be a good one," Clay added.

Magnolia sat up straighter. "I was in Brisbane when that happened, and that nuke was meant to kill me and Xavier, the former king. You want to hear the real fucking story?"

Donny also sat up straighter. "Real story, eh?"

"I'm aware of the truth," Namath said. "Rumors spread through our ranks like they do yours, I'm sure. Donny, Clay, I can assure you, Magnolia had nothing to do with that bomb, or she wouldn't be with us right now." He looked hard at Magnolia. "That doesn't mean I trust you."

"Fair enough," she replied.

"Good, now that we have that cleared up, I'd like to hear about your past."

Magnolia shrugged one shoulder. "What do you want to know?"

"About your airship, your diving, your people, how you ended up at the islands."

"That's all a very long story." Magnolia let out a deep sigh and closed her eyes again, letting the past unreel in her mind. The moment she stepped into the launch bay to meet X after being caught stealing... That first dive to the surface, which X didn't return from for ten years... All those horrible months and years without him replayed in her mind, right up to the day they finally found him. And then the wars that followed: with the Cazadores, the skinwalkers, and eventually the machines... Memories of falling in love with the quirky son of a clockmaker surfaced, along with the marriage of Tin and Layla, seeing Bray born, and Sofia giving birth to Rhino Jr. A rush of memories followed, from the outpost in Panama to the search for the Coral Castle. Losing Rodger, Arlo, Edgar—so many of the people she cared deeply for.

"You fall asleep, or what?" Donny asked.

"Nope, just thinking," Magnolia said. She shook her head. "For most of the last two and a half centuries, my people were passengers on an airship called the *Hive*, keeping to the skies above the former United States. We dived into green zones to search for supplies, but then we found the Cazadores, or rather, they found some of us. After a brief war, we set out across the planet to search for survivors and bring them into the sun. We found some in Rio de Janeiro, but eventually we learned about the machines at Mount Kilimanjaro, where they lured airships and survivors over the decades, as you mentioned."

"And your people destroyed them?" Clay asked.

Magnolia nodded.

"How?" Namath asked.

Magnolia told them how Captain Les Mitchells and other

heroes like Commander Michael Everhart went with Sofia and Arlo to rescue the civilians there and destroy the enemy with a cyber virus.

"I was off with Xavier dealing with the skinwalkers, a violent cult of Cazadores hell bent on killing everyone," she said. "In the end, we defeated both groups."

Namath, Clay, and Donny all listened actively. Even Mamoa seemed engaged there in the pilot seat. For the next few hours, they exchanged more stories, and slowly the walls between her and the knights seemed to come down. She realized that Captain Namath was nothing like the sadistic General Jack and that their people were more similar than she imagined—in ways both good and bad. The knights weren't the only civilization with a General Jack. The *Hive* had one in Captain Jordan. And *Victory* had Captain Rolo and Charmer.

"Well, you're right," Namath said when Magnolia finished.

"Right?"

"About us needing your experience. We're lucky to have you with us."

Even Donny and Clay nodded, and that simple response helped her relax. As their conversations waned, she rested her helmet against the hull again, hoping for sleep. But before she could drift off, the voice of Mamoa crackled over the team comms.

"Sir, I'm picking up a transmission from the islands."

"What is it?" Namath asked.

"The two knights who went missing before we left were found—dead, sir."

Namath hung his head.

"Good news, though," Mamoa said. *"General Jack has the killer in custody. The same man from that island, a Jorge Mata."*

Magnolia froze. It couldn't be true. She had watched them shoot his helicopter down.

Namath looked over to her and said, "This is the same man you were supposed to help us find?"

She nodded, hoping this didn't negate the progress they had made. But more than that, she hoped this wouldn't send the freak general on a violent rampage. One thing was for certain: if Jorge was indeed alive, he wouldn't be for long.

Namath unbuckled his harness and went to the cockpit. He returned a few minutes later.

"We're flying just east of Tierra del Fuego now," he announced. "We'll put down for Mamoa to rest before crossing the Southern Ocean and heading into Antarctica. We'll all grab a few hours of sleep—we'll need it when we arrive at Concordia Station."

He took a seat next to Magnolia this time, not leaving one between them. Then he leaned over.

"General Jack plans on executing Jorge in a few hours, along with three other Cazadores," he said. "It won't be pretty. He plans to make them examples, to make them suffer."

Magnolia met the captain's eyes and saw that he was anxious about the report.

"If he thinks that will subdue the Cazadores, he's got shit between his ears," she said. "Making an example of those warriors will only further alienate your people from them, and while I understand that Gran Jefe killed five of your people, torturing him will only turn him into a martyr."

Namath exhaled. "Let's hope it doesn't come to that."

*   *   *   *   *

After losing the trail of the monsters and Lucky, the team reached the idle snowmobiles left at the bottom. The goal was to outflank the beasts that had taken Lucky back to the reactors. But using the vehicles didn't mean moving quickly, especially with the animals

aboard. Valeria had tethered Jo-Jo to the back of her snowmobile to keep her from jumping off, and X carried Miles in a sling.

Kade led the way over fairly smooth ice. "Almost there!" he
called back.

Wind-whipped snow made it hard to see anything. X twisted
the throttle, gunning the vehicle up to Kade. They halted side by
side in the virtual whiteout. X heard, more than saw, the other
riders on their flanks, bulky machines growling softly below them.
The muted vibrations gave way to the distant growling of the
hybrid beasts protecting Concordia Station. They prowled in the
darkness, abominations that resembled some unholy blending of
bone beast and something even more sinister.

It was clear to X that Magnolia and the others weren't going
to make it in time to help, but there was no time to wait around
for them now that the creatures had taken Lucky. They had to
activate the reactors.

X could see all six of the reactors towering above the whiteout, a thousand feet ahead. The main facility was centered right
between the reactors. Unlike the reactors with their disk-shaped
tops, this building had at least five roof segments converging at
a central point, forming a pyramid top that looked almost as if it
could open. It reminded him of an exotic flower, with each piece
of roof a closed petal.

Josie raised infrared binoculars to her visor to scan the
terrain. After a few back-and-forth scans, she lowered them and
twisted in her seat to Kade.

"We have to come up with a new plan," she said. "Those
tunnels you accessed with your team will be guarded."

"What do you have in mind?" X asked.

"Bait, I'm afraid." She said to Kade, "You and Watt will drive
up on the snowmobiles and draw out the Cerebro while Xavier
and I get into position with our railguns."

"In this whiteout, we're going to need to get close," X said.

"Right, which is why we'll hoof it in on snowshoes." Josie turned back to Valeria. "You stay back and cover us. Once we're in position, Watt and Kade will head in and hopefully get us a shot."

Josie raised the binos again, did another scan, then handed them to X. "Take a look," she said. "Dial in on the first reactor."

He put the binos up to his visor.

"Check out the platform," Josie said.

Fifty feet off the ground, a mezzanine protruded off the base of the reactor. A closed door sealed off what was probably a maintenance shaft.

"If I can get up there without being seen, I'll have a direct shot from the facility," Josie said. "But just in case I can't, I want you on the ground with your dog, to try and get another angle. How about that snow mound about a hundred feet from the base?"

X panned the binos over to the hill. It looked solid enough.

"Okay," he said.

"Once we take out the Cerebro, we head inside to activate the reactors," Josie said.

"Understood." X handed the binos back, got off the snow-mobile, and undid the sling, releasing Miles onto the snow. "Okay, buddy, ready to hunt?"

Miles paced, tail wagging. Valeria dismounted and freed Jo-Jo. She slid off the back into the snow and knuckle-walked over to X.

"I don't like staying back," Valeria said. "We should be coming with you."

Jo-Jo grunted, as if in agreement. Miles nudged up against Valeria. X tried not to think about what could happen to them out there. But if this was the end of their journey, at least they would all be together.

"Let's move out," Josie said.

Watt hopped onto the other snowmobile and exchanged a nod with X.

"Good luck, Xavier," Kade said. "I'll buy you what time I can."

X heard the twinge of sadness in his voice. It was the same note he remembered hearing in the voices of divers over the years who had lost hope. X had heard the same tone in his own voice. He walked over and put his hand on Kade's neck.

"We can do this. It's not the end," he said.

They exchanged a last nod, and X set off with Miles. Josie unslung her railgun, leading the way across the frozen plain separating them from the main facility and the towering reactors of Concordia Station. Rolling mounds of snow provided some concealment on the way to the first reactor.

Miles went ahead of Josie, sniffing and listening as X lowered his head and fought against the relentless wind. About one hundred feet out from the snowmobiles, he turned to look at the others. Valeria and Jo-Jo were barely visible silhouettes behind them.

He hurried after Josie and Miles. They were coming up on the first reactor now, with no sign of hostiles. The distant howls had stopped, and the growl of the snowmobiles had long since faded away. It was just the three of them out here in the blustering wind. X hoped they weren't walking into a trap.

They snowshoed over to the base of the first reactor, which loomed overhead like a giant metal mushroom.

"Okay, upsy daisy," Josie said.

And slinging her railgun, she started up the ladder as X watched for hostiles. She climbed quickly, making it up to the mezzanine in less than a minute. As soon as she had mounted the railgun bipod to a strut on the mezzanine, X set off with Miles. The fresh powder was firm enough to trek up. At the top, he knelt down. He was just a few hundred feet from the station and had an unobstructed view of the main entrance. The double doors remained closed, just beyond a helicopter landing pad.

He raised a hand to Josie, signaling he was ready. She responded with a raised hand.

"Watt, Kade, you're up," she said over the comms.

X heard the distant growl of the snowmobiles firing up. He laid his assault rifle in the snow, then grabbed the railgun. He was glad for the cumbersome weapon's bipod, which he swung out and planted in the snow.

"Okay, watch my back, boy," X whispered, snugging the gun's butt against his shoulder.

The dog replied with a low growl that sounded so much like the snowmobiles, he eventually realized that Miles had been growling for several seconds. Taking his focus from the railgun sights, X checked his dog, who was staring off into the snow east of them.

X picked up the assault rifle, bringing the infrared scope up to his visor. A dozen signatures flickered amid the snow a hundred feet away. Indistinct figures trudged through the storm in the area Kade had marked, where his team had accessed the tunnels.

X relayed what he was seeing to Josie, but halted when he realized that these weren't the monsters they had encountered back in the city.

"Commander, these are… uh…" He squinted into his scope. In the crosshairs, he sighted up the pale features of a woman wearing a blue ITC uniform, her hair stiff in the freezing gusts of wind. At first, she looked like some sort of zombie, but this woman was very much alive. She was one of the inhabitants of the cryo-pods.

Kade's voice broke over the channel. *"Those people are controlled by the Cerebro,"* he warned. *"Don't let them get close!"*

"*Shoot to kill, Xavier,*" Josie said.

X motioned for Miles to get behind him. The snowmobiles growled louder, closing in on the facility. X trained his rifle on the woman with frozen hair.

"Help us!" she shouted. "We need help!"

Two more women staggered in the wind behind her. They appeared to be in their early twenties. A young man with a shaved head and square jaw joined them, wearing the same blue ITC uniform caked with snow.

The snowmobiles raced across the ice, blasting toward the front entrance. More of the cryo-sleepers were emerging from the tunnels, as if drawn by the engine noise. One batch was burned and covered in bandages. They looked harmless enough until X saw the knife in the closest woman's hand.

"I'm sorry," X said quietly as he fingered the trigger. He fired a three-round burst into her chest, and she sank onto the snow. The next woman looked in his direction just as he took off the top of her head.

He mowed the third female down as Kade and Watt covered the last fifty yards to the entrance of the facility. Someone, or something, had opened the doors to the dark interior. But nothing emerged from the shadows.

"Josie, get ready," X said.

He fired burst after burst, cutting down the advancing humans, who were now scattering in all directions as they emerged from the tunnels. There were easily fifty of them.

Muted shouting rang out in the distance, followed by a transmission from Valeria.

"*Contacts,*" she said. "*They have Lucky!*"

What X heard next sent a chill up his back—Jo-Jo's roar blended with the howls of the hybrid bone beasts. He turned with his rifle back the way he had come as the beasts' ethereal cries rose in volume. They were being attacked on two fronts, and he had yet to see the Cerebro.

Jo-Jo roared louder, and Valeria's shotgun boomed. The answering screech made X turn.

"Xavier, hold position," Josie said over the comms.

Kade and Watt circled around outside the base, firing their weapons into the group of sleepers.

"Kade, go help Valeria," Josie said. *"Save Lucky if you can, but if you can't, don't hesitate. We can't let anyone fall into their hands."*

"Understood," Kade replied. He pulled away from the battle, gunning his snowmobile over the ice.

X palmed in a fresh magazine and pulled back the charging handle. Firing selectively, he cut down the trudging figures, nailing head shot after head shot.

Watt sped toward a cluster of five sleepers, firing a pistol at them. A male ran out from behind the others, holding something above his head. It exploded in a shock wave of body parts. A second later, the snowmobile punched out the other side with Watt listing sideways.

More blasts came from flashing lights that X traced back to the facility's open doors. There in the shadows, he glimpsed the metallic torso of the Cerebro.

"I've got eyes on the target," he said.

"Copy that," Josie said. *"I see it."*

X again swapped weapons, slinging the assault rifle and grabbing the railgun.

Watt turned his snowmobile back toward the scattered procession of sleepers as the mechanical beast skittered out into the open. It raised three arms fitted with an arsenal of weapons that could telescope in and out of its thick spider legs. Laser barrels blazed from three of those legs. Flashing bolts chased Watt, flashing just above his helmet.

"Taking the shot," Josie said.

The railgun's electrical discharge ionized the air, creating a streak of plasma. The fiery glow slammed into one of the Cerebro's legs, shearing it off. X fired a second later, his shot going over the dome and missing by inches as the thing recoiled from the first shot.

"Damn," he grumbled.

Before he could fire again, other legs flitted out, blasting in several directions, including at him. He slid down the hill as bolts vaporized the snow at the top. On his back, he watched Watt's snowmobile swerve away, then turn headlong into a laser. The vehicle exploded from behind, hitting a mound of snow and flying up in the air as Watt cartwheeled off.

X scrambled back up the hill, but he no longer had a shot.

"Moving for another angle," he said over the comm. Miles bounded after him as he slid down the slope to level ground.

"I've almost got a shot," Josie said. "Stand by."

The ground beneath X rumbled with enough force to knock him to the ground. Ice cracked and groaned behind him. He got back up to see a fissure snaking across the white expanse, sending plumes of icy flakes into the sky. The crack yawned wider into a cavernous opening.

"Xavier, there's a…" Josie began to shout.

He turned just as she leaped off the mezzanine on the reactor tower, flailing down into the drifted snow. A second later, the entire mezzanine vanished in an explosion.

"Kade, Valeria, sitrep," X asked.

"We're safe with Jo-Jo, but they still have Lucky," Valeria said.

"Those sleepers have changed course and are all heading for that big crevasse in the ice," Kade said. "Can't see what's down there yet, though."

X kept moving until he saw that the horde of sleepers was

shambling toward the opening in the ice. The grinding noise continued, as if something was rising toward the surface.

"Miles, come on," X said. They ran toward Josie, who lay squirming on the ground. Watt, too, was moving, injured but alive.

"Xavier," Josie called out. She was pointing at the crack in the ground. "We have to stop that ship," she called out.

X turned to see what the hell she was talking about. "What in the wastes…" he stammered.

A huge airship rose slowly up on some sort of hydraulic platform. X recognized it right away. This monster aircraft was the same model as the *Trident*. And like the *Trident*, it was fully equipped with cannons and machine-gun turrets. The sleepers rushed toward it like moths to a flame.

An engine whined, and X turned with his rifle, lowering it as Kade thumped over on the snowmobile, with Valeria on the back. Jo-Jo ran up after them, with fresh blood on her fur from enemies she had torn apart.

They gathered next to Josie.

"One of the beasts escaped with Lucky. I lost sight of them, but they took him inside the facility to the Cerebro," Kade said.

"Then it will soon have the location of the Vanguard Islands," Josie said.

X stared at the ship and suddenly understood. The flying behemoth would soon head to their home and erase it forever.

Watt limped over to them. "Commander, what do we do?" he asked.

Josie pushed up off the ground, gripping what was clearly a broken arm. She looked at the ship, then to the base, and finally to the reactors.

"Watt, Valeria, and Kade will have to destroy the Cerebro," she said. "Then turn on the reactors. I'll stay here with Xavier to stop that ship from taking off. We'll help if we can, but we can't let it leave."

"What about the *Trident*?" X asked. "Can't you call it in for a bombing run?"

"And risk it getting blown out of the sky?" She shook her head. "This is on us."

"Understood." X handed his railgun to Kade. "Take this. You'll need it."

Over Valeria's shoulder, he watched the crazed ITC sleepers still slogging toward the ship, which was almost aboveground.

"Come on," Kade said, reaching out. Valeria got back on the snowmobile, and Jo-Jo bounded ahead. As they drove away, Valeria looked over her shoulder at X.

By the time X started toward the airship with Miles and Josie, it had emerged fully. A ramp extended down toward the group of sleepers waiting to board. If this ship got in the sky, it would be the end of the Vanguard Islands, and then of humanity forever.

"Okay, Commander," X said. "You got any ideas on how we're going to stop that thing?"

"I was hoping you might have a thought," she said.

"Still working on it, but I'll come up with something."

TWENTY-EIGHT

Gran Jefe strained against the shackles chaining him to the hull in the brig of the *Frog*. The warship was now another weapon in the enemy's arsenal. He was completely alone here. No other prisoners. Not even Frank the AI was here to keep him company. Truth be told, he had started to like the ghost man, even considered him an *amigo*. But he would likely never see the AI again, as the knights had taken the handheld drive from Gran Jefe when he was captured.

At this point, he doubted he would see anyone he cared about again.

Soon, the knights would come to execute him. Probably in a public way, to deter others from resisting the invaders. A seed of hope remained in his head that maybe he could get off this vessel alive, but he didn't entertain any grand illusions about it. He just wanted to be able to put up a fight when they came, maybe bring a few more of these tin-can *pendejos* with him.

Gran Jefe looked down at his shackled wrists and ankles. Just to be sure he would never escape, the knights had even put a clamp around his neck, connecting the cable to the ceiling.

But he still drew breath, and that was their mistake.

Clenching his jaw, Gran Jefe pulled, trying with every bit of muscle to rip the chains free from the hull. Pulling up memories of the general holding his son captive to fuel him, he let the rage surge through him as he gathered his strength. The chains went taut, groaning under the weight. Dust rained from overhead.

He let out a long grunt, then took in deep breaths, chest heaving. Blinking, he focused on the sunlight streaming through the bars at the end of the corridor. His cell was beyond the reach of its warm glow, completely enshrouded in shadow.

In the past, he had felt alone. On Sint Eustatius, under the volcano known as Quill. Then again on Saint John. This entire time, he had been fighting the enemy on his own. By himself. Anger filled him at the realization. Sitting here now, like a chained animal, he felt the powerful heat of rage unlike any he had ever known. Rage at the sky people who had left him to fight on his own and at his own people for not avenging General Forge.

He filled his lungs and did what everyone else seemed to have given up doing—he continued the fight. He simply could not accept defeat, and he could not accept that he had failed his son.

He pulled harder on the chains attached to his shackled wrists. At the same time, he tugged his head back, the cable going taut overhead. His vision began to blur, his face warming and veins bulging from his neck.

Come on, come on, come on!

"I'd save my strength."

Footsteps clanked down the corridor, and General Jack walked up to his cage. Two knights followed a step behind.

"Then again, I guess strength isn't the issue. It will all be over soon." The general stepped up with a hard sort of grin. "I'm going to enjoy cutting you to pieces, but first I have a surprise for you.

I'm going to do it right in front of your boy, so he can see what happens if he grows up to be a barbarian like his old man."

Gran Jefe pushed against the neck restraints with all his might, ripping the bolts from the ceiling. He whipped his head to the side, slamming the bars with the loose chain. Both knights stepped back, but the general stayed put.

"Crikey, you are one violent brute, aren't you?" Jack said with a chuckle. "But I'd be civilized for a few minutes if I were you, for I'm going to give you an opportunity topside to fight for your freedom. And if you win, you will also win the freedom of the other prisoners."

Gran Jefe had a hard time understanding everything he was saying, especially in that dumb accent, but he understood most of it.

"You lie," he growled.

"I am many things, but I'm not a liar." Jack turned to his guards. "Get him out of there and bring him to the top deck. If he tries anything, cut off his head."

"Yes, sir," replied the knights in unison.

One of them stepped forward and opened the gate to the brig. The other drew his sword, placing the blade against the back of Gran Jefe's neck as his ankle chains were unlocked.

"Move," said the man at the gate.

They took off through the brig, passing empty cells. The hatch opened to the top deck of the *Frog*, and the eyes of his comrades fell upon him. Three warriors, two male and one female, rose up to the bars of the shipping container where they were being held. More were in an adjacent container. These once-proud warriors looked on with dread, their sense of defeat evident in their hollow gazes.

Tiger, the former captain promoted to admiral of the Vanguard fleet, was there. The young man was the only one of all the warriors who looked at Gran Jefe with any hope in his gaze, but Gran Jefe looked away, unable to give him any reassurance. This was the end of the line for him, and he knew it.

Holding up his hand, Gran Jefe shielded his face from the glow of the sun to search for his son on the deck. But the only people among the cannons and machine-gun turrets were knights. He turned to the capitol tower, where hundreds of people watched from their terraces.

He turned to starboard, where two huge cruise ships were anchored. Hundreds of civilians from the Coral Castle looked down from the balconies.

General Jack walked out with a bullhorn in his hand. He held it up into the air. "Citizens of the Trident," he intoned, "today, we are here to witness the end of this violent society, with the death of the last Barracuda."

Gran Jefe squinted in the sunlight at the faces of people looking down at him as if he were some monster. But he wasn't the only monster here. General Jack would hate to discover that he himself was more of a barbarian even than Gran Jefe. Soon, the psychopath would execute the rest of the Cazadores who had stood against him when the gargantuan sky horse rained hell down on the capitol tower. Worst of all, the bastard had gunned down General Forge—his better in every conceivable way.

Gran Jefe was ready to die, but he would love more than anything to bring this shithead along with him. He glared at Jack, anger warming his veins.

"This Cazador brute killed five of our own, including two of our hunters," the general droned on.

Angry shouting and booing came from the cruise ship. People threw things off their balconies and decks, some of them carrying far enough to hit the deck of the *Frog*.

"He killed my brother!" someone shouted.

"And my son!" yelled an elderly man.

"My husband," cried a woman.

Gran Jefe looked at her. She had a child with her, a boy not much older than his own. There was a moment of regret, in which he pondered the pain he had caused this family, but the feeling quickly passed. To save his son, he would slay the general a thousand times over.

"But I'm a fair man," Jack said into the bullhorn. "This barbarian is still a soldier, and he fought for his people, as I have fought for mine. Therefore, I'm granting him a death by duel. A duel with me. If he wins, he will earn his freedom and the freedom of his mates."

Boos and shouts arose from the ships around them.

Jack raised a hand to silence them and then turned to look at Gran Jefe.

"I will slay Jorge Mata unaided," he said.

A cutlass was tossed at Gran Jefe's feet, about five feet beyond his shackled hands.

"Today, I will cut this cancer out of their society before it can spread to their offspring," Jack said. He gestured to someone behind Gran Jefe.

Gran Jefe knew before he turned what he was about to see.

"Pablo," Gran Jefe said.

The boy looked at him, confused. Gran Jefe took a step back, but the guard holding the sword to his back pushed it to his flesh.

"Don't move," he said. "You will have your chance."

Gran Jefe stared at his son, his words all gone now. He had thought about what he would tell his boy, but now the words wouldn't come.

It's not what you should say, he realized. *It's what you should do.*

He would prove what he was at heart: a warrior. A *Barracuda.* Gran Jefe would pick up that sword, and he would slay this general.

The second knight standing guard walked over and bent down with a key.

"Hold still, or my mate will lop off your head," he said.

"That's my job," said Jack, to general merriment.

Gran Jefe smiled back, ready to prove them wrong. As the guard inserted the key and unlocked his cuffs, he felt something prick his arm. Glancing down, he saw that the knight had stuck a needle into his muscle. Within seconds, a flood of warmth rushed through his body. Whatever they had injected into him worked fast.

By the time the cuffs were off and the guards stepped away, his legs were already feeling weak. He blinked, his vision blurring slightly.

He should have known this wouldn't be a fair fight.

General Jack pulled a helmet over his head and buckled it into place. He reached out, and a knight handed him a spear. He put his robotic hand on the hilt of his sword but kept it sheathed.

Gran Jefe strode forward and bent down to pick up the sword, nearly falling to the deck. He looked up in a moment of clarity to see his son watching him with wide eyes. That look of fear gave Gran Jefe a shot of adrenaline that pushed back at whatever toxins had been injected into his system.

He scooped up the sword and lunged at Jack, striking sparks from the shoulder of his armor. The surprised general thrust his spear, but Gran Jefe ducked and grabbed the shaft. He pulled the general toward him.

At his best, Gran Jefe would have skewered the bastard through the heart. But his equilibrium was off, and the cutlass missed. Jack drew his own sword and used it to parry Gran Jefe's next blow, meant for the neck of the helmet.

Metal met metal with a loud clash.

The Trident spectators cheered, and so did the Cazador prisoners.

"Get him, Jefe!" Tiger shouted.

Gran Jefe stepped back, bees darting about in his field of vision. In that terrifying moment, he was carried back to his training. He recalled hunting monsters in the darkness beneath the Quill volcano on Sint Eustatius. To rely on his other senses when one had been compromised.

The spear jumped at his head, but he slipped to the side, the blade streaking past his face. He sliced at the shaft, but it held.

Shouts rang out—some angry, most surprised.

"Kill him!" Tiger yelled.

Jack lunged forward, jabbing his sword at Gran Jefe. The point nicked his right arm. He bled, but the warmth felt good, and it pushed back the numbness from the toxins.

The spectators erupted with applause when Gran Jefe grabbed his arm slick with blood. Jack strode forward, and Gran Jefe spat, hitting him square in the Trident symbol on the forehead of his helmet.

Every cheer and shout stopped abruptly, and there was only the whistling of the wind.

Jack took a step forward, then another. "I'm going to enjoy handing your head to your little bastard," he said.

"You got this, Jefe," Tiger said behind him. "You can beat this shithead, brother."

Gran Jefe wanted to believe that, but his body was starting to fade from his control. His muscles twitched, and his vision dimmed. He stumbled back and fell to one knee.

"Come on, Jefe, don't give up," Tiger said.

The voice was close, and Gran Jefe turned to see the shipping container. In his mind's eye, he remembered some of the lessons that Rhino had taught him all those years ago in Texas—specifically, to always use the terrain to your advantage.

Gran Jefe pushed up as a knight tossed Jack a new spear.

He cocked it back in one arm but then lowered it. "Too easy," he scoffed. And he charged. He thrust the shaft outward, the blade whizzing toward Gran Jefe. At the last instant, Gran Jefe jerked to his right, and the spear glanced harmlessly off the steel of the container behind him.

Holding his cutlass in both hands, he brought it down on the shaft, splintering it. Jack swung backhand with his sword, but Gran Jefe had already jumped back, several inches out of reach. The general followed through with a forward swing, and the only thing that kept Gran Jefe's head attached to his body was the edge of his cutlass meeting and turning the next slash. The powerful stroke nearly knocked the cutlass from his grip, but Gran Jefe held on.

He ducked under the general's sword arm and away, his comrades' mantra pulsing in his ears. "Gran Jefe! Gran Jefe!"

Across the deck, some thirty feet away, his son watched anxiously, in the firm grip of two guards. Gran Jefe held the boy's gaze, watching in his peripheral as Jack charged. As the general swung the big sword, Gran Jefe flattened his body and arched back, right under the blade's arc. Jack lunged past, the victim of his own momentum.

As the force of his attack carried him past his target, Gran Jefe put his back foot down, tripping him. Jack crashed to the deck, rolling to his back just as Gran Jefe jabbed his cutlass into the armor over his belly. The dull, weathered blade broke through, punching into soft flesh. The general howled as his head flipped back with such force his helmet slid off.

A flurry of shocked voices called out, but they quickly faded away. Not even the Cazador prisoners said a word. Gran Jefe twisted the blade deeper, and Jack's mouth drooled blood. He stared with the shocked eyes of someone who realized, too late, that he was not the better man.

"*Puto,*" Gran Jefe growled. He drove the blade deeper until he felt it grind against the steel deck, and twisted it free. Jack convulsed in agony.

Gran Jefe raised the blade over his head in both hands, then flinched from a sharp pain in his upper back.

"Watch out!" Tiger shouted.

"*¡Papá!*" Pablo wailed.

Gran Jefe jerked again as something cold ripped into his back. Whatever it was, he didn't feel any pain this time. He glanced down to see two arrowheads protruding from his chest. He kept the sword above his head, glaring down at Jack. He should have known that even in death, the man wouldn't keep his word.

Two more arrows slammed into his back, but they didn't stop him from delivering the death blow. He plunged the full breadth of the machete's blade through the center of the general's face.

All sense of time seemed to slow as the blood left Gran Jefe's body. He collapsed over the remains of the general. Lying there, he blinked through the stars, seeing the containers and the faces of the Cazadores who would be freed now that he had killed Jack.

Pablo broke free from the guards and ran over to kneel by his side.

"It's okay; this is a good death," Gran Jefe whispered in Spanish. "I love you, my son."

His vision suddenly clear, he looked at his boy to see a tear running down his face. But there was no longer confusion there, or fear. Pablo nodded with pride, and Gran Jefe took his hand. He drew his last breath knowing he had died showing his son what a Cazador warrior was.

TWENTY-NINE

Darkness shrouded the fortress. The slavers knew that any shining light made them a target. They also were smart enough to know that their voices could get them killed. Together, the surviving men had figured out that there was still another hunter out there.

Michael peeked over the stone wall with his night-vision optics, searching for hostiles. He could see six: three on the ground level, where the prison and surrounding shacks were. Two more on the walls, and a sixth at the far end, near the gate by a paddock of horses. Those were just the ones he could see.

The remaining slavers spread out, laying down a net to capture any prisoners who hadn't escaped, as well as Michael and the kids he protected.

Hearing a whimper from the girl he had shielded with his body, he lowered his head and whispered, "You have to be quiet. I'm not going to let them hurt you."

He didn't know how much English she understood, but she stopped whimpering. The terror she and the other children were experiencing broke his heart. And for that reason more than any other, he didn't regret staying to help them. He was going to get them out of here.

First, though, he had to find a way out. He was still pinned down on the bridge, shielded somewhat by the broken-down parapet wall. Worse, a section ahead had collapsed, blocking the route he had selected to get the kids to safety. They had crawled for the past hour, maybe more. Michael had lost track of time. Each second felt like a minute, and minutes like hours. He currently had the comms offline to keep as silent as possible.

A few feet ahead of him, the other four kids hugged the stone ground. Confident they were hidden for now, Michael decided to give the go-ahead.

"Okay, when I tell you to jump, you jump over that gap," he whispered.

The older boy nodded back, then whispered something to the other kids.

Michael had a bad feeling about this, but it was their only option right now. Pinning the girl down gently with his lower body, he freed his arm and grabbed his laser rifle.

"Get ready," he said to the kids ahead.

A nod.

"Okay. Go!" he said, going up on a knee and spraying laser bolts in a wild arc while keeping the girl down with his knee. One by one, the other kids all jumped across the broken bridge, landing safely on the other side.

Return fire zipped past Michael. Leaning down against the girl, he stared ahead. Getting this little girl across was going to be extremely dangerous, especially now with their position exposed.

"Timothy, I want you to lower the ship and give me a way out," Michael said. "Stay in the cloud cover, do you understand?"

"*Copy that, Chief.*"

Layla's voice surged over the channel. *"Michael, are you okay?"*

"I'm still pinned down with the kids and need an eye in the sky. An *eye*, Layla—not you diving down. Do you understand?"

He heard a brief pop of radio static.

"Layla, earlier I saw a girl lose her mom. I can't let that happen to Bray."

Michael clutched the crying girl against his chest.

"Layla, I need you to say—"

"Yes, I understand," Layla said. *"We're lowering now."*

Gunfire peppered the wall, chipping flakes of the ancient stone over Michael as he shielded the girl with his armor.

"We have to crawl," he said. "Do you understand?"

She stared up at him, clearly in shock. As bullets whizzed over them, he crawled over the top of her and practically dragged her to the edge of the collapsed bridge. All four kids on the other side stared as he prepared to launch the girl. The older boy held out his arms to signal he was ready.

Heaving with all his strength, Michael launched the girl across. She landed in the arms of the oldest boy, who fell on his back, unhurt.

Relief flooded over Michael until a bullet zipping past his helmet told him he had poked his head up too far. He squirmed back from the bridge. Then he pushed himself up and ran as fast as he could, rounds chasing him as he jumped.

He slid to a stop, going down on his side. Somehow, he hadn't gotten shot. He reached for the wailing girl again and clutched her against his chest, too afraid she might stand up. A hundred feet of open ground stretched between his little group and the stairs. It might as well be a mile. He craned his neck to look at the first lookout tower they had left over an hour ago, knowing they could be flanked via the ladder that led up inside.

So far, no one was back there, but he heard muffled voices. These weren't prisoners but slavers, wearing masks.

"Almost there," Timothy reported over the comms.

The other four kids kept going and were almost to the stairs when an explosion shook the stone bridge. It had taken an RPG round, or something else big. The realization hit Michael: another round like that could bring down the bridge. It was also the type of firepower that could take out the airship.

He checked his HUD to find the ship at 2,500 feet—almost visible through the clouds. Michael had to take out the launcher, but first he needed to hand the little girl off and get the kids out of here. The oldest boy looked back at him, and Michael set her down on the stone, signaling he was going to hand her off.

The boy nodded back, and Michael pushed her over to him. The boy scrambled over, keeping low over her body. Heaving a sigh of relief, Michael unslung his laser rifle. He edged up against the parapet, then sneaked a glance, easily seeing a vapor trail across the fortress, not far from where he had killed the sniper. Sure enough, a man was reloading an RPG.

Bullets forced Michael down. He crawled a few paces ahead, stopping to take a deep breath. Popping up, he aimed at the slaver with the launcher and fired a bolt. It missed his vital areas but took out his legs. Down he went, firing at the same moment. A rocket streaked across the fortress, slamming into a stone turret in a shower of rock and flame.

"Watch out, Chief, twelve o'clock," Timothy said over the comms.

Michael looked ahead, seeing nothing but the kids crawling ahead of him.

"I mean six!" Timothy yelled.

Michael rolled to his side, raised his rifle, and fired at the tower before he even had a target. The man standing there with a pistol didn't get his shot off before a bolt flashed through him. The guy crumpled, smoldering from several holes through his torso.

"Nice shooting, Chief," Timothy said.

"How many more are there?"

"I'm seeing at least three hostiles, all moving toward your position. I'll mark them on your HUD, but you need to get out of there fast."

"And the prisoners?"

"I've detected fifteen heat signatures spreading out into the surrounding city, with three more inside the prison still, either hiding or injured."

So I'm on my own, Michael thought.

He had faced worse odds before.

"Got any flares left?" he asked.

"Yes, Chief—just enough to create a final light show."

Michael checked his HUD, seeing the three hostiles Timothy had identified. Two were on the ground below, and one was on a bridge across the fortress.

"Use them on the hostile mounting the eastern wall. I'll deal with the other two as soon as you do."

"Copy that, Chief," said Timothy.

"I am ready when you are, Pepper."

A second later, flares streaked out of the clouds. In the bright bursts, Michael identified the first slaver on the ground. The man turned, providing the perfect shot. Michael put a laser through the side of his head.

"One down," he confirmed.

Moving positions again, he found a nice ledge for the laser rifle. He propped it up, but not soon enough to take out the slaver on the ground level running for cover behind a shack. Michael searched for the third hostile and caught him in the glow of the parachute flares drifting overhead. The soldier was crouched behind a parapet across the prison. Michael fired a laser bolt at the exposed head. It went high, but the next bolt sheared off the back of his skull.

Before the slaver's body hit the ground, Michael had crouched and run to a new position. A few feet away, he tried to sight up the guy behind the shack, but he remained hidden. So Michael just started firing into the flimsy sheet-metal structure, punching holes through the sides. The slaver ran, and Michael shot him in the back without remorse.

"Three up, three down," he said into his headset.

Layla replied over the comms, but Michael didn't catch it as flares continued to burst overhead. He looked over at the kids, seeing two of them pointing at him.

"Yeah, we did it!" Michael said with a grin.

That grin faded when he saw a shadow behind him. He turned right into a spiked club that smacked him in the chest, denting his armor and knocking him backward. The slaver swung again as Michael turned to the side. The club caught him with a glancing blow in the shoulder. Pain shot up his neck and down his arm. He backed up, trying to get some distance, but the slaver swung the club into his stomach armor, knocking the air from his lungs and bringing him to his knees.

The man walked over to him, giving him no time before he swung again—a glancing blow to the helmet. Red broke across his vision as he crashed to the stone. Dimly he saw the kids still there, yelling and snarling at the man as he walked over. He stopped, standing right above Michael.

"Run," Michael mumbled.

He tried to push up but fell back down. Warm blood ran down his forehead. Voices called out over the comms, but he couldn't make anything out.

A boot pushed down on his back. Then the man kicked

Michael to his side and pushed his helmet up, to look down at his face. Michael lay there stunned. Looking up at the man who was about to take his life. The slaver lifted his own helmet for a look at Michael—probably just as curious to see who he was and where he came from.

As the man leaned down, Michael found himself surprised by his youthful features. He had expected to see a scarred, older face and greasy hair, yellow teeth, and hard eyes. But this man had an innocent look and couldn't be much older than twenty-five.

They were almost the same age, but while Michael had spent his life protecting people, this young man had spent it inflicting horrors. Their eyes locked for a long moment. Then the man raised the spiked club in both hands above his head, preparing to bring it down on Michael's unprotected face.

Behind him, young voices shouted, cried, and pleaded for the slaver to spare Michael. In this final moment, he thought of Bray and how he had failed not only his boy but *all* these kids, who would no doubt soon be paying a heavy price.

Michael tried to get up but only got another boot to the chest, knocking his helmetless head back onto the stone. His skull throbbed as the young slaver brought up the club again, his face empty of emotion. Fear gripped Michael's heart, but he spent his last second looking at the sky.

"Goodbye, Layla. Goodbye, Bray, I love you forever," he whispered.

Blinking, he noticed a flicker. Something was up there. The airship maybe, or a huge bird...

A black canopy blossomed, and a moment later he understood what he was seeing. This wasn't some bird, Siren, or hang glider, but a Hell Diver. It was Layla.

"Hey, up here, asshole!" she called out.

She flared, then released the toggles, stopping her backward momentum and swinging herself forward as the slaver turned. Her boots caught him in the chest with her full weight. The force knocked him backward onto the parapet wall, where he flipped over and fell eighty feet onto the ocean rocks.

Layla crashed to the ground but was up a moment later, a rifle in her hands. She went to the side of the wall to check over the side, then hurried to Michael as the children gathered around.

"Tin, can you hear me?" she shouted.

He lay there a moment, unable to move much at all.

"Michael Everhart," she said.

Managing to move a few fingers, he found her hand and squeezed. "Did we get 'em all?" he whispered.

"Yes, I think you did." She looked up as the kids huddled around. They no longer shed tears or stared wide eyed. He saw smiles. Real smiles.

With a small assist from Layla, Michael sat up. The little girl he had carried walked over and hugged his arm. He leaned his head down.

"It's okay. You're safe now," he said. Three of the other kids moved in, hugging his waist and patting his dented armor.

The oldest boy raised his fist in the air and shouted, "¡Libertad!"

As the word echoed, Michael looked over the parapet at figures across the fortress. Timid and cautious, they moved slowly toward the gates. These were former slaves, now free and returning to search for their loved ones.

Layla cradled her rifle, cautious. "What do we do now?" she asked.

"I hadn't gotten that far yet," Michael said. "But we do have plenty of room on the airship…"

He glanced down at the little girl still gripping his leg.

"And it's about time Bray had some friends his own age."

* * * * *

The maze of steel and shadows stretched before Kade. This evil place devoured lives. But it didn't just kill people; it used them. If he didn't stop the Cerebro mastermind behind it all, Lucky would soon be another forever-enslaved component of the system, joining Zen, Nobu, and Tia.

The thought of Tia brought back the deep agony and made it fresh again. But he couldn't let that eat his insides. He had to push on, had to finish the mission. An image of Alton came to mind, back at the islands and twirling a loop of rope over his head like a performing cowboy. That was what Kade still had to fight for—something that X had reminded him of just hours ago.

Kade flashed a hand signal, motioning for Valeria, Jo-Jo, and Watt to follow him inside the base. They moved cautiously into the dimly lit corridor. An eerie quiet had settled over the facility, as if they had entered a sealed-off bunker. Every footstep seemed to echo in the silence.

But his small team wasn't alone.

The Cerebro dwelled in the darkness, and it had Lucky.

Kade relied on the night-vision goggles that painted the passage in green as he searched for the beast. The small team crossed through several passages, working its way deeper inside. At the next intersection, a distant whirring resonated off the frozen walls. A grinding came next, followed by what sounded like cracking bones. Kade held up a hand, stopping Watt and Valeria.

Raising the railgun, Kade moved around the corner, clearing the left side, then the right. The noise sounded to be coming from the labs. He remembered the corridor well, for it led to the room where he had destroyed the thing that Tia had become. And it seemed that was where he must go to find Lucky. The grinding paused and quickly resumed.

"I'll deal with this bastard," Kade said. "You two go turn on the reactors."

Watt and Valeria slipped away in the darkness with Jo-Jo, heading to the command center. Heaving a deep breath, Kade moved toward the whirring noise. He crossed the hall and made his way to the laboratory entrance. Shattered glass lay strewn across the floor inside. Skirting around it, he moved into the labs, his heart now thumping loud enough that he could hear it over the grinding.

That grinding gave way to a muffled hiss, like an alarmed snake, or a helium bladder losing gas. Kade halted midstep, with one foot suspended over a shard of glass. He held it there, listening, trying to control his breathing as his heart thumped louder. After interminable seconds, he slowly put his foot down.

The pneumatic hissing grew louder before suddenly being eclipsed by a message over the comms.

"We've reached the command center," Watt said.

Metal scraped loudly on metal. Something had received the message. Kade held the railgun steady, waiting for a shot. A few seconds passed before he realized that the sounds were growing fainter, more distant. He took off running, throwing stealth to the winds and crushing glass under his boots. Cradling the heavy railgun, he ran until he saw a body sprawled on the floor behind a lab station in the next room.

At first, Kade thought he had found Tia's corpse, but as he moved around the lab station, he saw the bandages that he himself had applied to Lucky's torso, leaving no doubt that this was his friend.

"Kade," hissed a pained voice.

Kade took a step closer but realized the voice wasn't coming from the body in front of him. It couldn't, he realized, for the body was headless.

He whirled with his rifle as the Cerebro lowered from an overhead utility shaft that Kade had missed. A narrow limb like a hinged stiletto lanced into Kade with amazing speed, puncturing through his upper left chest and out his back. He tried to raise his rifle, but his left arm went limp and his right wasn't strong enough to raise it unaided.

"Kade, Kade you—"

The beast dropped from the darkness of the utility shaft, landing on the lab floor with a heavy thud in front of Kade. The source of the mumbling words revealed itself as it leaned its domed head down. Kade looked up at the twisted face of his friend, now trapped in the mass of flesh behind the glass dome.

"Lucky," Kade said.

"Help . . . me, Kade," Lucky said. His face twitched and grimaced. Somehow, the machine had transplanted his head with the others on the brain's surface. Veins bulged across his forehead, as if Lucky was fighting assimilation into the hive mind.

The only way to help Lucky now was to end his suffering. Kade tried again to raise the railgun, but it was too heavy. He set it down and reached for the pistol known as the Monster Hunter.

"Your people have failed," Lucky said in a sudden change of tone. The other faces said the same thing, their unblinking eyes staring at Kade.

"Soon, we will journey to your primitive civilization and destroy the last of your species," they said.

"No, you won't!" shouted a female voice.

A shotgun boomed behind Kade, the blast shattering the glass dome. He felt heat in his lower body, just as a light flashed against his legs.

The shotgun fired again, punching into the flesh left exposed by the shattered dome. The blade arm withdrew from Kade, and his body slumped to the floor. Lying on his belly, he fumbled with his right arm, propping the railgun up and aiming it at Lucky's face.

"I'm sorry," Kade whispered. He pulled the trigger, sending

the electrical charge right into the center of the mass, which exploded, painting the walls with its pulp.

Kade let go of the weapon as the mechanical beast thrashed on the floor. An armored figure moved in front of him, pumped a shell into a shotgun, and fired again. Finally, the twitching machine fell limp. For good measure, the figure fired a final shot into the slurry of destroyed flesh under the smashed glass dome. The fighter turned and bent down to Kade. The blurred face he saw was familiar. But it couldn't be real.

"Tia," he said.

"Kade, you did it," she said.

Another figure emerged—a ghostly vision of Raph, standing with his daughter.

"You can stop fighting now, brother," Raph said. "You can rest."

"Come with us," said another voice.

His eyes flitted to four more figures that stepped forward in a group—his wife and their three sons. They were standing together, all smiling, gesturing for him to join them.

"Come on, Dad!" Rich said. "We've been waiting so long!"

Kade smiled back, the pain in his heart relieved.

"Love you, Daddy!" Sean called out.

"We have so much to show you!" Jack said.

Mikah smiled at him. "It's time, my love."

Her voice faded to another female voice—the one that had called out before the shotgun blasts.

"Stay with me, Kade," she said.

He blinked away the ghostly images to see Valeria. She reached into her med pack, pulling out bandages. His eyes flitted down to the blood pooling around his body. There was too much. He knew then there was no coming back from this. Even if the Forerunner's technology might be able to give him new parts, he didn't want that.

"No," he murmured as she brought the bandages down to his wounds, packing them around his body. "Leave me... Go activate the reactors. Help Xavier..."

She held a bandage to him, not listening at first.

"Leave me," he said louder. "I'm done; you know it—"

Their eyes connected, and she drew her hand away with a blood-soaked bandage.

"Tell X... tell him I would have followed him forever," Kade said.

Valeria sniffled, then nodded.

"And tell Alton I love him, that I wish I could be with him in the new world," Kade said. "Tell him I'll always be with him... in his heart." Kade choked on blood. He blinked and lay there watching Valeria hurry off. But he didn't feel alone. As his vision faded, he heard the voices of his family.

"It's okay now, Dad," Jack said. "We can all be together again."

"Come to us, Kade," Mikah soothed.

"I love you, Daddy," Sean's sweet little voice chimed in.

Kade heaved a deep breath, his broken heart no longer hurting. He had finished what he needed to finish, and was ready for what came next: to be with his family. Closing his eyes, he embraced the darkness with a smile on his face.

THIRTY

"Kade's gone," Valeria said over the comms.

The message hit X like one of the bullets streaking over his head. He hunched behind a crate in the cargo hold of the enemy airship, pinned down with Miles on one side, Josie on the other. Gunfire pounded into their position from the now fully armed group of sleepers that had made it to the armory before X and Josie could stop them.

She held a pistol in one hand, her broken arm hanging uselessly by her side.

The engines rumbled deep inside the vessel.

"We have to get to the bridge," Josie said. She peeked over the crate but was forced right back down by gunfire. For people that had been in cryo-sleep for their entire existence, they were decent shots, but X figured that had something to do with the devices implanted on the backs of their heads.

"Stay down," X said.

Josie leaned down. "What's the status of the reactors?" she said over the open channel.

"Working on it, Commander," Watt replied. *"We got two hostiles hunting us."*

X could hear howling in the background, but he also heard Jo-Jo's roar. Miles barked, but it wasn't in response to the monkey. A hostile sleeper charged their position, leaping onto the crate with a submachine gun. X slid on his back, bringing up his rifle and firing a burst into the man, knocking him backward in a bloody spray.

Another male sleeper came around the side holding a knife and a pistol. As he lunged, Josie fired a bullet into his arm, knocking the pistol away.

X swung his rifle over, aimed, and pulled the trigger, cursing when the round jammed. Rather than waste time clearing the jam, he let the weapon sag and pulled out his .357 Magnum pistol. By the time he had it up, the snarling man was on top of Josie and pushing his knife down with both hands, toward the gap between her helmet and chest armor. She had gripped his wrist, but with only one functioning hand, she couldn't hold him back.

Miles barked again just as X pulled the trigger. The bullet hit the man in the chest, jerking him upward and allowing Josie to flip onto her side. As X aimed to finish the knife attacker, a third hostile stormed their position, firing at X. Bullets slammed into his armor from close range, punching into his side before he could take a shot.

X hit the deck as Josie snatched up her pistol and did what X had tried to do seconds earlier, blowing a hole through the third sleeper's skull. Then she turned to the man who had shot X and fired two shots into his gut. The guy crashed against the crate, gripping his belly with one hand but somehow still managing to level his submachine gun at Josie with the other. Miles lunged for the neck and shook until the man fell limp, the head lolling over at an impossibly sharp angle.

X pushed up, his side in agony from the bullet impacts. The armor stopped the rounds, but for a moment he couldn't move from the shock. He fell back down to the deck, groaning from the pain.

Josie put down covering fire for them, holding back anyone else who might have bold ideas about storming their position.

"We have to move," she said.

X took another moment, then picked up his rifle, freeing the jammed cartridge and swapping out the almost-spent magazine. He rose up, firing a burst while he took in the room. He could see four more hostiles holding down the area at the hatch leading into the airship.

"I'll cover you to the next crates," X said.

Josie nodded. "Watt, what's your status?" she asked over the channel. Static broke up the transmission. The ship was in the air now, out of range from surface fire.

X laid down a covering burst to keep them honest, giving himself time to sight up his targets. A woman had ducked behind a crate, but not quite enough. He lined up the crosshairs and took the top of her head off with a burst to the hairline.

Josie slid safely behind the next crate. She rose up, popping off single shots while X took off. He fired as he ran, hitting a second person in the arm. Miles moved in for the kill. Instead of stopping by Josie at the next crate, X kept going while laying down bursts at the last two hostiles.

Return fire whizzed past his head, and a round clipped his leg armor, knocking him to the deck. His shin felt as if a bone beast had kicked him. But at least the bullet hadn't penetrated the plate. Pushing up, he saw the shooter adjusting his aim when his head suddenly ejected a poof of bloody mist from Josie's bullet. Even with one arm, she was a hell of a shot.

Miles had the injured shooter X had shot in the arm. The man's screams died away to a gurgling sigh as the dog moved on.

Down to one hostile remaining, X strode forward, squeezing off individual shots to keep the man down. Only ten feet away now, he whistled for Miles. The dog barked as commanded, and the man peeked out from behind the crate. X squeezed off an easy shot between the eyes.

"On me," X said.

Josie and Miles joined him at the hatch. An alarm wailed, the lights flickering off in the cargo hold. The exterior hatch hummed behind them, opening and extending the ramp. The ship tilted as the thrusters fired.

Checking his HUD, X saw they were already at ten thousand feet and climbing.

"Hold on!" He searched desperately for something, anything, to hold on to as the sleepers resorted to trying to blast them out of the cargo hold. About two hundred feet away, he saw a mesh net hanging from what looked like a secured pallet of smaller crates.

"There," he said, pointing.

He started toward it, the deck slanting more with each step. Miles slid and X grabbed the dog by the collar, practically tossing him toward the secured crates. Josie crashed to the deck but got back up and raced over to the netting. She looped her good arm inside, and X tied up Miles with his collar and limbs looped through.

With his dog and Josie secure, X focused on finding a way out. The ship continued to rise up at an angle, giving them a view of the clouds below. He looked back out of the hold and into the ship. The only hatch he could see was at least fifty feet away.

An idea took shape in his mind as he remembered the thrusters built into the suit.

"Hold here!" he shouted over the howl of the freezing wind. Josie nodded, hanging on to the net. After a quick check of Miles, he said, "I'll be right back, buddy."

X tapped the control panel under an armored slot on his wrist, activating the thrusters. He angled his body, then blasted away from the net, but too fast. He slammed into the hull and slid down the wildly tilting deck.

Using his thrusters again, he shot back up to the interior hatch, fumbling for the holstered .357 Magnum pistol. Seeing someone looking at him through the glass viewport, he aimed, cocked the hammer, and fired. Blood burst across the cracked glass. He hit the hatch and punched his robotic hand through, breaking out the shards. Then he reached through and flipped the locking mechanism.

Gunfire came through the opening hatch from a second sleeper in the corridor. X retracted his robotic hand but lost his grip and fell back from the hatch, onto the deck. Sliding away on his stomach, he reached down to tap the thrusters back online. His body blasted upward, right toward the sleeper now aiming a machine pistol out of the open hatch. A wild spray of gunfire streaked away, hitting the deck and overhead. He felt a stab of pain from a round that nicked his suit between armored plates. Another bullet slammed into his shoulder. The impacts knocked him off target, and he missed the shot.

Gunfire popped to his right, where Josie was firing her pistol with an arm looped through the netting. The bullets hit the shooter in the open doorway, sending him falling. His muted scream echoed out through the cargo hold, silenced when he slammed into a crate. The unconscious body somersaulted down into the hold and into the black clouds.

Bleeding from his neck, X fought back to the open hatch, hoping no other hostiles waited for him this time. He used his thrusters to blast back up to the opening, grabbing the side and looking left and right in the corridor for more contacts.

Seeing none, he pulled his body inside and began scrambling toward the dashboard that controlled the exterior hatches. The panel wasn't far, and he tapped it, shutting them. Not a moment later, the ship began to right itself. Why, he couldn't say. Maybe the pilots thought X and his friends were dead.

He stood there a moment, breathing hard and feeling his neck. Blood trickled down, but he knew that if the bullet had hit a major vessel he would be on the deck, bleeding out. He looked down at the dented plate over his shoulder and saw that the armor had stopped the bullet.

X unslung his rifle and covered the corridors while Miles and Josie made their way inside the corridor from the cargo hold.

"Good work," she said. "You okay?"

X nodded. "Just a flesh wound."

Blood dripped from his chest, exploding into little red stars as it hit the deck. He swung his rifle up to watch their six. "We have to get out of the open," he said.

They could hear voices already descending on their position.

"This ship looks identical to the *Trident*," Josie said. "If it is, then I know a shortcut to the bridge. Follow me."

X backed away from the hatch with her and Miles. They took off running to the next intersection, but Miles began to growl right before they reached it.

"Hold," X said.

He moved ahead of Josie, listening to two approaching voices. With his back to the hull, X checked his weapon, then nodded. Dropping to the deck, he darted a glance around the corner and sighted up the two sleepers, who didn't look low enough, soon enough. They wore no armor, and the bullets easily cut them down.

"Clear," he said.

Josie came up behind X. He stayed there a moment, watching the far end of the corridor for more hostiles. At this point, there couldn't be many more, but it would take only one lucky shot to kill him, Miles, or Josie.

"If I'm right, the bridge isn't far," she said. "Just around the next bend."

They passed two closed hatches, one with a sign that read *Mess*, and the other reading *Saloon*. Nearing the intersection, they heard the hiss of pneumatic valves and meshing of gears. Miles heard it, too, and barked to warn X. He raised his rifle and fired at an armored robot ten feet tall that strode into the passage. At first, he thought it was another Cerebro, but then X saw that it was actually a sleeper piloting a mech suit. Now he knew where the Forerunner had gotten the base for his own model.

"Back!" X shouted.

A chain gun on the robotic right arm spun to life, whirring and spitting a storm of lead down the corridor. Rounds punched into the overhead, hulls, deck, and bulkheads in a devastating wave of destruction. In what seemed like slow motion, X turned and scooped up Miles, shielding the dog with his armor. In front of them, bullets slammed into Josie, knocking her backward with a broken arm and leg.

Rounds hit X in his thick shoulder plate, and he fell to the deck with Miles under him. They slid to a halt in front of the two hatches. X tried the one to the saloon. It opened.

Bullets zipped past him as he ducked down and shoved Miles inside. Clambering in after him, X turned and leaned out into the corridor to grab Josie by her hand, not realizing it was her broken arm. He pulled her inside as she let out a howl of pain.

Falling to his back, X kicked the hatch shut. He tried to raise his prosthetic arm, but it wouldn't respond after taking damage from gunfire. Sparks shot out as he pulled Josie down by her good arm. The large space had tables, couches, and chairs bolted to the deck and, beyond these, a metal bar that looked like the best cover. He pulled her behind it.

"Can you hear me?" he asked.

She managed a nod, and X turned to deal with the approaching threat. The thudding feet approached fast in the corridor, giving X only seconds to figure out a plan—one that got them out of here before they both bled out.

Miles stood at the hatch, barking at it.

"Back!" X shouted.

The dog retreated behind the bar. A bright flash filled the saloon, but it wasn't coming from inside. X looked to the far hull, its portholes suddenly lit up by a missile streaking into the sky beyond. A second later, the clouds swallowed it.

"They did it," Josie breathed.

The realization gave X a little reprieve from the fear and pain. Valeria and Watt had activated the reactors. But that wouldn't matter if this airship made it to the Vanguard Islands and wiped out the last known bastion of humanity.

X had to stop this vessel.

Something pounded the hatch from outside, and he got up with his assault rifle hanging over his chest. He crossed the space in a hurry to draw the fire, but then realized something else when he saw the portholes. Shooting in here would be a huge risk since, armored or not, the loss of pressure could bring the entire ship down—a risk this sleeper would likely not be programmed to take.

He aimed at the hatch, hoping his rounds would penetrate the armor of the suit. A shot to the visor was his best hope. Pounding came from the other side of the hatch. With each loud bang, a new dent appeared. X could see it wasn't going to hold. Keeping his rifle up, he waited for his shot. It came a few seconds later as the hatch finally gave way, shearing open and falling off its hinges.

The sleeper pilot strode forward in the mech suit, lowering the robotic hand it had used to bash the hatch in and raising a chain gun.

Standing in the open now, X realized his vital error, and his heart sank. The formidable weapon whirred to life again. Rounds punched into the deck and overhead. So much for his theory that the attacker wouldn't endanger the airship. He jumped, but a round hit his foot. It felt as if he had been stung by a mutant bullet ant.

Out of the corner of his eye, he saw a furry dark blur, his mind processing the image before his good foot hit the deck. The chain gun turned on that shadow of fur.

"No!" X screamed.

He fired his assault rifle at the mounted weapon, hitting the barrel and pushing it away as the dog sprang. Miles slammed into the chest of the mech suit and bit down on an exposed hose. The pilot reached up to grab the dog.

Dragging his shot foot, X moved fast, fighting the pain. He threw a forward elbow, cracking the visor.

Miles dropped to the ground but lunged again, snarling and biting down on a leg. X smashed the visor with his fist, breaking shards into the pilot's eyes. His next punch knocked the helmet back so hard, the mech suit collapsed on its back. He climbed on top and hammered the broken visor until there was nothing but pulp on the other side.

The adrenaline eventually ebbed, and X slid off and looked over to the bar he had hidden Josie behind. She was crawling over to him, holding in her hand a small metal fork with three tines.

"Take this key," she whispered. "It will allow you to override the system."

He reached out and took the trident-shaped key.

It was on him now.

Weak from blood loss, he pushed up and instantly fell back down. Miles nudged him in the side, whining.

"I'm okay, boy," he said.

X pushed up to his knees, then up on his good foot, and hopped one legged to the open hatch. Pulling out the .357 Magnum pistol, he started down the passage with Miles right behind him. X stopped halfway down, bracing himself with a robotic hand on the hull.

He took in a deep breath, then continued.

Turning the corner, he saw the way clear to the bridge. The hatches were open, revealing an abandoned command center that had to be running on autopilot. Woozy, he staggered around the various workstations. At the helm, he saw a digital map. X slumped into the leather seat and looked at the screen to see the Virgin Islands in the Caribbean Sea. He checked another screen and saw that the ballistic missiles on board were armed and ready to fire.

X took out the key, fumbled it, dropped it to the deck. His blood dripped onto the deck. His vision dimmed, and he let out a groan. Miles bent down and picked up the key in his mouth, pushing it against his fingers.

"Thanks, buddy," X said.

He sat up, grimacing in pain, and carefully inserted the key into the dashboard.

"System override authorized," said a robotic voice. "Countdown to self-destruct now active."

X stared down. "Wait. No!" he muttered.

His fogged brain quickly made sense of what was happening. There was no disarming this ship or putting it back down. The only way to stop it was to blow it up—something Josie must have known all along.

X looked down at Miles and then slid out of the seat next to him on the blood-smeared deck. He reached out and pulled his dog close.

"I'm sorry, boy." He pushed up his helmet. "I'm sorry I couldn't save us."

Miles licked at his beard as a hot tear fell from his eye. The countdown ticked down on the monitor in front of them. Nine minutes remained. The irony wasn't lost on X. In the end, he knew exactly how much time he had left.

He hugged his best friend, grateful that they were together and that it would be peaceful—the way he had always hoped they would go.

THIRTY-ONE

The relentless Antarctic wind battered the Jayhawk. Magnolia stared out the cockpit windshield as they closed in on their destination. Forty-five hours after leaving the Vanguard Islands, they were just a half hour from Concordia Station. But Magnolia had accepted now that they were probably too late.

"Still nothing from the ground team or the airship," reported Lieutenant Mamoa for what seemed like the fifth time.

Captain Namath sat in the copilot's seat, helping the pilot navigate in the limited visibility against the merciless wind. The chopper had handled most of the trip well, considering its age and the distance traveled, but the whine of the engines told Magnolia the machine was redlining now.

Mamoa, looking exhausted, glanced from the instruments to the barely visible horizon. Namath relayed the coordinates of the rendezvous—a small city a few miles away from Concordia Station. From what Magnolia understood, this was where Xavier and his team had gone to meet Kade and Lucky, and the site of the first team's drop.

"Listen up," Namath called over the comms. *"We're almost there. Get your domes on right and prepare for the worst."*

Sergeant Donny and Master Chief Clay sat across the cabin from Magnolia, loading their rifles.

"You going to give me something to defend myself with?" She recalled something she had heard back in Australia. "I didn't come here to fuck spiders."

Namath looked back from the cockpit, then turned when Mamoa pointed.

"Crikey, what the bloody shit stain is that?" asked the pilot.

Namath leaned forward. *"Looks like smoke."*

Magnolia unbuckled her harness, freeing her numb buns from the seat she had been strapped into for most of the journey. She moved up with Clay and Donny for a view as the chopper flew over the ice sheet. Despite the limited visibility, it wasn't hard to see the smoke plumes fingering up from wreckage in the distance.

"Is that the city?" Donny asked.

"Negative," Mamoa said. *"We're fifty miles out."*

"So what's burning?"

"Shit . . ." Mamoa pushed against his harness. *"I think, I think . . . uh."*

"My God, that's the Trident," Namath said.

"We're too late," Magnolia whispered. She grabbed a handhold, holding on steady while the chopper swooped low. Magnolia searched the debris field for any sign of life, but she knew that nothing would have survived the crash. Shards of metal lay scattered in a halo around an impact crater, which the Jayhawk circled.

From all appearances, the ship had come down like a suicidal Hell Diver. It was apparent now that the storms and interference weren't the reason they had lost contact with the ground teams—there was simply nothing left of them.

Magnolia felt the reality of the situation setting in. If X, Miles,

Kade, and everyone else were truly dead, she was now completely alone.

This was rock bottom.

No, she thought.

This was the end of everything. There would be no coming back from this emotionally. She had lost literally everyone she cared about except for Michael and his family. And even they could well be gone forever.

"I've seen enough," Namath said. *"Change course for Concordia Station; bypass the city. We'll set down at the edge of the reactors and head in on our own."*

The chopper pulled away from the wreckage, a somber mood settling over the cabin as Donny and Clay returned to their seats. Magnolia did the same, but the numbness in her legs had spread to her heart.

She shook away the invasive negative thoughts. X could still be out there.

Magnolia allowed herself to hope that by some fluke, maybe X and Miles were alive somehow. That they weren't on the *Trident* and that they had survived despite all odds. It wouldn't be the first time for X, but there would eventually be a last, and this just might be it.

"As soon as we set down, you pull out of here, Mamoa," Namath said. *"If we don't make it, you—"*

"All due respect, Captain, but you'll need me on the ground, and if you don't make it, I ain't going home alone."

Their eyes met, and Namath nodded.

"Okay, prepare for combat," said the captain. *"For the Trident."*

"For the *Trident,*" his men repeated.

He returned to the cabin with Clay, Donny, and Magnolia. They finished the last of their gear checks over the next few minutes. Magnolia checked her suit and HUD, then took a swig of water from the straw in her helmet.

"I see the reactors," Mamoa called back.

Magnolia turned to look out the cockpit, and there they were. The giant disk-shaped Delta Cloud fusion reactors broke the horizon like ancient monuments from a bygone era—which, she realized, they were. In the center of the clustered reactors sat a domed facility: Concordia Station.

"Taking us down!" Mamoa yelled. The chopper raced low over the ice, toward the facility. Donny got up and grabbed the door lever, sliding it open.

"Captain, I got eyes on bodies," Mamoa said.

Namath glanced up, then motioned to keep going. "We don't stop!" he shouted.

Magnolia went to the open door for a view with the other knights. The chopper rolled over a battlefield, the rotors blasting away fresh snow from the frozen bodies littering the basin below. Closer to the base, a snowmobile lay on its side.

"Take us down!" Namath ordered.

Mamoa lowered until the wheels touched down with a jolt. Magnolia hopped out under the spinning rotors. The knights followed her, setting up a perimeter with their rifles while Mamoa shut down the bird. He climbed out of the cockpit and joined them.

Namath walked a few steps from the group to the closest body and brushed snow off a frozen face.

"It's human," he said.

Magnolia peered down at the youthful face of a woman. She moved to another corpse—a male, also in his twenties. Bending down, she dusted the snow from the ITC logo on a blue uniform.

"These must have been people from the pods," she said.

"Pods?" Namath asked.

"Yes. Cryo-pods—most of the bunkers I've been to have them."

The team moved on and soon came across a very large carcass, not human. She nudged it with her boot, and the shoulder flopped over to reveal the hideous face of a bone beast.

"What in the name of all things unholy is *that*?" Watt asked.

Namath came over to check it out, then shook his head. "Never seen anything like it before."

"I have, but this one is different," Magnolia said. "Genetically designed to survive out here, and *hunt* out here."

She looked to Namath. He reached down to a holstered pistol, drawing it and handing it to her. "Do not make me regret—"

"You won't regret it if those things are still out there," she said. Magnolia took the weapon, pulling back the slide to chamber a round.

Namath had Donny, Clay, and Mamoa fan out in combat intervals as they continued toward the base. Both front doors were wide open, partially blocked by drifts of snow. Along the way, Magnolia stopped when she saw something else: paw prints near the snowmobile, where they had sheltered from the wind.

Miles had been here.

She looked around, turning in all directions, resisting the urge to call out. Namath waved her onward, and she followed them to the doors, where Donny and Clay were digging a path through the icy rubble.

Soon, the rest of the team got a view of more bodies in the corridor beyond the entrance. Bullet casings lay scattered across the tile floor on the other side of the snowdrift. A battle had raged here, but there was no sign of recent activity. Even Miles's tracks were old.

Magnolia gripped the pistol as they entered the icy corridor. Namath flashed more hand signals, splitting the team. Mamoa and Clay headed straight while Magnolia went with Donny and Namath into a stairwell.

They went down a level, finding the door open to more carnage. A sprawled carcass of the same bearlike bone beast creature lay on the ground, a gaping hole in its head from a shotgun blast. Frozen brain matter stippled the wall.

Namath pushed on until they reached the command center. Magnolia followed the men inside, gripping her pistol in both hands and scanning the empty space. Donny went over to a glowing monitor.

"Captain," he said.

Namath went over. "What is it?"

"Uh . . ." Donny looked down, then back up. "The reactors are active. I, uh, crikey, sir, I think they've already been activated."

Before anyone had a chance to make sense of it, a growl resonated through the base.

"Watch out!" someone shouted from another room.

"That's Clay," Namath said. "On me!"

Magnolia was the first out of the command room.

"Hold up," Namath called.

She was already in the stairwell and moving up when she heard the roar of a monster. Namath and Donny pounded up the stairs behind her. The first to the top of the stairs, Magnolia stepped out almost into the path of an armored figure. It landed on its back with a crunch on the tile just left of the doorway. She pulled back a beat, then peeked around the corner with her pistol. Eight feet to her right, she saw the silhouette of a bulky, dark creature raising both arms above its head. The thing went down on all fours and came bolting forward. A dropped flashlight illuminated the spiky black fur that Magnolia recognized even before she saw the gleaming liquid black eyes.

"Jo-Jo, stop!" she yelled.

The beast slid over the ice on her knuckles, coming to a stop just a foot away from Magnolia. She reached out her hand. "It's me, Jo-Jo," she said. "Mags."

Jo-Jo lowered her head, snorting as she looked into the stairwell where Donny and Namath stood.

"It's okay," Magnolia said. "This is a friend."

"Keep that thing back," Clay groaned from where Jo-Jo had thrown him.

"Easy," Magnolia said. "This animal is part of the second team."

"So where's the rest of them?" Namath asked.

Magnolia looked down to Jo-Jo, who was the only one that might know. The animal knuckle-walked forward, passing Clay, who backed up against the wall.

"Where's it going?" Namath asked.

"I think she's trying to show us something," Magnolia said. "Come on."

She followed Jo-Jo down the corridor, in the opposite direction of the way they had entered the facility. The animal picked up speed, and Magnolia jogged after her, the knights clanking in their wake. When they turned at the next intersection, howling wind greeted them. Drafts blasted in through another open door to the facility. Jo-Jo bounded toward it, vanishing outside before Magnolia could stop her. She hesitated and decided to wait for the soldiers to catch up. The wind, mixed with a light snow, created a sheet of white outside. It was beautiful in a way. Serene, even.

In a pause of the gusting wind, she heard what sounded like barking. She stepped out into the wind to hear.

The barking came again.

Heart skipping, Magnolia stumbled out into snow that came up to her knees. She waded out toward the noise, hope arising inside her.

Could it be? Was Miles out there?

HELL DIVERS XII: HEROES

"Hold up," Namath called.

But Magnolia kept going. She found the path Jo-Jo had taken between the drifts, using it to move even faster. The barking faded in the whistling wind. Magnolia climbed up over a mound but face-planted at the top.

When she lifted her head, she saw something at the bottom of a hill. A big something—a sleek black airship that looked to be all in one piece. She turned as the knights arrived.

"Is that...?" Mamoa asked.

"It looks like the *Trident*," Namath said. "But how?"

The group slid and stumbled through the snow out to a basin where the airship sat. Even at a hundred yards, Magnolia could tell that it had sustained damage from laser fire and rockets. She followed the tracks from Jo-Jo to the ramp. There, a four-legged animal sat on its haunches next to Jo-Jo.

Miles barked when he saw Magnolia, then leaped out into the snow.

"Miles!" she yelled.

The dog bounded toward her, struggling through the chest-high powder. Tail wagging, Miles looked spryer than she had seen him in years. She plowed over to him until they met.

A voice came from the ramp, where Jo-Jo still waited. Magnolia looked over to see a knight standing there.

"Captain Namath, is that really you?"

"Watt, you did it!" Namath shouted.

"Had some help," said a second voice.

A woman with her arm in a sling and one foot in an orthopedic boot limped over.

"Commander Hallsey," Namath said. The knights all saluted as the woman hobbled to the edge of the ramp.

Magnolia was about to ask where Kade and X were, when she saw two more figures slowly approaching in the dim cargo hold. As they stepped into the light, she saw that it was Valeria, helping X.

Miles hopped back into the snow, leading the way to the ramp. At first, Magnolia stood and stared, unsure whether to believe her eyes.

X stopped next to the knights, with Valeria helping him stand.

"Mags," he said with a laugh. "What took you so long?"

She gave a snort and a sniffle, then hurried over and up the ramp. When she was face to face with X again, she stopped short of embracing him. Like Commander Hallsey, he had one arm in a sling, and one foot in a medical boot.

"Let's get out of the cold, yeah?" he said.

The group went inside, to the cargo hold.

"So you going to tell me what happened down here?" Magnolia asked.

"How about I *show* you," X said.

They went to the medical chamber full of glowing blue pods where she had earlier seen X. Suspended in one of them was the half-human, half-robotic body of the Forerunner.

"Commander Hallsey, Miles, and I boarded the enemy ship that was armed to strike the Vanguard Islands," X said. "After eliminating the hostile forces aboard, we had no choice but to activate the self-destruct sequence."

He stepped up to the pod, placing his robotic fingers on it. "Noah used the last of his strength to save us."

"Noah..." Magnolia whispered with realization. She studied the man on the other side of the glass. Tubes snaked away from his cyborg body, keeping him alive. X looked on with empathy and respect—a huge change since Magnolia saw him last.

"Miles, Josie, and I are alive right now because of his final actions," X said. "After Watt and Valeria activated the reactors with Jo-Jo, the Forerunner took control of the *Trident* from this very pod, extracting Watt and Valeria, who in turn extracted us before the airship went down. They pulled us out and patched us up."

Commander Hallsey stepped up to the pod.

"Noah has two final wishes," she said.

She turned and looked to the knights, then to Magnolia, and finally back to X.

"For our people all to live in peace," she said.

"And the second?" Magnolia asked.

Josie put a hand up to the glass. "Noah told me that if X could activate the reactors, then the prophecy was true," she said. "That he is the one to lead humanity into the new future—that he should return to the islands as king."

*   *   *   *   *

"Open the shutters," Michael commanded.

"Stand by, sir," Timothy said.

The airship cut through the skies over the South Atlantic Ocean, making good time through what should normally be turbulent skies. Layla rose out of her seat next to him, both of them staring in disbelief as the lowering shutters revealed what they had been seeing for days now.

"Not dark," Bray said. He stood between them, pointing at the brightening viewports. "Sun comin'."

"Yeah," Michael said in awe.

"Not dark outside, Ma-ma."

Layla smiled, picking him up and holding him up to see. Shafts of sunlight broke through the electrical storms in all directions, chasing them away. All across the horizon, the flashing clouds weakened and retreated.

"Sir, based on these readings and what you're seeing now, I

would say this isn't coincidence or luck," Timothy said. "I believe someone did this."

Michael scratched his bruised chin, still not quite believing that was possible—or that his eyes were telling him the truth. His right eye was still puffy from the beating he took at the slaver prison, but he was healing nicely. He was lucky—very lucky.

But there was no denying the evidence. For the past two weeks after they left the fortress of Agadir Oufella, the storms had gradually weakened, and now that process seemed to be picking up steam. In those two weeks, Michael had observed the skies, thinking it was just a random occurrence, or a weak spot like the one they had experienced back at Lanzarote in the Canary Island chain. But now he believed Timothy was right.

Something had caused this. Some*one*.

"They turned on the weather-mod units," he said.

"Who?" Layla asked.

"Who, Da-da?" Bray asked.

"Heroes."

"Hee-roooo," Bray said.

Michael couldn't help but chuckle. Layla laughed too, her dimpled cheeks warming with color. The sadness they both had felt about leaving what they once hoped to be their forever home at Lanzarote had all but dissipated with this discovery. It meant there would be more Lanzarotes out there. Many more.

"We need to tell Victor and prepare an announcement," Layla said.

Michael nodded. "Timothy, you have the bridge. When I tell you, transmit over the PA system in Spanish and again in Arabic for all passengers to meet in the launch bay."

Layla carried Bray out of the bridge but set him down in the corridor.

"I walk," he said.

Michael took him by the hand, and Layla took his other hand. Bray loved swinging while holding their hands, giggling as he hung there with his knees up. They did that for the first stretch of hallway, until the boy decided he was finished. He let go of their fingers and broke into a run all the way to the farm hatch. The scent of freshly sprayed produce wafted out of the chamber as Michael opened it.

"Up, Da-da," said Bray.

Michael picked him up, and they walked inside. Ten former prisoners from the slaver fortress were working in the long field. Gabi was here too, a basket in one hand overflowing with vegetables for the soup she planned to make with Layla.

"Hi," Bray said, waving.

Everyone waved back, some even smiling.

The first week, these people had acted much the way that Gabi had when she first joined Michael's family and Victor in the caves. But now they were slowly starting to relax—Michael and Layla, too. Not letting their guard down, necessarily, but trying to spend more time with these people whose lives had just been transformed. From community meetings in the launch bay to games in the mess hall.

Michael stepped out of the room and went to the quarters where Victor had settled back in. Layla knocked on his hatch, next to theirs. They heard rustling on the other side. Bray reached out as Victor opened the door, dressed in shorts and a tattered T-shirt. He gazed into the light with one eye still partly closed.

"Sorry to wake you, but we have some good—*great*—news," Michael said. "Bray, want to tell him what you saw?"

"Hi, Unka Victa," Bray said.

"Hello, my friend," Victor said with a smile as he opened the hatch all the way. "What did you see?"

Bray looked timid and shy at first, but he grinned when Victor reached out and tickled his neck.

"Tell him, bud," Michael said. "What did you see in the sky?"

"Not dark outside," Bray said.

"Did you see the sun?" Layla asked.

"Yes." Bray nodded. "Yup."

"We don't think this is a fluke anymore," Michael said. "We think someone turned on the weather-tech machines."

"Who?" A brow rose on Victor's still-bruised face.

"We don't know, but we're going to make an announcement shortly."

Victor opened the hatch all the way and went back inside, throwing on some pants over his shorts and then a buttoned shirt. They set off together while Timothy made the announcement for all passengers to head to the launch bay. When they arrived, they all went to the center of the room.

Their new friends entered in twos and threes—the kids, too. The older boy who had helped Michael during the battle ran over with a big grin on his face.

"*Hola, Jaifa*," Michael said. "*¿Cómo estás?*"

"*¡Bien, bien!*" he replied.

Bray giggled as Jaifa ran and skipped around the large deck. The kid loved to dance, and he had plenty of space to do it here. The airship had always seemed small to Michael growing up, but Jaifa's people had been cooped up in a prison much smaller than this ship. They were deliriously happy to move around, and the kids had a place to play.

The other children, all eight of them, rushed into the room, laughing and shouting with their parents and caretakers. After the battle at the fortress, more prisoners had emerged from hiding spots, including three additional kids. In total, there were twenty-six men, women, and children. Michael knew everyone by name now and greeted each individually.

Timothy's hologram appeared, bringing more excited laughter

from the kids, several of whom rushed through his translucent form.

"Pepper, will you translate for me?" Michael asked. "I'll kick us off but might need your help after."

"Certainly, Chief."

Michael cleared his throat. "*Todos reúnanse*," he said. "Gather around, everyone."

The parents corralled the children in front of Michael, Layla, Bray, Gabi, and Victor. Timothy also walked over to join in.

"Thanks for coming, everyone," Michael started. "We're here today to celebrate something that I wasn't sure would ever happen, and while I'm not sure *how* it happened, the evidence is undeniable."

Timothy gave a running translation. Even the kids listened quietly.

"Pepper, lower the shutters," he said.

All at once, the shields over the viewports lowered. Sunlight speared inside, making the space so bright, everyone had to raise their hands over their eyes.

"We don't know who, but we believe that a team of heroes set off to the poles and activated weather technology to clear the storms," Michael said. "What this means is that we won't have to stay on this airship forever."

He waited for Timothy's translation to catch up.

Jaifa raised a brow to Michael.

"It means we will find a new home in the sun—on the ground, where it's safe," Michael said. "A place where we all can live in peace and start over."

Again Timothy translated, sparking several side conversations. Some people cheered. Others just smiled. Kids looked up, some too young to understand exactly what he was saying, but most of them grinning anyway.

"Start ova," Bray said.

Michael reached down and lifted his son up. "Yes, Bray. We're going to find a new home, I promise you."

"Anything else?" Timothy asked.

"Yes, one last thing," Michael said. "Layla, you have something, right?"

"*Esta noche, tenemos una sopa especial para celebrar,*" she said. "*Vengan con apetito.*"

"*Muy bien,*" Gabi said.

Michael nodded, also impressed with his wife's command of Spanish.

There was more cheering. People embraced, and the kids tore around the space, screaming with joy.

"I'm going to take Bray to play with the other kids," Layla said as the group dispersed. "Want to come?"

"I do, but I have some work I'd like to get done," Michael replied. "I'll be on the bridge if you need me."

Bray had already run after his new playmates, and Layla hurried to catch up. Michael watched them go, then returned to the bridge, his own promise fresh on his mind. He opened the hatch to the captain's office. Maps lay over the desk in front of a computer that he had used to access the archives. He had already started the search for places that might soon be habitable, relying on the old maps as much as the archives to piece together information lost over the decades.

With the sun returning, he was searching for a green zone that would be radiation-free, not near a major Old World city that had been bombed.

"Chief, would you like some help?" Timothy offered.

"Not right now, thank you," Michael said.

After closing the hatch, he sat down at the desk. For the next few hours, he lost himself in his search, scouring the maps and archives. A knock on the hatch commanded his attention at five in the afternoon, and he looked up as Bray rushed in.

"Da-da!"

Michael reached down as Bray tried to crawl up on his lap. Layla walked over, taking in the maps and tablet.

"Find anything yet?" she asked.

"Maybe. I'm thinking about a place in Patagonia."

"Sounds beautiful," she said. "Let's look before bed. But right now let's head over and get some food. Soup's on."

Michael picked Bray up and followed Layla to the mess hall. People had already gathered in a line outside the kitchen, where Gabi was ladling out steaming vegetable broth into bowls that each recipient seemed to stare down at as if this couldn't be real. They all were very thin, and one of Michael and crew's first tasks was to work with Timothy and get these people healthy. That meant daily rations of healthy, nutrient-rich food and plenty of clean water. It seemed to be working.

Michael joined the line, thanked Gabi for his bowl, and sat down. As he lifted the first spoonful of soup to his lips, Timothy's hologram emerged.

"Chief, may I speak with you?" he asked.

"Is it an emergency?" Michael said.

"Sir, I believe it is."

Michael set the spoon back into his soup and looked at Layla. "I'll be right back," he said.

Bray held out his spoon in a shaky hand. "Here, Da-da."

"I'll be back, buddy," Michael said.

Layla gave him a concerned look as he backed away and discreetly left the room. The last thing he wanted to do was scare anyone. But as he walked out into the passageway, he realized that it might be unavoidable.

"Chief, I've picked something up on radar," Timothy said. "A ship."

Michael went completely still. "An *air*ship?"

"Yes, sir. Heading toward us at forty knots."

"How long until they reach us?"

"Ten minutes, sir."

"Can we outrun them?"

"I don't think so, sir," Timothy called out to Michael's receding form, but he was already running to the bridge.

Had Charmer somehow found an airship and hunted them down?

He rushed into the bridge, anger and fear vying for supremacy within him.

"Have they tried to hail us?" he asked.

"Negative, Chief. Would you like me to try?"

Michael wasn't sure what to do. There was no way to outrun whoever this was, and they didn't have enough firepower to take out another vessel this large.

All his bubbling optimism about the future evaporated.

"Timothy, do we have anything we can fire to defend ourselves?" Michael asked.

"Afraid not, Chief."

Michael put a hand on the back of the leather chair, staring as the craft inched closer on the radar. His mind spun with fight-or-flight scenarios and solutions, but there was little he could do.

"Sir, I'm receiving a transmission," Timothy said.

"Bring it online."

Michael squeezed the leather tightly.

"To the crew of the Vanguard, *does anyone copy?"*

That voice ... Michael knew that voice. It was the voice of a ghost.

Timothy looked over at Michael.

"Sir, I can say with certainty that is the voice of Xavier Rodriguez," said the AI.

The hatch opened, and Layla entered with Bray in her arms. "Michael, what's going on?"

He slowly rose from his seat, trying to make sense of what he had just heard.

"To the crew of the Vanguard," said the same gravelly voice.

"Michael, who is that?" Layla asked, grabbing his shoulders. "That must be a trick. It can't be—"

Michael reached down and tapped the comms.

"This is Chief Everhart. To whom am I speaking?" He watched the radar blip closing in on their position. "I repeat, who is this?"

Layla hovered over Michael, Bray in her arms.

"Michael, is it you?" came that same rough voice.

"Identify yourself," Michael said.

"It's me, Michael. It's X."

"It can't be. You're ... Charmer said you were dead."

"Not the first time somebody got that wrong, is it, now?"

A chuckle came over the channel. Clear as could be. It was X.

"Michael, Layla, you're alive!" said a second voice, this one female.

"*Mags?*" Michael gasped.

Layla just stared, finally saying, "Is this real, Tin?"

"I ... I think so. And I think we know who turned on the poles." Michael reached for his son. "Say hello to the heroes, buddy."

Bray reached down to the radio. "Hello, hee-ro."

More chuckles broke out.

"Well, you gonna invite us over, or what?" X asked.

EPILOGUE

"What's on the agenda now?" X asked. He pushed the lever on the elevator cart, lifting himself and Imulah toward the rooftop of the capitol tower. It was midmorning, and he had just finished meeting with Martino on the piers to discuss fishing hauls and the ragtag fleet of trawlers.

"Take a look, sir," Imulah said. He handed X a clipboard. "After your council meeting, you are due at the engineering rig today to discuss energy curtailments with Chief Everhart, and then you have—"

X listened as Imulah rattled off his duties as king for another day. Things that kept the gears turning. But as boring as most of these things were, they sure beat the old way of life: of killing and war. As they rose up the side of the tower, X studied the chains that once held the cage containing Charmer. The cage was gone, but the chains remained, reminders of bloodshed and betrayals past.

"Looks like storm clouds, Your Majesty," Imulah said.

X watched the wall of clouds to the west, quickening over the ocean.

"Sight for sore eyes," he said. "Now, there's something I didn't think I'd ever say."

It certainly wasn't a response he would have made before they activated the Delta Cloud fusion reactors two months ago. But with storms clearing across the world, rain was something the islands needed for the crops to feed their growing population. It was also a reminder of the past.

Also a reminder of how far you've come, he thought.

"Should we secure the airship?" Imulah asked.

X nodded when he saw the former *Hive* in the path of the approaching black wall. The airship was currently lowering crates over the two Trident ships that were once used to take thousands of tourists across the world on holidays.

"That's the last of the harvest from the airship," Imulah said. "Those crates, along with the harvest from the hybrid seeds we used on the rigs, should produce plenty of food to support our new populations over the next six months."

"Good," X said. "Full bellies promote peace."

Looking out over the ocean, he had no illusions about this being easy. Even with the sun shining all across the world now, they couldn't just go plant food. In most places, the soil remained poisoned. It would be difficult to produce enough for everyone, which could lead to future struggles, either here or with survivors emerging from bunkers around the world after living underground for over two and a half centuries. It was not a matter of if but of where, when, and how.

X had no illusions that their home was still safe, and he didn't want anyone to grow complacent with this peace. One of his first acts as king was to prepare for external threats by keeping the navy and airpower in tip-top condition.

The *Frog* patrolled in the open water. It was pocked with bullet holes and scars from battles, and on its deck sat a Jayhawk.

Farther out, he spotted the destroyer that once belonged to the madman Crixus and his cult. War boats once used by el Pulpo, also bearing battle scars, patrolled the waters.

There were more new additions to the navy with the arrival of the Trident armada, led by two ships once used as cruise vessels. Several smaller craft that had made the voyage all the way from the Sunshine Coast were now spread out across the islands. Some had been decommissioned from naval duties to fish the vast waters, or to transport goods between the fourteen surviving oil rigs.

The cage clanked to the top, right within line of sight of their biggest asset—the *Trident* airship that had helped them save the world, now moored on top of the tower.

"King Xavier," said a familiar voice.

Victor walked over from beneath a shady tree, spear in hand. X smiled at his old friend, grateful to have him watching his back again.

He patted Victor on the shoulder, and they set off across the rooftop, to the airship *Trident*. Imulah hurried after them, his sheaf of papers fluttering in the breeze. Barking came from the dense stand of tropical trees that had survived the past years of warfare. Miles burst out of the foliage, a gaggle of joyful kids racing after him. At the head of the pack was Alton, with five of the kids Michael had rescued from the slavers' compound on the western coast of Africa. Supervising the herd of ankle biters was Layla. She carried Bray on her back, the boy giggling as Miles reached up to lick his naked toes.

"School out for the day?" X asked.

"It's a rest day," Layla said.

"Doesn't look all that restful to me." He chuckled as the kids swarmed Miles, who broke free and took off across the dirt.

HELL DIVERS XII: HEROES

"Where's Michael?" X asked. "You look like you could use some help."

"At the engineering rig—battery issue."

Layla smiled and then turned as X reached out to Bray. The boy extended a finger to meet one of X's skeletal metal fingers. X jerked back, pretending he'd been shocked, to the boy's great delight.

"I better go after them," Layla said.

"Have fun," X said.

He continued across the rooftop with Imulah and Victor to the airship. A crew worked outside, preparing it for flight. Among them was Magnolia. It wasn't a huge surprise when she had told X she would be heading out on the first mission. As always, searching for her next adventure.

Wearing a tank top and cargo pants, she loaded crates of supplies. Commander Hallsey would depart soon for Concordia Station, where she would be in charge of salvaging the equipment that was designed to create a new colony at the end of the world. With the storms clearing, that invaluable equipment could be used to create a colony somewhere far more hospitable to humanity. Though she would be on a different mission, Magnolia had decided to go with her, and for that, X couldn't blame her.

"Hey, X," she said, grinning and wiping her brow.

"You're sure in a hurry to leave, aren't you?"

She shrugged. "Not much left for me here."

X could argue with her about that, but this was her choice, her life. Selfishly, he wanted her to stay at the islands, to settle down. But he knew that this place was too painful for her.

"King Xavier," said a female voice.

X turned to the open cargo hold. Standing on the ramp was Commander Josie Hallsey, in a spotless blue uniform.

"Ready?" he asked.

She gave a stern nod.

They heard a bark, and Miles ran over, tail wagging. Jo-Jo wasn't far behind. She knuckle-walked over to X but didn't greet him with her usual excitement. She had become melancholy in recent weeks. Not even the sun, fruit, or fresh fish seemed to pull her out of her funk.

"Let's go," Josie said.

Magnolia threw on a shirt and followed the commander with X up the ramp and into the airship. They walked through to an oval hatch that opened to a bowl-shaped recessed space with three levels of seating surrounding a central table below. Six empty chairs were positioned around it. This was the same place X had been brought after General Jack shot Jonah and Valeria.

The other knights who had stood around him with their swords out were all gone now. Blue Blood, Nobu, Zen, and Lucky. Just like Kade and Slayer. X felt the darkness trying to claw its way up inside him, but he wrestled it down, reminding himself that those people had paved the way for a better world. Standing in their place was the next generation of warriors.

Watt was here, along with Sergeant Donny, Master Chief Clay, Lieutenant Mamoa, and Captain Namath. In the audience were their new allies: Cazadores Valeria and Tiger, Hell Divers Sofia Walters and Pedro, and of course the many sky people represented by X.

Everyone looked to him, including Commander Josie Hallsey, who stood where the Forerunner had once sat in his chair.

X thought of the man once more, grateful for the lessons he had shared in such a short time. Today, X would honor him in his speech as they announced the next mission. He cleared his throat and swept the room with his gaze, trying to connect with each person there.

"Today, we are gathered to reinforce our ironclad alliance to protect our home," X said. "As we look to this future of peace between our peoples, we must also look to protecting them from exterior threats. The sun is shining across the world, and survivors we didn't know existed will be coming out."

He nodded to Magnolia.

"Commander Katib will be leading expeditions to locate these survivors and, perhaps, form trade relationships with them, but exercising the utmost caution," X said. "It's a new world, and we will face it together, without fear, without regret, and with a confidence as strong and resilient as our alliance."

Nods all around the room.

X looked to Captain Namath. They had met in private several times over the past two months, and X found him to be a genuinely good man—just the sort of man he needed to help protect this place. A man like Rhino and Forge.

"I'm promoting Captain Namath to general and placing him in charge of our defenses, working closely with me," X announced. "Tiger will be admiral of the naval forces, and Sofia Walters will train a new generation of Hell Divers."

Magnolia exchanged a nod with her best friend, who didn't want her to leave any more than X did. But also like X, Sofia understood that Magnolia needed this.

"Commander Hallsey will depart in two days," X said. "We wish you well, Commander. Good luck out there."

X stepped back as the knights raised their swords to the Trident. Then they turned and did something he wasn't expecting.

In unison, they said, "Long live the Immortal. May he lead us to a life of prosperity and peace."

"I'll die before I let you all down," X said. He stepped back, and the room began to clear. Namath walked over to him, and X reached out his hand.

"Congratulations, General," he said.

"Thank you, sir. In our first order of business, I have news," he said. "That island you were looking for—I believe we've found it. I can have the Jayhawk ready shortly if you'd like."

X looked to Valeria, who waited with Magnolia and Victor. "Yes. Fire it up," he said. "Pick up Michael on the way here."

"Will do, sir."

X left the ship with his friends and went to the rooftop's plot of tropical forest, where Jo-Jo lounged under the leafy canopy. Miles sat there on his haunches, tongue hanging out and panting after all that play.

"Jo-Jo, come here," X said.

Valeria stood next to him. "You're sure about this?" she asked.

"Oh, very," X said. He motioned for Jo-Jo. "Come, I have a surprise for you."

The animal gingerly came out from the shadows. Hearing the distant chop of the Jayhawk, she looked up.

"Miles, come," X said with a pat to his thigh.

The dog bolted out of the forest, and Jo-Jo joined them as they crossed over to the helicopter. It landed near the Sky Arena, and the door slid open. Michael already sat inside. Victor, Valeria, and X ran under the rotor blast with Jo-Jo and Miles in tow, and the motley group piled inside the chopper.

"Sir," said Lieutenant Mamoa from the cockpit. The pilot gripped the controls of the Jayhawk, ready to fly. For a moment, X stared, second-guessing his decision, but a glance at Jo-Jo confirmed that this was the right move.

He took a seat in the chopper as Watt came aboard, shutting the door behind him. X tried to relax as they pulled away from the tower. He watched out the viewports as they flew over the rigs and out into the blue beyond. The border of light and dark was nowhere to be seen—nothing but endless sunshine. *"This is it,"* Mamoa said.

X looked down at Jo-Jo, feeling even more conflicted in what he was about to do—but as she looked up with her loving gaze, he knew this was the right thing. After all she had been through with his people, it was the least she deserved.

"Take us down, Lieutenant," X said.

Mamoa flew over a beach strewn with the crushed hulls of boats. He took them down to a few hundred feet for a look at the vast jungles covering the island.

"There they are!" Mamoa shouted.

He pointed to a troop of beasts swinging from the trees as the chopper passed overhead. Watt, carrying a light machine gun, moved into the back of the cabin and opened the door. Everyone inside was armed, but they weren't here for a fight. They were here to release Jo-Jo back into the wild, on the island where Ada Winslow had found her years ago.

The animal nudged up to the Plexiglass, tilting her head at the distant grunts and hoots. X and Valeria moved behind Jo-Jo as Miles nudged up for a look out the open door. Sure enough, several big, furry anthropoid-looking creatures drifted into focus. X wasn't sure they were related to Jo-Jo, but he was hoping they would accept her. If not, he would bring her right back to the islands.

There was also a third alternative—one that X didn't like but was prepared for, and the reason they all carried weapons. He hoped it didn't come to that, but despite three months of relative peace, he hadn't let his guard down. The world was still infested with monsters that might see him and his comrades as a snack.

"Set down on the beach," X said.

"You got it, boss," Mamoa said.

The chopper cut back toward the shore, whipping the canopy below. Watt hopped out and started up the beach to hold security while the rest of the crew disembarked.

Jo-Jo hopped out and ran toward the jungle, Miles bolting after her.

"Slow down, boy!" X shouted.

The dog halted next to Jo-Jo, who had stopped on a sandy hump a hundred paces from the deep, dim jungle. The calls of birds and chirring of insects formed an orchestra of sounds. Somewhere just beneath all that, X picked up the rustle of leaves and snapping of branches.

Victor and Watt moved out with their weapons, watching for threats while X, Michael, Magnolia, and Valeria stayed with the animals.

The grunts and calls drew closer as, all across the jungle, the insects, birds, and frogs went silent. A flurry of what sounded like chest beats pierced the stillness, followed by a guttural howling rumble.

X motioned for the others to retreat. All but the dog slowly stepped back. A tap to his leg got even Miles to part reluctantly from his friend. Jo-Jo tilted her head, curious of the guttural call.

Suddenly, a massive monkey emerged from the shadows. Two dark, intelligent eyes took in Jo-Jo, then the humans behind her. The beast moved forward on its knuckles, muscles flexing across its broad chest and back.

Behind it, the curious but docile eyes of four smaller monkeys peeked from behind trees. Their leader pounded his chest again.

"Don't look at him," Valeria whispered.

X gazed downward.

Slowly, the giant animal came out of the jungle. He looked at Jo-Jo, sniffing the air. X risked a glance to see Jo-Jo remaining calm and fearless. The animal roared at them, snarling.

Valeria slowly backed away, and X got the message. He, too, retreated with the group. They made their way back down to the beach as the beast stood on the bank, watching them.

Jo-Jo turned and looked at them, and X thought he saw a wistfulness in her eyes.

"Go," he said. "You're free now, pal."

"Bye, Jo-Jo," Michael said.

Magnolia raised a hand. "I'll miss you, girl."

The animal looked at them all in turn and finally to Miles. The dog let out a sad whine but then wagged his tail as if to say, *It's okay. Go home, my friend.*

Jo-Jo gazed back at them another moment, then turned back up the sand bank, joining the troop. At the edge of the tree line, she glanced back at them one last time. And then she was gone, swallowed by the shadows.

"So long, pal," X said.

Miles whined, and Valeria bent down to console him.

"You can come visit her again, boy," X said.

He whistled, and Miles trotted after him, tail up and wagging again. They got back into the chopper, where Mamoa sat with feet up, arms folded over his chest, and a cigar clamped between his teeth, fast asleep.

"Nap time's over," X said. "I have work to do back home."

Mamoa shot up. "Sir."

The rotors turned, and the Jayhawk lifted back into the sky. X looked down at the canopy below. But Jo-Jo and her new family were gone.

Valeria leaned her head against his shoulder on the ride back. An hour later, they were back in Vanguard territory. The storm clouds had already passed, leaving the rigs shiny with rain. Mamoa flew toward the trading-post rig, where X had one final surprise for the day. Smoke wafted, filling the air with the savory scent of barbecue. Boats motored up, disgorging occupants wearing a tapestry of colors.

"What's going on down there?" Michael asked.

"You'll see soon," X said.

The chopper set down, and they disembarked on a rooftop bustling with activity. People from everywhere were here, gathered for the celebration X had planned. Waiting for them on the main trading deck were tables laden with garden vegetables, fresh fish, and a pig slow-roasting over an open pit of embers.

X took a ladder with Miles up to a raised platform. In the crowd, he noticed Chano, Jada, and Pablo looking up at him. He nodded down, thinking of Gran Jefe. The warrior with a checkered past would be missed. As would Forge, Slayer, and all the other Barracudas before them. Tonight was for them as much as anyone.

X stepped up to the railing to scan the growing crowd. Michael stood with his wife, who held Bray. Timothy stood next to them in holographic form. Pedro, Sofia, and her son, Rhino Jr., were here, too. Imulah and Martino led a small group of Cazadores. Alton and Phyl were with Katherine. Josie, Watt, and Namath came in uniform only, having left their armor behind.

X gripped the railing and whistled to get everyone's attention. As the eyes turned up to him, he breathed in the appetizing smells.

"Tonight, we celebrate the harvest by coming together to break bread, as we once did before the war," X said. "This will become a tradition for us, and it is possible thanks to the heroes who are here tonight. And those who are not. Let us take a moment to think of those who can't be with us."

Heads went down, and prayers were murmured.

X said his own to whatever higher being might be out there listening.

"Please give me the strength to lead these people to a better future," he said quietly. Then he looked up, sweeping his gaze over friends old and new. His eyes met Magnolia's. It saddened him knowing he wouldn't see her for a while. But he knew she would find what she was looking for out there. He caught Michael and Layla looking at him. They were the kids he never had, but kids had to find their own way in the world, just like Bray would eventually.

A tear formed in his eye as X realized he was finally letting go. They could take care of themselves.

His gaze went skyward to the airship formerly known as the *Hive*, where it all began. God, they had come so far since those dark days in the sky!

X exhaled, as if letting go of all the despair before turning back to the crowd.

"Let us eat, and celebrate in the name of all our heroes!" he shouted.

As his hand shot up, the crowd erupted in cheers. Music started up from the mariachi band. As he walked away from the railing, a chant started with an energetic beat, quickly growing louder.

"Long live the Immortal!"

X thought of Noah. The cyborg was right—immortality was a curse. But ready as X was to retire, he could see all the work yet to be done. He also knew that life wasn't all about work.

Looking down, he motioned for Valeria. She climbed up to the platform. Miles wagged his tail as Valeria scratched his head and then joined X by his side.

"Time to find you a companion, too," he whispered down to Miles.

Michael, Layla, Bray, and Magnolia all watched them, wearing big grins as the crowd danced and celebrated around them.

X took Valeria's hand. After all he had accomplished here, something was still missing.

The islands needed a queen, and now they would have one.

Dear readers,

Is this really the end? Yes and no. For X and Miles, their story likely ends here, in retirement, where they can enjoy the sunshine after years of battling the darkness. There are younger characters, however, that will have plenty of battles ahead of them as they rebuild and explore the planet now that the storms are clearing. Perhaps someday in the future I'll write a spin-off about the youth, but for now, I'm focusing on a story fans have wanted for almost a decade—a prequel.

This tale will focus on the end of the world, how it unfolded, and the aftermath. It will be loaded with action, suspense, and new characters that I think you'll really come to love. Speaking of, many of you have asked for a General Rhino origin story, and I'm just finishing that now. It is the tale of Nick Baker, born in a bunker and captured by the Cazadores. Conscripted into their war machine, Nick is thrown into the wastes on raids, where he earns his nickname and becomes the legendary warrior Rhino. Through his eyes, we will explore the culture and violence of the Cazador society and meet other survivors they encounter in the wastes, including a civilization called the Horse Lords. I really think fans will love it.

And that's not all, as many of you already know, I've been working on some new Hell Diver concepts. *The Lost Years, Part I: X and Miles* has already shown up in e-book, and more stories will follow. I have ideas featuring the origin stories of Al Timothy Pepper, the Forerunner, and an entirely new group of characters set in Japan. A large chunk of my 2024 writing schedule will be dedicated to writing these tales, and if all goes to plan, they will start rolling out in 2025.

After that, I suppose it's up to you, the reader. I have enjoyed and continue to enjoy writing in this world more than any other NSS universe. Ironic, considering I thought the first book would be so limiting with one airship. The way the series has expanded and the enjoyment fans show continue to amaze me. I will be forever grateful to you all.

Another reason I keep writing more Hell Diver stories is due to Blackstone Publishing, especially CEO Josh Stanton. Thank you for the ironclad support and for believing in Hell Divers. I couldn't have gotten this far without the team there or my world-class editor Michael Carr, who is truly like a real-life X. I also want to thank R. C. Bray, the voice of X, and a huge reason why Hell Divers has reached this level of success. Thank you, Bob—you are a legend.

I'd be remiss if I didn't also mention the possibility of a movie. For the past two years I've been working with Ari Arad of Arad Productions and his fantastic team. It will take a lot more work to bring Hell Divers to the big screen, but with the support of the community behind Hell Divers, I believe it is possible.

Thank you all from the bottom of my heart.

The dives aren't over…

All the best,
Nick

ABOUT THE AUTHOR

Nicholas Sansbury Smith is the *New York Times* and *USA Today* bestselling author of more than forty novels with two million copies sold. He is best known for his dystopian sci-fi Hell Divers series, set to be a major motion picture under Arad Productions. Before his writing career, Nicholas served at Iowa Homeland Security and Emergency Management, a background that inspired many of his story concepts. A two-time Ironman triathlete, he enjoys running, biking, and hiking. He also loves traveling, especially to his cabin in Northern Minnesota where he weaves his tales. He lives in Iowa with his wonderful wife and their son and daughter.

Join Nicholas on social media:
Facebook: Nicholas Sansbury Smith
Twitter: @GreatWaveInk
Website: www.NicholasSansburySmith.com